THE MORTAL INSTRUMENTS

City of Lost Souls

Also by Cassandra Clare

THE MORTAL INSTRUMENTS

City of Bones

City of Ashes

City of Glass

City of Fallen Angels

City of Lost Souls

City of Heavenly Fire

THE INFERNAL DEVICES

Clockwork Angel

Clockwork Prince

Clockwork Princess

The Shadowhunter's Codex

With Joshua Lewis

The Bane Chronicles

With Sarah Rees Brennan
and Maureen Johnson

THE MORTAL INSTRUMENTS

City of Lost Souls

Book Five

CASSANDRA CLARE

Margaret K. McElderry Books
NEW YORK LONDON TORONTO SYDNEY NEW DELHI

MARGARET K. McELDERRY BOOKS
An imprint of Simon & Schuster Children's Publishing Division
1230 Avenue of the Americas, New York, New York 10020

For information about special discounts for bulk purchases, please contact Simon & Schuster
Special Sales at 1-866-506-1949 or business@simonandschuster.com.
The Simon & Schuster Speakers Bureau can bring authors to your live event.
For more information or to book an event, contact the Simon & Schuster Speakers Bureau
at 1-866-248-3049 or visit our website at www.simonspeakers.com.
Also available in a Margaret K. McElderry Books hardcover edition
Cover design by Russell Gordon
Interior design by Mike Rosamilia
Map illustration by Drew Willis
The text for this book is set in Dolly.
Manufactured in the United States of America
This Margaret K. McElderry Books paperback edition September 2015
12 14 16 18 20 19 17 15 13 11
The Library of Congress has cataloged the hardcover edition as follows:
Clare, Cassandra.
City of lost souls / Cassandra Clare.
p. cm.—(The mortal instruments ; bk. 5)
Summary: When Jace vanishes with Sebastian, Clary and the Shadowhunters struggle to piece
together their shattered world and Clary infiltrates the group planning the world's destruction.
ISBN 978-1-4424-1686-4 (hardcover)
ISBN 978-1-4424-1688-8 (eBook)
[1. Supernatural—Fiction. 2. Demonology—Fiction. 3. Magic—Fiction.
4. Vampires—Fiction.
5. New York (N.Y.)—Fiction. 6. Horror stories.] I. Title.
PZ7.C5265Ckl 2012
[Fic]—dc23
2011042547
ISBN 978-1-4814-5600-5 (repackaged pbk)

For Nao,
Tim, David,
and Ben

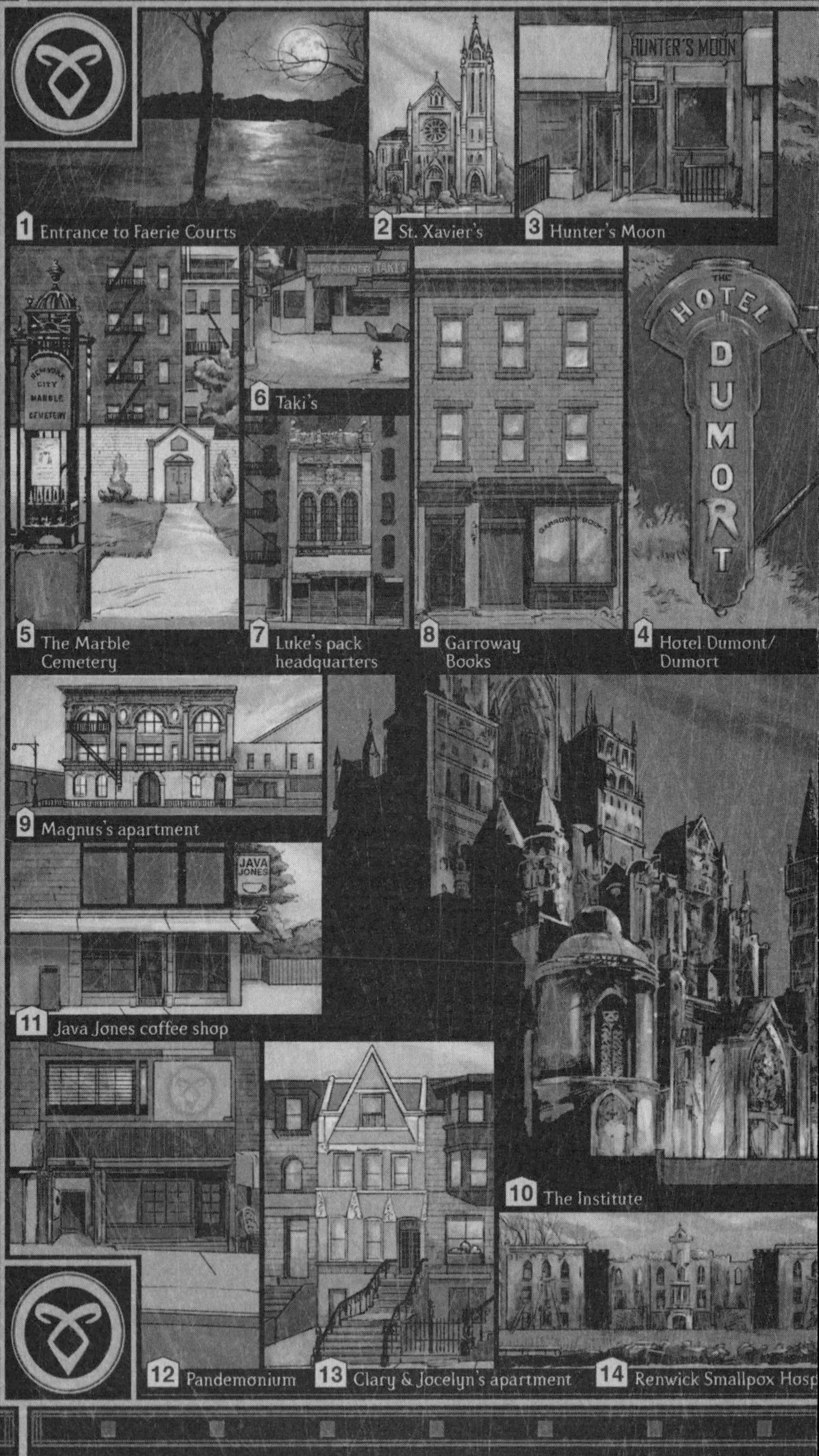
1 Entrance to Faerie Courts
2 St. Xavier's
3 Hunter's Moon
HUNTER'S MOON
5 The Marble Cemetery
6 Taki's
7 Luke's pack headquarters
8 Garroway Books
4 Hotel Dumont/ Dumort
THE HOTEL DUMORT
9 Magnus's apartment
JAVA JONES
11 Java Jones coffee shop
10 The Institute
12 Pandemonium
13 Clary & Jocelyn's apartment
14 Renwick Smallpox Hosp

UPPER WEST SIDE
UPPER EAST SIDE
LINCOLN SQUARE
HELL'S KITCHEN
ASTORIA
MIDTOWN
QUEENS
MANHATTAN
CHELSEA
WEST VILLAGE
EAST VILLAGE
GREENPOINT
CHINATOWN
WILLIAMSBURG
FINANCIAL DISTRICT
BUSHWICK
FORT GREENE
COBBLE HILL
BROOKLYN
BEDFORD-STUYVESANT
CARROLL GARDENS
RED HOOK
PROSPECT HEIGHTS
GOWANUS
PARK SLOPE
1
2
3
4
5
6
7
8
9
10
11
12
13
14

Foreword

All the stories are true.

That's what Jace Wayland tells Clary Fray in the first book of the Shadowhunters chronicles, *City of Bones.*

Jace means, of course, more than one thing by this. He means that everything she'd always been told didn't exist—vampires, werewolves, faeries, ghosts, and monsters of all shape, size, and intention—did exist after all and that, in fact, the world is full of them. He means that the stories we believe in our hearts—stories in which we are the heroes, stories in which there are good people who rise up to defeat the evil, stories in which there is always hope—are also true. Clary ends *City of Bones* feeling a true sense of wonder as she flies over New York City, seeing revealed below all the magic and enchantment that had been previously hidden from her.

All the stories are true.

When I set out to write *City of Bones*, I was in love with stories about vampires and faeries and warlocks, but I was also in love with the mythological tales of angels and demons. I was fascinated by *Paradise Lost* and Dante's *Inferno* and Mike Carey's *Lucifer*. I was fascinated with the way that human beings had grappled with the ideas of absolute evil and absolute good tempered with love and free will. I wanted to create a world that was rich in folklore, the tales people tell each other about things that go bump and bite in the night, but which also incorporated the existence of figures of myth—angels so powerful that one look at them would blind you. Demons so evil that their blood could change the nature of your soul from good to evil. I wanted to make real that which is so shrouded in myth and history that it has become symbolic: when Valentine frees Jace from his prison in the Silent City, he carries with him a sword and explains, "This is the blade with which the Angel drove Adam and Eve out of the garden. *And he placed at the east of the garden of Eden Cherubim, and a flaming sword which turned every way.*" Later, Simon comes into possession of the sword of the Archangel Michael. The idea that these objects of immense power and history were real things our heroes could touch and use delighted me.

The existence of angels and demons in the world of Shadowhunters is the ur-myth from which every other aspect of the stories is derived. Shadowhunters were created from the blood of angels. Faeries are part angel, part demon. Warlocks are the offspring of humans and demons. Werewolves and vampires are humans who bear demon diseases. I wanted to create a universe where myth and folklore dovetailed, where every story of magic could be explained.

All the stories are true.

The idea of Shadowhunters came to me in part from the stories of Nephilim in the Bible. The offspring of humans and angels, they were enormous monsters who laid waste to the earth. As writers often do, I adapted what seemed compelling to me from the myth—angels having children, when that is such a human thing to do! (Of course the Shadowhunters are only created from angel blood, but Raziel still seems to have a fatherly interest in them.) The idea of being part angel, partly a symbol of goodness, and yet being beset by all the weaknesses inherent to humanity: frailty, cruelty, greed, selfishness, despair. It seemed a way to take an ancient story and ring a twist on it that would allow any reader to imagine what it might mean to be part divine, to have immense power—and as Spider-Man likes to remind us, the immense responsibility that goes with it.

All the stories are true.

Of course, what Jace means ultimately is that stories are how we make sense of the world. The Mortal Instruments is the story of Clary above everything else: the story of a girl who starts out ordinary and becomes a hero. A girl who first is blind to the magic in the world all around her, but comes not just to see it, but to be able to master and control it. Clary is an artist and a shaper of runes, the magical language of angels, and in using that language she shapes her own story and her own destiny. Clary and her friends are heroes who *make* their stories true—as, in the end, do we all.

No man chooses evil because it is evil.
He only mistakes it for happiness, the good he seeks.
—Mary Wollstonecraft

Prologue

Simon stood and stared numbly at the front door of his house.

He'd never known another home. This was the place his parents had brought him back to when he was born. He had grown up within the walls of the Brooklyn row house. He'd played on the street under the leafy shade of the trees in the summer, and had made improvised sleds out of garbage can lids in the winter. In this house his family had sat shivah after his father had died. Here he had kissed Clary for the first time.

He had never imagined a day when the door of the house would be closed to him. The last time he had seen his mother, she had called him a monster and prayed at him that he would go away. He had made her forget that he was a vampire, using glamour, but he had not known how long the glamour would last. As he stood in the cold autumn air, staring in front of him, he knew it had not lasted long enough.

The door was covered with signs—Stars of David splashed on in paint, the incised shape of the symbol for *Chai*, life. Tefillin were bound to the doorknob and knocker. A *hamsa*, the Hand of God, covered the peephole.

Numbly he put his hand to the metal mezuzah affixed to the right side of the doorway. He saw the smoke rise from the place where his hand touched the holy object, but he felt nothing. No pain. Only a terrible empty blankness, rising slowly into cold rage.

He kicked the bottom of the door and heard the echo through the house. "Mom!" he shouted. "Mom, it's me!"

There was no reply—only the sound of the bolts being turned on the door. His sensitized hearing had recognized his mother's footsteps, her breathing, but she said nothing. He could smell acrid fear and panic even through the wood. "Mom!" His voice broke. "Mom, this is ridiculous! Let me in! It's *me*, Simon!"

The door juddered, as if she had kicked it. "Go away!" Her voice was rough, unrecognizable with terror. "Murderer!"

"I don't kill people." Simon leaned his head against the door. He knew he could probably kick it down, but what would be the point? "I told you. I drink animal blood."

"You killed my son," she said. "You killed him and put a monster in his place."

"I *am* your son—"

"You wear his face and speak with his voice, but you are not him! You're not Simon!" Her voice rose to almost a scream.

"Get away from my house before I kill you, monster!"

"Becky," he said. His face was wet; he put his hands up to touch it, and they came away stained: His tears were bloody. "What have you told Becky?"

"Stay away from Rebecca." Simon heard a clattering from inside the house, as if something had been knocked over.

"Mom," he said again, but this time his voice wouldn't rise. It came out as a hoarse whisper. His hand had begun to throb. "I need to know—is Becky there? Mom, open the door. Please—"

"Stay away from Becky!" She was backing away from the door; he could hear it. Then came the unmistakeable squeal of the kitchen door swinging open, the creak of the linoleum as she walked on it. The sound of a drawer being opened. Suddenly he imagined his mother grabbing for one of the knives.

Before I kill you, monster.

The thought rocked him back on his heels. If she struck out at him, the Mark would rise. It would destroy her as it had destroyed Lilith.

He dropped his hand and backed up slowly, stumbling down the steps and across the sidewalk, fetching up against the trunk of one of the big trees that shaded the block. He stood where he was, staring at the front door of his house, marked and disfigured with the symbols of his mother's hate for him.

No, he reminded himself. She didn't hate him. She thought he was dead. What she hated was something that didn't exist. *I am not what she says I am.*

He didn't know how long he would have stood there, staring, if his phone hadn't begun to ring, vibrating his coat pocket.

He reached for it reflexively, noticing that the pattern from the front of the mezuzah—interlocked Stars of David—was burned into the palm of his hand. He switched hands and put the phone to his ear. "Hello?"

"Simon?" It was Clary. She sounded breathless. "Where are you?"

"Home," he said, and paused. "My mother's house," he amended. His voice sounded hollow and distant to his own ears. "Why aren't you back at the Institute? Is everyone all right?"

"That's just it," she said. "Just after you left, Maryse came back down from the roof where Jace was supposed to be waiting. There was no one there."

Simon moved. Without quite realizing he was doing it, like a mechanical doll, he began walking up the street, toward the subway station. "What do you mean, there was no one there?"

"Jace was gone," she said, and he could hear the strain in her voice. "And so was Sebastian."

Simon stopped in the shadow of a bare-branched tree. "But Sebastian was dead. He's dead, Clary—"

"Then you tell me why his body isn't there, because it isn't," she said, her voice finally breaking. "There's nothing up there but a lot of blood and broken glass. They're both gone, Simon. Jace is gone. . . ."

Part One
No Evil Angel

Love is a familiar. Love is a devil. There is no evil angel but Love.
—William Shakespeare, *Love's Labour's Lost*

TWO WEEKS LATER

1

THE LAST COUNCIL

"How much longer will the verdict take, do you think?" Clary asked. She had no idea how long they'd been waiting, but it felt like ten hours. There were no clocks in Isabelle's black and hot-pink powder-puff bedroom, just piles of clothes, heaps of books, stacks of weapons, a vanity overflowing with sparkling makeup, used brushes, and open drawers spilling lacy slips, sheer tights, and feather boas. It had a certain backstage-at-*La-Cage-aux-Folles* design aesthetic, but over the past two weeks Clary had spent enough time among the glittering mess to have begun to find it comforting.

Isabelle, standing over by the window with Church in her arms, stroked the cat's head absently. Church regarded her with baleful yellow eyes. Outside the window a November storm was in full bloom, rain streaking the windows like clear paint. "Not much longer," she said slowly. "Five minutes, probably."

Clary, sitting on Izzy's bed between a pile of magazines and a rattling stack of seraph blades, swallowed hard against the bitter taste in her throat. *I'll be back. Five minutes.*

That had been the last thing she had said to the boy she loved more than anything else in the world. Now she thought it might be the last thing she would ever get to say to him.

Clary remembered the moment perfectly. The roof garden. The crystalline October night, the stars burning icy white against a cloudless black sky. The paving stones smeared with black runes, spattered with ichor and blood. Jace's mouth on hers, the only warm thing in a shivering world. Clasping the Morgenstern ring around her neck. *The love that moves the sun and all the other stars.* Turning to look for him as the elevator took her away, sucking her back down into the shadows of the building. She had joined the others in the lobby, hugging her mother, Luke, Simon, but some part of her, as it always was, had still been with Jace, floating above the city on that rooftop, the two of them alone in the cold and brilliant electric city.

Maryse and Kadir had been the ones to get into the elevator to join Jace on the roof and to see the remains of Lilith's ritual. It was another ten minutes before Maryse returned, alone. When the doors had opened and Clary had seen her face—white and set and frantic—she had known.

What had happened next had been like a dream. The crowd of Shadowhunters in the lobby had surged toward Maryse; Alec had broken away from Magnus, and Isabelle had leaped to her feet. White bursts of light cut through the darkness like the soft explosions of camera flashes at a crime scene as, one after another, seraph blades lit the shadows. Pushing her way forward, Clary heard the story in broken pieces—the rooftop garden was empty; Jace was gone. The glass coffin that had held Sebastian had been smashed open; glass was lying everywhere in fragments. Blood, still fresh, dripped down the pedestal on which the coffin had sat.

The Shadowhunters were making plans quickly, to spread out in a radius and search the area around the building. Magnus was there, his hands sparking blue, turning to Clary to ask if she had something of Jace's they could track him with. Numbly, she gave him the Morgenstern ring and retreated into a corner to call Simon. She had only just closed the phone when the voice of a Shadowhunter rang out above the rest. "Tracking? That'll work only if he's still alive. With that much blood it's not very likely—"

Somehow that was the last straw. Prolonged hypothermia, exhaustion, and shock took their toll, and she felt her knees give. Her mother caught her before she hit the ground. There was a dark blur after that. She woke up the next morning in her bed at Luke's, sitting bolt upright with her heart going like a trip-hammer, sure she had had a nightmare.

As she struggled out of bed, the fading bruises on her arms and legs told a different story, as did the absence of her ring. Throwing on jeans and a hoodie, she staggered out into the living room to find Jocelyn, Luke, and Simon seated there with somber expressions on their faces. She didn't even need to ask, but she did anyway: "Did they find him? Is he back?"

Jocelyn stood up. "Sweetheart, he's still missing—"

"But not dead? They haven't found a body?" She collapsed onto the couch next to Simon. "No—he's not dead. I'd *know*."

She remembered Simon holding her hand while Luke told her what they did know: that Jace was still gone, and so was Sebastian. The bad news was that the blood on the pedestal had been identified as Jace's. The good news was that there was less of it than they had thought; it had mixed with the water from the coffin to give the impression of a greater volume of blood than there had really been. They now thought it was quite possible he had survived whatever had happened.

"*But what happened?*" she demanded.

Luke shook his head, blue eyes somber. "Nobody knows, Clary."

Her veins felt as if her blood had been replaced with ice water. "I want to help. I want to do something. I don't want to just sit here while Jace is missing."

"I wouldn't worry about that," Jocelyn said grimly. "The Clave wants to see you."

Invisible ice cracked in Clary's joints and tendons as she stood up. "Fine. Whatever. I'll tell them anything they want if they'll find Jace."

"You'll tell them anything they want because they have the Mortal Sword." There was despair in Jocelyn's voice. "Oh, baby. I'm so sorry."

And now, after two weeks of repetitive testimony, after scores of witnesses had been called, after she had held the Mortal Sword a dozen times, Clary sat in Isabelle's bedroom and waited for the Council to rule on her fate. She couldn't help but remember what it had felt like to hold the Mortal Sword. It was like tiny fishhooks embedded in your skin, pulling the truth out of you. She had knelt, holding it, in the circle of the Speaking Stars and had heard her own voice telling the Council everything: how Valentine had raised the Angel Raziel, and how she had taken the power of controlling the Angel from him by erasing his name in the sand and writing hers over it. She had told them how the Angel had offered her one wish, and she had used it to raise Jace from the dead; she told them how Lilith had possessed Jace and Lilith had planned to use Simon's blood to resurrect Sebastian, Clary's brother, whom Lilith regarded as a son. How Simon's Mark of Cain had ended Lilith, and they had thought Sebastian had been ended too, no longer a threat.

Clary sighed and flipped her phone open to check the time. "They've been in there for an hour," she said. "Is that normal? Is it a bad sign?"

Isabelle dropped Church, who let out a yowl. She came over to the bed and sat down beside Clary. Isabelle looked even more slender than usual—like Clary, she'd lost weight in the past two weeks—but elegant as always, in black cigarette pants and a fitted gray velvet top. Mascara was smudged all around Izzy's eyes, which should have made her look like a raccoon but just made her look like a French film star instead. She stretched her arms out, and her electrum bracelets with their rune charms jingled musically. "No, it's not a bad sign," she said. "It just means they have a lot to talk over." She twisted the Lightwood ring on her finger. "You'll be fine. You *didn't* break the Law. That's the important thing."

Clary sighed. Even the warmth of Isabelle's shoulder next to hers couldn't melt the ice in her veins. She knew that technically she had broken no Laws, but she also knew the Clave was furious at her. It was illegal for a Shadowhunter to raise the dead, but not for the Angel to do it; nevertheless it was such an enormous thing she had done in asking for Jace's life back that she and Jace had agreed to tell no one about it.

Now it was out, and it had rocked the Clave. Clary knew they wanted to punish her, if only because her choice had had such disastrous consequences. In some way she wished they *would* punish her. Break her bones, pull her fingernails out, let the Silent Brothers root through her brain with their bladed thoughts. A sort of devil's bargain—her own pain for Jace's safe return. It would have helped her guilt over having left Jace behind on that rooftop, even though Isabelle and the others had told her a hundred times she was being ridiculous—that they had all thought he was perfectly safe there, and that if Clary had stayed, she would probably now be missing too.

"Quit it," Isabelle said. For a moment Clary wasn't sure if Isabelle was talking to her or to the cat. Church was doing what he often did when dropped—lying on his back with all four legs in the air, pretending to be dead in order to induce guilt in his owners. But then Isabelle swept her black hair aside, glaring, and Clary realized she was the one being told off, not the cat.

"Quit what?"

"Morbidly thinking about all the horrible things that are going to happen to you, or that you wish would happen to you because you're alive and Jace is . . . missing." Isabelle's voice jumped, like a record skipping a groove. She never spoke of Jace as being dead or even gone—she and Alec refused to entertain the possibility. And Isabelle had never reproached Clary once for keeping such an enormous secret. Throughout everything, in fact, Isabelle had been her staunchest defender. Meeting her every day at the door to the Council Hall, she had held Clary firmly by the arm as she'd marched her past clumps of glaring, muttering Shadowhunters. She had waited through endless Council interrogations, shooting dagger glances at anyone who dared look at Clary sideways. Clary had been astonished. She and Isabelle had never been enormously close, both of them being the sort of girls who were more comfortable with boys than other female companionship. But Isabelle didn't leave her side. Clary was as bewildered as she was grateful.

"I can't help it," Clary said. "If I were allowed to patrol—if I were allowed to do *anything*—I think it wouldn't be so bad."

"I don't know." Isabelle sounded weary. For the past two weeks she and Alec had been exhausted and gray-faced from sixteen-hour patrols and searches. When Clary had found out she was banned from patrolling or searching for Jace in any way until the Council decided what to do about the fact that she had brought him back from the dead, she had kicked a hole in her bedroom door. "Sometimes it feels so futile," Isabelle added.

Ice crackled up and down Clary's bones. "You mean you think he's dead?"

"No, I don't. I mean I think there's no way they're still in New York."

"But they're patrolling in other cities, right?" Clary put a hand to her throat, forgetting that the Morgenstern ring no longer hung there. Magnus was still trying to track Jace, though no tracking had yet worked.

"Of course they are." Isabelle reached out curiously and touched the delicate silver bell that hung around Clary's neck now, in place of the ring. "What's that?"

Clary hesitated. The bell had been a gift from the Seelie Queen. No, that wasn't quite right. The Queen of the faeries didn't give *gifts*. The bell was meant to signal the Seelie Queen that Clary wanted her help. Clary had found her hand wandering to it more and more often as the days dragged on with no sign of Jace. The only thing that stopped Clary was the knowledge that the Seelie Queen never gave anything without the expectation of something terrible in return.

Before Clary could reply to Isabelle, the door opened. Both girls sat up ramrod straight, Clary clutching one of Izzy's pink pillows so hard that the rhinestones on it dug into the skin of her palms.

"Hey." A slim figure stepped into the room and shut the door. Alec, Isabelle's older brother, was dressed in Council wear—a black robe figured with silver runes, open now over jeans and a long-sleeved black T-shirt. All the black made his pale skin look paler, his crystal-blue eyes bluer. His hair was black and straight like his sister's, but shorter, cut just above his jawline. His mouth was set in a thin line.

Clary's heart started to pound. Alec didn't look happy. Whatever the news was, it couldn't be good.

It was Isabelle who spoke. "How did it go?" she said quietly. "What's the verdict?"

Alec sat down at the vanity table, swinging himself around the chair to face Izzy and Clary over the back. At another time it would have been comical—Alec was very tall, with long legs like a dancer, and the way he folded himself awkwardly around the chair made it look like dollhouse furniture.

"Clary," he said. "Jia Penhallow handed down the verdict. You're cleared of any wrongdoing. You broke no Laws, and Jia feels that you've been punished enough."

Isabelle exhaled an audible breath and smiled. For just

a moment a feeling of relief broke through the layer of ice over all of Clary's emotions. She wasn't going to be punished, locked up in the Silent City, trapped somewhere where she couldn't help Jace. Luke, who as the representative of the werewolves on the Council had been present for the verdict, had promised to call Jocelyn as soon as the meeting ended, but Clary reached for her phone anyway; the prospect of giving her mother good news for a change was too tempting.

"Clary," Alec said as she flipped her phone open. "Wait."

She looked at him. His expression was still as serious as an undertaker's. With a sudden sense of foreboding, Clary put her phone back down on the bed. "Alec—what is it?"

"It wasn't your verdict that took the Council so long," said Alec. "There was another matter under discussion."

The ice was back. Clary shivered. "Jace?"

"Not exactly." Alec leaned forward, folding his hands along the back of the chair. "A report came in early this morning from the Moscow Institute. The wardings over Wrangel Island were smashed through yesterday. They've sent a repair team, but having such important wards down for so long—that's a Council priority."

Wards—which served, as Clary understood it, as a sort of magical fence system—surrounded Earth, put there by the first generation of Shadowhunters. They could be bypassed by demons but not easily, and kept out the vast majority of them, preventing the world from being flooded by a massive demon invasion. She remembered something that Jace had said to her, what felt like years ago: *There used to be only small demon invasions into this world, easily contained. But even in my lifetime more and more of them have spilled in through the wardings.*

"Well, that's bad," Clary said. "But I don't see what it has to do with—"

"The Clave has its priorities," Alec interrupted. "Searching for Jace and Sebastian has been top priority for the past two weeks. But they've scoured everything, and there's no sign of either of them in any Downworld haunt. None of Magnus's tracking spells have worked. Elodie, the woman who brought up the real Sebastian Verlac, confirmed that no one's tried to get in touch with her. That was a long shot, anyway. No spies have reported any unusual activity among the known members of Valentine's old Circle. And the Silent Brothers haven't been able to figure out exactly what the ritual Lilith performed was supposed to do, or whether it succeeded. The general consensus is that Sebastian—of course, they call him Jonathan when they talk about him—kidnapped Jace, but that's not anything we didn't know."

"So?" Isabelle said. "What does that mean? More searching? More patrolling?"

Alec shook his head. "They're not discussing expanding the search," he said quietly. "They're de-prioritizing it. It's been two weeks and they haven't found anything. The specially commissioned groups brought over from Idris are going to be sent home. The situation with the *wards* is taking priority now. Not to mention that the Council has been in the middle of delicate negotiations, updating the Laws to allow for the new makeup of the Council, appointing a new Consul and Inquisitor, determining different treatment of Downworlders—they don't want to be thrown completely off track."

Clary stared. "They don't want Jace's disappearance to throw them off the track of changing a bunch of stupid old Laws? They're *giving up*?"

"They're not giving up—"

"*Alec,*" Isabelle said sharply.

Alec took a breath and put his hands up to cover his face. He had long fingers, like Jace's, scarred like Jace's were as well. The eye Mark of the Shadowhunters decorated the back of his right hand. "Clary, for you—for *us*—this has always been about searching for Jace. For the Clave it's about searching for Sebastian. Jace as well, but primarily Sebastian. He's the danger. He destroyed the wards of Alicante. He's a mass murderer. Jace is . . ."

"Just another Shadowhunter," said Isabelle. "We die and go missing all the time."

"He gets a little extra for being a hero of the Mortal War," said Alec. "But in the end the Clave was clear: The search will be kept up, but right now it's a waiting game. They expect Sebastian to make the next move. In the meantime it's third priority for the Clave. If that. They expect us to go back to normal life."

Normal life? Clary couldn't believe it. A normal life without Jace?

"That's what they told us after Max died," said Izzy, her black eyes tearless but burning with anger. "That we'd get over our grief faster if we just went back to normal life."

"It's supposed to be good advice," said Alec from behind his fingers.

"Tell that to Dad. Did he even come back from Idris for the meeting?"

Alec shook his head, dropping his hands. "No. If it's any consolation, there were a lot of people at the meeting speaking out angrily on behalf of keeping the search for Jace up at full strength. Magnus, obviously, Luke, Consul Penhallow, even Brother Zachariah. But at the end of the day it wasn't enough."

Clary looked at him steadily. "Alec," she said. "Don't you feel anything?"

Alec's eyes widened, their blue darkening, and for a moment Clary remembered the boy who had hated her when she'd first arrived at the Institute, the boy with bitten nails and holes in his sweaters and a chip on his shoulder that had seemed immovable. "I know you're upset, Clary," he said, his voice sharp, "but if you're suggesting that Iz and I care less about Jace than you do—"

"I'm not," Clary said. "I'm talking about your *parabatai* connection. I was reading about the ceremony in the *Codex*. I know being *parabatai* ties the two of you together. You can sense things about Jace. Things that will help you when you're fighting. So I guess I mean . . . can you sense if he's still alive?"

"Clary." Isabelle sounded worried. "I thought you didn't . . ."

"He's alive," Alec said cautiously. "You think I'd be this functional if he weren't alive? There's definitely something fundamentally *wrong*. I can feel that much. But he's still breathing."

"Could the 'wrong' thing be that he's being held prisoner?" said Clary in a small voice.

Alec looked toward the windows, the sheeting gray rain. "Maybe. I can't explain it. I've never felt anything like it before."

"But he's alive."

Alec looked at her directly then. "I'm sure of it."

"Then screw the Council. We'll find him ourselves," Clary said.

"Clary . . . if that were possible . . . don't you think we already would have—," Alec began.

"We were doing what the Clave wanted us to do before," said Isabelle. "Patrols, searches. There are other ways."

"Ways that break the Law, you mean," said Alec. He sounded hesitant. Clary hoped he wasn't going to repeat the Shadowhunters' motto when it came to the Law: *Sed lex, dura lex.* "The Law is harsh, but it is the Law." She didn't think she could take it.

"The Seelie Queen offered me a favor," Clary said. "At the fireworks party in Idris." The memory of that night, how happy she'd been, made her heart contract for a moment, and she had to stop and regain her breath. "And a way to contact her."

"The Queen of the Fair Folk gives nothing for free."

"I know that. I'll take whatever debt it is on my shoulders." Clary remembered the words of the faerie girl who had handed her the bell. *You would do anything to save him, whatever it cost you, whatever you might owe to Hell or Heaven, would you not?* "I just want one of you to come with me. I'm not good with translating faerie-speak. At least if you're with me you can limit whatever the damage is. But if there's anything she can do—"

"I'll go with you," Isabelle said immediately.

Alec looked at his sister darkly. "We already talked to the Fair Folk. The Council questioned them extensively. And they can't lie."

"The Council asked them if they knew where Jace and Sebastian were," Clary said. "Not if they'd be willing to look for them. The Seelie Queen knew about my father, knew about the angel he summoned and trapped, knew the truth about my blood and Jace's. I think there's not much that happens in this world that she *doesn't* know about."

"It's true," said Isabelle, a little animation entering into her voice. "You know you have to ask faeries the exact right things to get useful information out of them, Alec. They're very hard to question, even if they do have to tell the truth. A favor, though, is different."

"And its potential for danger is literally unlimited," said Alec. "If Jace knew I let Clary go to the Seelie Queen, he'd—"

"I don't care," Clary said. "He'd do it for me. Tell me he wouldn't. If I were missing—"

"He'd burn the whole world down till he could dig you out of the ashes. I know," Alec said, sounding exhausted. "Hell, you think I *don't* want to burn down the world right now? I'm just trying to be . . ."

"An older brother," said Isabelle. "I get it."

Alec looked as if he were fighting for control. "If something happened to you, Isabelle—after Max, and Jace—"

Izzy got to her feet, went across the room, and put her arms around Alec. Their dark hair, precisely the same color, mixed together as Isabelle whispered something into her brother's ear; Clary watched them with not a little envy. She had always wanted a brother. And she had one now. Sebastian. It was like always wanting a puppy for a pet and being handed a hell-hound instead. She watched as Alec tugged his sister's hair affectionately, nodded, and released her. "We should all go," he said. "But I have to tell Magnus, at least, what we're doing. It wouldn't be fair not to."

"Do you want to use my phone?" Isabelle asked, offering the battered pink object to him.

Alec shook his head. "He's waiting downstairs with the others. You'll have to give Luke some kind of excuse too, Clary.

I'm sure he's expecting you to go home with him. And he says your mother's been pretty sick about this whole thing."

"She blames herself for Sebastian's existence." Clary got to her feet. "Even though she thought he was dead all those years."

"It's not her fault." Isabelle pulled her golden whip down from where it hung on the wall and wrapped it around her wrist so that it looked like a ladder of shining bracelets. "No one blames her."

"That never matters," said Alec. "Not when you blame yourself."

In silence, the three of them made their way through the corridors of the Institute, oddly crowded now with other Shadowhunters, some of whom were part of the special commissions that had been sent out from Idris to deal with the situation. None of them really looked at Isabelle, Alec, or Clary with much curiosity. Initially Clary had felt so much as if she were being stared at—and had heard the whispered words "Valentine's daughter" so many times—that she'd started to dread coming to the Institute, but she'd stood up in front of the Council enough times now that the novelty had worn off.

They took the elevator downstairs; the nave of the Institute was brightly lit with witchlight as well as the usual tapers and was filled with Council members and their families. Luke and Magnus were sitting in a pew, talking to each other; beside Luke was a tall, blue-eyed woman who looked just like him. She had curled her hair and dyed the gray brown, but Clary still recognized her—Luke's sister, Amatis.

Magnus got up at the sight of Alec and came over to talk to him; Izzy appeared to recognize someone else across the pews and darted away in her usual manner, without pausing to say where she was going. Clary went to greet Luke and Amatis; both of them looked tired, and Amatis was patting Luke's shoulder sympathetically. Luke rose to his feet and hugged Clary when he saw her. Amatis congratulated Clary on being cleared by the Council, and she nodded; she felt only half-there, most of her numb and the rest of her responding on autopilot.

She could see Magnus and Alec out of the corner of her eye. They were talking, Alec leaning in close to Magnus, the way couples often seemed to curve into each other when they spoke, in their own contained universe. She was happy to see them happy, but it hurt, too. She wondered if she would ever have that again, or ever even want it again. She remembered Jace's voice: *I don't even want to want anyone but you.*

"Earth to Clary," said Luke. "Do you want to head home? Your mother is dying to see you, and she'd love to catch up with Amatis before she goes back to Idris tomorrow. I thought we could have dinner. You pick the restaurant." He was trying to hide the concern in his voice, but Clary could hear it. She hadn't been eating much lately, and her clothes had started to hang more loosely on her frame.

"I don't really feel like celebrating," she said. "Not with the Council de-prioritizing the search for Jace."

"Clary, it doesn't mean they're going to stop," said Luke.

"I know. It's just— It's like when they say a search and rescue mission is now a search for bodies. That's what it sounds like." She swallowed. "Anyway, I was thinking of going to Taki's for dinner with Isabelle and Alec," she said. "Just . . . to do something normal."

Amatis squinted toward the door. "It's raining pretty hard out there."

Clary felt her lips stretch into a smile. She wondered if it looked as false as it felt. "I won't melt."

Luke folded some money into her hand, clearly relieved she was doing something as normal as going out with friends. "Just promise to eat something."

"Okay." Through the twinge of guilt, she managed a real half smile in his direction before she turned away.

Magnus and Alec were no longer where they had been a moment ago. Glancing around, Clary saw Izzy's familiar long black hair through the crowd. She was standing by the Institute's large double doors, talking to someone Clary couldn't see. Clary headed toward Isabelle; as she drew closer, she recognized one of the group, with a slight shock of surprise, as Aline Penhallow. Her glossy black hair had been cut stylishly just above her shoulders. Standing next to Aline was a slim girl with pale white-gold hair that curled in ringlets; it was drawn back from her face, showing that the tips of her ears were slightly pointed. She wore Council robes, and as Clary came closer she saw that the girl's eyes were a brilliant and unusual blue-green, a color that made Clary's fingers yearn for her Prismacolor pencils for the first time in two weeks.

"It must be weird, with your mother being the new Consul," Isabelle was saying to Aline as Clary joined them. "Not that Jia isn't *much* better than— Hey, Clary. Aline, you remember Clary."

The two girls exchanged nods. Clary had once walked in on Aline kissing Jace. It had been awful at the time, but the memory held no sting now. She'd be relieved to walk in on Jace kissing someone else at this point. At least it would mean he was alive.

"And this is Aline's *girlfriend*, Helen Blackthorn." Isabelle said with heavy emphasis. Clary shot her a glare. Did Isabelle think she was an idiot? Besides, she remembered Aline telling her that she'd kissed Jace only as an experiment to see if any guy were her type. Apparently the answer had been no. "Helen's family runs the Los Angeles Institute. Helen, this is Clary Fray."

"Valentine's daughter," Helen said. She looked surprised and a little impressed.

Clary winced. "I try not to think about that too much."

"Sorry. I can see why you wouldn't." Helen flushed. Her skin was very pale, with a slight sheen to it, like a pearl. "I voted for the Council to keep prioritizing the search for Jace, by the way. I'm sorry we were overruled."

"Thanks." Not wanting to talk about it, Clary turned to Aline. "Congratulations on your mother being made Consul. That must be pretty exciting."

Aline shrugged. "She's busy a lot more now." She turned to Isabelle. "Did you know your dad put his name in for the Inquisitor position?"

Clary felt Isabelle freeze beside her. "No. No, I didn't know that."

"I was surprised," Aline added. "I thought he was pretty committed to running the Institute here—" She broke off, looking past Clary. "Helen, I think your brother is trying to make the world's biggest puddle of melted wax over there. You might want to stop him."

Helen blew out an exasperated breath, muttered something about twelve-year-old boys, and vanished into the crowd just as Alec pushed his way forward. He greeted Aline with a hug—Clary forgot, sometimes, that the Penhallows and the

Lightwoods had known each other for years—and looked at Helen in the crowd. "Is that your girlfriend?"

Aline nodded. "Helen Blackthorn."

"I heard there's some faerie blood in that family," said Alec.

Ah, Clary thought. That explained the pointed ears. Nephilim blood was dominant, and the child of a faerie and a Shadowhunter would be a Shadowhunter as well, but sometimes the faerie blood could express itself in odd ways, even generations down the line.

"A little," said Aline. "Look, I wanted to thank you, Alec."

Alec looked bewildered. "What for?'

"What you did in the Hall of Accords," Aline said. "Kissing Magnus like that. It gave me the push I needed to tell my parents . . . to come out to them. And if I hadn't done that, I don't think, when I met Helen, I would have had the nerve to say anything."

"Oh." Alec looked startled, as if he'd never considered what impact his actions might have had on anyone outside his immediate family. "And your parents—were they good about it?"

Aline rolled her eyes. "They're sort of ignoring it, like it might go away if they don't talk about it." Clary remembered what Isabelle had said about the Clave's attitude toward its gay members. *If it happens, you don't talk about it.* "But it could be worse."

"It could definitely be worse," said Alec, and there was a grim edge to his voice that made Clary look at him sharply.

Aline's face melted into a look of sympathy. "I'm sorry," she said. "If your parents aren't—"

"They're fine with it," Isabelle said, a little too sharply.

"Well, either way. I shouldn't have said anything right now.

Not with Jace missing. You must all be so worried." She took a deep breath. "I know people have probably said all sorts of stupid things to you about him. The way they do when they don't really know what to say. I just—I wanted to tell you something." She ducked away from a passer-by with impatience and moved closer to the Lightwoods and Clary, lowering her voice. "Alec, Izzy—I remember once when you guys came to see us in Idris. I was thirteen and Jace was—I think he was twelve. He wanted to see Brocelind Forest, so we borrowed some horses and rode there one day. Of course, we got lost. Brocelind's impenetrable. It got darker and the woods got thicker and I was terrified. I thought we'd die there. But Jace was never scared. He was never anything but sure we'd find our way out. It took hours, but he did it. He got us out of there. I was so grateful but he just looked at me like I was crazy. Like of course he'd get us out. Failing wasn't an option. I'm just saying—he'll find his way back to you. I know it."

Clary had rarely ever seen Izzy cry, and she was clearly trying not to now. Her eyes were suspiciously wide and shining. Alec was looking at his shoes. Clary felt a wellspring of misery wanting to leap up inside her but forced it down; she couldn't think about Jace when he was twelve, couldn't think about him lost in the darkness, or she'd think about him now, lost somewhere, trapped somewhere, needing her help, expecting her to come, and she'd break. "Aline," she said, seeing that neither Isabelle nor Alec could speak. "Thank you."

Aline flashed a shy smile. "I mean it."

"Aline!" It was Helen, her hand firmly clamped around the wrist of a younger boy whose hands were covered with blue wax. He must have been playing with the tapers in the huge candelabras that decorated the sides of the nave. He looked about twelve, with an impish grin and the same shocking blue-green eyes as his sister, though his hair was dark brown. "We're back. We should probably go before Jules destroys the whole place. Not to mention that I have no idea where Ty and Livvy have gone."

"They were eating wax," the boy—Jules—supplied helpfully.

"Oh, God," Helen groaned, and then looked apologetic. "Never mind me. I've got six younger brothers and sisters. It's always a zoo."

Jules looked from Alec to Isabelle and then at Clary. "How many brothers and sisters have you got?" he asked.

Helen paled. Isabelle said, in a remarkably steady voice, "There are three of us."

Jules's eyes stayed on Clary. "You don't look alike."

"I'm not related to them," Clary said. "I don't have any brothers or sisters."

"None?" Disbelief registered in the boy's tone, as if she'd told him she had webbed feet. "Is that why you look so sad?"

Clary thought of Sebastian, with his ice-white hair and black eyes. *If only*, she thought. *If only I didn't have a brother, none of this would have happened.* A little throb of hatred went through her, warming her icy blood. "Yes," she said softly. "That's why I'm sad."

2
Thorns

Simon was waiting for Clary, Alec, and Isabelle outside the Institute, under an overhang of stone that only just protected him from the worst of the rain. He turned as they came out through the doors, and Clary saw that his dark hair was pasted to his forehead and neck. He pushed it back and looked at her, a question in his eyes.

"I'm cleared," she said, and as he started to smile, she shook her head. "But they're de-prioritizing the search for Jace. I—I'm pretty sure they think he's dead."

Simon looked down at his wet jeans and T-shirt (a wrinkled gray ringer tee that said CLEARLY I HAVE MADE SOME BAD DECISIONS on the front in block lettering). He shook his head. "I'm sorry."

"The Clave can be like that," Isabelle said. "I guess we shouldn't have expected anything else."

"Basia coquum," Simon said. "Or whatever their motto is."

"It's *'Descensus Averno facilis est.'* 'The descent into hell is easy,'" said Alec. "You just said "Kiss the cook."

"Dammit," said Simon. "I knew Jace was screwing with me." His wet brown hair fell back into his eyes; he flicked it away with a gesture impatient enough that Clary caught a flashing glimpse of the silvery Mark of Cain on his forehead. "Now what?"

"Now we go see the Seelie Queen," said Clary. As she touched the bell at her throat, she explained to Simon about Kaelie's visit to Luke and Jocelyn's reception, and her promises to Clary about the Seelie Queen's help.

Simon looked dubious. "The red-headed lady with the bad attitude who made you kiss Jace? I didn't like her."

"*That's* what you remember about her? That she made Clary kiss Jace?" Isabelle sounded annoyed. "The Seelie Queen is dangerous. She was just playing around that time. Usually she likes to drive at least a few humans to screaming madness every day before breakfast."

"I'm not human," Simon said. "Not anymore." He looked at Isabelle only briefly, dropped his gaze, and turned to Clary. "You want me with you?"

"I think it would be good to have you there. Daylighter, Mark of Cain—some things have to impress even the Queen."

"I wouldn't bet on it," said Alec.

Clary glanced past him and asked, "Where's Magnus?"

"He said it would be better if he didn't come. Apparently he and the Seelie Queen have some kind of history."

Isabelle raised her eyebrows.

"Not that kind of history," said Alec irritably. "Some kind of feud. Though," he added, half under his breath, "the way he got around before me, I wouldn't be surprised."

"Alec!" Isabelle dropped back to talk to her brother, and Clary opened her umbrella with a snap. It was one Simon had bought her years ago at the Museum of Natural History and had a pattern of dinosaurs on the top. She saw his expression change to one of amusement as he recognized it.

"Shall we walk?" he inquired, and offered his arm.

The rain was coming down steadily, creating small rills out of the gutters and splashing water up from the wheels of passing taxis. It was odd, Simon thought, that although he didn't feel cold, the sensation of being wet and clammy was still irritating. He shifted his gaze slightly, looking at Alec and Isabelle over his shoulder; Isabelle hadn't really met his eyes since they'd come out of the Institute, and he wondered what she was thinking. She seemed to want to talk to her brother, and as they paused at the corner of Park Avenue, he heard her say, "So, what do you think? About Dad putting his name in for the Inquisitor position."

"I think it sounds like a boring job." Isabelle was holding an umbrella. It was clear plastic, decorated with decals of colorful flowers. It was one of the girliest things Simon had ever seen, and he didn't blame Alec for ducking out from under it and taking his chances with the rain. "I don't know why he'd want it."

"I don't care if it's *boring*," Isabelle whisper-hissed. "If he takes it, he'll be in Idris all the time. Like, *all the time*. He can't run the Institute and be the Inquisitor. He can't have two jobs at once."

"If you've noticed, Iz, he's in Idris all the time anyway."

"Alec—" The rest of what she said was lost as the light changed and traffic surged forward, spraying icy water up onto the pavement. Clary dodged a geyser of it and nearly knocked into Simon. He took her hand to steady her.

"Sorry," she said. Her hand felt small and cold in his. "Wasn't really paying attention."

"I know." He tried to keep the worry out of his voice. She hadn't really been "paying attention" to anything for the past two weeks. At first she'd cried, and then been angry—angry that she couldn't join the patrols looking for Jace, angry at the Council's endless grilling, angry that she was being kept virtually a prisoner at home because she was under suspicion from the Clave. Most of all she'd been angry at herself for not being able to come up with a rune that would help. She would sit at her desk at night for hours, her stele clutched so tightly in whitening fingers that Simon was afraid it would snap in half. She'd try to force her mind to present her with a picture that would tell her where Jace was. But night after night nothing happened.

She looked older, he thought as they entered the park through a gap in the stone wall on Fifth Avenue. Not in a bad way, but she was different from the girl she'd been when they had walked into the Pandemonium Club on that night that had changed everything. She was taller, but it was more than that. Her expression was more serious, there was more grace and force in the way she walked, her green eyes were less dancing, more focused. She was starting to look, he realized with a jolt of surprise, like Jocelyn.

Clary paused in a circle of dripping trees; the branches blocked most of the rain here, and Isabelle and Clary leaned their umbrellas against the trunks of nearby trees. Clary unclasped the chain around her neck and let the bell slide into her palm. She looked around at all of them, her expression serious. "This is a risk," she said, "and I'm pretty sure if I take it, I can't go back from it. So if any of you don't want to come with me, it's all right. I'll understand."

Simon reached out and put his hand over hers. There was no need to think. Where Clary went, he went. They had been through too much for it to be any other way. Isabelle followed suit, and lastly Alec; rain dripped off his long black lashes like tears, but his expression was resolute. The four of them held hands tightly.

Clary rang the bell.

There was a sensation as if the world were spinning—not the same sensation as being flung through a Portal, Clary thought, into the heart of a maelstrom, but more as if she were sitting on a merry-go-round that had begun to spin faster and faster. She was dizzy and gasping when the sensation stopped suddenly and she was standing still again, her hand clasped with Isabelle's, Alec's, and Simon's.

They released one another, and Clary glanced around. She had been here before, in this dark brown, shining corridor that looked as if it had been carved out of a tiger's eye gemstone. The floor was smooth, worn down by the passage of thousands of years' worth of faerie feet. Light came from glinting chips of gold in the walls, and at the end of the passage was a multicolored curtain that swayed back and forth as if moved by wind, though there was no wind here underground. As Clary drew near to it, she saw that it was sewed out of butterflies. Some of them were still alive, and their struggles made the curtain flutter as if in a stiff breeze.

She swallowed back the acid taste in her throat. "Hello?" she called. "Is anyone there?"

The curtain rustled aside, and the faerie knight Meliorn stepped out into the hallway. He wore the white armor Clary remembered, but there was a sigil over his left breast now—the four *Cs* that also decorated Luke's Council robes, marking him as a member. There was a scar, also, on Meliorn's face that was new, just under his leaf-colored eyes. He regarded her frigidly. "One does not greet the Queen of the Seelie Court with the barbarous human 'hello,'" he said, "as if you were hailing a servant. The proper address is 'Well met.'"

"But we haven't met," said Clary. "I don't even know if she's here."

Meliorn looked at her with scorn. "If the Queen were not present and ready to receive you, ringing the bell would not have brought you. Now come: follow me, and bring your companions with you."

Clary turned to gesture at the others, then followed Meliorn through the curtain of tortured butterflies, hunching her shoulders in the hopes that no part of their wings would touch her.

One by one the four of them stepped into the Queen's chamber. Clary blinked in surprise. It looked entirely different from how it had the last time she'd been here. The Queen reclined on a white and gold divan, and all around her stretched a floor made of alternating squares of black and white, like a great checkerboard. Strings of dangerous-looking thorns hung from the ceiling, and on each thorn was impaled a will-o'-the-wisp, its normally blinding light flickering as it died. The room shimmered in their glow.

Meliorn went to stand beside the Queen; other than him the room was empty of courtiers. Slowly the Queen sat up straight. She was as beautiful as ever, her dress a diaphanous mixture of silver and gold, her hair like rosy copper as she arranged it gently over one white shoulder. Clary wondered why she was bothering. Of all of them there, the only one likely to be moved by her beauty was Simon, and he hated her.

"Well met, Nephilim, Daylighter," she said, inclining her head in their direction. "Daughter of Valentine, what brings you to me?"

Clary opened her hand. The bell shone there like an accusation. "You sent your handmaiden to tell me to ring this if I ever needed your help."

"And you told me you wanted nothing from me," said the Queen. "That you had everything you desired."

Clary thought back desperately to what Jace had said when they had had an audience with the Queen before, how he had flattered and charmed her. It was as if he had suddenly acquired a whole new vocabulary. She glanced back over her shoulder at Isabelle and Alec, but Isabelle only made an irritable motion at her, indicating that she should keep going.

"Things change," Clary said.

The Queen stretched her legs out luxuriously. "Very well. What is it you want from me?"

"I want you to find Jace Lightwood."

In the silence that followed, the sound of the will-o'-the-wisps, crying in their agony, was softly audible. At last the Queen said, "You must think us powerful indeed if you believe the Fair Folk can succeed where the Clave has failed."

"The Clave wants to find Sebastian. I don't care about Sebastian. I want *Jace*," Clary said. "Besides, I already know you know more than you're letting on. You predicted this would happen. No one else knew, but I don't believe you sent me that bell when you did—the same night Jace disappeared—without knowing something was brewing."

"Perhaps I did," said the Queen, admiring her shimmering toenails.

"I've noticed the Fair Folk often say '*perhaps*' when there is a truth they want to hide," Clary said. "It keeps you from having to give a straight answer."

"Perhaps so," said the Queen with an amused smile.

"'Mayhap' is a good word too," Alec suggested.

"Also 'perchance,'" Izzy said.

"I see nothing wrong with 'maybe,'" said Simon. "A little modern, but the gist of the idea comes across."

The Queen waved away their words as if they were annoying bees buzzing around her head. "I do not trust you, Valentine's daughter," she said. "There was a time I wanted a favor from you, but that time is over. Meliorn has his place on the Council. I am not sure there is anything you can offer me."

"If you thought that," said Clary, "you never would have sent the bell."

For a moment their eyes locked. The Queen was beautiful, but there was something behind her face, something that made Clary think of the bones of a small animal, whitening in the sun. At last the Queen said, "Very well. I may be able to help you. But I will desire recompense."

"Shocker," Simon muttered. He had his hands jammed into his pockets and was looking at the Queen with loathing.

Alec laughed.

The Queen's eyes flashed. A moment later Alec staggered back with a cry. He was holding his hands out before him, gaping, as the skin on them wrinkled and his hands curved inward, bent, the joints swollen. His back hunched, his hair graying, his blue eyes fading and sinking into deep wrinkles. Clary gasped. Where Alec had been, an old man, bent and white-haired, stood trembling.

"How swift mortal loveliness does fade," the Queen gloated. "Look at yourself, Alexander Lightwood. I give you a glimpse of yourself in a mere threescore years. What will your warlock lover say then of your beauty?"

Alec's chest was heaving. Isabelle stepped quickly to his side and took his arm. "Alec, it's nothing. It's a glamour." She turned on the Queen. "Take it off him! *Take it off!*"

"If you and yours will speak to me with more respect, then I might consider it."

"We will," Clary said quickly. "We apologize for any rudeness."

The Queen sniffed. "I rather miss your Jace," she said. "Of all of you, he was the prettiest and the best-mannered."

"We miss him too," said Clary in a low voice. "We didn't mean to be ill-mannered. We humans can be difficult in our grief."

"Hmph," said the Queen, but she snapped her fingers and

the glamour fell from Alec. He was himself again, though white-faced and stunned-looking. The Queen shot him a superior look, and turned her attention to Clary.

"There is a set of rings," said the Queen. "They belonged to my father. I desire the return of these objects, for they are faerie-made and possess great power. They allow us to speak to one another, mind to mind, as your Silent Brothers do. At present I have it on good authority that they are on display in the Institute."

"I remember seeing something like that," Izzy said slowly. "Two faerie-work rings in a glass case on the second floor of the library."

"You want me to steal something from the Institute?" Clary said, surprised. Of all the favors she might have guessed the Queen would ask for, this one wasn't high on the list.

"It is not theft," said the Queen, "to return an item to its rightful owners."

"And then you'll find Jace for us?" said Clary. "And don't say 'perhaps.' What will you do exactly?"

"I will assist you in finding him," said the Queen. "I give you my word that my help would be invaluable. I can tell you, for instance, why all of your tracking spells have been for naught. I can tell you in what city he is most likely to be found—"

"But the Clave questioned you," interrupted Simon. "How did you lie to them?"

"They never asked the correct questions."

"*Why* lie to them?" demanded Isabelle. "Where is your allegiance in all this?"

"I have none. Jonathan Morgenstern could be a powerful ally if I do not make him an enemy first. Why endanger him or earn his ire at no benefit to ourselves? The Fair Folk are an old people; we do not make hasty decisions but first wait to see in what direction the wind blows."

"But these rings mean enough to you that if we get them, you'll risk making him angry?" Alec asked.

But the Queen only smiled, a lazy smile, ripe with promise. "I think that is quite enough for today," she said. "Return to me with the rings and we will speak again."

Clary hesitated, turning to look at Alec, and then Isabelle. "You're all right with this? Stealing from the Institute?"

"If it means finding Jace," Isabelle said.

Alec nodded. "Whatever it takes."

Clary turned back to the Queen, who was watching her with an expectant gaze. "Then, I think we have ourselves a bargain."

The Queen stretched and gave a contented smile. "Fare thee well, little Shadowhunters. And a word of warning, though you have done nothing to deserve it. You might well consider the wisdom of this hunt for your friend. For as is often the happenstance with that which is precious and lost, when you find him again, he may well not be quite as you left him."

It was nearly eleven when Alec reached the front door of Magnus's apartment in Greenpoint. Isabelle had persuaded Alec to come to Taki's for dinner with Clary and Simon, and though he had protested, he was glad he had. He had needed a few hours to settle his emotions after what had happened in the Seelie Court. He did not want Magnus to see how badly the Queen's glamour had shaken him.

He no longer had to ring the bell for Magnus to buzz him upstairs. He had a key, a fact he was obscurely proud of. He unlocked the door and headed upstairs, passing Magnus's first-floor neighbor as he did so. Though Alec had never seen the occupants of the first-floor loft, they seemed to be engaged in a tempestuous romance. Once there had been a bunch of someone's belongings strewn all over the landing with a note attached to a jacket lapel addressed to "A lying liar who lies." Right now there was a bouquet of flowers taped to the door with a card tucked among the blooms that read I'M SORRY. That was the thing about New York: you always knew more about your neighbors' business than you wanted to.

Magnus's door was cracked slightly open, and the sounds of music playing softly wafted out into the hall. Today it was Tchaikovsky. Alec felt his shoulders relax as the door of the apartment shut behind him. He could never be quite sure how the place was going to look—it was minimalist right now, with white couches, red stacking tables, and stark black-and-white photos of Paris on the walls—but it had begun to feel increasingly familiar, like home. It smelled like the things he associated with Magnus: ink, cologne, Lapsang Souchong tea, the burned-sugar smell of magic. He scooped up Chairman Meow, who was dozing on a windowsill, and made his way into the study.

Magnus looked up as Alec came in. He was wearing what for Magnus was a somber ensemble—jeans and a black T-shirt with rivets around the collar and cuffs. His black hair was down, messy and tangled as if he'd run his hands through it multiple times in annoyance, and his cat's eyes were heavy-lidded with tiredness. He dropped his pen when Alec appeared, and grinned. "The Chairman likes you."

"He likes anyone who scratches behind his ears," Alec said,

shifting the dozing cat so that his purring seemed to rumble through Alec's chest.

Magnus leaned back in his chair, the muscles in his arms flexing as he yawned. The table was strewn with pieces of paper covered in small, cramped handwriting and drawings—the same pattern over and over, variations on the design that had been splattered across the floor of the rooftop from which Jace had disappeared. "How was the Seelie Queen?"

"Same as usual."

"Raging bitch, then?"

"Pretty much." Alec gave Magnus the condensed version of what had happened in the faerie court. He was good at that—keeping things short, not a word wasted. He never understood people who chattered on incessantly, or even Jace's love of overcomplicated wordplay.

"I worry about Clary," said Magnus. "I worry she's getting in over her little red head."

Alec set Chairman Meow down on the table, where he promptly curled up into a ball and went back to sleep. "She wants to find Jace. Can you blame her?"

Magnus's eyes softened. He hooked a finger into the top of Alec's jeans and pulled him closer. "Are you saying you'd do the same thing if it were me?"

Alec turned his face away, glancing at the paper Magnus had just set aside. "You looking at these again?"

Looking a little disappointed, Magnus let Alec go. "There's got to be a key," he said. "To unlocking them. Some language I haven't looked at yet. Something ancient. This is old black magic, very dark, not like anything I've ever seen before." He looked at the paper again, his head tilted to the side. "Can you hand me that snuffbox over there? The silver one, on the edge of the table."

Alec followed the line of Magnus's gesture and saw a small silver box perched on the opposite side of the big wooden table. He reached over and picked it up. It was like a miniature metal chest set on small feet, with a curved top and the initials *W.S.* picked out in diamonds across the top.

W, he thought. *Will?*

Will, Magnus had said when Alec had asked him about the name Camille had taunted him with. *Dear God, that was a long time ago.*

Alec bit his lip. "What is this?"

"It's a snuffbox," said Magnus, not looking up from his papers. "I told you."

"Snuff? As in snuffing people out?" Alec eyed it.

Magnus looked up and laughed. "As in tobacco. It was very popular around the seventeenth, eighteenth century. Now I use the box to keep odds and ends in."

He held out his hand, and Alec gave the box up. "Do you ever wonder," Alec began, and then started again. "Does it bother you that Camille's out there somewhere? That she got away?" *And that it was my fault?* Alec thought but didn't say. There was no need for Magnus to know.

"She's always been out there somewhere," said Magnus. "I know the Clave isn't terribly pleased, but I'm used to imagining her living her life, not contacting me. If it ever bothered me, it hasn't in a long time."

"But you did love her. Once."

Magnus ran his fingers over the diamond insets in the snuffbox. "I thought I did."

"Does she still love you?"

"I don't think so," Magnus said dryly. "She wasn't very pleasant the last time I saw her. Of course that could be because I've got an eighteen-year-old boyfriend with a stamina rune and she doesn't."

Alec sputtered. "As the person being objectified, I . . . object to that description of me."

"She always was the jealous type." Magnus grinned. He was awfully good at changing the subject, Alec thought. Magnus had made it clear that he didn't like talking about his past love life, but somewhere during their conversation, Alec's sense of familiarity and comfort, his feeling of being at home, had vanished. No matter how young Magnus looked—and right now, barefoot, with his hair sticking up, he looked about eighteen—uncrossable oceans of time divided them.

Magnus opened the box, took out some tacks, and used them to fix the paper he had been looking at to the table. When he glanced up and saw Alec's expression, he did a double take. "Are you okay?"

Instead of replying, Alec reached down and took Magnus's hands. Magnus let Alec pull him to his feet, a questioning look in his eyes. Before he could say anything, Alec drew him closer and kissed him. Magnus made a soft, pleased sound, and gripped the back of Alec's shirt, rucking it up, his fingers cool on Alec's spine. Alec leaned into him, pinning Magnus between the table and his own body. Not that Magnus seemed to mind.

"Come on," Alec said against Magnus's ear. "It's late. Let's go to bed."

Magnus bit his lip and glanced over his shoulder at the papers on the table, his gaze fixed on ancient syllables in forgotten languages. "Why don't you go on ahead?" he said. "I'll join you—five minutes."

"Sure." Alec straightened up, knowing that when Magnus was deep in his studies, five minutes could easily become five hours. "I'll see you there."

"Shhh."

Clary put her finger to her lips before motioning for Simon to go before her through the front door of Luke's house. All the lights were off, and the living room was dark and silent. She shooed Simon toward her room and headed into the kitchen to grab a glass of water. Halfway there she froze.

Her mother's voice was audible down the hall. Clary could hear the strain in it. Just like losing Jace was Clary's worst nightmare, she knew that her mother was living her worst nightmare too. Knowing that her son was alive and out there in the world, capable of anything, was ripping her apart from the inside out.

"But they cleared her, Jocelyn," Clary overheard Luke reply, his voice dipping in and out of a whisper. "There won't be any punishment."

"All of it is my fault." Jocelyn sounded muffled, as if she had buried her head against Luke's shoulder. "If I hadn't brought that . . . creature into the world, Clary wouldn't be going through this now."

"You couldn't have known . . ." Luke's voice faded off into a murmur, and though Clary knew he was right, she had a brief, guilty flash of rage against her mother. Jocelyn should have killed Sebastian in his crib before he'd ever had a chance to grow up and ruin all their lives, she thought, and was instantly horrified at herself for thinking it. She turned and swung back toward the other end of the house, darting into her bedroom and closing the door behind her as if she were being followed.

Simon, who had been sitting on the bed playing with his DS, looked up at her in surprise. "Everything okay?"

She tried to smile at him. He was a familiar sight in this room—they'd slept over at Luke's often enough when they were growing up. She'd done what she could to make this room hers instead of a spare room. Photos of herself and Simon, the Lightwoods, herself with Jace and with her family, were stuck haphazardly into the frame of the mirror over the dresser. Luke had given her a drawing board, and her art supplies were sorted neatly into a stack of cubbyholes beside it. She had tacked up posters of her favorite animes: *Fullmetal Alchemist*, *Rurouni Kenshin*, *Bleach*.

Evidence of her Shadowhunter life lay scattered about as well—a fat copy of *The Shadowhunter's Codex* with her notes and drawings scribbled into the margins, a shelf of books on the occult and paranormal, her stele atop her desk, and a new globe, given to her by Luke, that showed Idris, bordered in gold, in the center of Europe.

And Simon, sitting in the middle of her bed, cross-legged, was one of the few things that belonged both to her old life and her new one. He looked at her with his eyes dark in his pale face, the glimmer of the Mark of Cain barely visible on his forehead.

"My mom," she said, and leaned against the door. "She's really not doing well."

"Isn't she relieved? I mean about you being cleared?"

"She can't get past thinking about Sebastian. She can't get past blaming herself."

"It wasn't her fault, the way he turned out. It was Valentine's."

Clary said nothing. She was recalling the awful thing she had just thought, that her mother should have killed Sebastian when he was born.

"Both of you," said Simon, "blame yourselves for things that aren't your fault. You blame yourself for leaving Jace on the roof—"

She jerked her head up and looked at him sharply. She wasn't aware she'd ever said she blamed herself for that, though she did. "I never—"

"You do," he said. "But I left him, Izzy left him, Alec left him—and Alec's his *parabatai*. There's no way we could have known. And it might have been worse if you'd stayed."

"Maybe." Clary didn't want to talk about it. Avoiding Simon's gaze, she headed into the bathroom to brush her teeth and pull on her fuzzy pajamas. She avoided looking at herself in the mirror. She hated how pale she looked, the shadows under her eyes. She was strong; she wasn't going to fall apart. She had a plan. Even if it was a little insane, and involved robbing the Institute.

She brushed her teeth and was pulling her wavy hair back into a ponytail as she left the bathroom, just catching Simon slipping back into his messenger bag a bottle of what was almost surely the blood he'd bought at Taki's.

She came forward and ruffled his hair. "You can keep the bottles in the fridge, you know," she said. "If you don't like it room temperature."

"Ice-cold blood is worse than room temperature, actually. Warm is best, but I think your mom would balk at me heating it up in saucepans."

"Does Jordan care?" Clary asked, wondering if in fact Jordan even still remembered Simon lived with him. Simon had been at her house every night for the past week. In the first few days after Jace had disappeared, she hadn't been able to sleep. She had piled five blankets over herself, but she'd been unable to get warm. Shivering, she would lie awake imagining her veins sluggish with frozen blood, ice crystals weaving a coral-like shining net around her heart. Her dreams were full of black seas and ice floes and frozen lakes and Jace, his face always hidden from her by shadows or a breath of cloud or his own shining hair as he turned away from her. She would fall asleep for minutes at a time, always waking up with a sick drowning feeling.

The first day the Council had interrogated her, she'd come home and crawled into bed. She'd lain there wide awake until there'd been a knock on her window and Simon had crawled inside, nearly tumbling onto the floor. He'd climbed onto the bed and stretched out beside her without a word. His skin had been cold from the outside, and he'd smelled like city air and oncoming winter chill.

She had touched her shoulder to his, dissolving a tiny part of the tension that clamped her body like a clenched fist. His hand had been cold, but it had been familiar, like the texture of his corduroy jacket against her arm.

"How long can you stay?" she had whispered into the darkness.

"As long as you want."

She'd turned on her side to look at him. "Won't Izzy mind?"

"She's the one who told me I should come over here. She said you weren't sleeping, and if having me with you will make you feel better, I can stay. Or I could just stay until you fall asleep."

Clary had exhaled her relief. "Stay all night," she'd said. "Please."

He had. That night she had had no bad dreams.

As long as he was there, her sleep was dreamless and blank, a dark ocean of nothingness. A painless oblivion.

"Jordan doesn't really care about the blood," Simon said now. "His whole thing is about me being comfortable with what I am. Get in touch with your inner vampire, blah, blah."

Clary slid next to him onto the bed and hugged a pillow. "Is your inner vampire different from your . . . outer vampire?"

"Definitely. He wants me to wear midriff-baring shirts and a fedora. I'm fighting it."

Clary smiled faintly. "So your inner vampire is Magnus?"

"Wait, that reminds me." Simon dug around in his messenger bag and produced two volumes of manga. He waved them triumphantly before handing them to Clary. "*Magical Love Gentleman* volumes fifteen and sixteen," he said. "Sold out everywhere but Midtown Comics."

She picked them up, looking at the colorful back-to-front covers. Once upon a time she would have waved her arms in fangirl joy; now it was all she could do to smile at Simon and thank him, but he had done it for her, she reminded herself, the gesture of a good friend. Even if she couldn't even imagine distracting herself with reading right now. "You're awesome," she said, bumping him with her shoulder. She lay down against the pillows, the manga books balanced on her lap. "And thanks for coming with me to the Seelie Court. I know it brings up sucky memories for you, but—I'm always better when you're there."

"You did great. Handled the Queen like a pro." Simon lay down next to her, their shoulders touching, both of them looking up at the ceiling, the familiar cracks in it, the old glow-in-the-dark paste-on stars that no longer shed light. "So you're going to do it? Steal the rings for the Queen?"

"Yes." She let out her held breath. "Tomorrow. There's a local Conclave meeting at noon. Everyone'll be in it. I'm going in then."

"I don't like it, Clary."

She felt her body tighten. "Don't like what?"

"You having anything to do with faeries. Faeries are liars."

"They *can't* lie."

"You know what I mean. 'Faeries are misleaders' sounds lame, though."

She turned her head and looked at him, her chin against his collarbone. His arm came up automatically and circled her shoulders, pulling her against him. His body was cool, his shirt still damp from the rain. His usually stick-straight hair had dried in windblown curls. "Believe me, I don't like getting mixed up with the Court. But I'd do it for you," she said. "And you'd do it for me, wouldn't you?"

"Of course I would. But it's still a bad idea." He turned his head and looked at her. "I know how you feel. When my father died—"

Her body tightened. "Jace isn't dead."

"I know. I wasn't saying that. It's just— You don't need to say you're better when I'm there. I'm always there with you. Grief makes you feel alone, but you're not. I know you don't believe in—in religion—the same way I do, but you can believe you're surrounded by people who love you, can't you?" His eyes were wide, hopeful. They were the same dark brown they had always been, but different now, as if another layer had been added to their color, the same way his skin seemed both poreless and translucent at the same time.

I believe it, she thought. *I'm just not sure it matters.* She knocked her shoulder gently against his again. "So, do you mind if I ask you something? It's personal but important."

A note of wariness crept into his voice. "What is it?"

"With the whole Mark of Cain thing, does that mean if I accidentally kick you during the night, I get kicked in the shins seven times by an invisible force?"

She felt him laugh. "Go to sleep, Fray."

3
Bad Angels

"Man, I thought you'd forgotten you lived here," Jordan said the moment Simon walked into the living room of their small apartment, his keys still dangling in his hand. Jordan was usually to be found sprawled out on their futon, his long legs dangling over the side, the controller for their Xbox in his hand. Today he *was* on the futon, but he was sitting up straight, his broad shoulders hunched forward, his hands in the pockets of his jeans, the controller nowhere to be seen. He sounded relieved to see Simon, and in a moment Simon realized why.

Jordan wasn't alone in the apartment. Sitting across from him in a nubbly orange velvet armchair—none of Jordan's furniture matched—was Maia, her wildly curling hair contained in two braids. The last time Simon had seen her, she'd been glamorously dressed for a party. Now she was back in uniform: jeans with frayed cuffs, a long-sleeved T-shirt, and a caramel leather jacket. She looked as uncomfortable as Jordan did, her back straight, her gaze straying to the window. When she saw Simon, she clambered gratefully to her feet and gave him a hug. "Hey," she said. "I just stopped by to see how you were doing."

"I'm fine. I mean, as fine as I could be with everything going on."

"I didn't mean about the whole Jace thing," she said. "I meant about *you*. How are you holding up?"

"Me?" Simon was startled. "I'm all right. Worried about Isabelle and Clary. You know the Clave was investigating her—"

"And I heard she got cleared. That's good." Maia let him go. "But I was thinking about you. And what happened with your mom."

"How did you know about that?" Simon shot Jordan a look, but Jordan shook his head, almost imperceptibly. He hadn't told.

Maia pulled on a braid. "I ran into Eric, of all people. He told me what happened and that you'd backed out of Millenium Lint's gigs for the past two weeks because of it."

"Actually, they changed their name," Jordan said. "They're Midnight Burrito now."

Maia shot Jordan an irritated look, and he slid down a little in his seat. Simon wondered what they'd been talking about before he'd gotten home. "Have you talked to anyone else in your family?" Maia asked, her voice soft. Her amber eyes were full of concern. Simon knew it was churlish, but there was something about being looked at like that that he didn't like. It was as if her concern made the problem real, when otherwise he could pretend it wasn't happening.

"Yeah," he said. "Everything's fine with my family."

"Really? Because you left your phone here." Jordan picked it up from the side table. "And your sister's been calling you about every five minutes all day. And yesterday."

A cold feeling spread through Simon's stomach. He took the phone from Jordan and looked at the screen. Seventeen missed calls from Rebecca.

"Crap," he said. "I was hoping to avoid this."

"Well, she's your sister," said Maia. "She was going to call you eventually."

"I know, but I've been sort of fending her off—leaving messages when I knew she wouldn't be there, that kind of thing. I just . . . I guess I was avoiding the inevitable."

"And now?"

Simon set the phone down on the windowsill. "Keep avoiding it?"

"Don't." Jordan took his hands out of his pockets. "You should talk to her."

"And say what?" The question came out more sharply than Simon had intended.

"Your mother must have told her something," said Jordan. "She's probably worried."

Simon shook his head. "She'll be coming home for Thanksgiving in a few weeks. I don't want her to get mixed up in what's going on with my mom."

"She's already mixed up in it. She's your family," said Maia. "Besides, *this*—what's going on with your mom, all of it—this is your life now."

"Then, I guess I want her to stay out of it." Simon knew he was being unreasonable, but he didn't seem to be able to help it. Rebecca was—special. Different. From a part of his life that had so far remained untouched by all this weirdness. Maybe the only part.

Maia threw her hands up and turned to Jordan. "Say something to him. You're his Praetorian guard."

"Oh, come on," said Simon before Jordan could open his mouth. "Are either of you in touch with your parents? Your families?"

They exchanged quick looks. "No," Jordan said slowly, "but neither of us had good relationships with them *before*—"

"I rest my case," said Simon. "We're all orphans. Orphans of the storm."

"You can't just ignore your sister," insisted Maia.

"Watch me."

"And when Rebecca comes home and your house looks like the set of *The Exorcist*? And your mom has no explanation for where you are?" Jordan leaned forward, his hands on his knees. "Your sister will call the police, and your mom will end up committed."

"I just don't think I'm ready to hear her voice," Simon said, but he knew he'd lost the argument. "I have to head back out, but I promise, I'll text her."

"Well," Jordan said. He was looking at Maia, not Simon, as he said it, as if he hoped she'd notice he'd made progress with Simon and be pleased. Simon wondered if they'd been seeing each other at all during the past two weeks when he'd been largely absent. He would have guessed no from the awkward way they'd been sitting when he'd come in, but with these two it was hard to be sure. "It's a start."

***

The rattling gold elevator stopped at the third floor of the Institute; Clary took a deep breath and stepped out into the hallway. The place was, as Alec and Isabelle had promised her it would be, deserted and quiet. The traffic on York Avenue outside was a soft murmur. She imagined she could hear the brush of dust motes against one another as they danced in the window light. Along the wall were the pegs where the residents of the Institute hung their coats when they came inside. One of Jace's black jackets still dangled from a hook, the sleeves empty and ghostly.

With a shiver she set off down the hallway. She could remember the first time Jace had taken her through these corridors, his careless light voice telling her about Shadowhunters, about Idris, about the whole secret world she had never known existed. She had watched him as he'd talked—covertly, she'd thought, but she knew now that Jace noticed everything—watching the light glint off his pale hair, the quick movements of his graceful hands, the flex of the muscles in his arms as he'd gestured.

She reached the library without encountering another Shadowhunter and pushed the door open. The room still gave her the same shiver it had the first time she'd seen it. Circular because it was built inside a tower, the library had a second floor gallery, railed, that ran along the midpoint of the walls, just above the rows of bookshelves. The desk Clary still thought of as Hodge's rested in the center of the room, carved from a single slab of oak, the wide surface rested on the backs of two kneeling angels. Clary half-expected Hodge to stand up behind it, his keen-eyed raven, Hugo, perched on his shoulder.

Shaking off the memory, she headed quickly for the circular staircase at the far end of the room. She was wearing jeans and rubber-soled sneakers, and a soundless rune was carved into her ankle; the silence was almost eerie as she bounded up the steps and onto the gallery. There were books up here too, but they were locked away behind glass cases. Some looked very old, their covers frayed, their bindings reduced to a few strings. Others were clearly books of dark or dangerous magic—*Unspeakable Cults*, *The Demon's Pox*, *A Practical Guide to Raising the Dead.*

Between the locked bookshelves were glass display cases. Each held something of rare and beautiful workmanship—a delicate glass flacon whose stopper was an enormous emerald; a crown with a diamond in the center that did not look as if it would fit any human head; a pendant in the shape of an angel whose wings were clockwork cogs and gears; and in the last case, just as Isabelle had promised, a pair of gleaming golden rings shaped like curling leaves, the faerie work as delicate as baby's breath.

The case was locked, of course, but the Opening rune—Clary biting her lip as she drew it, careful not to make it too powerful lest the glass case burst apart and bring people running—unsnapped the lock. Carefully she eased the case open. It was only as she slid her stele back into her pocket that she hesitated.

Was this really her? Stealing from the Clave to pay the Queen of the Fair Folk, whose promises, as Jace had told her once, were like scorpions, with a barbed sting in the tail?

She shook her head as if to clear the doubts away—and froze. The door to the library was opening. She could hear the creak of wood, muffled voices, footsteps. Without another thought she dropped to the ground, flattening herself against the cold wooden floor of the gallery.

"You were right, Jace," came a voice—coolly amused, and horribly familiar—from below. "The place is deserted."

The ice that had been in Clary's veins seemed to crystallize, freezing her in place. She could not move, could not breathe. She had not felt a shock this intense since she had seen her father run a sword through Jace's chest. Very slowly she inched toward the edge of the gallery and looked down.

And bit down on her lip savagely to keep herself from screaming.

The sloping roof above rose to a point and was set with a glass skylight. Sunlight poured down through the skylight, lighting a portion of the floor like a spotlight on a stage. She could see that the chips of glass and marble and bits of semi-precious stone that were inlaid in the floor formed a design—the Angel Raziel, the cup and the sword. Standing directly on one of the Angel's outspread wings was Jonathan Christopher Morgenstern.

Sebastian.

So this was what her brother looked like. *Really* looked like, alive and moving and animated. A pale face, all angles and planes, tall and slim in black gear. His hair was silvery white, not dark as it had been when she had first seen him, dyed to match the color of the real Sebastian Verlac's. His own pale color suited him better. His eyes were black and snapping with life and energy. The last time she'd seen him, floating in a glass coffin like Snow White, one of his hands had been a bandaged stump. Now that hand was whole again, with a silver bracelet glittering on the wrist, but nothing visible showed that it had ever been damaged—and more than damaged, had been *missing*.

And there beside him, golden hair shimmering in the pale sunlight, was Jace. Not Jace as she had imagined him so often over the past two weeks—beaten or bleeding or suffering or starving, locked away in some dark cell, screaming in pain or calling out for her. This was Jace as she remembered him, when she let herself remember—flushed and healthy and vibrant and beautiful. His hands were careless in the pockets of his jeans, his Marks visible through his white T-shirt. Over it was thrown an unfamiliar tan suede jacket that brought out the gold undertones to his skin. He tipped his head back, as if enjoying the feeling of sun on his face. "I'm always right, Sebastian," he said. "You ought to know that about me by now."

Sebastian gave him a measured look, and then a smile. Clary stared. It had every appearance of being a real smile. But what did she know? Sebastian had smiled at her before, and that had turned out to be one big lie. "So where are the books on summoning? Is there any order to the chaos here?"

"Not really. It's not alphabetized. It follows Hodge's special system."

"Isn't he the one I killed? Inconvenient, that," said Sebastian. "Perhaps I should take the upstairs level and you the downstairs."

He moved toward the staircase that led up to the gallery. Clary's heart began to pound with fear. She associated Sebastian with murder, blood, pain, and terror. She knew that Jace had fought him and won once but had nearly died in the process himself. In a hand-to-hand fight she would never beat her brother. Could she fling herself from the gallery railing to the floor without breaking a leg? And if she did, what would happen then? What would Jace do?

Sebastian had his foot on the lowest step when Jace called out to him, "Wait. They're here. Filed under 'Magic, Nonlethal.'"

"Nonlethal? Where's the fun in that?" Sebastian purred, but he took his foot off the step and moved back toward Jace.

"This is quite a library," he said, reading off titles as he passed them. "*The Care and Feeding of Your Pet Imp. Demons Revealed.*" He plucked that one off the shelf and let out a long, low chuckle.

"What is it?" Jace looked up, his mouth curving upward. Clary wanted to run downstairs and throw herself at him so badly that she bit down on her lip again. The pain was acid sharp.

"It's pornography," said Sebastian. "Look. Demons . . . *revealed*."

Jace came up behind him, resting one hand on Sebastian's arm for balance as he read over his shoulder. It was like watching Jace with Alec, someone he was so comfortable with, he could touch them without thinking about it—but horrible, backward, inside out. "Okay, how can you *tell*?"

Sebastian shut the book and hit Jace lightly on the shoulder with it. "Some things I know more about than you. Did you get the books?"

"I got them." Jace scooped up a stack of heavy-looking tomes from a nearby table. "Do we have time to go by my room? If I could get some of my stuff . . ."

"What do you want?"

Jace shrugged. "Clothes mostly, some weapons."

Sebastian shook his head. "Too dangerous. We need to get in and out fast. Only emergency items."

"My favorite jacket is an emergency item," Jace said. It was so much like hearing him talk to Alec, to any of his friends. "Much like myself, it is both snuggly *and* fashionable."

"Look, we have all the money we could want," said Sebastian. "*Buy* clothes. And you'll be ruling this place in a few weeks. You can run your favorite jacket up the flagpole and fly it like a pennant."

Jace laughed, that soft rich sound Clary loved. "I'm warning you, that jacket is sexy. The Institute could go up in sexy, sexy flames."

"Be good for the place. Too dismal right now." Sebastian grabbed the back of Jace's current jacket with a fist and pulled him sideways. "Now we're going. Hold on to the books." He glanced down at his right hand, where a slim silver ring glittered; with the hand that wasn't holding on to Jace, he used his thumb to twist the ring.

"Hey," Jace said. "Do you think—" He broke off, and for a moment Clary thought that it was because he had looked up and seen her—his face was tilted upward—but even as she sucked in her breath, they both vanished, fading like mirages against the air.

Slowly Clary lowered her head onto her arm. Her lip was bleeding where she had bitten it; she could taste the blood in her mouth. She knew she should get up, move, run away. She wasn't supposed to be here. But the ice in her veins had grown so cold, she was terrified that if she moved, she would shatter.

Alec woke to Magnus's shaking his shoulder. "Come on, sweet pea," he said. "Time to rise and face the day."

Alec unfolded himself groggily out of his nest of pillows and blankets and blinked at his boyfriend. Magnus, despite having gotten very little sleep, looked annoyingly chipper. His hair was wet, dripping onto the shoulders of his white shirt and making it transparent. He wore jeans with holes in them and fraying hems, which usually meant he was planning to spend the day without leaving his apartment.

"'Sweet pea'?" Alec said.

"I was trying it out."

Alec shook his head. "No."

Magnus shrugged. "I'll keep at it." He held out a chipped blue mug of coffee fixed the way Alec liked it—black, with sugar. "Wake up."

Alec sat up, rubbing at his eyes, and took the mug. The first bitter swallow sent a tingle of energy through his nerves. He remembered lying awake the night before and waiting for Magnus to come to bed, but eventually exhaustion had overtaken him and he had fallen asleep at around five a.m. "I'm skipping the Council meeting today."

"I know, but you're supposed to meet your sister and the others in the park by Turtle Pond. You told me to remind you."

Alec swung his legs over the side of the bed. "What time is it?"

Magnus took the mug gently out of his hand before the coffee spilled and set it on the bedside table. "You're fine. You've got an hour." He leaned forward and pressed his lips against Alec's; Alec remembered the first time they had ever kissed, here in this apartment, and he wanted to wrap his arms around his boyfriend and pull him close. But something held him back.

He stood up, disentangling himself, and went over to the bureau. He had a drawer where his clothes were. A place for his toothbrush in the bathroom. A key to the front door. A decent amount of real estate to take up in anyone's life, and yet he couldn't shake the cold fear in his stomach.

Magnus had rolled onto his back on the bed and was watching Alec, one arm crooked behind his head. "Wear that scarf," he said, pointing to a blue cashmere scarf hanging on a peg. "It matches your eyes."

Alec looked at it. Suddenly he was filled with hate—for the scarf, for Magnus, and most of all for himself. "Don't tell me," he said. "The scarf's a hundred years old, and it was given to you by Queen Victoria right before she died, for special services to the Crown or something."

Magnus sat up. "What's gotten into you?"

Alec stared at him. "Am I the newest thing in this apartment?"

"I think that honor goes to Chairman Meow. He's only two."

"I said newest, not youngest," Alec snapped. "Who's *W.S.*? Is it Will?"

Magnus shook his head like there was water in his ears. "What the hell? You mean the snuffbox? *W.S.* is Woolsey Scott. He—"

"Founded the Praetor Lupus. I know." Alec pulled on his jeans and zipped them up. "You mentioned him before, and besides, he's a historical figure. And his snuffbox is in your junk drawer. What else is in there? Jonathan Shadowhunter's toenail clippers?"

Magnus's cat eyes were cold. "Where is all this coming from, Alexander? I don't lie to you. If there's anything about me you want to know, you can ask."

"Bull," Alec said bluntly, buttoning his shirt. "You're kind and funny and all those great things, but what you're not is forthcoming, *sweet pea*. You can talk all day about other people's problems, but you won't talk about yourself or your history, and when I do ask, you wriggle like a worm on a hook."

"Maybe because you can't ask me about my past without picking a fight about how I'm going to live forever and you're not," Magnus snapped. "Maybe because immortality is rapidly becoming the third person in our relationship, Alec."

"Our relationship isn't supposed to *have* a third person."

"Exactly."

Alec's throat tightened. There were a thousand things he

wanted to say, but he had never been good with words like Jace and Magnus were. Instead he grabbed the blue scarf off its peg and wrapped it defiantly around his neck.

"Don't wait up," he said. "I might patrol tonight."

As he slammed out of the apartment, he heard Magnus yell after him, "And that scarf, I'll have you know, is from the *Gap*! I got it *last year*!"

Alec rolled his eyes and jogged down the stairs to the lobby. The single bulb that usually lit the place was out, and the space was so dim that for a moment he didn't see the hooded figure slipping toward him from the shadows. When he did, he was so startled that he dropped his key chain with a rattling clang.

The figure glided toward him. He could tell nothing about it—not age or gender or even species. The voice that came from beneath the hood was crackling and low. "I have a message for you, Alec Lightwood," it said. "From Camille Belcourt."

"Do you want to patrol together tonight?" Jordan asked, somewhat abruptly.

Maia turned to look at him in surprise. He was leaning back against the kitchen counter, his elbows on the surface behind him. There was an unconcern about his posture that was too studied to be sincere. That was the problem with knowing someone so well, she thought. It was very hard to pretend around them, or to ignore it when they were pretending, even when it would be easier.

"Patrol together?" she echoed. Simon was in his room, changing clothes; she'd told him she'd walk to the subway with him, and now she wished she hadn't. She knew she should have contacted Jordan since the last time she'd seen him, when, rather unwisely, she'd kissed him. But then Jace had vanished and the whole world seemed to have blown into pieces and it had given her just the excuse she'd needed to avoid the whole issue.

Of course, not thinking about the ex-boyfriend who had broken your heart and turned you into a werewolf was a lot easier when he wasn't standing right in front of you, wearing a green shirt that hugged his leanly muscled body in all the right places and brought out the hazel color of his eyes.

"I thought they were canceling the patrol searches for Jace," she said, looking away from him.

"Well, not canceling so much as cutting down. But I'm Praetor, not Clave. I can look for Jace on my own time."

"Right," she said.

He was playing with something on the counter, arranging it, but his attention was still on her. "Do you, you know . . . You used to want to go to college at Stanford. Do you still?"

Her heart skipped a beat. "I haven't thought about college since . . ." She cleared her throat. "Not since I Changed."

His cheeks flushed. "You were— I mean, you always wanted to go to California. You were going to study history, and I was going to move out there and surf. Remember?"

Maia shoved her hands into the pockets of her leather jacket. She felt as if she ought to be angry, but she wasn't. For a long time she had blamed Jordan for the fact that she'd stopped dreaming of a human future, with school and a house and a family, maybe, someday. But there were other wolves in the police station pack who still pursued their dreams, their art. Bat, for instance. It had been her own choice to stop her life short. "I remember," she said.

His cheeks flushed. "About tonight. No one's searched the

Brooklyn Navy Yard, so I thought . . . but it's never much fun doing it on my own. But if you don't want to . . ."

"No," she said, hearing her own voice as if it were someone else's. "I mean, sure. I'll go with you."

"Really?" His hazel eyes lit up, and Maia cursed herself inwardly. She shouldn't get his hopes up, not when she wasn't sure how she felt. It was just so hard to believe that he cared that much.

The Praetor Lupus medallion gleamed at his throat as he leaned forward, and she smelled the familiar scent of his soap, and under that—wolf. She flicked her eyes up toward him, just as Simon's door opened and he came out, shrugging on a hoodie. He stopped dead in his doorway, his eyes moving from Jordan to Maia, his eyebrows slowly rising.

"You know, I can make it to the subway on my own," he said to Maia, a faint smile tugging the corner of his mouth. "If you want to stay here . . ."

"No." Maia hastily took her hands out of her pockets, where they had been balled into nervous fists. "No, I'll come with you. Jordan, I'll—I'll see you later."

"Tonight," he called after her, but she didn't turn around to look at him; she was already hurrying after Simon.

Simon trudged alone up the low rise of the hill, hearing the shouts of the Frisbee players in the Sheep Meadow behind him, like distant music. It was a bright November day, crisp and windy, the sun lighting what remained of the leaves on the trees to brilliant shades of scarlet, gold, and amber.

The top of the hill was strewn with boulders. You could see how the park had been hacked out of what had once been a wilderness of trees and stone. Isabelle sat atop one of the boulders, wearing a long dress of bottle-green silk with an embroidered black and silver coat over it. She looked up as Simon strode toward her, pushing her long, dark hair out of her face. "I thought you'd be with Clary," she said as he drew closer. "Where is she?"

"Leaving the Institute," he said, sitting down next to Isabelle on the rock and shoving his hands into his Windbreaker pockets. "She texted. She'll be here soon."

"Alec's on his way—," she began, and broke off as his pocket buzzed. Or, more accurately, the phone in his pocket buzzed. "I think someone's messaging you."

He shrugged. "I'll check it later."

She gave him a look from under her long eyelashes. "Anyway, I was saying, Alec's on his way too. He had to come all the way from Brooklyn, so—"

Simon's phone buzzed again.

"All right, that's it. If you're not getting it, I will." Isabelle leaned forward, against Simon's protests, and slipped her hand into his pocket. The top of her head brushed his chin. He smelled her perfume—vanilla—and the scent of her skin underneath. When she pulled the phone out and drew back, he was both relieved and disappointed.

She squinted at the screen. "Rebecca? Who's *Rebecca?*"

"My sister."

Isabelle's body relaxed. "She wants to meet you. She says she hasn't seen you since—"

Simon swiped the phone out of her hand and flipped it off before shoving it back into his pocket. "I know, I know."

"Don't you want to see her?"

"More than—more than almost anything else. But I don't

want her to *know*. About me." Simon picked up a stick and threw it. "Look what happened when my mom found out."

"So set up a meeting with her somewhere public. Where she can't freak out. Far from your house."

"Even if she can't freak out, she can still look at me like my mother did," Simon said in a low voice. "Like I'm a monster."

Isabelle touched his wrist lightly. "My mom tossed out Jace when she thought he was Valentine's son and a spy—then she regretted it horribly. My mom and dad are coming around to Alec's being with Magnus. Your mom will come around too. Get your sister on your side. That'll help." She tilted her head a little. "I think sometimes siblings understand more than parents. There's not the same weight of expectations. I could never, ever cut Alec off. No matter what he did. Never. Or Jace." She squeezed his arm, then dropped her hand. "My little brother died. I won't ever see him again. Don't put your sister through that."

"Through what?" It was Alec, coming up the side of the hill, kicking dried leaves out of his path. He was wearing his usual ratty sweater and jeans, but a dark blue scarf that matched his eyes was wrapped around his throat. Now, that had to have been a gift from Magnus, Simon thought. No way would Alec have thought to buy something like that himself. The concept of matching seemed to be beyond him.

Isabelle cleared her throat. "Simon's sister—"

She got no further than that. There was a blast of cold air, bringing with it a swirl of dead leaves. Isabelle put her hand up to shield her face from the dust as the air began to shimmer with the unmistakeable translucence of an opening Portal, and Clary appeared before them, her stele in one hand and her face wet with tears.

4

And Immortality

"And you're totally sure it was Jace?" Isabelle asked, for what seemed to Clary like the forty-seventh time.

Clary bit down on her already sore lip and counted to ten. "It's me, Isabelle," she said. "You honestly think I wouldn't recognize *Jace?*" She looked up at Alec standing over them, his blue scarf fluttering like a pennant in the wind. "Could you mistake someone else for Magnus?"

"No. Not ever," he said without missing a beat. His blue eyes were troubled, dark with worry. "I just— I mean, of course we're asking. It doesn't make any sense."

"He could be a hostage," said Simon, leaning back against a boulder. The autumn sunlight turned his eyes the color of coffee grounds. "Like, Sebastian is threatening him that if Jace doesn't go along with his plans, Sebastian will hurt someone he cares about."

All eyes went to Clary, but she shook her head in frustration. "You didn't see them together. Nobody acts like that when they're a hostage. He seemed totally happy to be there."

"Then he's possessed," Alec said. "Like he was by Lilith."

"That was what I thought at first. But when he was possessed by Lilith, he was like a robot. He just kept saying the same things over and over. But this was *Jace*. He was making jokes like Jace does. Smiling like him."

"Maybe he has Stockholm syndrome," Simon suggested. "You know, when you get brainwashed and start sympathizing with your captor."

"It takes *months* to develop Stockholm syndrome," Alec objected. "How did he look? Hurt, or sick in any way? Can you describe them both?"

It wasn't the first time he'd asked. The wind blew dry leaves around their feet as Clary told them again how Jace had looked—vibrant and healthy. Sebastian, too. They had seemed completely calm. Jace's clothes had been clean, stylish, ordinary. Sebastian had been wearing a long black wool trench coat that had looked expensive.

"Like an evil Burberry ad," Simon said when she was done.

Isabelle shot him a look. "Maybe Jace has a plan," she said. "Maybe he's tricking Sebastian. Trying to get into his good graces, figure out what his plans are."

"You'd think that if he were doing that, he'd have figured out a way to tell us about it," Alec said. "Not to leave us panicking. That's too cruel."

"Unless he couldn't risk sending a message. He'd believe we

would trust him. We *do* trust him." Isabelle's voice rose, and she shivered, wrapping her arms around herself. The trees lining the gravel path they stood on rattled their bare branches.

"Maybe we *should* tell the Clave," Clary said, hearing her own voice as if from a distance. "This is— I don't see how we can handle this on our own."

"We can't tell the Clave." Isabelle's voice was hard.

"Why not?"

"If they think he's cooperating with Sebastian, the mandate will be to kill him on sight," Alec said. "That's the Law."

"Even if Isabelle's right? Even if he's just playing along with Sebastian?" Simon said, a note of doubt in his voice. "Trying to get on his side to get information?"

"There's no way to prove it. And if we claimed it was what he's doing, and that got back to Sebastian, he'd probably kill Jace," said Alec. "If Jace is possessed, the Clave will kill him themselves. We can't tell them anything." His voice was hard. Clary looked at him in surprise; Alec was normally the most rule-abiding of them all.

"This is Sebastian we're talking about," said Izzy. "There's no one the Clave hates more, except Valentine, and he's dead. But practically everyone knows someone who died in the Mortal War, and Sebastian's the one who took the wards down."

Clary scuffed at the gravel underfoot with her sneaker. The whole situation seemed like a dream, like she might wake up at any moment. "Then, what next?"

"We talk to Magnus. See if he has any insight." Alec tugged on the corner of his scarf. "He won't go to the Council. Not if I ask him not to."

"He'd better not," said Isabelle indignantly. "Otherwise, worst boyfriend *ever*."

"I said he wouldn't—"

"Is there any point now?" Simon said. "In seeing the Seelie Queen? Now that we know Jace is possessed, or maybe hiding out on purpose—"

"You don't miss an appointment with the Seelie Queen," Isabelle said firmly. "Not if you value your skin the way it is."

"But she'll just take away the rings from Clary and we won't learn anything," Simon argued. "We know more now. We have different questions for her now. She won't answer them, though. She'll just answer the old ones. That's how faeries *work*. They don't do favors. It's not like she's going to let us go talk to Magnus and then come back."

"It doesn't matter." Clary rubbed her hands across her face. They came away dry. At some point her tears had stopped coming, thank God. She hadn't wanted to face the Queen looking like she'd just been bawling her eyes out. "I never got the rings."

Isabelle blinked. "What?"

"After I saw Jace and Sebastian, I was too shaken to get them. I just raced out of the Institute and Portaled here."

"Well, we can't see the Queen, then," said Alec. "If you didn't do what she asked you to, she'll be furious."

"She'll be more than furious," said Isabelle. "You saw what she did to Alec last time we went to the Court. And that was just a glamour. She'll probably turn Clary into a lobster or something."

"She knew," Clary said. "She said, 'When you find him again, he may well not be quite as you left him.'" The Seelie Queen's voice drifted through Clary's head. She shivered.

She could understand why Simon hated faeries so much. They always knew exactly the right words that would lodge like a splinter in your brain, painful and impossible to ignore or remove. "She's just playing around with us. She wants those rings, but I don't think there's any chance she'll really help us."

"Okay," Isabelle said doubtfully. "But if she knew that much, she might know more. And who else is going to be able to help us, since we can't go to the Clave?"

"Magnus," Clary said. "He's been trying to decode Lilith's spell all this time. Maybe if I tell him what I saw, it'll help."

Simon rolled his eyes. "It's a good thing we know the person who's dating Magnus," he said. "Otherwise, I get the feeling we'd all just lie around all the time wondering what the hell to do next. Or try to raise the money to hire Magnus by selling lemonade."

Alec looked merely irritated by this comment. "The only way you could raise enough money to hire Magnus by selling lemonade is if you put meth in it."

"It's an expression. We are all aware that your boyfriend is expensive. I just wish we didn't have to go running to him with every problem."

"So does he," said Alec. "Magnus has another job today, but I'll talk to him tonight and we can all meet at his loft tomorrow morning."

Clary nodded. She couldn't even imagine getting up the next morning. She knew the sooner they talked to Magnus the better, but she felt drained and exhausted, as if she'd left pints of her blood on the library floor in the Institute.

Isabelle had moved closer to Simon. "I guess that leaves us

the rest of the afternoon," she said. "Should we go to Taki's? They'll serve you blood."

Simon glanced over at Clary, clearly worried. "Do you want to come?"

"No, it's okay. I'll grab a cab back to Williamsburg. I should spend some time with my mom. All of this stuff with Sebastian has her falling apart already, and now . . ."

Isabelle's black hair flew in the wind as she whipped her head back and forth. "You can't tell her what you saw. Luke's on the Council. He can't keep it from them, and you can't ask her to keep it from him."

"I know." Clary looked at the three anxious gazes fixed on her. *How had this happened?* she thought. She, who had never kept secrets from Jocelyn—not real ones, anyway—was about to go home and hide something enormous from both her mother and Luke. Something she could talk about only with people like Alec and Isabelle Lightwood and Magnus Bane, people that six months ago she hadn't known existed. It was strange how your world could shift on its axis and everything you trusted could invert itself in what seemed like no time at all.

At least she still had Simon. Constant, permanent Simon. She kissed him on the cheek, waved her good-bye to the others, and turned away, aware that all three of them were watching her worriedly as she strode away across the park, the last of the dead fall leaves crunching under her sneakers as if they were tiny bones.

Alec had lied. It wasn't Magnus who had something to do that afternoon. It was himself.

He knew what he was doing was a mistake, but he couldn't

help himself: it was like a drug, this needing to know more. And now, here he was, underground, holding his witchlight and wondering just what the hell he was doing.

Like all New York subway stations, this one smelled of rust and water, metal and decay. But unlike any other station Alec had ever been in, it was eerily quiet. Aside from the marks of water damage, the walls and platform were clean. Vaulted ceilings, punctuated by the occasional chandelier, rose above him, the arches patterned in green tile. The nameplate tiles on the wall read CITY HALL in block lettering.

The City Hall subway station had been out of use since 1945, though the city still kept it in order as a landmark; the 6 train ran through it on occasion to make a turnaround, but no one ever stood on this platform. Alec had crawled through a hatch in City Hall Park surrounded by dogwood trees to reach this place, dropping down a distance that would probably have broken a mundane's legs. Now he stood, breathing in the dusty air, his heart rate quickening.

This was where the letter the vampire subjugate had handed him in Magnus's entryway had directed him to go. At first he had determined he would never use the information. But he had not been able to bring himself to throw it away. He had balled it up and shoved it into his jeans pocket, and all through the day, even in Central Park, it had eaten at the back of his mind.

It was like the whole situation with Magnus. He couldn't seem to help worrying at it the way one might worry at a diseased tooth, knowing you were making the situation worse but not being able to stop. Magnus had done nothing wrong. It wasn't his fault he was hundreds of years old, and that he had been in love before. But it corroded Alec's peace of mind just the same. And now, knowing both more and less about Jace's situation than he had yesterday—it was too much. He needed to talk to someone, go somewhere, *do something.*

So here he was. And here *she* was, he was sure of it. He moved slowly down the platform. The ceiling vaulted overhead, a central skylight letting in light from the park above, four lines of tiles radiating out from it like a spider's legs. At the end of a platform was a short staircase, which led up into gloom. Alec could detect the presence of a glamour: any mundane looking up would see a concrete wall, but he saw an open doorway. Silently, he headed up the steps.

He found himself in a gloomy, low-ceilinged room. An amethyst-glass skylight let in a little light. In a shadowy corner of the room sat an elegant velvet sofa with an arched, gilded back, and on the sofa sat Camille.

She was as beautiful as Alec remembered, though she had not been at her best the last time he had seen her, filthy and chained to a pipe in a building under construction. She wore a neat black suit now with high-heeled red shoes, and her hair spilled down her shoulders in waves and curls. She had a book open on her lap—*La Place de l'Étoile* by Patrick Modiano. He knew enough French to translate the title. "*The Place of the Star.*"

She looked at Alec as if she had expected to see him.

"Hello, Camille," he said.

She blinked slowly. "Alexander Lightwood," she said. "I recognized your footsteps on the stairs."

She put the back of her hand against her cheek and smiled at him. There was something distant about her smile. It had all the warmth of dust. "I don't suppose you have a message from Magnus for me."

Alec said nothing.

"Of course not," she said. "Silly me. As if he knows where you are."

"How did you know it was me?" he said. "On the stairway."

"You're a Lightwood," she said. "Your family never gives up. I knew you wouldn't let well enough alone after what I said to you that night. The message today was just to prod your memory."

"I didn't need to be reminded of what you promised me. Or were you lying?"

"I would have said anything to get free that night," she said. "But I wasn't lying." She leaned forward, her eyes bright and dark at the same time. "You are Nephilim, of the Clave and Council. There is a price on my head for murdering Shadowhunters. But I already know you have not come here to bring me to them. You want answers."

"I want to know where Jace is," he said.

"You want to know that," she said. "But you know there's no reason I'd have the answer, and I don't. I'd give it to you if I did. I know he was taken by Lilith's son, and I have no reason to have any loyalty to her. She is gone. I know there have been patrols out looking for me, to discover whatever I might know. I can tell you now, I know nothing. I would tell you where your friend is if I knew. I have no reason to further antagonize the Nephilim." She ran a hand through her thick blond hair. "But that's not why you're here. Admit it, Alexander."

Alec felt his breath quicken. He had thought of this moment, lying awake at night beside Magnus, listening to the warlock breathing, hearing his own breaths, numbering them out. Each breath a breath closer to aging and dying. Each night spinning him closer to the end of everything.

"You said you knew a way to make me immortal," said Alec. "You said you knew a way Magnus and I could be together forever."

"I did, didn't I? How interesting."

"I want you to tell it to me now."

"And I will," she said, setting down her book. "For a price."

"No price," said Alec. "I freed you. Now you'll tell me what I want to know. Or I'll give you to the Clave. They'll chain you on the roof of the Institute and wait for sunrise."

Her eyes went hard and flat. "I do not care for threats."

"Then give me what I want."

She stood up, brushing her hands down the front of her jacket, smoothing the wrinkles. "Come and take it from me, Shadowhunter."

It was as if all the frustration, panic, and despair of the past weeks exploded out of Alec. He leaped for Camille, just as she started for him, her fang teeth snapping outward.

Alec barely had time to draw his seraph blade from his belt before she was on him. He had fought vampires before; their swiftness and force was stunning. It was like fighting the leading edge of a tornado. He threw himself to the side, rolled onto his feet, and kicked a fallen ladder in her direction; it stopped her briefly enough for him to lift the blade and whisper, *"Nuriel."*

The light of the seraph blade shot up like a star, and Camille hesitated—then flung herself at him again. She attacked, ripping her long nails along his cheek and shoulder. He felt the warmth and wetness of blood. Spinning, he slashed at her, but she rose into the air, freeing herself from gravity the way some older vampires could. She darted just out of reach, laughing and taunting him.

He ran for the stairs leading down to the platform. She rushed after him; he dodged aside, spun, and pushed off the wall into the air, leaping toward her just as she dived. They collided in midair, her screaming and slashing at him, him keeping a firm hold on her arm, even as they crashed to the ground, almost getting the wind knocked out of him. Keeping her earthbound was the key to winning the fight, and he silently thanked Jace, who had made him practice flips over and over in the training room until he could use almost any surface to get himself airborne for at least a moment or two.

He slashed with the seraph blade as they rolled across the floor, and she deflected his blows easily, moving so fast she was a blur. She kicked at him with her high heels, stabbing his legs with their points. He winced and swore, and she responded with an impressive torrent of filth that involved his sex life with Magnus, *her* sex life with Magnus, and there might have been more had they not reached the center of the room, where the skylight above beamed a circle of sunshine onto the floor. Seizing her wrist, Alec forced Camille's hand down, into the light.

She screamed as enormous white blisters appeared on her skin. Alec could feel the heat from her bubbling hand. Fingers laced with hers, he jerked her hand upright, back into the shadows. She snarled and snapped at him. He elbowed her in the mouth, splitting her lip. Vampire blood—shimmering bright red, brighter than human blood—dripped from the corner of her mouth.

"Have you had enough?" he snarled. "Do you want more?" He began to force her hand back toward the sunlight. It had already begun to heal, the red, blistered skin fading to pink.

"No!" She gasped, coughed, and began to tremble, her whole body spasming. After a moment he realized she was *laughing*—laughing up at him through the blood. "That made me feel alive, little Nephilim. A good fight like that—I should thank you."

"Thank me by giving me the answer to my question," Alec said, panting. "Or I'll ash you. I'm sick of your games."

Her lips stretched into a smile. Her cuts had healed already, though her face was still bloody. "There is no way to make you immortal. Not without black magic or turning you into a vampire, and you have rejected both options."

"But you said—you said there was another way we could be together—"

"Oh, there is." Her eyes danced. "You may not be able to give yourself immortality, little Nephilim, at least not on any terms that would be acceptable to you. *But you can take Magnus's away.*"

Clary sat in her bedroom at Luke's, a pen clutched in her hand, a piece of paper spread out on the desk in front of her. The sun had gone down, and the desk light was on, blazing down on the rune she had just begun.

It had started to come to her on the L train home as she'd stared unseeingly out the window. It was nothing that had ever existed before, and she had rushed home from the station while the image was still fresh in her mind, brushing away her mother's inquiries, closing herself in her room, putting pen to paper—

A knock came on the door. Quickly Clary slid the paper she was drawing on under a blank sheet as her mother came into the room.

"I know, I know," Jocelyn said, holding up a hand against Clary's protest. "You want to be left alone. But Luke made dinner, and you should eat."

Clary gave her mother a look. "So should you." Jocelyn, like her daughter, was given to loss of appetite under stress, and her face looked hollow. She should have been preparing for her honeymoon now, getting ready to pack her bags for somewhere beautiful and far away. Instead the wedding was postponed indefinitely, and Clary could hear her crying through the walls at night. Clary knew that kind of crying, born out of anger and guilt, a crying that said *This is all my fault*.

"I'll eat if you will," Jocelyn said, forcing a smile. "Luke made pasta."

Clary turned her chair around, deliberately angling her body to block her mother's view of her desk. "Mom," she said. "There was something I wanted to ask you."

"What is it?"

Clary bit the end of her pen, a bad habit she'd had since she started to draw. "When I was in the Silent City with Jace, the Brothers told me that there's a ceremony performed on Shadowhunters at birth, a ceremony that protects them. That the Iron Sisters and the Silent Brothers have to perform it. And I was wondering . . ."

"If the ceremony was ever performed on you?"

Clary nodded.

Jocelyn exhaled and pushed her hands through her hair. "It was," she said. "I arranged it through Magnus. A Silent Brother was present, someone sworn to secrecy, and a female warlock who took the place of the Iron Sister. I almost didn't want to do it. I didn't want to think you could be in danger from the supernatural after I'd hidden you so carefully. But Magnus talked me into it, and he was right."

Clary looked at her curiously. "Who was the female warlock?"

"Jocelyn!" It was Luke calling from the kitchen. "The water's boiling over!"

Jocelyn dropped a quick kiss on Clary's head. "Sorry. Culinary emergency. See you in five?"

Clary nodded as her mother hurried from the room, then turned back to her desk. The rune she had been creating was still there, teasing the edge of her mind. She began to draw again, completing the design she had started. As she finished, she sat back and stared at what she'd made. It looked a little like the Opening rune but wasn't. It was a pattern as simple as a cross and as new to the world as a just-born baby. It held a sleeping threat, a sense that it had been born out of her rage and guilt and impotent anger.

It was a powerful rune. But though she knew exactly what it meant and how it could be used, she couldn't think of a single way in which it could possibly be helpful in the current situation. It was like having your car break down on a lonely road, rooting desperately around in the trunk, and triumphantly pulling out an electrical extension cord instead of jumper cables.

She felt as if her own power was laughing at her. With a curse, she dropped her pen onto the desk and put her face in her hands.

***

The inside of the old hospital had been carefully whitewashed, lending an eerie glow to each of the surfaces. Most of the windows were boarded up, but even in the dim light Maia's enhanced sight could pick out details—the sifted dusting of plaster along the bare hallway floors, the marks where construction lights had been put in, bits of wiring glued to the walls by clumps of paint, mice scrabbling in the darkened corners.

A voice spoke from behind her. "I've searched the east wing. Nothing. What about you?"

Maia turned. Jordan stood behind her, wearing dark jeans and a black sweater half-zipped over a green T-shirt. She shook her head. "Nothing in the west wing either. Some pretty rickety staircases. Nice architectural detailing, if that sort of thing interests you."

He shook his head. "Let's get out of here, then. This place gives me the creeps."

Maia agreed, relieved not to be the one who had to say it. She fell into step beside Jordan as they made their way down a set of stairs whose banister was so flaked with crumbling plaster that it resembled snow. She wasn't sure why exactly she'd agreed to patrol with him, but she couldn't deny that they made a decent team.

Jordan was easy to be with. Despite what had happened between them just before Jace had disappeared, he was respectful, keeping his distance without making her feel awkward. The moonlight was bright on both of them as they came out of the hospital and into the open space in front of it. It was a great white marble building whose boarded-over windows looked like blank eyes. A crooked tree, shedding its last leaves, hunched before the front doors.

"Well, that was a waste of time," said Jordan. Maia looked over at him. He was staring at the old naval hospital, which was how she preferred it. She liked looking at Jordan when he wasn't looking at her. That way she could watch the angle of his jawline, the way his dark hair curled against the back of his neck, the curve of his collarbone under the *V* of his T-shirt, without feeling like he expected anything from her for looking.

He'd been a pretty hipster boy when she'd met him, all angles and eyelashes, but he was older-looking now, with scarred knuckles and muscles that moved smoothly under his close-fitting green T-shirt. He still had the olive tone to his skin that echoed his Italian heritage, and the hazel eyes she remembered, though they had the gold-ringed pupils of lycanthropy now. The same pupils she saw when she looked in the mirror every morning. The pupils she had because of him.

"Maia?" He was looking at her quizzically. "What do you think?"

"Oh." She blinked. "I, ah— No, I don't think there was much point in searching the hospital. I mean, to be honest, I can't see why they sent us down here at all. The Brooklyn Navy Yard? Why would Jace be here? It's not like he had a thing for boats."

Jordan's expression went from quizzical to something much darker. "When bodies wind up in the East River, a lot of times they wash up here. The navy yard."

"You think we're looking for a *body*?"

"I don't know." With a shrug he turned and started walking. His boots rustled in the dry, choppy grass. "Maybe at this point I'm just searching because it feels wrong to give up."

His pace was slow, unhurried; they walked shoulder to shoulder, nearly touching. Maia kept her eyes fixed on the Manhattan skyline across the river, a wash of brilliant white light reflecting in the water. As they neared the shallow Wallabout Bay, the arch of the Brooklyn Bridge came into view, and the lit-up rectangle of the South Street Seaport across the water. She could smell the polluted miasma of the water, the dirt and diesel of the navy yard, the scent of small animals moving in the grass.

"I don't think Jace is dead," she said finally. "I think he doesn't want to be found."

At that, Jordan did look at her. "Are you saying we shouldn't be looking?"

"No." She hesitated. They had come out by the river, near a low wall; she trailed her hand along the top of it as they walked. There was a narrow strip of asphalt between them and the water. "When I ran away to New York, I didn't want to be found. But I would have liked the idea that someone was looking for me as hard as everyone's looking for Jace Lightwood."

"Did you like Jace?" Jordan's voice was neutral.

"Like him? Well, not like *that*."

Jordan laughed. "I didn't mean like that. Although, he seems to be generally considered stunningly attractive."

"Are you going to pull that straight-guy thing where you pretend that you can't tell whether other guys are attractive or not? Jace, the hairy guy at the deli on Ninth, they all look the same to you?"

"Well, the hairy guy has that mole, so I think Jace comes out slightly ahead. If you like that whole chiseled, blond, Abercrombie-and-Fitch-wishes-they-could-afford-me thing." He looked at her through his eyelashes.

"I always liked dark-haired boys," she said in a low voice.

He looked at the river. "Like Simon."

"Well—yeah." Maia hadn't thought about Simon that way in a while. "I guess so."

"And you like musicians." He reached up and pulled a leaf off a low-hanging branch overhead. "I mean, I'm a singer, and Bat was a DJ, and Simon—"

"I like music." Maia pushed her hair back from her face.

"What else do you like?" Jordan tore at the leaf in his fingers. He paused and hoisted himself up to sit on the low wall, swinging around to face her. "I mean, is there anything you like so much you think you might want to do it for, like, a living?"

She looked at him in surprise. "What do you mean?"

"Do you remember when I got these?" He unzipped his sweater and shrugged it off. The shirt he wore underneath was short-sleeved. Wrapped around each of his biceps were the Sanskrit words of the Shanti Mantras. She remembered them well. Their friend Valerie had inked them, after hours, for free, in her tattoo shop in Red Bank. Maia took a step toward him. With him sitting and her standing, they were nearly eye to eye. She reached out and hesitantly ran her fingers around the letters inked on his left arm. His eyes fluttered shut at her touch.

"*Lead us from the unreal to the real*," she read aloud. "*Lead us from darkness to light. Lead us from death to immortality.*" His skin felt smooth under her fingertips. "From the Upanishads."

"They were your idea. You were the one who was always reading. You were the one who knew everything. . . ." He opened his eyes and looked at her. His eyes were shades lighter than the water behind him. "Maia, whatever you want to do, I'll help you. I've saved up a lot of my salary from the Praetor. I could give it to you. . . . It could cover your tuition to Stanford. Well, most of it. If you still wanted to go."

"I don't know," she said, her mind whirling. "When I joined the pack, I thought you couldn't be a werewolf and anything else. I thought it was just about living in the pack, not really having an identity. I felt safer that way. But Luke, he has a life. He owns a bookstore. And you, you're in the Praetor. I guess . . . you can be more than one thing."

"You always have been." His voice was low, throaty. "You know, what you said earlier—that when you ran away you would have liked to think someone was looking for you." He took a deep breath. "I was looking for you. I never stopped."

She met his hazel eyes. He didn't move, but his hands, gripping his knees, were white-knuckled. Maia leaned forward, close enough to see the faint stubble along his jaw, to smell the scent of him, wolf-smell and toothpaste and boy. She placed her hands over his. "Well," she said. "You found me."

Their faces were only inches away from each other. She felt his breath against her lips before he kissed her, and she leaned into it, her eyes closing. His mouth was as soft as she remembered, his lips brushing hers gently, sending shivers all through her. She raised her arms to wind them around his neck, to slide her fingers under his curling dark hair, to lightly touch the bare skin at the nape of his neck, the edge of the worn collar of his shirt.

He pulled her closer. He was shaking. She felt the heat of his strong body against hers as his hands slid down her back. "Maia," he whispered. He started to lift the hem of her sweater, his fingers gripping the small of her back. His lips moved against hers. "I love you. I never stopped loving you."

You're mine. You'll always be mine.

Her heart hammering, she jerked away from him, pulling her sweater down. "Jordan—stop."

He looked at her, his expression dazed and worried. "I'm sorry. Was that not any good? I haven't kissed anyone but you, not since . . ." He trailed off.

She shook her head. "No, it's just— I can't."

"All right," he said. He looked very vulnerable, sitting there, dismay written all over his face. "We don't have to do anything—"

She groped for words. "It's just too much."

"It was only a kiss."

"You said you loved me." Her voice shook. "You offered to give me your savings. I can't take that from you."

"Which?" he said, hurt sparking in his voice. "My money, or the love part?"

"Either. I just can't, okay? Not with you, not right now." She started to back away. He was staring after her, his lips parted. "Don't follow me, please," she said, and turned to hurry back the way they had come.

5
Valentine's Son

She was dreaming of icy landscapes again. Bitter tundra that *stretched in all directions, ice floes drifting out on the black waters of the Arctic sea, snow-capped mountains, and cities carved out of ice whose towers sparkled like the demon towers of Alicante.*

In front of the frozen city was a frozen lake. Clary was skidding down a steep slope, trying to reach the lake, though she was not sure why. Two dark figures stood out in the center of the frozen water. As she neared the lake, skidding on the surface of the slope, her hands burning from contact with the ice, and snow filling her shoes, she saw that one was a boy with black wings that spread out from his back like a crow's. His hair was as white as the ice all around them. Sebastian. And beside Sebastian was Jace, his gold hair the only color in the frozen landscape that was not black or white.

As Jace turned away from Sebastian and began to walk toward Clary, wings burst from his back, white-gold and shimmering. Clary slid the last few feet to the frozen surface of the lake and collapsed to her knees, exhausted. Her hands were blue and bleeding, her lips cracked, her lungs seared with each icy breath.

"Jace," she whispered.

And he was there, lifting her to her feet, his wings wrapping around her, and she was warm again, her body thawing from her heart down through her veins, bringing her hands and feet to life with half-painful, half-pleasurable tingles. "Clary," he said, stroking her hair tenderly. "Can you promise me that you won't scream?"

Clary's eyes opened. For a moment she was so disoriented that the world seemed to swing around her like the view from a moving carousel. She was in her bedroom at Luke's—the familiar futon beneath her, the wardrobe with its cracked mirror, the strip of windows that looked out onto the East River, the radiator spitting and hissing. Dim light spilled through the windows, and a faint red glow came from the smoke alarm over the closet. Clary was lying on her side, under a heap of blankets, and her back was deliciously warm. An arm was draped along her side. For a moment, in the half-conscious dizzy space between waking and sleeping, she wondered if Simon had crawled in the window while she slept and lain down beside her.

But Simon had no body heat.

Her heart skittered in her chest. Now entirely awake, she twisted around under the covers. Beside her was Jace, lying on his side, looking down at her, his head propped on his hand. Dim moonlight made a halo out of his hair, and his eyes glittered gold like a cat's. He was fully dressed, still wearing the short-sleeved white T-shirt she had seen him in earlier that day, and his bare arms were twined with runes like climbing vines.

She sucked in a startled breath. Jace, *her* Jace, had never looked at her like that. He had looked at her with desire, but not with this lazy, predatory, *consuming* look that made her heart pulse unevenly in her chest.

She opened her mouth—to say his name or to scream, she wasn't sure, and she never got the chance to find out; Jace moved so fast she didn't even see it. One moment he was lying beside her, and the next he was on top of her, one hand clamped down over her mouth. His legs straddled her hips; she could feel his lean, muscled body pressed against hers.

"I'm not going to hurt you," he said. "I'd never hurt you. But I don't want you screaming. I need to talk to you."

She glared at him.

To her surprise he laughed. His familiar laugh, hushed to a whisper. "I can read your expressions, Clary Fray. The minute I take my hand off your mouth, you're going to yell. Or use your training and break my wrists. Come on, promise me you won't. Swear on the Angel."

This time she rolled her eyes.

"Okay, you're right," he said. "You can't exactly swear with my hand over your mouth. I'm going to take it off. And if you yell—" He tilted his head to the side; pale gold hair fell across his eyes. "I'll disappear."

He took his hand away. She lay still, breathing hard, the pressure of his body on hers. She knew he was faster than her, that there was no move she could make that he wouldn't outpace, but for the moment he seemed to be treating their interaction as a game, something playful. He bent closer to her, and she realized her tank top had pulled up, and she could feel the muscles of his flat, hard stomach against her bare skin. Her face flushed.

Despite the heat in her face, it felt as if cold needles of ice were running up and down her veins. "What are you doing here?"

He drew back slightly, looking disappointed. "That isn't really an answer to my question, you know. I was expecting more of a 'Hallelujah Chorus.' I mean, it's not every day your boyfriend comes back from the dead."

"I already knew you weren't dead." She spoke through numb lips. "I saw you in the library. With—"

"Colonel Mustard?"

"Sebastian."

He let his breath out in a low chuckle. "I knew you were there too. I could feel it."

She felt her body tighten. "You let me think you were gone," she said. "Before that. I thought you— I really thought there was a chance you were—" She broke off; she couldn't say it. *Dead.* "It's unforgivable. If I'd done that to you—"

"Clary." He leaned down over her again; his hands were warm on her wrists, his breath soft in her ear. She could feel everywhere that their bare skin touched. It was horribly distracting. "I had to do it. It was too dangerous. If I'd told you, you would have had to choose between telling the Council I was still alive—and letting them hunt me—and keeping a secret that would make you an accomplice in their eyes. Then, when you saw me in the library, I had to wait. I needed to know if you still loved me, if you would go to the Council or not about what you'd seen. You didn't. I had to know you cared more about me than the Law. You do, don't you?"

"I don't know," she whispered. "I don't know. Who are you?"

"I'm still Jace," he said. "I still love you."

Hot tears welled up in her eyes. She blinked, and they spilled down her face. Gently he ducked his head and kissed her cheeks, and then her mouth. She tasted her own tears, salty on his lips, and he opened her mouth with his, carefully, gently. The familiar taste and feel of him washed over her, and she leaned into him for a split second, her doubts subsumed in her body's blind, unreasoning recognition of the need to keep him close, to keep him *there*—just as the door of her bedroom opened.

Jace let go of her. Clary instantly jerked away from him, scrambling to pull down her tank top. Jace stretched himself into a sitting position with unhurried, lazy grace, and grinned up at the person standing in the doorway. "Well, well," Jace said. "You may have the worst timing since Napoléon decided the dead of winter was the right moment to invade Russia."

It was Sebastian.

Close up, Clary could more clearly see the differences in him since she had known him in Idris. His hair was paper white, his eyes black tunnels fringed by lashes as long as spider's legs. He wore a white shirt, the sleeves pulled up, and she could see a red scar ringing his right wrist, like a ridged bracelet. There was a scar across the palm of his hand, too, looking new and harsh.

"That's my sister you're defiling there, you know," he said, moving his black gaze to Jace. There was amusement in his expression.

"Sorry." Jace didn't sound sorry. He was leaning back against the blankets, catlike. "We got carried away."

Clary sucked in a breath. It sounded harsh in her own ears. "Get *out*," she said, to Sebastian.

He leaned against the door frame, elbow and hip, and she was struck by the similarity in movement between him and Jace. They didn't look alike, but they *moved* alike. As if—

As if they'd been trained to move by the same person.

"Now," he said, "is that any way to talk to your big brother?"

"Magnus should have left you a coatrack," Clary spat.

"Oh, you remember that, do you? I thought we had a pretty good time that day." He smirked a little, and Clary, with a sick drop in her stomach, remembered how he had taken her to the burned remains of her mother's house, how he had kissed her among the rubble, knowing all along who they really were to each other and delighting in the fact that she didn't.

She glanced sideways at Jace. He knew perfectly well that Sebastian had kissed her. Sebastian had taunted him with it, and Jace had nearly killed him. But he didn't look angry now; he looked amused, and mildly annoyed to have been interrupted.

"We should do it again," Sebastian said, examining his nails. "Have some family time."

"I don't care what you think. You're not my brother," Clary said. "You're a murderer."

"I really don't see how those things cancel each other out," said Sebastian. "It's not like they did in the case of dear old Dad." His gaze drifted lazily back to Jace. "Normally I'd hate to get in the way of a friend's love life, but I really don't care for standing out here in this hallway indefinitely. Especially since I can't turn on any lights. It's boring."

Jace sat up, tugging his shirt down. "Give us five minutes."

Sebastian sighed an exaggerated sigh and swung the door shut. Clary stared at Jace. "What the *f*—"

"Language, Fray." Jace's eyes danced. "Relax."

Clary jabbed her hand toward the door. "You heard what he said. About that day he kissed me. He *knew* I was his sister. Jace—"

Something flashed in his eyes, darkening their gold, but when he spoke again, it was as if her words had hit a Teflon surface and bounced off, making no impression.

She drew back from him. "Jace, aren't you listening to anything I'm saying?"

"Look, I understand if you're uncomfortable with your brother waiting outside in the hallway. I wasn't *planning* on kissing you." He grinned in a way that at another time she would have found adorable. "It just seemed like a good idea at the time."

Clary scrambled out of the bed, staring down at him. She reached for the robe that hung on the post of her bed and wrapped it around herself. Jace watched, making no move to stop her, though his eyes shone in the dark. "I—I don't even understand. First you disappear, and now you come back with *him*, acting like I'm not even supposed to notice or care or *remember*—"

"I told you," he said. "I had to be sure of you. I didn't want to put you in the position of knowing where I was while the Clave was still investigating you. I thought it would be hard for you—"

"*Hard* for me?" She was almost breathless with rage. "Tests are hard. Obstacle courses are hard. You disappearing like that practically killed me, Jace. And what do you think you've done to Alec? Isabelle? Maryse? Do you know what it's been like? Can you imagine? Not knowing, the searching—"

That odd look passed over his face again, as if he were hearing her but not hearing her at the same time. "Oh, yes, I was going to ask." He smiled like an angel. "*Is* everyone looking for me?"

"Is everyone—" She shook her head, pulling the robe closer. Suddenly she wanted to be covered up in front of him, in front of all that familiarity and beauty and that lovely predatory smile that said he was willing to do whatever with her, *to* her, no matter who was waiting in the hall.

"I was hoping they'd put up flyers like they do for lost cats," he said. "*Missing, one stunningly attractive teenage boy. Answers to 'Jace,' or 'Hot Stuff.'*"

"You did not just say that."

"You don't like 'Hot Stuff'? You think 'Sweet Cheeks' might be better? 'Love Crumpet'? Really, that last one's stretching it a bit. Though, technically, my family *is* British—"

"Shut up," she said savagely. "And get out."

"I . . ." He looked taken aback, and she remembered how surprised he'd been outside the Manor, when she'd pushed him away. "All right, fine. I'll be serious. Clarissa, I'm here because I want you to come with me."

"Come where with you?"

"Come with me," he said, and then hesitated, "and Sebastian. And I'll explain everything."

For a moment she was frozen, her eyes locked on his. Silvery moonlight outlined the curves of his mouth, the shape of his cheekbones, the shadow of his lashes, the arch of his throat. "The last time I 'came with you somewhere,' I wound up knocked unconscious and dragged into the middle of a black magic ceremony."

"That wasn't me. That was Lilith."

"The Jace Lightwood I know wouldn't be in the same room with Jonathan Morgenstern without killing him."

"I think you'll find that would be self-defeating," Jace said lightly, shoving his feet into his boots. "We are bound, he and I. Cut him and I bleed."

"Bound? What do you mean, *bound?*"

He tossed his light hair back, ignoring her question. "This is bigger than you understand, Clary. He has a plan. He's willing to work, to sacrifice. If you'd give me a chance to explain—"

"He killed Max, Jace," she said. "Your little brother."

He flinched, and for a moment of wild hope she thought she'd broken through to him—but his expression smoothed over like a wrinkled sheet pulled tight. "That was—it was an accident. Besides, Sebastian's just as much my brother."

"No." Clary shook her head. "He's not your brother. He's mine. God knows, I wish it weren't true. He should never have been born—"

"How can you say that?" Jace demanded. He swung his legs out of the bed. "Have you ever considered that maybe things aren't so black and white as you think?" He bent over to grab his weapons belt and buckle it on. "There was a war, Clary, and people got hurt, but—things were different then. Now I know Sebastian would never harm anyone I loved intentionally. He's serving a greater cause. Sometimes there's collateral damage—"

"Did you just call your own brother *collateral damage?*" Her voice rose in an incredulous half shout. She felt as if she could barely breathe.

"Clary, you're not listening. This is important—"

"Like what Valentine thought he was doing was important?"

"Valentine was wrong," he said. "He was right that the Clave was corrupt but wrong about how to go about fixing things. But Sebastian is right. If you'd just hear us out—"

"'Us,'" she said. "God. Jace . . ." He was staring at her from the bed, and even as she felt her heart breaking, her mind was racing, trying to remember where she had left her stele, wondering if she could get to the X-Acto knife in the drawer of her nightstand. Wondering if she could bring herself to use it if she did.

"Clary?" Jace tilted his head to the side, studying her face. "You do—you still love me, don't you?"

"I love Jace Lightwood," she said. "I don't know who *you* are."

His face changed, but before he could speak, a scream shattered the silence. A scream, and the sound of breaking glass.

Clary knew the voice instantly. It was her mother.

Without another glance at Jace, she yanked the bedroom door open and bolted down the hallway, into the living room. The living room in Luke's house was large, divided from the kitchen by a long counter. Jocelyn, in yoga pants and a frayed T-shirt, her hair pulled back in a messy bun, stood by the counter. She had clearly come into the kitchen for something to drink. A glass lay shattered at her feet, the water soaking into the gray carpeting.

All the color had drained from her face, leaving her as pale as bleached sand. She was staring across the room, and even before Clary turned her head, she knew what her mother was looking at.

Her son.

Sebastian was leaning against the living room wall, near the door, with no expression on his angular face. He lowered his eyelids and looked at Jocelyn through his lashes. Something about his posture, the look of him, could have stepped out of Hodge's photograph of Valentine at seventeen years old.

"Jonathan," Jocelyn whispered. Clary stood frozen, even as Jace burst out of the hallway, took in the scene in front of him in one moment, and came to a halt. His left hand was at his weapons belt; his slim fingers were inches from the hilt of one of his daggers, but Clary knew it would take him less than seconds to free it.

"I go by 'Sebastian' now," said Clary's brother. "I concluded that I wasn't interested in keeping the name you and my father gave me. Both of you betrayed me, and I would prefer as little association with you as possible."

Water spread out from the pool of broken glass at Jocelyn's feet in a dark ring. She took a step forward, her eyes searching, running up and down Sebastian's face. "I thought you were dead," she whispered. "*Dead.* I saw your bones turned to ashes."

Sebastian looked at her, his black eyes quiet and narrow. "If you were a real mother," he said, "a good mother, you would have known I was alive. There was a man once who said that mothers carry the key of our souls with them all our lives. But you threw mine away."

Jocelyn made a sound in the back of her throat. She was leaning against the counter for support. Clary wanted to run to her, but her feet felt frozen to the ground. Whatever was happening between her brother and her mother, it was something that had nothing to do with her.

"Don't tell me you aren't even a little glad to see me, Mother," Sebastian said, and though his words were pleading, his voice was flat. "Aren't I everything you could want in a son?" He spread his arms wide. "Strong, handsome, looks just like dear old Dad."

Jocelyn shook her head, her face gray. "What do you want, Jonathan?"

"I want what everyone wants," said Sebastian. "I want what's owed to me. In this case the Morgenstern legacy."

"The Morgenstern legacy is blood and devastation," said Jocelyn. "We are not Morgensterns here. Not me, and not my daughter." She straightened up. Her hand was still gripping the counter, but Clary could see some of the old fire returning to her mother's expression. "If you go now, Jonathan, I won't tell the Clave you were ever here." Her eyes flicked to Jace. "Or you. If they knew you were cooperating, they would kill you both."

Clary moved to stand in front of Jace, reflexively. He looked past her, over her shoulder, at her mother. "You care if I die?" Jace said.

"I care about what it would do to my daughter," said Jocelyn. "And the Law *is* hard—*too* hard. What has happened to you—maybe it can be undone." Her eyes moved back to Sebastian. "But for you—my Jonathan—it's much too late."

The hand that had been gripping the counter swept forward, holding Luke's long-handled *kindjal* blade. Tears shone on Jocelyn's face. But her grip on the knife was steady.

"I look just like him, don't I?" Sebastian said, not moving. He seemed barely to notice the knife. "Valentine. That's why you're looking at me like that."

Jocelyn shook her head. "You look like you always did, from the moment I first saw you. You look like a demon thing." Her voice was achingly sad. "I'm so sorry."

"Sorry for what?"

"For not killing you when you were born," she said, and came out from behind the counter, spinning the *kindjal* in her hand.

Clary tensed, but Sebastian didn't move. His dark eyes followed his mother as she came toward him. "Is that what you want?" he said. "For me to die?" He opened his arms, as if he meant to embrace Jocelyn, and took a step forward. "Go ahead. Commit filicide. I won't stop you."

"*Sebastian*," said Jace. Clary shot him an incredulous look. Did he actually sound *concerned?*

Jocelyn moved another step forward. The knife was a blur in her hand. When it came to a stop, the tip was pointed directly at Sebastian's heart.

Still, he didn't move.

"Do it," he said softly. He cocked his head to the side. "Or can you bring yourself to? You could have killed me when I was born. But you didn't." His voice lowered. "Maybe you know that there is no such thing as conditional love for a child. Maybe if you loved me enough, you could save me."

For a moment they stared at each other, mother and son, ice-green eyes meeting coal-black ones. There were sharp lines at the corners of Jocelyn's mouth that Clary could have sworn hadn't been there two weeks ago. "You're pretending," she said, her voice shaking. "You don't feel anything, Jonathan. Your father taught you to feign human emotion the way one might teach a parrot to repeat words. It doesn't understand what it's saying, and neither do you. I wish—oh, God, I wish—that you did. But—"

Jocelyn brought the blade up in a swift, clean, cutting arc. A perfectly placed blow, it should have driven up under Sebastian's ribs and into his heart. It would have, if he had not moved even faster than Jace; he spun away and back, and the tip of the blade cut only a shallow slash along his chest.

Beside Clary, Jace sucked in his breath. She whirled to look at him. There was a spreading red stain across the front of his shirt. He touched his hand to it; his fingertips came away bloody. *We are bound. Cut him and I bleed.*

Without another thought Clary darted across the room, throwing herself between Jocelyn and Sebastian. "Mom," she gasped. "Stop."

Jocelyn was still holding the knife, her eyes on Sebastian. "Clary, get out of the way."

Sebastian began to laugh. "Sweet, isn't it?" he said. "A little sister defending her big brother."

"I'm not defending *you*." Clary kept her eyes fixed on her mother's face. "Whatever happens to Jonathan happens to Jace. Do you understand, Mom? If you kill him, Jace dies. He's already bleeding. Mom, please."

Jocelyn was still gripping the knife, but her expression was uncertain. "Clary . . ."

"Gracious, how awkward," Sebastian observed. "I'll be interested to see how you resolve this. After all, I've got no reason to leave."

"Yes, actually," came a voice from the hallway, "you do."

It was Luke, barefoot and in jeans and an old sweater. He looked tousled, and oddly younger without his glasses. He also had a sawed-off shotgun balanced at his shoulder, the barrel trained directly on Sebastian. "This is a Winchester twelve-gauge pump-action shotgun. The pack uses it to put down wolves who've gone rogue," he said. "Even if I don't kill you, I can blow your leg off, Valentine's son."

It was as if everyone in the room took a quick gasp of breath all at once—everyone except Luke. And Sebastian, who, a grin splitting his face in half, turned and walked toward Luke, as if oblivious of the gun. "'*Valentine's son*,'" he said. "Is that really how you think of me? Under other circumstances you could have been my godfather."

"Under other circumstances," said Luke, sliding his finger onto the trigger, "you could have been human."

Sebastian stopped in his tracks. "The same could be said of you, werewolf."

The world seemed to have slowed down. Luke sighted along the barrel of the rifle. Sebastian stood smiling.

"Luke," Clary said. It was like one of those dreams, a nightmare where she wanted to scream but all that would scrape past her throat was a whisper. "Luke, *don't do it*."

Her stepfather's finger tightened on the trigger—and then Jace exploded into movement, launching himself from beside Clary, flipping over the sofa, and slamming into Luke just as the shotgun went off.

The shot flew wide; one of the windows shattered outward as the bullet struck it. Luke, knocked off balance, staggered back. Jace yanked the gun from his hands and threw it. It hurtled through the broken window, and Jace turned back toward the older man.

"Luke—," he began.

Luke hit him.

Even knowing everything she knew, the shock of it, seeing Luke, who had stood up for Jace countless times to her mother, to Maryse, to the Clave—Luke, who was basically gentle and kind—seeing him actually strike Jace across the face was as if he had hit Clary instead. Jace, totally unprepared, was thrown backward into the wall.

And Sebastian, who had so far shown no real emotion beyond mockery and disgust, snarled—snarled and drew from his belt a long, thin dagger. Luke's eyes widened, and he began to twist away, but Sebastian was faster than him—faster than anyone else Clary had ever seen. Faster than Jace. He drove the dagger into Luke's chest, twisting it hard before jerking it back out, red to the hilt. Luke fell back against the wall—then slid down it, leaving a smear of blood behind as Clary stared in horror.

Jocelyn screamed. The sound was worse than the sound of the bullet shattering the window, though Clary heard it as if it came from a distance away, or underwater. She was staring at Luke, who had collapsed to the floor, the carpet around him rapidly turning red.

Sebastian raised the dagger again—and Clary flung herself at him, slamming as hard as she could into his shoulder, trying to knock him off balance. She barely moved him, but he did drop the dagger. He turned on her. He was bleeding from a split lip. Clary didn't know why, not until Jace swung into her field of vision and she saw the blood on his mouth where Luke had hit him.

"Enough!" Jace grabbed Sebastian by the back of the jacket. He was pale, not looking at Luke, or at Clary, either. "Stop it. This isn't why we came here."

"Let me go—"

"No." Jace reached around Sebastian and grabbed his hand. His eyes met Clary's. His lips shaped words—there was a flash of silver, the ring on Sebastian's finger—and then both of them were gone, winking out of existence between one breath and another. Just as they vanished, a streak of something metallic shot through the air where they had been standing, and buried itself in the wall.

Luke's *kindjal*.

Clary turned to look at her mother, who had thrown the knife. But Jocelyn wasn't looking at Clary. She was darting to Luke's side, dropping to her knees on the bloody carpet, and pulling him up into her lap. His eyes were closed. Blood trickled from the corners of his mouth. Sebastian's silver dagger, smeared with more blood, lay a few feet away.

"Mom," Clary whispered. "Is he—"

"The dagger was silver." Jocelyn's voice shook. "He won't heal fast like he should, not without special treatment." She touched Luke's face with her fingertips. His chest was rising and falling, Clary saw with relief, if shallowly. She could taste tears burning in the back of her throat and for a moment was amazed at her mother's calm. But then this was the woman who had once stood in the ashes of her home, surrounded by the blackened bodies of her family, including her parents and son, and had gone on from that. "Get some towels from the bathroom," her mother said. "We have to stop the bleeding."

Clary staggered to her feet and went almost blindly into Luke's small, tiled bathroom. There was a gray towel hanging from the back of the door. She yanked it down, went back into the living room. Jocelyn was holding Luke in her lap with one hand; the other hand held a cell phone. She dropped it and reached for the towel as Clary came in. Folding it in half, she laid it over the wound in Luke's chest and pressed down. Clary watched as the edges of the gray towel began to turn scarlet with blood.

"Luke," Clary whispered. He didn't move. His face was an awful gray color.

"I just called his pack," Jocelyn said. She didn't look at her daughter; Clary realized Jocelyn had not asked her a single question about Jace and Sebastian, or why she and Jace had emerged from her bedroom, or what they had been doing there. She was entirely focused on Luke. "They have some members patrolling the area. As soon as they get here, we have to leave. Jace will come back for you."

"You don't know that—," Clary began, whispering past her dry throat.

"I do," said Jocelyn. "Valentine came back for me after fifteen years. That's what the Morgenstern men are like. They don't ever give up. He'll come for you again."

Jace isn't Valentine. But the words died on Clary's lips. She wanted to drop to her knees and take Luke's hand, hold it tightly, tell him she loved him. But she remembered Jace's hands on her in the bedroom and didn't. This was her fault. She didn't deserve to get to comfort Luke, or herself. She deserved the pain, the guilt.

The scrape of footsteps sounded on the porch, the low murmur of voices. Jocelyn's head jerked up. The pack.

"Clary, go and get your things," she said. "Take what you think you'll need but not more than you can carry. We're not coming back to this house."

6

No Weapon in This World

Little flakes of early snow had begun to fall from the steel-gray sky like feathers as Clary and her mother hurried along Greenpoint Avenue, their heads bent against the chill wind coming off the East River.

Jocelyn had not spoken a word since they had left Luke at the disused police station that served as pack headquarters. The whole thing had been a blur—the pack carrying their leader in, the healing kit, Clary and her mother struggling to get a glimpse of Luke as the wolves seemed to close ranks against them. She knew why they couldn't take him to a mundane hospital, but it had been hard, beyond hard, to leave him there in the whitewashed room that served as their infirmary.

It wasn't that the wolves didn't *like* Jocelyn or Clary. It was that Luke's fiancée and her daughter weren't part of the pack. They never would be. Clary had looked around for Maia, for an ally, but she hadn't been there. Eventually Jocelyn had sent Clary out to wait in the corridor since the room had been too crowded, and Clary had slumped on the floor, cradling her knapsack on her lap. It had been two in the morning, and she had never felt so alone. If Luke died . . .

She could barely remember a life without him. Because of him and her mother, she knew what it was like to be loved unconditionally. Luke swinging her up to perch her in the fork of an apple tree on his farm upstate was one of her earliest memories. In the infirmary he had been taking rattling breaths while his third in command, Bat, had unpacked the healing kit. People were supposed to take rattling breaths when they died, she'd remembered. She couldn't remember the last thing she'd said to Luke. Weren't you supposed to remember the last thing you said to someone before they died?

When Jocelyn had come out of the infirmary at last, looking exhausted, she'd held out a hand to Clary and had helped her up off the floor.

"Is he . . . ," Clary had begun.

"He's stabilized," Jocelyn had said. She'd looked up and down the hallway. "We should go."

"Go where?" Clary had been bewildered. "I thought we'd stay here, with Luke. I don't want to leave him."

"Neither do I." Jocelyn had been firm. Clary had thought of the woman who'd turned her back on Idris, on everything she'd ever known, and had walked away from it to start a new life alone. "But we can't lead Jace and Jonathan here either. It's not safe for the pack, or Luke. And this is the first place Jace will look for you."

"Then where . . . ," Clary had started, but she'd realized, even before she'd finished her own sentence, and had shut her mouth. Where did they ever go when they needed help these days?

Now there was a sugary dusting of white along the cracked pavement of the avenue. Jocelyn had put on a long coat before they'd left the house, but beneath it she still wore the clothes that were stained with Luke's blood. Her mouth was set, her gaze unwavering on the road before her. Clary wondered if this was how her mother had looked walking out of Idris, her boots clogged with ashes, the Mortal Cup hidden in her coat.

Clary shook her head to clear it. She was being fanciful, imagining things she hadn't been present to see, her mind skittering away, perhaps, from the awfulness of what she just *had* seen.

Unbidden, the image of Sebastian driving the knife into Luke came into her head, and the sound of Jace's familiar and beloved voice saying "*collateral damage.*"

For as is often the happenstance with that which is precious and lost, when you find him again, he may well not be quite as you left him.

Jocelyn shivered and flipped her hood up to cover her hair. White flakes of snow had already begun to mix with the bright red strands. She was still silent, and the street, lined with Polish and Russian restaurants in between barbershops and beauty parlors, was deserted in the white and yellow night. A memory flashed before the backs of Clary's eyelids—a real one this time, not a wisp of imagination. *Her mother was hurrying her down a night-black street between piles of heaped and dirty snow. A lowering sky, gray and leaden . . .*

She had seen the image before, the first time the Silent Brothers had dug into her mind. She realized what it was now. Her memory of a time her mother had taken her to Magnus's to have her memories altered. It must have been in the dead of winter, but she recognized Greenpoint Avenue in the memory.

The redbrick warehouse Magnus lived in rose above them. Jocelyn pushed open the glass doors to the entryway, and they crowded inside, Clary trying to breathe through her mouth as her mother pushed the buzzer for Magnus one, two, and three times. At last the door opened and they hurried up the stairs. The door to Magnus's apartment was open, and the warlock was leaning against the architrave, waiting for them. He was wearing canary-yellow pajamas, and on his feet were green slippers with alien faces, complete with sproingy antennae. His hair was a tangled, curly, spiky mass of black, and his gold-green eyes blinked tiredly at them.

"Saint Magnus's Home for Wayward Shadowhunters," he said in a deep voice. "Welcome." He threw an arm wide. "Spare bedrooms are that way. Wipe your boots on the mat." He stepped back into the apartment, letting them pass through in front of him before shutting the door. Today the place was done up in a sort of faux-Victorian decor, with high-backed sofas and large gilt mirrors everywhere. The pillars were strung with lights in the shape of flowers.

There were three spare rooms down a short corridor off the main living room; at random Clary chose one on the right. It was painted orange, like her old bedroom in Park Slope, and had a sofa bed and a small window that looked out on the darkened windows of a closed diner. Chairman Meow was curled up on the bed, nose tucked under his tail. She sat down beside him and petted his ears, feeling the purring that vibrated through his small furry body. As she stroked him, she caught sight of the sleeve of her sweater. It was stained dark and crusted with blood. Luke's blood.

She stood up and yanked the sweater off violently. From her backpack she took a clean pair of jeans and a black V-necked thermal shirt and changed into them. She glanced at herself briefly in the window, which showed her a pale reflection, her hair hanging limply, damp with snow, her freckles standing out like paint splotches. Not that it mattered what she looked like. She thought of Jace kissing her—it felt like days ago instead of hours—and her stomach hurt as if she'd swallowed tiny knives.

She held on to the edge of the bed for a long moment until the pain subsided. Then she took a deep breath and went back out into the living room.

Her mother was seated on one of the gilt-backed chairs, her long artist's fingers wrapped around a mug of hot water with lemon. Magnus was slumped on a hot-pink sofa, his green slippers up on the coffee table. "The pack stabilized him," Jocelyn was saying in an exhausted voice. "They don't know for how long, though. They thought there might have been silver powder on the blade, but it appears to be something else. The tip of the knife —" She glanced up, saw Clary, and fell silent.

"It's okay, Mom. I'm old enough to hear what's wrong with Luke."

"Well, they don't know exactly what it is," Jocelyn said softly. "The tip of the blade Sebastian used broke off against one of his ribs and lodged in the bone. But they can't retrieve it. It . . . moves."

"It moves?" Magnus looked puzzled.

"When they tried to dig it out, it burrowed into the bone and nearly snapped it," Jocelyn said. "He's a werewolf, he heals fast, but it's in there gashing up his internal organs, keeping the wound from closing."

"Demon metal," said Magnus. "Not silver."

Jocelyn leaned forward. "Do you think you can help him? Whatever it costs, I'll pay—"

Magnus stood up. His alien slippers and rumpled bed-head seemed extremely incongruous given the gravity of the situation. "I don't know."

"But you healed Alec," said Clary. "When the Greater Demon wounded him . . ."

Magnus had begun to pace. "I knew what was wrong with him. I *don't* know what kind of demon metal this is. I could experiment, try different healing spells, but it won't be the fastest way to help him."

"What's the fastest way?" Jocelyn said.

"The Praetor," said Magnus. "The Wolf Guard. I knew the man who founded it—Woolsey Scott. Because of certain . . . incidents, he was fascinated with minutiae about the way demon metals and demon drugs act on lycanthropes, the same way the Silent Brothers keep records of the ways Nephilim can be healed. Over the years the Praetor have become very closed-off and secretive, unfortunately. But a member of the Praetor could access their information."

"Luke's not a member," Jocelyn said. "And their roster is secret—"

"But Jordan," said Clary. "Jordan's a member. He can find out. I'll call him—"

"*I'll* call him," said Magnus. "I can't get into Praetor headquarters, but I can pass on a message that ought to hold some extra weight. I'll be back." He padded off to the kitchen, the antennae on his slippers waving gently like seaweed in a current.

Clary turned back to her mother, who was staring down at her mug of hot water. It was one of her favorite restoratives, though Clary could never figure out why anyone would want to drink warm sour water. The snow had soaked her mother's hair, and now that it was drying, it was beginning to curl, like Clary's did in humid weather.

"Mom," Clary said, and her mother looked up. "That knife you threw—back at Luke's—was it at Jace?"

"It was at Jonathan." She would never call him Sebastian, Clary knew.

"It's just . . ." Clary took a deep breath. "It's almost the same thing. You saw. When you stabbed Sebastian, Jace started to bleed. It's like they're—mirrored in some way. Cut Sebastian, Jace bleeds. Kill him, and Jace dies."

"Clary." Her mother rubbed her tired eyes. "Can we not discuss this now?"

"But you said you think he'll come back for me. Jace, I mean. I need to know that you won't hurt him—"

"Well, you can't know that. Because I won't promise it, Clary. I can't." Her mother looked at her with unflinching eyes. "I saw the two of you come out of your bedroom."

Clary flushed. "I don't want to—"

"To what? Talk about it? Well, too bad. You brought it up.

You're lucky I'm not in the Clave anymore, you know. How long have you known where Jace was?"

"I *don't* know where he is. Tonight is the first time I've talked to him since he disappeared. I *saw* him in the Institute with Seb—with Jonathan, yesterday. I told Alec and Isabelle and Simon. But I couldn't tell anyone else. If the Clave got hold of him— I can't let that happen."

Jocelyn raised her green eyes. "And why not?"

"Because he's Jace. Because I love him."

"He's *not* Jace. That's just it, Clary. He's not who he was. Can't you see that—"

"Of course I can see it. I'm not stupid. But I have faith. I saw him possessed before, and I saw him break free of it. I think Jace is still inside there somewhere. I think there's a way to save him."

"What if there isn't?"

"Prove it."

"You can't prove a negative, Clarissa. I understand that you love him. You always have loved him, too much. You think I didn't love your father? You think I didn't give him every chance? And look what came of that. Jonathan. If I hadn't stayed with your father, he wouldn't exist—"

"Neither would I," said Clary. "In case you forgot, I came *after* my brother, not before." She looked at her mother, hard. "Are you saying it would be worth it never to have had me, if you could get rid of Jonathan?"

"No, I—"

There was the grating sound of keys in a lock, and the apartment door swung open. It was Alec. He wore a long leather duster open over a blue sweater, and there were white flakes of snow in his black hair. His cheeks were candy-apple red from the cold, but his face was otherwise pale.

"Where's Magnus?" he said. As he looked toward the kitchen, Clary saw a bruise on his jaw, below his ear, about the size of a thumbprint.

"Alec!" Magnus came skidding into the living room and blew a kiss to his boyfriend across the room. Having discarded his slippers, he was barefoot now. His cat's eyes shone as he looked at Alec.

Clary knew that look. That was herself looking at Jace. Alec didn't return the gaze, though. He was shucking off his coat and hanging it on a hook on the wall. He was visibly upset. His hands were trembling, his broad shoulders tightly set.

"You got my text?" Magnus asked.

"Yeah. I was only a few blocks away anyway." Alec looked at Clary, and then at her mother, anxiety and uncertainty warring in his expression. Though Alec had been invited to Jocelyn's reception party, and had met her several times besides that, they did not by any measure know each other well. "It's true, what Magnus said? You saw Jace again?"

"And Sebastian," said Clary.

"But Jace," Alec said. "How was—I mean, how did he seem?"

Clary knew exactly what he was asking; for once she and Alec understood each other better than anyone else in the room. "He's not playing a trick on Sebastian," she replied softly. "He really has changed. He isn't like himself at all."

"How?" Alec demanded, with an odd blend of anger and vulnerability. "How is he different?"

There was a hole in the knee of Clary's jeans; she picked at it, scraping the skin underneath. "The way he talks—he believes in Sebastian. Believes in what he's doing, whatever that is. I reminded him that Sebastian killed Max, and he didn't even seem to care." Her voice cracked. "He said Sebastian was just as much his brother as Max was."

Alec whitened, the red spots on his cheeks standing out like bloodstains. "Did he say anything about me? Or Izzy? Did he ask about us?"

Clary shook her head, hardly able to stand the look on Alec's face. Out of the corner of her eye, she could see Magnus watching Alec too, his face almost blank with sadness. She wondered if he was jealous of Jace still, or just hurt on Alec's behalf.

"Why did he come to your house?" Alec shook his head. "I don't get it."

"He wanted me to come with him. To join him and Sebastian. I guess he wants their evil little duo to be an evil little trio." She shrugged. "Maybe he's lonely. Sebastian can't be the greatest company."

"We don't know that. He could be absolutely fantastic at Scrabble," said Magnus.

"He's a murdering psychopath," said Alec flatly. "And Jace knows it."

"But Jace isn't Jace right now—," Magnus began, and broke off as the phone rang. "I'll get that. Who knows who else might be on the run from the Clave and need a place to stay? It's not like there are hotels in this city." He padded off toward the kitchen.

Alec flung himself down on the sofa. "He's working too hard," he said, looking worriedly after his boyfriend. "He's been up all night every night trying to decipher those runes."

"Is the Clave employing him?" Jocelyn wanted to know.

"No," Alec said slowly. "He's doing it for me. Because of what Jace means to me." He tapped his shoulder, where his *parabatai* rune was hidden by his shirt.

"You knew Jace wasn't dead," Clary said, her mind beginning to tick over thoughts. "Because you're *parabatai*, because of that tie between you. But you said you felt something wrong."

"Because he's possessed," Jocelyn said. "It's changed him. Valentine said that when Luke became a Downworlder, he felt it. That sense of wrongness."

Alec shook his head. "But when Jace was possessed by Lilith, I didn't *feel* it," he said. "Now I can feel something . . . wrong. Something off." He looked down at his shoes. "You can feel it when your *parabatai* dies—like there was a cord tying you to something and it has snapped, and now you're falling." He looked at Clary. "I felt it, once, in Idris, during the battle. But it was so brief—and when I returned to Alicante, Jace was alive. I convinced myself I had imagined it."

Clary shook her head, thinking of Jace and the blood-soaked sand by Lake Lyn. *You didn't.*

"What I feel now is different," he went on. "I feel like he's absent from the world but not dead. Not imprisoned . . . Just not *here*."

"That's just it," Clary said. "Both times I've seen him and Sebastian, they've vanished into thin air. No Portal, just one minute they were here and the next they were gone."

"When you talk about *there* or *here*," said Magnus, coming back into the room with a yawn, "and this world and that world, what you're talking about are dimensions. There are only a few warlocks who can do dimensional magic. My old friend Ragnor could. Dimensions don't lie side by side—they're folded together, like paper. Where they intersect, dimensional pockets can be created that prevent magic from being able to find you. After all, you're not *here*—you're *there*."

"Maybe that's why we can't track him? Why Alec can't feel him?" said Clary.

"Could be." Magnus sounded almost impressed. "It would mean there's literally no way to find them if they don't want to be found. And no way to get a message back to us if you *did* find them. That's complicated, expensive magic. Sebastian must have some connections—" The door buzzer sounded, and they all jumped. Magnus rolled his eyes. "Everyone calm down," he said, and vanished into the entryway. He was back a moment later with a man wrapped in a long parchment-colored robe, the back and sides inked with patterns of runes in dark red-brown. Though his hood was up, shadowing his face, he looked completely dry, as if not a flake of snow had fallen on him. When he pushed the hood back, Clary was not at all surprised to see the face of Brother Zachariah.

Jocelyn set her mug down suddenly on the coffee table. She was looking at the Silent Brother. With his hood pushed back, you could see his dark hair, but his face was shadowed so that Clary could not see his eyes, only his high, rune-scarred cheekbones. "You," Jocelyn said, her voice trailing off. "But Magnus told me that you would never—"

Unexpected events call for unexpected measures. Brother Zachariah's voice floated out, touching the inside of Clary's head; she knew from the expressions on the faces of the others that they could hear him too. *I will say nothing to the Clave or Council of anything that transpires tonight. If the chance comes before me to save the last of the Herondale bloodline, I consider that of higher importance than the fealty I render the Clave.*

"So that's settled," Magnus said. He made a strange pair with the Silent Brother beside him, one of them pale and blanched in robes, the other in bright yellow pajamas. "Any new insight into Lilith's runes?"

I have studied the runes carefully and listened to all the testimony given in the Council, said Brother Zachariah. *I believe that her ritual was twofold. First she used the Daylighter's bite to revive Jonathan Morgenstern's consciousness. His body was still weak, but his mind and will were alive. I believe that when Jace Herondale was left alone on the roof with him, Jonathan drew on the power of Lilith's runes and forced Jace to enter the enspelled circle that surrounded him. At that point Jace's will would have been subject to his. I believe he would have drawn on Jace's blood for the strength to rise and escape the roof, taking Jace with him.*

"And somehow all that created a connection between them?" Clary said. "Because when my mother stabbed Sebastian, Jace started to bleed."

Yes. What Lilith did was a sort of twinning ritual, not unlike our own parabatai *ceremony but much more powerful and dangerous. The two are now bound inextricably. Should one die, the other will follow. No weapon in this world can wound only one of them.*

"When you say they're bound inextricably," Alec said, leaning forward, "does that mean— I mean, Jace *hates* Sebastian. Sebastian murdered our brother."

"And I don't see how Sebastian can be all that fond of Jace, either. He was horribly jealous of him all his life. He thought Jace was Valentine's favorite," added Clary.

"Not to mention," Magnus noted, "that Jace killed him. That would put anyone off."

"It's like Jace doesn't remember that any of these things happened," Clary said in frustration. "No, not like he doesn't remember them—like he doesn't *believe* them."

He remembers them. But the power of the binding is such that Jace's thoughts will pass over and around those facts, like water passing around rocks in a riverbed. It was like the spell that Magnus cast upon your mind, Clarissa. When you saw pieces of the Invisible World, your mind would reject them, turn away from them. There is no point reasoning with Jace about Jonathan. The truth cannot break their connection.

Clary thought of what had happened when she had reminded Jace that Sebastian had killed Max, how his face had temporarily furrowed in thought, then smoothed out as if he had forgotten what she had said as quickly as she'd said it.

Take some small comfort in the fact that Jonathan Morgenstern is as bound as your Jace is. He cannot harm or hurt Jace, nor would he want to, Zachariah added.

Alec threw his hands up. "So they love each other now? They're best friends?" The hurt and jealousy was plain in his tone.

No. They are each other now. They see as the other sees. They know the other is somehow indispensable to them. Sebastian is the leader, the primary of the two. What he believes, Jace will believe. What he wants, Jace will do.

"So he's possessed," Alec said flatly.

In a possession there is often some part of the person's original consciousness left intact. Those who have been possessed speak of watching their own actions from the outside, crying out but unable to be heard. But Jace is fully inhabiting his body and mind. He believes himself sane. He believes that this is what he wants.

"So what did he want from me?" Clary demanded in a shaking voice. "Why did he come to my room tonight?" She hoped her cheeks didn't burn. She tried to push back the memory of kissing him, the pressure of his body against hers in the bed.

He still loves you, said Brother Zachariah, and his voice was surprisingly gentle. *You are the central point about which his world spins. That has not changed.*

"And that's why we had to leave," Jocelyn said tensely. "He'll come back for her. We couldn't stay at the police station. I don't know where will be safe—"

"Here," Magnus said. "I can put up wards that will keep Jace and Sebastian out."

Clary saw relief flood her mother's eyes. "Thank you," Jocelyn said.

Magnus waved an arm. "It's a privilege. I do love fending off angry Shadowhunters, especially of the possessed variety."

He is not possessed, Brother Zachariah reminded them.

"Semantics," said Magnus. "The question is, what are the two of them up to? What are they planning?"

"Clary said that when she saw them in the library, Sebastian told Jace he'd be running the Institute soon enough," said Alec. "So they're up to *something.*"

"Carrying on Valentine's work, probably," said Magnus. "Down with Downworlders, kill all recalcitrant Shadowhunters, blah blah."

"Maybe." Clary wasn't sure. "Jace said something about Sebastian serving a greater cause."

"The Angel only knows what that indicates," Jocelyn said. "I was married to a zealot for years. I know what 'a greater cause' means. It means torturing the innocent, brutal murder, turning your back on your former friends, all in the name of something that you believe is bigger than yourself but is no more than greed and childishness dressed up in fanciful language."

"Mom," Clary protested, worried to hear Jocelyn sound so bitter.

But Jocelyn was looking at Brother Zachariah. "You said no weapon in this world can wound only one of them," she said. "No weapon you know of . . ."

Magnus's eyes glowed suddenly, like a cat's when caught in a beam of light. "You think . . ."

"The Iron Sisters," said Jocelyn. "They are the experts on weapons and weaponry. They might perhaps have an answer."

The Iron Sisters, Clary knew, were the sister sect to the Silent Brothers; unlike their brethren, they did not have their mouths or eyes sewed shut but instead lived in almost total solitude in a fortress whose location was unknown. They were not fighters—they were creators, the hands who shaped the weapons, the steles, the seraph blades that kept the Shadowhunters alive. There were runes only they could carve, and only they knew the secrets of molding the silvery-white substance called *adamas* into demon towers, steles, and witchlight runestones. Rarely seen, they did not attend Council meetings or venture into Alicante.

It is possible, Brother Zachariah said after a long pause.

"If Sebastian could be killed—if there is a weapon that could kill him but leave Jace alive—does that mean Jace would be free of his influence?" Clary asked.

There was an even longer pause. Then, *Yes,* said Brother Zachariah. *That would be the most likely outcome.*

"Then, we should go to see the Sisters." Exhaustion hung

on Clary like a cloak, weighting her eyes, souring the taste in her mouth. She rubbed her eyes, trying to scrub it away. "Now."

"I can't go," said Magnus. "Only female Shadowhunters can enter the Adamant Citadel."

"And you're not going," Jocelyn said to Clary in her sternest No-you-are-not-going-out-clubbing-with-Simon-after-midnight voice. "You're safer here, where you're warded."

"Isabelle," said Alec. "Isabelle can go."

"Do you have any idea where she is?" Clary said.

"Home, I'd imagine," said Alec, one shoulder lifting in a shrug. "I can call her—"

"I'll take care of it," Magnus said, smoothly removing his cell phone from his pocket and punching in a text with the skill of the long-practiced. "It's late, and we don't need to wake her up. Everyone needs rest. If I'm to send any of you through to the Iron Sisters, it will be tomorrow."

"I'll go with Isabelle," Jocelyn said. "No one's looking for me specifically, and it's better that she not go alone. Even if I'm not technically a Shadowhunter, I was once. It's only required that one of us be in good standing."

"This isn't fair," Clary said.

Her mother didn't even look at her. "Clary . . ."

Clary rose to her feet. "I've been practically a prisoner for the past two weeks," she said in a shaking voice. "The Clave wouldn't let me look for Jace. And now that he came to me—*to me*—you won't even let me come with you to the Iron Sisters—"

"It isn't *safe*. Jace is probably tracking you—"

Clary lost it. "Every time you try to keep me safe, you wreck my life!"

"No, the more involved you get with Jace the more *you*

wreck your life!" her mother snapped back. "Every risk you've taken, every danger you've been in, is because of him! He held a knife to your throat, Clarissa—"

"That wasn't him," Clary said in the softest, deadliest voice she could imagine. "Do you think I'd stay for one second with a boy who threatened me with a knife, even if I loved him? Maybe you've been living too long in the mundane world, Mom, but *there is magic*. The person who hurt me wasn't Jace. It was a demon wearing his face. And the person we're looking for now isn't Jace. But if he dies . . ."

"There's no chance of getting Jace back," said Alec.

"There may already be no chance," said Jocelyn. "God, Clary, look at the evidence. You thought you and Jace were brother and sister! You sacrificed everything to save his life, and a Greater Demon used him to get to you! When are you going to face the fact that the two of you are *not meant to be together*?"

Clary jerked back as if her mother had hit her. Brother Zachariah stood as still as a statue, as if no one were shouting at all. Magnus and Alec were staring; Jocelyn was red-cheeked, her eyes glittering with anger. Not trusting herself to speak, Clary spun on her heel, stalked down the hallway to Magnus's spare bedroom, and slammed the door behind her.

"All right, I'm here," Simon said. A cold wind was blowing across the flat expanse of the roof garden, and he stuffed his hands into the pockets of his jeans. He didn't really feel the cold, but he felt like he ought to. He raised his voice. "I showed up. Where are you?"

The roof garden of the Greenwich Hotel—now closed, and therefore empty of people—was done up like an English garden, with carefully shaped dwarf box trees, elegantly scattered wicker and glass furniture, and Lillet umbrellas that flapped in the stiff wind. The trellises of climbing roses, bare in the cold, spider-webbed the stone walls that surrounded the roof, above which Simon could see a gleaming view of downtown New York. "I am here," said a voice, and a slender shadow detached itself from a wicker armchair and rose. "I had begun to wonder if you were coming, Daylighter."

"Raphael," Simon said in a resigned voice. He walked forward, across the hardwood planks that wound between the flower borders and artificial pools lined with shining quartz. "I was wondering myself."

As he came closer, he could see Raphael clearly. Simon had excellent night vision, and only Raphael's skill at blending with the shadows had kept him hidden before. The other vampire was wearing a black suit, turned up at the cuffs to show the gleam of cuff links in the shape of chains. He still had the face of a little boy angel, though his gaze as he regarded Simon was cold. "When the head of the Manhattan vampire clan calls you, Lewis, you come."

"And what would you do if I didn't? Stake me?" Simon spread his arms wide. "Take a shot. Do whatever you want to me. Go nuts."

"*Dios*, but you are boring," said Raphael. Behind him, by the wall, Simon could see the chrome gleam of the vampire motorcycle he'd ridden to get here.

Simon lowered his arms. "You're the one who asked me to meet you."

"I have a job offer for you," said Raphael.

"Seriously? You short-staffed at the hotel?"

"I need a bodyguard."

Simon eyed him. "Have you been watching *The Bodyguard?* Because I am *not* going to fall in love with you and carry you around in my burly arms."

Raphael looked at him sourly. "I would pay you extra money to remain entirely silent while you worked."

Simon stared at him. "You're serious, aren't you?"

"I would not bother coming to see you if I were not serious. If I were in a joking mood, I would spend that time with someone I liked." Raphael sat back down in the armchair. "Camille Belcourt is free in the city of New York. The Shadowhunters are entirely caught up with this stupid business with Valentine's son and will not be bothered to track her down. She represents an immediate danger to me, for she wishes to reassert her control of the Manhattan clan. Most are loyal to me. Killing me would be the fastest way for her to put herself back at the top of the hierarchy."

"Okay," Simon said slowly. "But why me?"

"You are a Daylighter. Others can protect me during the night, but you can protect me in the day, when most of our kind are helpless. And you carry the Mark of Cain. With you between me and her, she would not dare to strike at me."

"That's all true, but I'm not doing it."

Raphael looked incredulous. "Why not?"

The words exploded out of Simon. "Are you kidding? Because you have never done one single thing for me in the entire time since I became a vampire. Instead you have done your level best to make my life miserable and then end it. So—if you want it in vampire language—it affords me great pleasure, my liege, to say to you now: *Hell, no.*"

"It is not wise for you to make an enemy of me, Daylighter. As friends—"

Simon laughed incredulously. "Wait a second. Were we *friends*? That was friends?"

Raphael's fang teeth snapped out. He was very angry indeed, Simon realized. "I know why you refuse me, Daylighter, and it is not out of some pretended sense of rejection. You are so involved with the Shadowhunters, you think you are one of them. We have seen you with them. Instead of spending your nights in the hunt, as you should, you spend them with Valentine's daughter. You live with a werewolf. You are a disgrace."

"Do you act like this with every job interview?"

Raphael bared his teeth. "You must decide if you are a vampire or a Shadowhunter, Daylighter."

"I'll take Shadowhunter, then. Because from what I've experienced of vampires, you mostly suck. No pun intended."

Raphael stood up. "You are making a grave mistake."

"I already told you—"

The other vampire waved a hand, cutting him off. "There is a great darkness coming. It will sweep the Earth with fire and shadow, and when it is gone, there will be no more of your precious Shadowhunters. We, the Night Children, will survive it, for we live in darkness. But if you persist in denying what you are, you too will be destroyed, and none shall lift a hand to help you."

Without thinking, Simon raised his hand to touch the Mark on his forehead.

Raphael laughed soundlessly. "Ah, yes, the Angel's brand upon you. In the time of darkness even the angels will be destroyed. Their strength will not aid you. And you had better pray, Daylighter, that you do not lose that Mark before the war comes. For if you do, there will be a line of enemies waiting their turn to kill you. And I will be at the head of it."

Clary had been lying on her back on Magnus's sofa bed for a long time. She had heard her mother come down the hall and go into one of the other spare bedroom, shutting the door behind her. Through her own door she could hear Magnus and Alec talking in low voices in the living room. She supposed she could wait for them to go to sleep, but Alec had said Magnus had been up until all hours lately studying the runes; even though Brother Zachariah appeared to have interpreted them, she couldn't trust that Alec and Magnus would retire soon.

She sat up on the bed next to Chairman Meow, who made a fuzzy noise of protest, and rummaged in her backpack. She drew out of it a clear plastic box and flipped it open. There were her Prismacolor pencils, some stumps of chalk—and her stele.

She stood up, slipping the stele into her jacket pocket. Taking her phone off the desk, she texted MEET ME AT TAKI'S. She watched as the message went through, then tucked the phone into her jeans and took a deep breath.

This wasn't fair to Magnus, she knew. He'd promised her mother he'd look after her, and that didn't include her sneaking out of his apartment. But she had kept her mouth shut. She hadn't promised anything. And besides, it was Jace.

You would do anything to save him, whatever it cost you, whatever you might owe to Hell or Heaven, would you not?

She took out her stele, set the tip to the orange paint of the wall, and began to draw a Portal.

***

The sharp banging noise woke Jordan out of a sound sleep. He bolted upright instantly and rolled out of bed to land in a crouch on the floor. Years of training with the Praetor had left him with fast reflexes and a permanent habit of sleeping lightly. A quick sight-scent scan told him the room was empty—just moonlight pooling on the floor at his feet.

The banging came again, and this time he recognized it. It was the sound of someone pounding on the front door. He usually slept in just his boxer shorts; yanking on jeans and a T-shirt, he kicked the door of his room open and strode out into the hallway. If this was a bunch of drunk college kids amusing themselves by knocking on all the doors in the building, they were about to get a faceful of angry werewolf.

He reached the door—and paused. The image came to him again, as it had in the hours it had taken him to fall asleep, of Maia running away from him at the navy yard. The look on her face when she'd pulled away from him. He'd pushed her too far, he knew, asked for too much, too fast. Blown it completely, probably. Unless—maybe she'd reconsidered. There had been a time when their relationship had been all passionate fights and equally passionate make-up sessions.

His heart pounding, he threw the door open. And blinked. On the doorstep stood Isabelle Lightwood, her long black glossy hair falling almost to her waist. She wore black suede knee-high boots, tight jeans, and a red silky top with her familiar red pendant around her throat, glittering darkly.

"*Isabelle?*" He couldn't hide the surprise in his voice, or, he suspected, the disappointment.

"Yeah, well, I wasn't looking for you, either," she said,

pushing past him into the apartment. She smelled of Shadowhunter—a smell like sun-warmed glass—and underneath that, a rosy perfume. "I was looking for Simon."

Jordan squinted at her. "It's two in the morning."

She shrugged. "He's a vampire."

"But I'm not."

"Ohhhhh?" Her red lips curled up at the corners. "Did I wake you up?" She reached out and flicked the top button on his jeans, the tip of her fingernail scraping across his flat stomach. He felt his muscles jump. Izzy was gorgeous, there was no denying that. She was also a little terrifying. He wondered how unassuming Simon managed to handle her at all. "You might want to button these all the way up. Nice boxers, by the by." She moved past him, toward Simon's bedroom. Jordan followed, buttoning his jeans and muttering about how there was nothing strange about having a pattern of dancing penguins on your underwear.

Isabelle ducked her head into Simon's room. "He's not here." She slammed the door behind her and leaned back against the wall, looking at Jordan. "You did say it was two in the morning?"

"Yeah. He's probably at Clary's. He's been sleeping there a lot lately."

Isabelle bit her lip. "Right. Of course."

Jordan was beginning to get that feeling he got sometimes, that he was saying something unfortunate, without knowing exactly what that thing was. "Is there a reason you came over here? I mean, did something happen? Is something wrong?"

"Wrong?" Isabelle threw up her hands. "You mean other than the fact that my brother has disappeared and has probably been brainwashed by the evil demon who murdered my *other* brother, and my parents are getting divorced and Simon is off with *Clary*—"

She stopped abruptly and stalked past him into the living room. He hurried after her. By the time he caught up, she was in the kitchen, rifling through the pantry shelves. "Do you have anything to drink? A nice Barolo? Sagrantino?"

Jordan took her by the shoulders and moved her gently out of the kitchen. "Sit," he said. "I'll get you some tequila."

"Tequila?"

"Tequila's what we have. That and cough syrup."

Sitting down at one of the stools that lined the kitchen counter, she waved a hand at him. He would have expected her to have long red or pink fingernails, buffed to perfection, to match the rest of her, but no—she was a Shadowhunter. Her hands were scarred, the nails squared off and filed down. The Voyance rune shone blackly on her right hand. "Fine."

Jordan grabbed the bottle of Cuervo, uncapped it, and poured her a shot. He pushed the glass across the counter. She downed it instantly, frowned, and slammed the glass down.

"Not enough," she said, reached across the counter, and took the bottle out of his hand. She tilted her head back and swallowed once, twice, three times. When she set the bottle back down, her cheeks were flushed.

"Where'd you learn to drink like that?" He wasn't sure if he should be impressed or frightened.

"The drinking age in Idris is fifteen. Not that anyone pays attention. I've been drinking wine mixed with water along with my parents since I was a kid." Isabelle shrugged. The gesture lacked a little of her usual fluid coordination.

"Okay. Well, is there a message you want me to give Simon, or anything I can say or—"

"No." She took another swig out of the bottle. "I got all liquored up and came over to talk to him, and of course he's at Clary's. Figures."

"I thought you were the one who told him he ought to go over there in the first place."

"Yeah." Isabelle fiddled with the label on the tequila bottle. "I did."

"So," Jordan said, in what he thought was a reasonable tone. "Tell him to stop."

"I can't do that." She sounded exhausted. "I owe her."

Jordan leaned on the counter. He felt a little like a bartender in a TV show, dispensing sage advice. "What do you owe her?"

"Life," Isabelle said.

Jordan blinked. This was a little beyond his bartending and advice-offering skills. "She saved your life?"

"She saved *Jace's* life. She could have had anything from the Angel Raziel, and she saved my brother. I've only ever trusted a few people in my life. Really trusted. My mother, Alec, Jace, and Max. I lost one of them already. Clary's the only reason I didn't lose another."

"Do you think you'll ever be able to really trust someone you aren't related to?"

"I'm not related to Jace. Not really." Isabelle avoided his gaze.

"You know what I mean," said Jordan, with a meaningful glance at Simon's room.

Izzy frowned. "Shadowhunters live by an honor code, werewolf," she said, and for a moment she was all arrogant Nephilim, and Jordan remembered why so many Downworlders disliked them. "Clary saved a Lightwood. I owe her my life. If I can't give her that—and I don't see how she has any use for it—I can give her whatever will make her less unhappy."

"You can't *give* her Simon. Simon's a person, Isabelle. He goes where he wants."

"Yeah," she said. "Well, he doesn't seem to mind going where she is, does he?"

Jordan hesitated. There was something about what Isabelle was saying that seemed off, but she wasn't *completely* wrong either. Simon had with Clary an ease that he never seemed to show with anyone else. Having been in love with only one girl in his life, and having stayed in love with her, Jordan didn't feel he was qualified to hand out advice on that front—though he remembered Simon warning him, with wryness, that Clary had "the nuclear bomb of boyfriends." Whether there had been jealousy under that wryness, Jordan wasn't sure. He wasn't sure whether you could ever completely forget the first girl you loved either. Especially when she was right there in front of you, every day.

Isabelle snapped her fingers. "Hey, you. Are you even paying attention?" She tilted her head to the side, blowing dark strands of hair out of her face, and looked at him hard. "What's going on with you and Maia, anyway?"

"Nothing." The single word held volumes. "I'm not sure she's ever going to stop hating me."

"She might not, at that," Isabelle said. "She's got good reason."

"Thanks."

"I don't do false reassurances," Izzy said, and pushed the

tequila bottle away from her. Her eyes, on Jordan, were lively and dark. "Come here, werewolf boy."

She'd dropped her voice. It was soft, seductive. Jordan swallowed against a suddenly dry throat. He remembered seeing Isabelle in her red dress outside the Ironworks and thinking, *That's the girl Simon was messing around on Maia with?* Neither of them was the sort of girl who gave the impression you could cheat on her and survive it.

And neither one of them was the sort of girl you said no to. Warily he moved around the counter toward Isabelle. He was a few steps away when she reached out and pulled him toward her by the wrists. Her hands slid up his arms, over the swell of his biceps, the muscles of his shoulders. His heartbeat quickened. He could feel the warmth coming off her and could smell her perfume and sweet tequila. "You're gorgeous," she said. Her hands slid around to flatten themselves against his chest. "You know that, right?"

Jordan wondered if she could feel his heart beating through his shirt. He knew the way girls looked at him on the street—boys, too, sometimes—knew what he saw in the mirror every day, but he never thought about it much. He had been so focused on Maia for so long that it never seemed to matter beyond whether *she* would still find him attractive if they ever saw each other again. He'd been chatted up plenty, but not often by girls who looked like Isabelle, and never by anyone so blunt. He wondered if she was going to kiss him. He hadn't kissed anyone but Maia since he was fifteen. But Isabelle was looking up at him, and her eyes were big and dark, and her lips were slightly parted and the color of strawberries. He wondered if they would taste like strawberries if he kissed her.

"And I just don't care," she said.

"Isabelle, I don't think— Wait. *What?*"

"I should care," she said. "I mean, there's Maia to think about, so I probably wouldn't just rip your clothes off blithely anyway, but the thing is, I don't *want* to. Normally I would want to."

"Ah," Jordan said. He felt relief, and also the tiniest twinge of disappointment. "Well . . . that's good?"

"I think about him *all the time*," she said. "It's awful. Nothing like this has ever happened to me before."

"You mean Simon?"

"Scrawny little mundane bastard," she said, and took her hands off Jordan's chest. "Except he isn't. Scrawny, anymore. Or a mundane. And I like spending time with him. He makes me laugh. And I like the way he smiles. You know, one side of his mouth goes up before the other one— Well, you live with him. You must have noticed."

"Not really," said Jordan.

"I miss him when he's not around," Isabelle confessed. "I thought . . . I don't know, after what happened that night with Lilith, things changed between us. But now he's with Clary all the time. And I can't even be angry with her."

"You lost your brother."

Isabelle looked up at him. "What?"

"Well, he's knocking himself out to make Clary feel better because she lost Jace," said Jordan. "But Jace is your brother. Shouldn't Simon be knocking himself out to make *you* feel better too? Maybe you're not mad at her, but you could be mad at him."

Isabelle looked at him for a long moment. "But we're not

anything," she said. "He's not my boyfriend. I just *like* him." She frowned. "Crap. I can't believe I said that. I must be drunker than I thought."

"I kind of figured it out from what you were saying before." He smiled at her.

She didn't smile back, but she lowered her lashes and looked up at him through them. "You're not so bad," she said. "If you want, I can say nice things to Maia about you."

"No, thanks," said Jordan, who wasn't sure what Izzy's version of nice things was, and feared finding out. "You know, it's normal, when you're going through a tough time, to want to be with the person you—" He was about to say "love," realized she had never used the word, and switched gears. "Care about. But I don't think Simon knows you feel that way about him."

Her lashes fluttered back up. "Does he ever say anything about me?"

"He thinks you're really strong," Jordan said. "And that you don't need him at all. I think he feels . . . superfluous to your life. Like, what can he give you when you're already perfect? Why would you want a guy like him?" Jordan blinked; he hadn't meant to run on like that, and he wasn't sure how much of what he'd said applied to Simon, and how much to himself and Maia.

"So you mean I should tell him how I feel?" said Isabelle in a small voice.

"Yes. Definitely. Tell him how you feel."

"Okay." She grabbed for the tequila bottle and took a swig. "I'll go over to Clary's right now and I'll tell him."

A small flower of alarm blossomed in his chest. "You can't. It's practically three in the morning—"

"If I wait, I'll lose my nerve," she said, in that reasonable tone that only very drunk people ever employed. She took another swig out of the bottle. "I"ll just go over there, and I'll knock on the window, and I'll tell him how I feel."

"Do you even know which window is Clary's?"

She squinted. "Nooo."

The horrible vision of a drunk Isabelle waking up Jocelyn and Luke floated through Jordan's head. "Isabelle, *no*." He reached up to take the tequila bottle from her, and she jerked it away from him.

"I think I'm changing my mind about you," she said in a semi-threatening tone that would have been more frightening if she'd been able to focus her eyes on him directly. "I don't think I like you so much after all." She stood up, looked down at her feet with a surprised expression—and fell over backward. Only Jordan's quick reflexes allowed him to catch her before she hit the floor.

7

A Sea Change

Clary was on her third cup of coffee at Taki's when Simon finally walked in. He was in jeans, a red zip-up sweatshirt (why bother with wool coats when you didn't feel the cold?), and engineer boots. People turned to look at him as he wove his way through the tables toward her. Simon had cleaned up nicely since Isabelle had started getting on his case about his clothes, Clary thought as he headed toward her among the tables. There were flakes of snow caught in his dark hair, but where Alec's cheeks had been scarlet from the cold, Simon's remained colorless and pale. He slid into the booth across from her and looked at her, his dark eyes reflective and shining.

"You called?" he asked, making his voice deep and resonant so that he sounded like Count Dracula.

"Technically, I texted." She slid the menu across the table toward him, flipping it to the page for vampires. She'd glanced at it before, but the thought of blood pudding and blood milk shakes made her shudder. "I hope I didn't wake you up."

"Oh, no," he said. "You wouldn't believe where I was . . ." His voice trailed off as he saw the expression on her face. "Hey." His fingers were suddenly under her chin, lifting her head. The laughter was gone from his eyes, replaced by concern. "What happened? Is there more news about Jace?"

"Do you know what you want?" It was Kaelie, the blue-eyed faerie waitress who had given Clary the Queen's bell. She looked at Clary now and grinned, a superior grin that made Clary grit her teeth.

Clary ordered a piece of apple pie; Simon ordered a mix of hot chocolate and blood. Kaelie took the menus away, and Simon looked at Clary with concern. She took a deep breath and told him about the night, every gritty detail—Jace's appearance, what he had said to her, the confrontation in the living room, and what had happened to Luke. She told him what Magnus had said about dimensional pockets and other worlds, and how there was no way to track someone hidden in a dimensional pocket or get a message through to them. Simon's eyes grew darker as she spoke, and by the end of the story, he had his head in his hands.

"Simon?" Kaelie had come and gone, leaving their food, which was untouched. Clary touched his shoulder. "What is it? Is it Luke—"

"It's my fault." He looked up at her, eyes dry. Vampires cried tears mixed with blood, she thought; she had read that somewhere. "If I hadn't bitten Sebastian . . ."

"You did it for me. So I'd live." Her voice was gentle. "You saved my life."

"You've saved mine six or seven times. It seemed fair." His voice cracked; she recalled him retching up Sebastian's black blood, on his knees in the roof garden.

"Assigning blame doesn't get us anywhere," Clary said. "And this isn't why I dragged you here, just to tell you what happened. I mean, I would have told you anyway, but I would have waited for tomorrow if it weren't that . . ."

He looked at her warily and took a sip from his mug. "Weren't that what?"

"I have a plan."

He groaned. "I was afraid of that."

"My plans are *not* terrible."

"Isabelle's plans are terrible." He pointed a finger at her. "*Your* plans are suicidal. At best."

She sat back, her arms crossed over her chest. "Do you want to hear it or not? You have to keep it a secret."

"I would pluck out my own eyes with a fork before I would give away your secrets," Simon said, then looked anxious. "Wait a second. Do you think that's likely to be required?"

"I don't know." Clary covered her face with her hands.

"Just tell me." He sounded resigned.

With a sigh she reached into her pocket and drew out a small velvet bag, which she upended on the table. Two gold rings fell out, landing with a soft clink.

Simon looked at them, puzzled. "You want to get married?"

"Don't be an idiot." She leaned forward, dropping her voice. "Simon, these are *the rings*. The ones the Seelie Queen wanted."

"I thought you said you never got them—" He broke off, raising his eyes to her face.

"I lied. I did take them. But after I saw Jace in the library, I didn't want to give them to the Queen anymore. I had a feeling we might need them sometime. And I realized she was never going to give us any useful information. The rings seemed more valuable than another round with the Queen."

Simon caught them up in his hand, hiding them from sight as Kaelie passed by. "Clary, you can't just take things the Seelie Queen wants and keep them for yourself. She's a very dangerous enemy to have."

She looked at him pleadingly. "Can we at least see if they work?"

He sighed and handed her one of the rings; it felt light but was as soft as real gold. She worried for a moment that it wouldn't fit, but as soon as she slipped it onto her right index finger, it seemed to mold to the shape of her finger, until it sat perfectly in the space below her knuckle. She saw Simon glancing down at his right hand, and realized the same thing had happened to him.

"Now we talk, I guess," he said. "Say something to me. You know, mentally."

Clary turned to Simon, feeling absurdly as if she were being asked to perform in a play whose lines she hadn't memorized. *Simon?*

Simon blinked. "I think— Could you do that again?"

This time Clary concentrated, trying to focus her mind on Simon—the Simon-ness of him, the shape of the way he thought, the feeling of hearing his voice, the sense of him close. His whispers, his secrets, the way he made her laugh. *So,* she thought conversationally, *now that I'm in your mind, want to see some naked mental pictures of Jace?*

Simon jumped. "I *heard* that! And, no."

Excitement fizzed in Clary's veins; it was *working*. "Think something back to me."

It took less than a second. She heard Simon, the way she heard Brother Zachariah, a voice without sound inside her mind. *You've seen him* naked?

Well, not entirely. But I—

"Enough," he said out loud, and though his voice was caught between amusement and anxiety, his eyes sparked. "They work. Holy crap. They really work."

She leaned forward. "So can I tell you my idea?"

He touched the ring on his finger, feeling its delicate tracery, the leaf-veins carved under his fingertips. *Sure.*

She began to explain, but she hadn't yet reached the end of her description when Simon interrupted, out loud this time. "No. Absolutely not."

"Simon," she said. "It's a perfectly fine plan."

"The plan where you follow Jace and Sebastian off to some unknown dimensional pocket and we use these rings to communicate so those of us over here in the *regular* dimension of Earth can track you down? That plan?"

"Yes."

"No," he said. "No, it isn't."

Clary sat back. "You don't just get to say no."

"This plan involves me! I get to say no! *No*."

"Simon—"

Simon patted the seat beside him as if someone were sitting there. "Let me introduce you to my good friend No."

"Maybe we can compromise," she suggested, taking a bite of pie.

"No."

"SIMON."

"'No' is a magical word," he told her. "Here's how it goes. You say, 'Simon, I have an insane, suicidal plan. Would you like to help me carry it out?' And I say, '*Why, no.*'"

"I'll do it anyway," she said.

He stared at her across the table. "What?"

"I'll do it whether you help me or not," she said. "If I can't use the rings, I'll still follow Jace to wherever he is and try to get word back to you guys by sneaking away, finding telephones, whatever. If it's possible. I'm going to do it, Simon. I just have a better chance of surviving if you help me. And there's no risk to you."

"I *don't care about risk to me*," he hissed, leaning forward across the table. "I care about what happens to you! Dammit, I'm practically indestructible. Let *me* go. You stay behind."

"Yes," Clary said, "Jace won't find that odd at all. You can just tell him you've always been secretly in love with him and you can't stand being parted."

"I could tell him I've given it thought and I completely agree with his and Sebastian's philosophy and decided to throw in my lot with theirs."

"You don't even know what their philosophy is."

"There is that. I might have better luck telling him I'm in love with him. Jace thinks everyone's in love with him anyway."

"But I," said Clary, "actually *am*."

Simon looked at her for a long time over the table, silently. "You're serious," he said finally. "You'd actually do this. Without me—without any safety net."

"There isn't anything I wouldn't do for Jace."

Simon leaned his head back against the plastic booth seat. The Mark of Cain glowed a gentle silver against his skin. "Don't say that," he said.

"Wouldn't you do anything for the people you love?"

"I'd do almost anything for you," Simon said quietly. "I'd die for you. You know that. But would I kill someone else, someone innocent? What about a *lot* of innocent lives? What about the whole world? Is it really love to tell someone that if it came down to picking between them and every other life on the planet, you'd pick them? Is that— I don't know, is that a moral sort of love at all?"

"Love isn't moral or immoral," said Clary. "It just is."

"I know," Simon said. "But the actions we take in the name of love, those are moral or immoral. And normally it wouldn't matter. Normally—whatever I think of Jace being annoying—he'd never ask you to do anything that went against your nature. Not for him, not for anyone. But he isn't exactly *Jace* anymore, is he? And I just don't know, Clary. I don't know what he might ask you to do."

Clary leaned her elbow on the table, suddenly very tired. "Maybe he isn't Jace. But he's the closest thing to Jace I've got. There's no way back to Jace without him." She raised her eyes to Simon's. "Or are you telling me it's hopeless?"

There was a long silence. Clary could see Simon's innate honesty warring with his desire to protect his best friend. Finally he said, "I'd never say that. I'm still Jewish, you know, even if I am a vampire. In my heart I remember and believe, even the words I can't say. G—" He choked and swallowed. "He made a covenant with us, just like the Shadowhunters believe

Raziel made a covenant with them. And we believe in his promises. Therefore you can never lose hope—*hatikva*—because if you keep hope alive, it will keep you alive." He looked faintly embarrassed. "My rabbi used to say that."

Clary slid her hand across the table and laid it atop Simon's. He rarely talked about his religion with her or anyone, though she knew he believed. "Does that mean you agree?"

He groaned. "I think it means you crushed my spirit and beat me down."

"Fantastic."

"Of course you realize you're leaving me in the position of being the one to tell everyone—your mother, Luke, Alec, Izzy, Magnus . . ."

"I guess I shouldn't have said there would be no risk to you," Clary said meekly.

"That's right," said Simon. "Just remember, when your mother's gnawing my ankle like a furious mama bear separated from her cub, I did it for you."

Jordan had only just fallen back asleep when the banging on the front door came again. He rolled over and groaned. The clock by the bed said 4:00 a.m. in blinking yellow numbers.

More banging. Jordan rolled reluctantly to his feet, dragged on his jeans, and staggered out into the hallway. Blearily he jerked the door open. "Look—"

The words died on his lips. Standing in the hallway was Maia. She was wearing jeans and a caramel-colored leather jacket, and her hair was pulled up behind her head with bronze chopsticks. A single loose curl fell against her temple. Jordan's fingers itched to reach out and tuck it behind her ear.

Instead he jammed his hands into the pockets of his jeans.

"Nice shirt," she said with a dry glance at his bare chest. There was a backpack slung over one of her shoulders. For a moment his heart jumped. Was she leaving town? Was she leaving town to get away from *him*? "Look, Jordan—"

"Who is it?" The voice behind Jordan was husky, as rumpled as the bed she'd probably just climbed out of. He saw Maia's mouth drop open, and he looked back over his shoulder to see Isabelle, wearing only one of Simon's T-shirts, standing behind him and rubbing at her eyes.

Maia's mouth snapped shut. "It's me," she said in a not particularly friendly tone. "Are you . . . visiting Simon?"

"What? No, Simon's not here." *Shut up, Isabelle*, Jordan thought frantically. "He's . . ." She gestured vaguely. "Out."

Maia's cheeks reddened. "It smells like a bar in here."

"Jordan's cheap tequila," said Isabelle with a wave of her hand. "You know . . ."

"Is that his shirt, too?" Maia inquired.

Isabelle glanced down at herself, and then back up at Maia. Belatedly she seemed to realize what the other girl was thinking. "Oh. No. Maia—"

"So first Simon cheated on me with you, and now you and Jordan—"

"Simon," Isabelle said, "also cheated on *me* with *you*. Anyway, nothing's going on with me and Jordan. I came over to see Simon, but he wasn't here so I decided to crash in his room. And I'm going back in there now."

"No," Maia said sharply. "Don't. Forget about Simon and Jordan. What I have to say, it's something you need to hear too."

Isabelle froze, one hand on Simon's door, her sleep-flushed face slowly paling. "Jace," she said. "Is that why you're here?"

Maia nodded.

Isabelle sagged against the door. "Is he—" Her voice cracked. She started again. "Have they found—"

"He came back," said Maia. "For Clary." She paused. "He had Sebastian with him. There was a fight, and Luke was injured. He's dying."

Isabelle made a dry little sound in her throat. "Jace? Jace hurt Luke?"

Maia avoided her eyes. "I don't know what happened exactly. Only that Jace and Sebastian came for Clary, and there was a fight. Luke was hurt."

"Clary—"

"Is all right. She's at Magnus's with her mother." Maia turned to Jordan. "Magnus called me and asked me to come and see you. He tried to reach you, but he couldn't. He wants you to put him in touch with the Praetor Lupus."

"Put him in touch with . . ." Jordan shook his head. "You can't just *call* the Praetor. It's not like 1-800-WEREWOLF."

Maia crossed her arms. "Well, how do you reach them, then?"

"I have a supervisor. He reaches me when he wants to, or I can call on him in an emergency—"

"This *is* an emergency." Maia hooked her thumbs through the belt loops on her jeans. "Luke could die, and Magnus says the Praetor might have information that could help." She looked at Jordan, her eyes big and dark. He ought to tell her, he thought. That the Praetor didn't like getting mixed up in affairs of the Clave; that they kept to themselves and their mission—to help new Downworlders. That there was no guarantee they would agree to help, and every likelihood that they would resent the request.

But Maia was asking him. This was something he could do for her that might be a step down the long road of making it up to her for what he'd done before.

"Okay," he said. "Then, we go to their headquarters and present ourselves in person. They're out on the North Fork of Long Island. Pretty far from anywhere. We can take my truck."

"Fine." Maia hoisted her backpack higher. "I thought we might have to go somewhere; that's why I brought my stuff."

"Maia." It was Isabelle. She hadn't said anything in so long that Jordan had almost forgotten she was there; he turned and saw her leaning against the wall by Simon's door. She was hugging herself as if she were cold. "Is he all right?"

Maia winced. "Luke? No, he—"

"Jace." Isabelle's voice was an indrawn breath. "Is Jace all right? Did they hurt him or catch him or—"

"He's fine," Maia said flatly. "And he's gone. He disappeared with Sebastian."

"And Simon?" Isabelle's gaze flicked to Jordan. "You said he was with Clary—"

Maia shook her head. "He wasn't. He wasn't there." Her hand was tight on the strap of her backpack. "But there's one thing we know now, and you're not going to like it. Jace and Sebastian are connected somehow. Hurt Jace, you hurt Sebastian. Kill him, and Sebastian dies. And vice versa. Straight from Magnus."

"Does the Clave know?" Isabelle demanded instantly. "They didn't tell the Clave, did they?"

Maia shook her head. "Not yet."

"They'll find out," said Isabelle. "The whole pack knows. Someone will tell. Then it'll be a manhunt. They'll kill him just to kill Sebastian. They'll kill him anyway." She reached up and pushed her hands through her thick black hair. "I want my brother," she said. "I want to see Alec."

"Well, that's good," Maia said. "Because after Magnus called me, he sent a follow-up text. He said he had a feeling you'd be here, and he had a message for you. He wants you to go to his apartment in Brooklyn, right away."

It was freezing out, so cold that even the *thermis* rune she'd put on herself—and the thin parka she'd swiped from Simon's closet—weren't doing much to keep Isabelle from shivering as she pushed open the door of Magnus's apartment building and ducked inside.

After being buzzed up, she headed up the stairs, trailing her hand along the splintering banister. Part of her wanted to rush up the steps, knowing Alec was there and would understand what she was feeling. The other part of her, the part that had hidden her parents' secret from her brothers all her life, wanted to curl up on the landing and be alone with her misery. The part that hated relying on anyone else—because wouldn't they just let you down?—and was proud to say that Isabelle Lightwood didn't *need* anyone reminded herself that she was here because they had asked for her. *They* needed *her*.

Isabelle didn't mind being needed. Liked it, in fact. It was why it had taken her longer to warm up to Jace when he had first stepped off the boat from Idris, a thin ten-year-old boy with haunted pale gold eyes. Alec had been delighted with him immediately, but Isabelle had resented his self-possession.

When her mother had told her that Jace's father had been murdered in front of him, she'd imagined him coming to her tearfully, for comfort and even advice. But he hadn't seemed to need anyone. Even at ten years old he'd had a sharp, defensive wit and an acidic temperament. In fact, Isabelle had thought, dismayed, that he was just like her.

In the end it was Shadowhunting they had bonded over—a shared love of sharp-edged weapons, gleaming seraph blades, the painful pleasure of burning Marks, the thought-numbing swiftness of battle. When Alec had wanted to go out hunting alone with Jace, leaving Izzy behind, Jace had spoken up for her: "We need her with us; she's the best there is. Aside from me, of course."

She had loved him just for that.

She was at the front door of Magnus's apartment now. Light poured through the crack under the door, and she heard murmuring voices. She pushed the door open, and a wave of warmth enveloped her. She stepped gratefully forward.

The warmth came from a fire leaping in the grated fireplace—though there were no chimneys in the building, and the fire had the blue-green tinge of enchanted flame. Magnus and Alec sat on one of the couches grouped near the fireplace. As she came in, Alec looked up and saw her, and sprang to his feet, hurrying barefoot across the room—he was wearing black sweatpants and a white T-shirt with a torn collar—to put his arms around her.

For a moment she stood still in the circle of his arms, hearing his heartbeat, his hands patting half-awkwardly up and down her back, her hair. "Iz," he said. "It's going to be okay, Izzy."

She pushed away from him, wiping at her eyes. God, she

hated crying. "How can you say that?" she snapped. "How can anything possibly be okay after this?"

"Izzy." Alec drew his sister's hair over one shoulder and tugged gently at it. It reminded her of the years when she used to wear her hair in braids and Alec would yank on them, with considerably less gentleness than he was showing now. "Don't go to pieces. We need you." He dropped his voice. "Also, did you know you smell like tequila?"

She looked over at Magnus, who was watching them from the sofa with his unreadable cat's eyes. "Where's Clary?" she said. "And her mother? I thought they were here."

"Asleep," said Alec. "We thought they needed a rest."

"And I don't?"

"Did *you* just see your fiancé or your stepfather nearly murdered in front of your eyes?" Magnus inquired dryly. He was wearing striped pajamas with a black silk dressing gown thrown over them. "Isabelle Lightwood," he said, sitting up and loosely clasping his hands in front of him. "As Alec said, we need you."

Isabelle straightened up, putting her shoulders back. "Need me for what?"

"To go to the Iron Sisters," said Alec. "We need a weapon that will divide Jace and Sebastian so that they can be hurt separately— Well, you know what I mean. So Sebastian can be killed without hurting Jace. And it's a matter of time before the Clave knows that Jace isn't Sebastian's prisoner, that he's working with him—"

"It's not *Jace*," Isabelle protested.

"It may not be Jace," said Magnus, "but if he dies, your Jace dies right along with him."

"As you know, the Iron Sisters will speak only to women,"

said Alec. "And Jocelyn can't go alone because she isn't a Shadowhunter anymore."

"What about Clary?"

"She's still in training. She won't know the right questions to ask or the way to address them. But you and Jocelyn will. And Jocelyn says she's been there before; she can help guide you once we Portal you to the edge of the wards around the Adamant Citadel. You'll be going, both of you, in the morning."

Isabelle considered it. The idea of finally having something to do, something definite and active and important, was a relief. She would have preferred a task that had something to do with killing demons or chopping off Sebastian's legs, but this was better than nothing. The legends surrounding the Adamant Citadel made it sound like a forbidding, distant place, and the Iron Sisters were seen far more rarely than the Silent Brothers. Isabelle had never met one.

"When do we leave?" she said.

Alec smiled for the first time since she'd arrived, and reached to ruffle her hair. "That's my Isabelle."

"Quit it." She ducked out from his reach and saw Magnus grinning at them from the sofa. He levered himself up and ran a hand through his already explosively spiky black hair.

"I've got three spare rooms," he said. "Clary's in one; her mother's in the other. I'll show you the third."

The rooms all branched off a narrow, windowless hallway that led from the living room. Two of the doors were closed; Magnus drew Isabelle through the third, into a room whose walls were painted hot-pink. Black curtains hung from silver bars over the windows, secured by handcuffs. The bedspread had a print of dark red hearts on it.

Isabelle glanced around. She felt jittery and nervous and not in the least like going to sleep. "Nice handcuffs. I can see why you didn't put Jocelyn in here."

"I needed something to hold the curtains back." Magnus shrugged. "Do you have anything to sleep in?"

Isabelle just nodded, not wanting to admit she'd brought Simon's shirt with her from his apartment. Vampires didn't really smell like anything, but the shirt still carried with it the faint, reassuring scent of his laundry soap. "It's kind of weird," she said. "You demanding I come over right away, only to put me to bed and tell me we're getting started tomorrow."

Magnus leaned against the wall by the door, his arms over his chest, and looked at her through slitted cat eyes. For a moment he reminded her of Church, only less likely to bite. "I love your brother," he said. "You know that, right?"

"If you want my permission to marry him, go right ahead," said Isabelle. "Autumn's a nice time for it too. You could wear an orange tux."

"He isn't happy," said Magnus, as if she hadn't spoken.

"Of course he isn't," Isabelle snapped. "Jace—"

"*Jace*," said Magnus, and his hands made fists at his sides. Isabelle stared at him. She had always thought that he didn't mind Jace; liked him, even, once the question of Alec's affections had been settled.

Out loud, she said, "I thought you and Jace were friends."

"It's not that," said Magnus. "There are some people—people the universe seems to have singled out for special destinies. Special favors and special torments. God knows we're all drawn toward what's beautiful and broken; *I* have been, but some people cannot be fixed. Or if they can be, it's only by love and sacrifice so great that it destroys the giver."

Isabelle shook her head slowly. "You've lost me. Jace is our brother, but for Alec— He's Jace's *parabatai*, too."

"I know about *parabatai*," said Magnus. "I've known *parabatai* so close they were almost the same person. Do you know what happens, when one of them dies, to the one who's left—"

"Stop it!" Isabelle clapped her hands over her ears, then lowered them slowly. "How dare you, Magnus Bane?" she said. "How dare you make this worse than it is."

"Isabelle." Magnus's hands loosened; he looked a little wide-eyed, as if his outburst had startled even him. "I am sorry. I forget, sometimes . . . that with all your self-control and strength, you possess the same vulnerability that Alec does."

"There is nothing weak about Alec," said Isabelle.

"No," said Magnus. "To love as you choose, that takes strength. The thing is, I wanted you here for him. There are things I can't do for him, can't give him." For a moment Magnus looked oddly vulnerable himself. "You have known Jace as long as he has. You can give him understanding I can't. And he loves you."

"Of course he loves me. I'm his sister."

"Blood isn't love," said Magnus, and his voice was bitter. "Just ask Clary."

Clary shot through the Portal as if through the barrel of a rifle and flew out the other end. She tumbled toward the ground and struck hard on her feet, sticking the landing at first. The pose lasted only a moment before, too dizzy from the Portal to concentrate, she overbalanced and hit the ground, her backpack cushioning her fall. She sighed—*someday* all the training really would kick in—and got to her feet, brushing dust from the seat of her jeans.

She was standing in front of Luke's house. The river sparkled over her shoulder, the city rising behind it like a forest of lights. Luke's house was just as they had left it, hours ago, locked and dark. Clary, standing on the dirt and stone path that led up to the front steps, swallowed hard.

Slowly she touched the ring on her right hand with the fingers of her left. *Simon?*

The reply came immediately. *Yeah?*

Where are you?

Walking toward the subway. Did you Portal home?

Luke's. If Jace comes like I think he will, this is where he'll come to.

A silence. Then, *Well, I guess you know how to get me if you need me.*

I guess I do. Clary took a deep breath. *Simon?*

Yeah?

I love you.

A pause. *I love you, too.*

And that was all. There was no click, as when you hung up a phone; Clary just sensed a severing of their connection, as if a cord had been cut inside her head. She wondered if this was what Alec meant when he talked about the breaking of the *parabatai* bond.

She moved toward Luke's house and slowly mounted the stairs. This was her home. If Jace was going to come back for her, as he had mouthed to her that he would, this is where he would come. She sat down on the top step, pulled her backpack onto her lap, and waited.

***

Simon stood in front of the refrigerator in his apartment and took a last swallow of cold blood as the memory of Clary's silent voice faded out of his mind. He had just gotten home, and the apartment was dark, the hum of the refrigerator loud, and the place smelled oddly of—tequila? Maybe Jordan had been drinking. His bedroom door was closed, anyway, not that Simon blamed him for being asleep; it was after four in the morning.

He shoved the bottle back into the fridge and headed for his room. It would be the first night he'd slept at home in a week. He'd grown used to having someone to share a bed with, a body to roll against in the middle of the night. He liked the way Clary fit against him, curled asleep with her head on her hand; and, if he had to admit it to himself, he liked that she couldn't sleep unless he was with her. It made him feel indispensable and needed—even if the fact that Jocelyn didn't appear to care whether he slept in her daughter's bed or not did underscore that Clary's mother apparently regarded him as about as sexually threatening as a goldfish.

Of course, he and Clary had shared beds often, from the time they were five until they were about twelve. That might have had something to do with it, he mused, pushing his bedroom door open. Most of those nights they'd spent engaged in torrid activities, like having contests to see who could take the longest to eat a single Reese's Peanut Butter Cup. Or they'd sneaked in a portable DVD player and—

He blinked. His room looked the same—bare walls, stacked plastic shelves with his clothes on them, his guitar hanging on the wall, and a mattress on the floor. But on the bed was a single piece of paper—a white square against the frayed black blanket. The scrawled, looping hand was familiar. Isabelle's.

He picked it up and read:

Simon, I've been trying to call you, but it seems like your phone is turned off. I don't know where you are right now. I don't know if Clary's already told you what happened tonight. But I have to go to Magnus's and I'd really like you to be there.

I'm never scared, but I'm scared for Jace. I'm scared for my brother. I never ask you for anything, Simon, but I'm asking you now. Please come.

Isabelle.

Simon let the letter fall from his hand. He was out of the apartment and on his way down the steps before it had even hit the floor.

When Simon came into Magnus's apartment, it was quiet. There was a fire flickering in the grate, and Magnus sat in front of it on an overstuffed sofa, his feet up on the coffee table. Alec was asleep, his head in Magnus's lap, and Magnus was twirling strands of Alec's black hair between his fingers. The warlock's gaze, on the flames, was remote and distant, as if he were looking back into the past. Simon couldn't help but remember what Magnus had said to him once, about living forever:

Someday you and I will be the only two left.

Simon shuddered, and Magnus looked up. "Isabelle called

you over, I know." he said, speaking in a low voice so as not to wake Alec. "She's down the hall that way—the first bedroom on the left."

Simon nodded and, with a salute in Magnus's direction, headed off down the hall. He felt unusually nervous, as if he were prepping for a first date. Isabelle, to his recollection, had never demanded his help or his presence before, had never acknowledged that she needed him in any way.

He pushed open the door to the first bedroom on the left and stepped inside. It was dark, the lights off; if Simon hadn't had vampire sight, he probably would have seen only blackness. As it was, he saw the outlines of a wardrobe, chairs with clothes thrown over them, and a bed, covers thrown back. Isabelle was asleep on her side, her black hair fanning out across the pillow.

Simon stared. He'd never seen Isabelle sleeping before. She looked younger than she usually did, her face relaxed, her long eyelashes brushing the tops of her cheekbones. Her mouth was slightly open, her feet curled up under her. She was wearing only a T-shirt—*his* T-shirt, a worn blue tee that said THE LOCH NESS MONSTER ADVENTURE CLUB: FINDING ANSWERS, IGNORING FACTS across the front.

Simon closed the door behind him, feeling more disappointed than he had expected. It hadn't occurred to him that she'd already be asleep. He'd been wanting to talk to her, to hear her voice. He kicked his shoes off and lay down beside her. She certainly took up more real estate on the bed than Clary did. Isabelle was tall, almost his height, although when he put his hand on her shoulder, her bones felt delicate under his touch. He ran his hand down her arm. "Iz?" he said. "Isabelle?"

She murmured and turned her face into the pillow. He leaned closer—she smelled like alcohol and rose perfume. Well, that answered that. He had been thinking about pulling her into his arms and kissing her gently, but "Simon Lewis, Molester of Passed-Out Women" wasn't really the epitaph by which he wanted to be remembered.

He lay down flat on his back and stared at the ceiling. Cracked plaster, marked by water stains. Magnus really ought to get someone in here to do something about that. As if sensing his presence, Isabelle rolled sideways against him, her soft cheek against his shoulder. "Simon?" she said groggily.

"Yeah." He touched her face lightly.

"You came." She stretched her arm across his chest, moving so that her head fit against his shoulder. "I didn't think you would."

His fingers traced patterns on her arm. "Of course I came."

Her next words were muffled against his neck. "Sorry I'm asleep."

He smiled to himself, a little, in the dark. "It's okay. Even if all you wanted was for me to come here and hold you while you sleep, I would have done it."

He felt her stiffen, and then relax. "Simon?"

"Yeah?"

"Can you tell me a story?"

He blinked. "What kind of story?"

"Something where the good guys win and the bad guys lose. And stay dead."

"So, like a fairy tale?" he said. He racked his brain. He knew only the Disney versions of fairy tales, and the first image that came to mind was Ariel in her seashell bra. He'd had a crush on her when he was eight. Not that this seemed like the time to mention it.

"No." The word was an exhaled breath. "We *study* fairy tales in school. A lot of that magic is real—but, anyway. No, I want something I haven't heard yet."

"Okay. I've got a good one." Simon stroked Isabelle's hair, feeling her lashes flutter against his neck as she closed her eyes. "A long time ago, in a galaxy far, far away . . ."

Clary didn't know how long she'd been sitting on Luke's front steps when the sun began to come up. It rose behind his house, the sky turning a dark pinkish-rose, the river a strip of steely blue. She was shivering, had been shivering so long that her whole body seemed to have contracted into a single hard shudder of cold. She had used two warming runes, but they hadn't helped; she had a feeling the shivering was psychological as much as anything else.

Would he come? If he was still as much Jace inside as she thought he was, he would; when he had mouthed that he would come back for her, she had known that he had meant as soon as possible. Jace was not patient. And he didn't play games.

But there was only so long she could wait. Eventually the sun would rise. The next day would begin, and her mother would be watching her again. She would have to give up on Jace, for at least another day, if not longer.

She shut her eyes against the brightness of the sunrise, resting her elbows on the step above and behind her. For just a moment she let herself float in the fantasy that everything was as it had been, that nothing had changed, that she would meet Jace this afternoon for practice, or tonight for dinner, and he would hold her and make her laugh the way he always did.

Warm tendrils of sunlight touched her face. Reluctantly her eyes fluttered open.

And he was there, walking toward her up the steps, as soundless as a cat, as always. He wore a dark blue sweater that made his hair look like sunlight. She sat up straight, her heart pounding. The brilliant sunshine seemed to outline him in light. She thought of that night in Idris, how the fireworks had streaked across the sky and she had thought of angels, falling in fire.

He reached her and held his hands out; she took them, and let him pull her to her feet. His pale gold eyes searched her face. "I wasn't sure you'd be here."

"Since when have you not been sure of me?"

"You were pretty angry before." He cupped the side of her face in his hand. There was a rough scar across his palm; she could feel it against her skin.

"So if I hadn't been here, what would you have done?"

He drew her close. He was shivering too, and the wind was blowing his curling hair, messy and bright. "How is Luke?"

At the sound of Luke's name, another shudder went through her. Jace, thinking she was cold, pulled her more tightly against him. "He'll be all right," she said guardedly. *It's your fault, your fault, your fault.*

"I never meant for him to get hurt." Jace's arms were around her, his fingers tracing a slow line up and down her spine. "Do you believe me?"

"Jace . . . ," Clary said. "Why are you here?"

"To ask you again. To come with me."

She closed her eyes. "And you won't tell me where that is?"

"Faith," he said softly. "You have to have faith. But you also have to know—once you come with me, there's no going back. Not for a long time."

She thought of the moment when she'd stepped outside of Java Jones and seen him waiting for her there. Her life had changed in that moment in a way that could never be undone.

"There never has been any going back," she said. "Not with you." She opened her eyes. "We should go."

He smiled, as brilliant as the sun coming out from behind the clouds, and she felt his body relax. "You're sure?"

"I'm sure."

He leaned forward and kissed her. Reaching up to hold him, she tasted something bitter on his lips; then darkness came down like a curtain signaling the end of the act of a play.

Part Two
Certain Dark Things

I love you as one loves certain dark things
—Pablo Neruda, "Sonnet XVII"

8

Fire Tests Gold

Maia had never been to Long Island, but when she thought of it at all, she'd always thought of it as being a lot like New Jersey—mostly suburban, a place where people who worked in New York or Philly actually lived.

She had dropped her bag into the back of Jordan's truck—startlingly unfamiliar. He'd driven a beaten-up red Toyota when they'd been dating, and it had always been littered with old, crumpled coffee cups and fast-food bags, the ashtray full of cigarettes smoked down to the filter. The cab of this truck was comparatively clean, the only detritus a stack of papers on the passenger seat. He moved them aside with no comment as she climbed in.

They hadn't spoken through Manhattan and onto the Long

Island Expressway, and eventually Maia had dozed, her cheek against the cool glass of the window. She'd finally woken when they'd gone over a bump in the road, jolting her forward. She'd blinked, rubbing at her eyes.

"Sorry," Jordan had said ruefully. "I was going to let you sleep until we got there."

She'd sat up, looking around. They'd been driving down a two-lane blacktop road, the sky around them just beginning to lighten. There were fields on either side of the road, the occasional farmhouse or silo, clapboard houses set far back with picket fences around them.

"It's pretty," she'd said in surprise.

"Yeah." Jordan had changed gears, clearing his throat. "Since you're up anyway . . . Before we get to the Praetor House, can I show you something?"

She'd hesitated only a moment before nodding. And now here they were, bumping down a one-lane dirt road, trees on either side. Most were leafless; the road was muddy, and Maia cranked the window down to smell the air. Trees, salt water, softly decaying leaves, small animals running through the high grass. She took another deep breath just as they bumped off the road and onto a small circular turnaround space. In front of them was the beach, stretching down to dark steel-blue water. The sky was almost lilac.

She looked over at Jordan. He was staring straight ahead. "I used to come here while I was training at the Praetor House," he said. "Sometimes just to look at the water and clear my head. The sunrises here . . . Every one is different, but they're all beautiful."

"Jordan."

He didn't look at her. "Yeah?"

"I'm sorry about before. About running off, you know, in the navy yard."

"It's fine." He let his breath out slowly, but she could tell by the tension in his shoulders, his hand gripping the gearshift, that it wasn't, not really. She tried not to look at the way the tension shaped the muscles in his arm, accenting the indentation of his bicep. "It was a lot for you to take in; I get that. I just . . ."

"I think we should take it slow. Work toward being friends."

"I don't want to be friends," he said.

She couldn't hide her surprise. "You don't?"

He moved his hands from the gearshift to the steering wheel. Warm air poured from the heater inside the car, mixing with the cooler air outside Maia's open window. "We shouldn't talk about this now."

"I want to," she said. "I want to talk about it now. I don't want to be stressing about *us* when we're in the Praetor House."

He slid down in his seat, chewing his lip. His tangled brown hair fell forward over his forehead. "Maia . . ."

"If you don't want to be friends, then what are we? Enemies again?"

He turned his head, his cheek against the back of the car seat. Those eyes, they were just as she remembered, hazel with flecks of green and blue and gold. "I don't want to be friends," he said, "because I still love you. Maia, you know I haven't even so much as kissed anyone since we broke up?"

"Isabelle . . ."

"Wanted to get drunk and talk about Simon." He took his hands off the steering wheel, reached for her, then dropped them back into his lap, a defeated look on his face. "I've only ever loved you. Thinking about you got me through my training. The idea that I might be able to make it up to you someday. And I will, in any way that I can except for one."

"You won't be my friend."

"I won't be *just* your friend. I love you, Maia. I'm *in* love with you. I always have been. I always will be. Just being your friend would kill me."

She looked out toward the ocean. The rim of the sun was just showing above the water, its rays lighting the sea in shades of purple and gold and blue. "It's so beautiful here."

"That's why I used to come here. I couldn't sleep, and I'd watch the sun come up." His voice was soft.

"Can you sleep now?" She turned back to him.

He closed his eyes. "Maia . . . if you're going to say no, you don't want to be anything but friends with me, . . . just say it. Rip the Band-Aid off, okay?"

He looked braced, as if for a blow. His eyelashes cast shadows on his cheekbones. There were pale white scars on the olive skin of his throat, scars she had made. She unclipped her seat belt and scooted across the bench seat toward him. She heard his gasp of breath, but he didn't move as she leaned in and kissed his cheek. She inhaled the scent of him. Same soap, same shampoo, but no lingering scent of cigarettes. Same boy. She kissed across his cheek, to the corner of his mouth, and finally, edging even closer, set her mouth over his.

His lips opened under hers and he growled, low in his throat. Werewolves weren't gentle with each other, but his hands were light on her as he lifted her and set her on his lap, wrapping his arms around her as their kiss deepened. The feel of him, the warmth of his corduroy-covered arms around her, the beat of his heart, the taste of his mouth, the clash of lips, teeth, and tongue, stole her breath. Her hands slipped around the back of his neck, and she melted against him as she felt the soft thick curls of his hair, exactly the same as it had always been.

When they finally drew apart, his eyes were glassy. "I've been waiting for that for years."

She traced the line of his collarbone with a finger. She could feel her own heart beating. For a few moments they hadn't been two werewolves on a mission to a deadly secret organization—they'd been two teenagers, making out in a car on the beach. "Did it live up to your expectations?"

"It was much better." His mouth crooked up at the corner. "Does this mean . . ."

"Well," she said. "That's not the sort of thing you do with your friends, right?"

"Isn't it? I'll have to tell Simon. He's going to be seriously disappointed."

"*Jordan.*" She hit him lightly in the shoulder, but she was smiling, and so was he, an uncharacteristically big, goofy grin spreading over his face. She bent close and put her face against the crook of his neck, breathing him in along with the morning.

They were battling across the frozen lake, the icy city glowing like a lamp in the distance. The angel with the golden wings and the angel with the wings like black fire. Clary stood on the ice as blood and feathers fell around her. The golden feathers burned like fire where they touched her skin, but the black feathers were as cold as ice.

Clary awoke with her heart pounding, tangled in a knot of blankets. She sat up, pushing the blankets to her waist. She was in an unfamiliar room. The walls were white plaster, and she was lying in a bed made of black wood, still wearing the clothes she'd worn the night before. She slid out of the bed, her bare feet hitting the cold stone floor, and looked around for her backpack.

She found it easily, propped on a black leather chair. There were no windows in the room; the only light came from a pendant glass light fixture overhead made of cut black glass. She swept her hand through the pack and realized to her annoyance, although without surprise, that someone had already gone through the contents. Her art box was gone, including her stele. All that remained was her hairbrush and a change of jeans and underwear. At least the gold ring was still on her finger.

She touched it lightly and *thought* at Simon. *I'm in.*

Nothing.

Simon?

There was no response. She swallowed back her uneasiness. She had no idea where she was, what time it was, or how long she'd been out cold. Simon could be asleep. She couldn't panic and assume the rings didn't work. She had to go on autopilot. Check out where she was, learn what she could. She'd try Simon again later.

She took a deep breath and tried to focus on her immediate surroundings. Two doors led off the bedroom. She tried the first, and found that it opened onto a small glass-and-chrome bathroom with a copper claw-footed bathtub. There were no windows in here either. She showered quickly and dried herself with a fluffy white towel, then changed into clean jeans and a sweater before padding back into the bedroom, picking up her shoes, and trying the second door.

Bingo. Here was the rest of the—house? Apartment? She was in a large room, half of which was devoted to a long glass table. More of the black pendant cut-glass lights hung from the ceiling, sending dancing shadows against the walls. Everything was very modern, from the black leather chairs to the large fireplace, framed in washed chrome. There was a fire blazing in it. So someone else must be home, or must have been very recently.

The other half of the room was taken up with a large television screen, a glossy black coffee table on which were scattered games and controllers, and low leather couches. A set of glass stairs led upward in a spiral. After a glance around Clary began to climb them. The glass was perfectly clear, and lent the impression that she was climbing an invisible staircase into the sky.

The second floor was much like the first—pale walls, black floor, a long corridor with doors opening off it. The first door led into what was clearly a master bedroom. A huge rosewood bed, hung with gauzy white curtains, took up most of the space. There were windows in here, tinted a dark blue. Clary went across the room to look out.

She wondered for a moment if she was back in Alicante. She was looking across a canal at another building, its windows covered in closed green shutters. The sky above was gray, the canal a dark greenish-blue, and there was a bridge visible just at her right, crossing the canal. Two people were standing on the bridge. One of them held a camera to his face and was industriously taking photos. Not Alicante, then. Amsterdam? Venice? She looked everywhere for a way to open the window, but there didn't appear to be one; she banged on the glass and shouted, but the bridge-crossers took no notice. After a few moments they moved on.

Clary turned back into the bedroom and went to one of the wardrobes, and threw it open. Her heart skipped a beat. The wardrobe was full of clothes—women's clothes. Gorgeous dresses—lace and satin and beads and flowers. The drawers held camisoles and underwear, tops in cotton and silk, skirts but no jeans or pants. There were even shoes lined up, sandals and heels, and folded pairs of stockings. For a moment she just stared, wondering if there were another girl staying here, or if Sebastian had taken to cross-dressing. But the clothes all had the tags on them, and all of them were near her size. Not only that, she realized slowly, staring. They were exactly the shapes and colors that would suit her—blues and greens and yellows, cut for a petite frame. Eventually she drew out one of the simpler tops, a dark green cap-sleeved blouse with silk lacing up the front. After discarding her worn top on the floor, she shrugged the blouse on and glanced at the mirror hanging inside the wardrobe.

It fit perfectly. Made the most of her small figure, clinging to her waist, darkening the green of her eyes. She yanked the tag off, not wanting to see how much it had cost, and hurried out of the room, feeling a shiver run down her spine.

The next room was clearly Jace's. She knew it the minute she walked in. It smelled like him, like his cologne and soap and the scent of his skin. The bed was ebonized wood with white sheets and blankets, perfectly made. It was as neat as his room at the Institute. Books were stacked by his bed, the titles in Italian and French and Latin. The silver Herondale dagger with its pattern of birds was jammed into the plaster wall. When she looked closer, she could see that it was pinning a photograph in place. A photograph of herself and Jace, taken by Izzy. She remembered it, a clear day in early October, Jace sitting on the front steps of the Institute, a book on his lap. She was sitting a step above him, her hand on his shoulder, leaning forward to see what he was reading. His hand covered hers, almost absently, and he was smiling. She hadn't been able to see his face that day, hadn't known he was smiling like that, not until now. Her throat contracted, and she went out of the room, catching her breath.

She couldn't act like this, she told herself sternly. As if each sight of Jace the way he was now was a sucker punch to the gut. She had to pretend that it didn't matter, as if she noticed no difference. She went into the next room, another bedroom, much like the one before it, but this one was a mess—the bed a tangle of black silk sheets and comforter, a glass and steel desk covered with books and papers, boy clothes scattered everywhere. Jeans and jackets and T-shirts and gear. Her eye fell on something that gleamed silver, propped on the nightstand near the bed. She moved forward, staring, unable to believe her eyes.

It was the small box of her mother's, the one with the initials *J.C.* on it. The one her mother used to take out every year, once a year, and weep over silently, the tears running down her face to splash onto her hands. Clary knew what was in the box—a lock of hair, as fine and white as dandelion fluff; scraps from a child's shirt; a baby shoe, small enough to fit inside the palm of her hand. Bits and pieces of her brother, a sort of collage of the child her mother had wanted to have, had dreamed of having, before Valentine had done what he had and turned his own son into a monster.

J.C.

Jonathan Christopher.

Her stomach twisted, and she backed up quickly out of the room—directly into a wall of living flesh. Arms came around her, wrapping her tight, and she saw that they were slim and muscular, downed with fine pale hair, and for a moment she thought it was Jace holding her. She began to relax.

"What were you doing in my room?" Sebastian said into her ear.

Isabelle had been trained to wake early every morning, rain or shine, and a slight hangover did nothing to prevent it from happening again. She sat up slowly and blinked down at Simon.

She'd never spent an entire night in a bed with anyone else, unless you counted crawling into her parents' bed when she was four and afraid of thunderstorms. She couldn't help staring at Simon as if he were some exotic species of animal. He lay on his back, his mouth slightly open, his hair in his eyes. Ordinary brown hair, ordinary brown eyes. His T-shirt was pulled up slightly. He wasn't muscular like a Shadowhunter. He had a smooth flat stomach but no six-pack, and there was still a hint of softness to his face. What *was* it about him that fascinated her? He was plenty cute, but she had dated gorgeous faerie knights, sexy Shadowhunters. . . .

"Isabelle," Simon said without opening his eyes. "Quit staring at me."

Isabelle sighed irritably and swung herself out of bed. She rummaged in her bag for her gear, retrieved it, and headed out to find the bathroom.

It was halfway down the hall, and the door was just opening, Alec emerging in a cloud of steam. He had a towel around his waist and another around his shoulders and was rubbing energetically at his wet black hair. Isabelle supposed she shouldn't be surprised to see him; he'd been trained to wake up early in the morning just like she had.

"You smell like sandalwood," she said by way of greeting. She hated the smell of sandalwood. She liked sweet scents—vanilla, cinnamon, gardenia.

Alec looked at her. "We like sandalwood."

Isabelle made a face. "Either that's the royal 'we' or you and Magnus are turning into one of those couples that think they're one person. '*We* like sandalwood.' '*We* adore the symphony.' '*We* hope you enjoy *our* Christmas present'—which, if you ask me, is just a cheap way of avoiding having to buy two gifts."

Alec blinked wet lashes at her. "You'll understand—"

"If you tell me I'll understand when I'm in love, I'll smother you with that towel."

"And if you keep preventing me from going back to my room and getting dressed, I'll get Magnus to summon up pixies to tie your hair in knots."

"Oh, get out of my way." Isabelle kicked at Alec's ankle until he moved, unhurriedly, down the hall. She had the feeling if she turned around and looked at him he'd be sticking his tongue out at her, so she didn't look. Instead she locked herself in the bathroom and turned on the shower, full steam. Then she looked at the rack of shower products and said an unladylike word.

Sandalwood shampoo, conditioner, and soap. Ugh.

When she finally emerged, dressed in her gear and with her hair up, she found Alec, Magnus, and Jocelyn waiting for her in the living room. There were doughnuts, which she didn't want, and coffee, which she did. She poured a liberal amount of milk into it and sat back, looking at Jocelyn, who was also dressed—to Isabelle's surprise—in Shadowhunter gear.

It was odd, she mused. People often told her she looked like her mother, though she didn't see it herself, and she wondered now if it was in the same way that Clary looked like Jocelyn. The same color hair, yes, but also the same cast of features, the same tilt of the head, the same stubborn set to the jaw. The same sense that this person might look like a porcelain doll but was steel underneath. Although, Isabelle wished that, in the same way that Clary had gotten her mother's green eyes, she'd gotten Maryse and Robert's blue ones. Blue was so much more interesting than black.

"As with the Silent City, there is only one Adamant Citadel, but there are many doors through which one may find it," said Magnus. "The closest to us is the old Augustinian Monastery on Grymes Hill, in Staten Island. Alec and I will Portal with you there and wait for you to return, but we can't go with you all the way."

"I know," said Isabelle. "Because you're *boys*. Cooties."

Alec pointed a finger at her. "Take this seriously, Isabelle. The Iron Sisters aren't like the Silent Brothers. They're way less friendly and they don't like being bothered."

"I promise I'll be on my best behavior," Isabelle said, and set her empty coffee mug down on the table. "Let's go."

Magnus looked at her suspiciously for a moment, then shrugged. His hair was gelled up today into a million sharp points, and his eyes were smudged with black, making them look more catlike than ever. He moved past her to the wall, already murmuring in Latin; the familiar outline of a Portal, its arcane door shape outlined with glittering symbols, began to take form. Wind rose, cool and sharp, blowing back the tendrils of Isabelle's hair.

Jocelyn stepped forward first, and walked through the Portal. It was a little like watching someone disappear into the side of a wave of water: A silvery haze seemed to swallow her in, dulling the color of her red hair as she vanished into it with a faint shimmer.

Isabelle went next. She was used to the stomach-dropping feeling of transportation by Portal. There was a soundless roar in her ears and no air in her lungs. She closed her eyes, then opened them again as the whirlwind released her and she fell into dry brush. She rose to her feet, brushing dead grass from her knees, and saw Jocelyn looking at her. Clary's mother opened her mouth—and closed it again as Alec appeared, dropping into the vegetation beside Isabelle, and then Magnus, the shimmering half-seen Portal closing behind him.

Even the trip through the Portal had not disarranged Magnus's hair spikes. He tugged on one proudly. "Check it out," he said to Isabelle.

"Magic?"

"Hair gel. $3.99 at Ricky's."

Isabelle rolled her eyes at him and turned to take in her new surroundings. They stood atop a hill, its peak covered in dry brush and withered grass. Lower down were autumn-blackened trees, and in the far distance Isabelle saw cloudless sky and the top of the Verrazano-Narrows Bridge connecting Staten Island to Brooklyn. As she turned, Isabelle saw the monastery behind her, rising out of the dull foliage. It was a large building of red brick, most of its windows smashed out or boarded over. It was tagged here and there with graffiti.

Turkey vultures, disturbed by the travelers' arrival, circled the dilapidated bell tower.

Isabelle squinted at it, wondering if there was a glamour to be peeled off. If so, it was a strong one. Try as she might, she couldn't see anything but the ruinous building before her.

"There's no glamour," said Jocelyn, startling Isabelle. "What you see is what you get."

Jocelyn trudged toward it, her boots crushing down the dry vegetation in front of her. After a moment Magnus shrugged and followed her, and Isabelle and Alec came after. There was no path; branches grew in tangles, dark against the clear air, and the foliage underfoot crackled with dryness. As they neared the building, Isabelle saw that patches of the dry grass were burned away where pentagrams and runic circles had been spray-painted into the grass.

"Mundanes," said Magnus, lifting a branch out of Isabelle's way. "Playing their little games with magic, not really understanding it. They're often drawn to places like this—centers of power—without really knowing why. They drink and hang out and spray-paint the walls, like you could leave a human mark on magic. You can't." They had reached a boarded-up door in the brick wall. "We're here."

Isabelle looked hard at the door. Again there was no sense that a glamour covered it, although if she concentrated hard, a faint shimmer grew visible, like sunshine glancing off water. A look passed between Jocelyn and Magnus. Jocelyn turned to Isabelle. "You're ready?"

Isabelle nodded, and without further ado Jocelyn stepped forward and vanished through the boards of the door. Magnus looked expectantly at Isabelle.

Alec leaned closer to her, and she felt the brush of his hand on her shoulder. "Don't worry," he said. "You'll be fine, Iz."

She raised her chin. "I know," she said, and followed Jocelyn through the door.

Clary sucked in her breath, but before she could reply, there was a step on the stairs, and Jace appeared at the end of the hallway. Sebastian immediately let her go and spun her around. With a smile like a wolf's, he ruffled her hair. "Good to see you, little sister."

Clary was speechless. Jace, though, wasn't; he moved toward them soundlessly. He was wearing a black leather jacket, a white T-shirt and jeans, and was barefoot. "Were you *hugging* Clary?" He looked at Sebastian in amazement.

Sebastian shrugged. "She's my sister. I'm pleased to see her."

"*You* don't hug people," Jace said.

"I ran out of time to bake a casserole."

"It was nothing," Clary said, waving a dismissive hand at her brother. "I tripped. He was just keeping me from falling over."

If Sebastian was surprised to hear her defend him, he didn't show it. He was expressionless as she moved across the corridor, toward Jace, who kissed her on the cheek, his fingers cool against her skin. "What were you doing up here?" Jace asked.

"Looking for you." She shrugged. "I woke up and couldn't find you. I thought maybe you were asleep."

"I see you discovered the clothes stash." Sebastian indicated her shirt with a gesture. "Do you like them?"

Jace shot him a look. "We were out getting food," he said to Clary. "Nothing fancy. Bread and cheese. You want lunch?"

Which was how, several minutes later, Clary found herself installed at the big glass and steel table. From the comestibles spread out over the table, she figured that her second guess had been right. They were in Venice. There was bread, Italian cheeses, salami and prosciutto, grapes and fig jam, and bottles of Italian wine. Jace sat across from her, Sebastian at the head of the table. She was eerily reminded of the night she had met Valentine, at Renwick's in New York, how he had put himself between Jace and Clary at the head of a table, how he had offered them wine and told them they were brother and sister.

She sneaked a glance at her real brother now. She thought of how her mother had looked when she'd seen him. *Valentine.* But Sebastian wasn't a carbon copy of their father. She had seen pictures of Valentine when he was their age. Sebastian's face tempered her father's hard features with her mother's prettiness; he was tall but less broad-shouldered, more lithe and catlike. He had Jocelyn's cheekbones and fine soft mouth, Valentine's dark eyes and white-blond hair.

He looked up then, as if he had caught her staring at him. "Wine?" He offered the bottle.

She nodded, though she had never much liked the taste of wine, and since Renwick's she had hated it. She cleared her throat as Sebastian filled the glass. "So," she said. "This place—is it yours?"

"It was our father's," said Sebastian, setting the bottle down. "Valentine's. It moves, in and out of worlds—ours and others. He used to use it as a retreat as well as a mode of travel. He brought me here a few times, showed me how to get in and out and how to make it travel."

"There's no front door."

"There is if you know how to find it," said Sebastian. "Dad was very clever about this place."

Clary looked at Jace, who shook his head. "He never showed it to me. I wouldn't have guessed it existed either."

"It's very . . . bachelor pad," Clary said. "I wouldn't have thought of Valentine as . . ."

"Owning a flat-screen TV?" Jace grinned at her. "Not that it gets channels, but you can watch DVDs on it. Back at the manor we had an old icebox powered by witchlight. Here he's got a Sub-Zero fridge."

"That was for Jocelyn," said Sebastian.

Clary looked up. "What?"

"All the modern stuff. The appliances. And the clothes. Like that shirt you're wearing. They were for our mother. In case she decided to come back." Sebastian's dark eyes met hers. She felt a little sick. *This is my brother, and we're talking about our parents.* She felt dizzy—too much happening too fast to take in, to process. She had never had time to think about Sebastian as her living, breathing brother. By the time she'd found out who he really was, he'd been gone.

"Sorry if it's weird," Jace said apologetically, indicating her shirt. "We can buy you some other clothes."

Clary touched the sleeve lightly. The fabric was silky, fine, expensive. Well, that explained that—everything close to her size, everything in colors that suited her. Because she looked just like her mother.

She took a deep breath. "It's fine," she said. "It's just— What do you do exactly? Just travel around inside this apartment and . . ."

"See the world?" Jace said lightly. "There's worse things."

"But you can't do that forever."

Sebastian hadn't eaten much, but he'd drunk two glasses of wine. He was on his third, and his eyes were glittering. "Why not?"

"Well, because—because the Clave is looking for both of you, and you can't spend forever running and hiding . . ." Clary's voice trailed off as she looked from one of them to the other. They were sharing a look—the look of two people who knew something, together, that no one else did. It was not a look Jace had shared with someone else in front of her in a very long time.

Sebastian spoke softly and slowly. "Are you asking a question or making an observation?"

"She has a right to know our plans," Jace said. "She came here knowing she couldn't go back."

"A leap of faith," said Sebastian, running his finger around the rim of his glass. It was something Clary had seen Valentine do. "In *you*. She loves you. That's why she's here. Isn't it?"

"So what if it is?" Clary said. She supposed she could pretend there was another reason, but Sebastian's eyes were dark and sharp, and she doubted he'd believe her. "I trust Jace."

"But not me," Sebastian said.

Clary chose her next words with extreme care. "If Jace trusts you, then I want to trust you," she said. "And you're my brother. That counts for something." The lie tasted bitter in her mouth. "But I don't really know you."

"Then, maybe you should spend a little time *getting* to know me," Sebastian said. "And then we'll tell you our plans."

We'll tell you. *Our* plans. In his mind there was a him and Jace; there was no Jace and Clary.

"I don't like keeping her in the dark," Jace said.

"We'll tell her in a week. What difference does a week make?"

Jace gave him a look. "Two weeks ago you were dead."

"Well, I wasn't suggesting *two* weeks," said Sebastian. "That would be insane."

Jace's mouth quirked up at the corner. He looked at Clary.

"I'm willing to wait for you to trust me," she said, knowing it was the right, smart thing to say. Hating to say it. "However long it takes."

"A week," Jace said.

"A week," agreed Sebastian. "And that means she stays here in the apartment. No communication with anyone. No unlocking the door for her, no going in and out."

Jace leaned back. "What if I'm with her?"

Sebastian gave him a long look from under lowered eyelashes. His look was calculating. He was deciding what he was going to allow Jace to do, Clary realized. He was deciding how much leash to give his "brother." "Fine," he said at last, his voice rich with condescension. "If you're with her."

Clary looked down at her wineglass. She heard Jace reply in a mumur but couldn't look at him. The idea of a Jace who was *allowed* to do things—Jace, who always did whatever he wanted—made her sick to her stomach. She wanted to get up and smash the wine bottle over Sebastian's head, but she knew it was impossible. *Cut one, and the other bleeds.*

"How's the wine?" It was Sebastian's voice, an undercurrent of amusement plain in his tone.

She drained the glass, choking on the bitter flavor. "Delicious."

Isabelle emerged in an alien landscape. A deep green plain swept out before her under a lowering gray-black sky. Isabelle pulled up the hood of her gear and peered out, fascinated. She had never seen such a great, overarching expanse of sky, or such a vast plain—it was shimmering, jewel-toned, the shade of moss. As Isabelle took a step forward, she realized it *was* moss, growing on and around the black rocks scattered across the coal-colored earth.

"It's a volcanic plain," Jocelyn said. She was standing beside Isabelle, and the wind was pulling red-gold strands of her hair out of its tightly pinned bun. She looked so much like Clary that it was eerie. "These were lava beds once. The whole area is probably volcanic to some degree. Working with *adamas*, the Sisters need incredible heat for their forges."

"You'd think it would be a little warmer, then," Isabelle muttered.

Jocelyn cast her a dry look, and started walking, in what seemed to Isabelle a randomly chosen direction. She scrambled to follow. "Sometimes you're so much like your mother you astound me a little, Isabelle."

"I take that as a compliment." Isabelle narrowed her eyes. No one insulted her family.

"It wasn't meant as an insult."

Isabelle kept her eyes on the horizon, where the dark sky met the jewel-green ground. "How well did you know my parents?"

Jocelyn gave her a quick sideways look. "Well enough, when we were all in Idris together. I hadn't seen them for years until recently."

"Did you know them when they got married?"

The path Jocelyn was taking had begun to slant uphill, so her reply was slightly breathless. "Yes."

"Were they . . . in love?"

Jocelyn stopped short and turned to look at Isabelle. "Isabelle, what is this about?"

"Love?" Isabelle suggested, after a moment's pause.

"I don't know why you'd think I'd be an expert on that."

"Well, you managed to keep Luke hanging around for his whole life, basically, before you agreed to marry him. That's impressive. I wish I had that kind of power over a guy."

"You do," said Jocelyn. "Have it, I mean. And it isn't something to wish for." She pushed her hands up through her hair, and Isabelle felt a little jolt. For all that Jocelyn looked like her daughter, her thin long hands, flexible and delicate, were Sebastian's. Isabelle remembered slicing one of those hands off, in a valley in Idris, her whip cutting through skin and bone. "Your parents aren't perfect, Isabelle, because no one's perfect. They're complicated people. And they just lost a child. So if this is about your father staying in Idris—"

"My father cheated on my mother," Isabelle blurted out, and nearly covered her own mouth with her hand. She had kept this secret, kept it for years, and to say it out loud to Jocelyn seemed like a betrayal, despite everything.

Jocelyn's face changed. It held sympathy now. "I know."

Isabelle took a sharp breath. "Does everyone know?"

Jocelyn shook her head. "No. I heard it from a warlock. Not Magnus."

"Who was it?" Isabelle demanded. "Who did he cheat on her with?"

"It was no one you know, Isabelle—"

"You don't know who I know!" Isabelle's voice rose. "And stop saying my name that way, as if I'm a little kid."

"It's not my place to tell you," Jocelyn said flatly, and began to walk again.

Isabelle scrambled after her, even as the path took a steeper turn upward, a wall of green rising to meet the thunderous sky.

"I have every right to know. They're my parents. And if you don't tell me, I—"

She stopped, inhaling sharply. They had reached the top of the ridge, and somehow, in front of them, a fortress had sprung like a fast-blooming flower out of the ground. It was carved of white-silver *adamas*, reflecting the cloud-streaked sky. Towers topped with electrum reached toward the sky, and the fortress was surrounded by a high wall, also of *adamas*, in which was set a single gate, formed of two great blades plunged into the ground at angles, so that they resembled a monstrous pair of scissors.

"The Adamant Citadel," said Jocelyn.

"Thanks," Isabelle snapped. "I figured that out."

Jocelyn made the noise that Isabelle was familiar with from her own parents. Isabelle was pretty sure it was parent-speak for "Teenagers." Then Jocelyn started down the hill to the fortress. Isabelle, tired of scrambling, stalked ahead of her. She was taller than Clary's mother and had longer legs, and saw no reason why she should wait for Jocelyn if the other woman was going to persist in treating her like a child. She stomped down the hill, crushing moss under her boots, ducked through the scissorlike gates—

And froze. She was standing on a small outcropping of rock. In front of her the earth dropped away into a vast chasm, at the bottom of which boiled a river of red-gold lava, encircling the fortress. Across the chasm, much too far to jump—even for a Shadowhunter—was the only visible entrance to the fortress, a closed drawbridge.

"Some things," said Jocelyn at her elbow, "are not as simple as they first appear."

Isabelle jumped, then glared. "*So* not the place to sneak up on someone."

Jocelyn simply crossed her arms over her chest and raised her eyebrows. "Surely Hodge taught you the proper method of approaching the Adamant Citadel," she said. "After all, it is open to all female Shadowhunters in good standing with the Clave."

"Of course he did," said Isabelle haughtily, scrambling mentally to remember. *Only those with Nephilim blood . . .* She reached up and took one of the metal chopsticks from her hair. When she twisted its base, it popped and clicked and unfolded into a dagger with a Rune of Courage on the blade.

Isabelle raised her hands over the chasm. "*Ignis aurum probat,*" she said, and used the dagger to cut open her left palm; it was a swift searing pain, and blood ran from the cut, a ruby stream that splattered into the chasm below. There was a flash of blue light, and a creaking noise. The drawbridge was slowly lowering.

Isabelle smiled and wiped the blade of her knife on her gear. After another twist, it had become a slim metal chopstick again. She slid it back into her hair.

"Do you know what that means?" asked Jocelyn, her eyes on the lowering bridge.

"What?"

"What you just said. The motto of the Iron Sisters."

The drawbridge was almost flat. "It means 'Fire tests gold.'"

"Right," said Jocelyn. "They don't just mean forges and metalwork. They mean that adversity tests one's strength of character. In difficult times, in dark times, some people shine."

"Oh, yeah?" said Izzy. "Well, I'm sick of dark and difficult times. Maybe I don't want to shine."

The drawbridge crashed at their feet. "If you're anything like your mother," said Jocelyn, "you won't be able to help it."

9

The Iron Sisters

Alec raised the witchlight rune-stone high in his hand, bril-liant light raying out from it, spotlighting now one corner of the City Hall station and then another. He jumped as a mouse squeaked, running across the dusty platform. He was a Shadowhunter; he had been in many dark places, but there was something about the abandoned air of this station that made a cold shiver run up his spine.

Perhaps it was the chill of disloyalty he had felt, slipping away from his guard post on Staten Island and heading down the hill to the ferry the moment Magnus had left. He hadn't thought about what he was doing; he'd just done it, as if he were on autopilot. If he hurried, he was sure he could be back before Isabelle and Jocelyn returned, before anyone realized he had ever been gone.

Alec raised his voice. "Camille!" he called. "Camille Belcourt!"

He heard a light laugh; it echoed off the walls of the station. Then she was there, at the top of the stairs, the brilliance of his witchlight rendering her a silhouette. "Alexander Lightwood," she said. "Come upstairs."

She vanished. Alec followed his darting witchlight up the steps, and found Camille where he had before, in the lobby of the station. She was dressed in the fashion of a bygone era—a long velvet dress nipped in at the waist, her hair dressed high in white-blond curls, her lips dark red. He supposed she was beautiful, though he wasn't the best judge of feminine appeal, and it didn't help that he hated her.

"What's with the costume?" he demanded.

She smiled. Her skin was very smooth and white, without dark lines—she had fed recently. "A masquerade ball downtown. I fed quite well. Why are you here, Alexander? Starved for good conversation?"

If he were Jace, Alec thought, he'd have a smart remark for that, some kind of pun or cleverly disguised put-down. Alec just bit his lip and said, "You told me to come back if I was interested in what you were offering."

She ran a hand along the back of the divan, the only piece of furniture in the room. "And you've decided that you are."

Alec nodded.

She chuckled. "You understand what you're asking for?"

Alec's heart was pounding. He wondered if Camille could hear it. "You said you could make Magnus mortal. Like me."

Her full lips thinned. "I did," she said. "I must admit, I doubted your interest. You left rather hastily."

"Don't play with me," he said. "I don't want what you're offering that badly."

"Liar," she said casually. "Or you wouldn't be here." She moved around the divan, coming close to him, her eyes raking his face. "Up close," she said, "you do not look so much like Will as I had thought. You have his coloring, but a different shape to your face . . . perhaps a slight weakness to your jaw—"

"Shut up," he said. Okay, it wasn't Jace-level wit, but it was something. "I don't want to hear about Will."

"Very well." She stretched, languorously, like a cat. "It was many years ago, when Magnus and I were lovers. We were in bed together, after quite a passionate evening." She saw him flinch, and grinned. "You know how it is with pillow talk. One reveals one's weaknesses. Magnus spoke to me of a spell that existed, one that might be undertaken to rid a warlock of their immortality."

"So why don't I just find out what the spell is and do it?" Alec's voice rose and cracked. "Why do I need you?"

"First, because you're a Shadowhunter; you've no idea how to work a spell," she said calmly. "Second, because if you do it, he'll know it was you. If I do it, he will assume it is revenge. Spite on my part. And I do not care what Magnus thinks. But you do."

Alec looked at her steadily. "And you're going to do this for me as a favor?"

She laughed, like tinkling bells. "Of course not," she said. "You do a favor for me, and I will do one for you. That is how these matters are conducted."

Alec's hand tightened around the witchlight rune-stone until the edges cut into his hand. "And what favor do you want from me?"

"It's very simple," she said. "I want you to kill Raphael Santiago."

The bridge that crossed the crevasse surrounding the Adamant Citadel was lined with knives. They were sunk, point upward, at random intervals along the path, so that it was possible to cross the bridge only very slowly, by picking your way with dexterity. Isabelle had little trouble but was surprised to see how lightly Jocelyn, who hadn't been an active Shadowhunter in fifteen years, made her way.

By the time Isabelle had reached the opposite side of the bridge, her *dexteritas* rune had vanished into her skin, leaving a faint white mark behind. Jocelyn was only a step behind her, and as aggravating as Isabelle found Clary's mother, she was glad in a moment, when Jocelyn raised her hand and a witchlight rune-stone blazed forth, illuminating the space they stood in.

The walls were hewn from white-silver *adamas*, so that a dim light seemed to glow from within them. The floor was demon-stone as well, and carved into the center of it was a black circle. Inside the circle the symbol of the Iron Sisters was carved—a heart punctured through and through by a blade.

Whispering voices made Isabelle tear her gaze from the floor and look up. A shadow had appeared inside one of the smooth white walls—a shadow growing ever clearer, ever closer. Suddenly a portion of the wall slid back and a woman stepped out.

She wore a long, loose white gown, bound tightly at the wrists and under her breasts with silver-white cord—demon wire. Her face was both unwrinkled and ancient. She could have been any age. Her hair was long and dark, hanging in a thick braid down her back. Across her eyes and temples was an intricately curlicued tattooed mask, encircling both her eyes, which were the orange color of leaping flames.

"Who calls on the Iron Sisters?" she said. "Speak your names."

Isabelle looked toward Jocelyn, who gestured that she should speak first. She cleared her throat. "I am Isabelle Lightwood, and this is Jocelyn Fr—Fairchild. We have come to ask your help."

"Jocelyn *Morgenstern*," said the woman. "Born Fairchild, but you cannot so easily erase the taint of Valentine from your past. Have you not turned your back on the Clave?"

"It is true," said Jocelyn. "I am outcast. But Isabelle is a daughter of the Clave. Her mother—"

"Runs the New York Institute," said the woman. "We are remote here but not without sources of information; I am no fool. My name is Sister Cleophas, and I am a Maker. I shape the *adamas* for the other sisters to carve. I recognize that whip you wind so cunningly around your wrist." She indicated Isabelle. "As for that bauble about your throat—"

"If you know so much," said Jocelyn, as Isabelle's hand crept to the ruby at her neck, "then do you know why we are here? Why we have come to you?"

Sister Cleophas's eyelids lowered and she smiled slowly. "Unlike our speechless brethren, we cannot read minds here in the Fortress. Therefore we rely upon a network of information, most of it very reliable. I assume this visit has something to do with the situation involving Jace Lightwood—as his sister is here—and your son, Jonathan Morgenstern."

"We have a conundrum," said Jocelyn. "Jonathan Morgenstern plots against the Clave, like his father. The Clave has issued a death warrant against him. But Jace—Jonathan Lightwood—is very much loved by his family, who have done no wrong, and by my daughter. The conundrum is that Jace and Jonathan are bound, by very ancient blood magic."

"Blood magic? What sort of blood magic?"

Jocelyn took Magnus's folded notes from the pocket of her gear and handed them over. Cleophas studied them with her intent fiery gaze. Isabelle saw with a start that the fingers of her hands were very long—not elegantly long but grotesquely so, as if the bones had been stretched so that each hand resembled an albino spider. Her nails were filed to points, each tipped with electrum.

She shook her head. "The Sisters have little to do with blood magic." The flame color of her eyes seemed to leap and then dim, and a moment later another shadow appeared behind the frosted-glass surface of the *adamas* wall. This time Isabelle watched more closely as a second Iron Sister stepped through. It was like watching someone emerge from a haze of white smoke.

"Sister Dolores," said Cleophas, handing Magnus's notes to the new arrival. She looked much like Cleophas—the same tall narrow form, the same white dress, the same long hair, though in this case her hair was gray, and bound at the ends of her two braids with gold wire. Despite her gray hair, her face was lineless, her fire-colored eyes bright. "Can you make sense of this?"

Dolores glanced over the pages briefly. "A twinning spell," she said. "Much like our own *parabatai* ceremony, but its alliance is demonic."

"What makes it demonic?" Isabelle demanded. "If the *parabatai* spell is harmless—"

"Is it?" said Cleophas, but Dolores shot her a quelling look.

"The *parabatai* ritual binds two individuals but leaves their wills free," Dolores explained. "This binds two but makes one subordinate to the other. What the primary of the two believes, the other will believe; what the first one wants, the second will want. It essentially removes the free will of the secondary partner in the spell, and that is why it is demonic. For free will is what makes us Heaven's creatures."

"It also seems to mean that when one is wounded, the other is wounded," said Jocelyn. "Might we presume the same about death?"

"Yes. Neither will survive the death of the other. This again is not part of our *parabatai* ritual, for it is too cruel."

"Our question to you is this," said Jocelyn. "Is there any weapon forged, or that you might create, that could harm one but not the other? Or that might cut them apart?

Sister Dolores looked down at the notes, then handed them to Jocelyn. Her hands, like those of her colleague, were long and thin and as white as floss. "No weapon we have forged or could ever forge might do that."

Isabelle's hand tightened at her side, her nails cutting into her palm. "You mean there's nothing?"

"Nothing in this world," said Dolores. "A blade of Heaven or Hell might do it. The sword of the Archangel Michael, that Joshua fought with at Jericho, for it is infused with heavenly fire. And there are blades forged in the blackness of the Pit that might aid you, though how one might be obtained, I do not know."

"And we would be prevented from telling you by the Law if

we did know," said Cleophas with asperity. "You understand, of course, that we will also have to tell the Clave about this visit of yours—"

"What about Joshua's sword?" interrupted Isabelle. "Can you get that? Or can we?"

"Only an angel can gift you that sword," said Dolores. "And to summon an angel is to be blasted with heavenly fire."

"But Raziel—," Isabelle began.

Cleophas's lips thinned into a straight line. "Raziel left us the Mortal Instruments that he might be called upon in a time of direst need. That one chance was wasted when Valentine summoned him. We shall never be able to compel his might again. It was a crime to use the Instruments in that manner. The only reason that Clarissa Morgenstern escapes culpability is that it was her father who summoned him, not herself."

"My husband also summoned another angel," said Jocelyn. Her voice was quiet. "The angel Ithuriel. He kept him imprisoned for many years."

Both Sisters hesitated before Dolores spoke. "It is the bleakest of crimes to entrap an angel," she said. "The Clave could never approve it. Even if you could summon one, you could never force it to do your bidding. There is no spell for that. You could never get an angel to give you the archangel's sword; you can take by force from an angel, but there is no greater crime. Better that your Jonathan die than that an angel be so besmirched."

At that, Isabelle, whose temper had been rising, exploded. "That's the problem with you—all of you, the Iron Sisters and the Silent Brothers. Whatever they do to change you from Shadowhunters to what you are, it takes all the feelings out of you. We might be part angel, but we're part human, too. You don't understand love, or the things people do for love, or family—"

The flame leaped in Dolores's orange eyes. "I had a family," she said. "A husband and children, all murdered by demons. There was nothing left to me. I had always had a skill with shaping things with my hands, so I became an Iron Sister. The peace it has brought me is peace I think I would never have found elsewhere. It is for that reason I chose the name Dolores, "sorrow." So do not presume to tell us what we do or do not know about pain, or humanity."

"You don't know anything," Isabelle snapped. "You're as hard as demon-stone. No wonder you surround yourselves with it."

"Fire tempers gold, Isabelle Lightwood," said Cleophas.

"Oh, shut up," Isabelle said. "You've been very unhelpful, both of you."

She turned on the heel of her boot, spun away, and stalked back across the bridge, barely taking note of where the knives turned the path into a death trap, letting her body's training guide her. She reached the other side and strode through the gates; only when she was outside them did she break down. Kneeling among the moss and volcanic rocks, under the great gray sky, she let herself shake silently, though no tears came.

It seemed ages before she heard a soft step beside her, and Jocelyn knelt and put her arms around her. Oddly, Isabelle found that she didn't mind. Though she had never much liked Jocelyn, there was something so universally *motherly* in her touch that Isabelle leaned into it, almost against her own will.

"Do you want to know what they said, after you left?" Jocelyn asked, after Isabelle's trembling had slowed.

"I'm sure something about how I'm a disgrace to Shadowhunters everywhere, *et cetera*."

"Actually, Cleophas said you'd make an excellent Iron Sister, and if you were ever interested to let them know." Jocelyn's hand stroked her hair lightly.

Despite everything, Isabelle choked back a laugh. She looked up at Jocelyn. "Tell me," she said.

Jocelyn's hand stop moving. "Tell you what?"

"Who it was. That my father had the affair with. You don't understand. Every time I see a woman my mother's age, I wonder if it was her. Luke's sister. The Consul. You—"

Jocelyn sighed. "It was Annamarie Highsmith. She died in Valentine's attack on Alicante. I doubt you ever knew her."

Isabelle's mouth opened, then closed again. "I've never even heard her name before."

"Good." Jocelyn tucked a lock of Isabelle's hair back. "Do you feel any better, now that you know?"

"Sure," Isabelle lied, staring down at the ground. "I feel a lot better."

After lunch Clary had returned to the downstairs bedroom with the excuse that she was exhausted. With the door firmly closed she had tried contacting Simon again, though she realized, given the time difference between where she was now—Italy—and New York, there was every chance he was asleep. At least she prayed he was asleep. It was far preferable to hope for that than to consider the possibility that the rings might not work.

She had been in the bedroom for only about half an hour when a knock sounded at the door. She called, "Come in," moving to lean back on her hands, her fingers curled in as if she could hide the ring.

The door swung open slowly, and Jace looked down at her

from the doorway. She remembered another night, summer heat, a knock on her door. *Jace. Clean, in jeans and a gray shirt, his washed hair a halo of damp gold. The bruises on his face were already fading from purple to faint gray, and his hands were behind his back.*

"Hey," he said. His hands were in plain sight now, and he was wearing a soft-looking sweater the color of bronze that brought out the gold in his eyes. There were no bruises on his face, and the shadows she had almost grown used to seeing under his eyes were gone.

Is he happy like this? Really happy? And if he is, what are you saving him from?

Clary pushed away the tiny voice in her head and forced a smile. "What's up?"

He grinned. It was a wicked grin, the kind that made the blood in Clary's veins run a little faster. "You want to go on a date?"

Caught off guard, she stammered. "A wh-what?"

"A date," Jace repeated. "Often 'a boring thing you have to memorize in history class,' but in this case, 'an offer of an evening of blisteringly white-hot romance with yours truly.'"

"Really?" Clary was not sure what to make of this. "Blisteringly white-hot?"

"It's me," said Jace. "Watching me play Scrabble is enough to make most women swoon. Imagine if I actually put in some effort."

Clary sat up and looked down at herself. Jeans, silky green top. She thought about the cosmetics in that odd shrine-like bedroom. She couldn't help it; she was wishing for a little lip gloss.

Jace held his hand out. "You look gorgeous," he said. "Let's go."

She took his hand and let him pull her to her feet. "I don't know . . ."

"Come on." His voice had that self-mocking, seductive tone she remembered from when they had first been getting to know each other, when he'd brought her up to the greenhouse to show her the flower that bloomed at midnight. "We're in Italy. Venice. One of the most beautiful cities in the world. Shame not to see it, don't you think?"

Jace pulled her forward, so she fell against his chest. The material of his shirt was soft under her fingers, and he smelled like his familiar soap and shampoo. Her heart took a sweeping dive inside her chest. "Or we could stay in," he said, sounding a little breathless.

"So I can swoon watching you make a triple-word score?" With an effort she pulled back from him. "And spare me the jokes about scoring."

"Dammit, woman, you read my mind," he said. "Is there no filthy wordplay you can't foresee?"

"It's my special magical power. I can read your mind when you're thinking dirty thoughts."

"So, ninety-five percent of the time."

She craned her head back to look up at him. "*Ninety-five* percent? What's the other five percent?"

"Oh, you know, the usual—demons I might kill, runes I need to learn, people who've annoyed me recently, people who've annoyed me not so recently, ducks."

"Ducks?"

He waved her question away. "All right. Now watch this." He took her shoulders and turned her gently, so they were both facing the same way. A moment later—she wasn't sure how—

the walls of the room seemed to melt away around them, and she found herself stepping out onto cobblestones. She gasped, turning to look behind her, and saw only a blank wall, windows high up in an old stone building. Rows of similar houses lined the canal they stood beside. If she craned her head to the left, she could see in the distance that the canal opened out into a much larger waterway, lined with grand buildings. Everywhere was the smell of water and stone.

"Cool, huh?" Jace said proudly.

She turned and looked at him. "Ducks?" she said again.

A smile tugged the edge of his mouth. "I hate ducks. Don't know why. I just always have."

It was early morning when Maia and Jordan arrived at Praetor House, the headquarters of the Praetor Lupus. The truck clanked and bumped over the long white drive that swept through manicured lawns to the massive house that rose like the prow of a ship in the distance. Behind it Maia could see strips of trees, and behind that, the blue water of the Sound some distance away.

"This is where you did your training?" she demanded. "This place is gorgeous."

"Don't be fooled," Jordan said with a smile. "This place is boot camp, emphasis on the 'boot.'"

She looked sideways at him. He was still smiling. He had been, pretty much nonstop, since she'd kissed him down by the beach at dawn. Part of Maia felt as if a hand had lifted her up and dropped her back into her past, when she'd loved Jordan beyond anything she'd ever imagined, and part of her felt totally adrift, as if she'd woken up in a completely foreign landscape, far from the familiarity of her everyday life and the warmth of the pack.

It was very peculiar. Not bad, she thought. Just . . . peculiar.

Jordan came to a stop at a circular drive in front of the house, which, up close, Maia could see was built of blocks of golden stone, the tawny color of a wolf pelt. Black double doors were set at the top of a massive stone staircase. In the center of the circular drive was a massive sundial, its raised face telling her that it was seven in the morning. Around the edge of the sundial, words were carved: I ONLY MARK THE HOURS THAT SHINE.

She unlocked her door and jumped down from the cab just as the doors of the house opened and a voice rang out: "Praetor Kyle!"

Jordan and Maia both looked up. Descending the stairs was a middle-aged man in a charcoal suit, his blond hair streaked with gray. Jordan, smoothing all expression from his face, turned to him. "Praetor Scott," he said. "This is Maia Roberts, of the Garroway pack. Maia, this is Praetor Scott. He runs the Praetor Lupus, pretty much."

"Since the 1800s the Scotts have always run the Praetor," said the man, glancing at Maia, who inclined her head, a sign of submission. "Jordan, I have to admit, we did not expect you back again so soon. The situation with the vampire in Manhattan, the Daylighter—"

"Is in hand," Jordan said hastily. "That's not why we're here. This concerns something quite different."

Praetor Scott raised his eyebrows. "Now you've piqued my curiosity."

"It's a matter of some urgency," said Maia. "Luke Garroway, our pack's leader—"

Praetor Scott gave her a sharp look, silencing her. Though he might have been packless, he was an alpha, that much was clear from his bearing. His eyes, under his thick eyebrows, were green-gray; around his throat, under the collar of his shirt, sparkled the bronze pendant of the Praetor, with its imprint of a wolf's paw. "The Praetor chooses what matters it will regard as urgent," he said. "Nor are we a hotel, open to uninvited guests. Jordan took a chance in bringing you here, and he knows that. If he were not one of our most promising graduates, I might well send you both away."

Jordan hooked his thumbs into the waistband of his jeans and looked at the ground. A moment later Praetor Scott set his hand on Jordan's shoulder.

"But," he said, "you *are* one of our most promising graduates. And you look exhausted; I can see you were up all night. Come, and we'll discuss this in my office."

The office turned out to be down a long and winding hallway, elegantly paneled in dark wood. The house was lively with the sound of voices, and a sign saying HOUSE RULES was pinned to the wall beside a staircase leading up.

HOUSE RULES

- No shape-shifting in the hallways.
- No howling.
- No silver.
- Clothes must be worn at all times. ALL TIMES.
- No fighting. No biting.
- Mark all your food before you put it in the communal refrigerator.

The smell of cooking breakfast wafted through the air, making Maia's stomach grumble. Praetor Scott sounded amused. "I'll have someone make us up a plate of snacks if you're hungry."

"Thanks," Maia muttered. They had reached the end of a hallway, and Praetor Scott opened a door marked OFFICE.

The older werewolf's eyebrows drew together. "Rufus," he said. "What are you doing here?"

Maia peered past him. The office was a large room, comfortably messy. There was a rectangular picture window that gave out onto wide lawns, on which groups of mostly young people were executing what looked like drill maneuvers, wearing black warm-up pants and tops. The walls of the room were lined with books about lycanthropy, many in Latin, but Maia recognized the word "*lupus*." The desk was a slab of marble set upon the statues of two snarling wolves.

In front of it were two chairs. In one of them sat a large man—a werewolf—hunched over, his hands gripped together. "Praetor," he said in a grating voice. "I had hoped to speak with you regarding the incident in Boston."

"The one in which you broke your assigned charge's leg?" the Praetor said dryly. "I will be speaking to you about it, Rufus, but not this moment. Something more pressing calls me."

"But, Praetor—"

"That will be all, Rufus," said Scott in the ringing tone of an alpha wolf whose orders were not to be challenged. "Remember, this is a place of rehabilitation. Part of that is learning to respect authority."

Muttering under his breath, Rufus rose from the chair. Only when he stood up did Maia realize, and react to, his enormous size. He towered over both her and Jordan, his black T-shirt straining over his chest, the sleeves about to split around his biceps. His head was closely shaved, his face scored with deep claw marks all across one cheek, like furrows dug in soil. He gave her a sour look as he stalked past them and out into the hall.

"Of course some of us," Jordan muttered, "are easier to rehabilitate than others."

As Rufus's heavy tread faded down the hall, Scott threw himself into the high-backed chair behind the desk and buzzed a joltingly modern-looking intercom. After requesting breakfast in a terse voice, he leaned back, hands clasped behind his head.

"I'm all ears," he said.

As Jordan recounted their story, and their request, to Praetor Scott, Maia couldn't keep her eyes and mind from wandering. She wondered what it would have been like to have been raised here, in this elegant house of rules and regulations, rather than with the comparatively lawless freedom of the pack. At some point a werewolf dressed all in black—it seemed to be the regulation outfit of the Praetor—came in with sliced roast beef, cheese, and protein drinks on a pewter tray. Maia eyed the breakfast with some dismay. It was true that werewolves needed more protein than normal people, much more, but roast beef for breakfast?

"You'll find," Praetor Scott said as Maia drank her protein shake gingerly, "that, in fact, refined sugar is harmful to werewolves. If you cease consuming it for a period of time, you will cease desiring it. Hasn't your pack leader told you that?"

Maia tried to imagine Luke, who liked to make pancakes in odd and amusing shapes, lecturing her about sugar, and failed.

Now was not the time to mention that, though. "No, he has, of course," she said. "I tend to, ah, backslide in times of stress."

"I understand your concern for your pack leader," said Scott. A gold Rolex glinted on his wrist. "Normally we maintain a strict policy of noninterference regarding matters not related to new-fledged Downworlders. We do not, in fact, prioritize werewolves over other Downworlders, though only lycanthropes are allowed into the Praetor."

"But that's exactly why we do need your help," said Jordan. "Packs are by their nature always moving, transitional. They have no opportunity to build up things like libraries of stored knowledge. I'm not saying they don't have wisdom, but everything is an oral tradition and every pack knows different things. We could go from pack to pack, and maybe someone would know how to cure Luke, but we don't have *time*. Here"—he gestured at the books lining the walls—"is the closest thing werewolves have to, say, the archives of the Silent Brothers or the Spiral Labyrinth of the warlocks."

Scott looked unconvinced. Maia set her protein shake down. "And Luke isn't just any pack leader," she said. "He's the lyncanthrope's representative on the Council. If you helped cure him, you would know that the Praetor would always have a Council voice in their favor."

Scott's eyes glinted. "Interesting," he said. "Very well. I'll have a look through the books. It'll probably take a few hours. Jordan, I suggest that if you're going to drive back to Manhattan you get some rest. We don't need you wrapping your truck around a tree."

"I could drive—," Maia began.

"You look equally exhausted. Jordan, as you know, there

will always be a room for you here at the Praetor House, even though you've graduated. And Nick is on assignment, so there's a bed for Maia. Why don't you both get some rest, and I'll call you down when I'm finished." He swiveled around in his chair to examine the books on the walls.

Jordan gestured to Maia that this was their cue to leave; she stood up, brushing crumbs off her jeans. She was halfway to the door when Praetor Scott spoke again.

"Oh, and Maia Roberts," he said, and his voice held a note of warning. "I hope you understand that when you make promises in other people's names, it falls upon your head to make sure they follow through."

Simon awoke still feeling exhausted, blinking in the darkness. The thick black curtains over the windows let in very little light, but his internal body clock told him it was daytime. That and the fact that Isabelle was gone, her side of the bed rumpled, the covers turned back.

Daytime, and he hadn't talked to Clary since she'd gone. He drew his hand out from under the covers and looked at the gold ring on his right hand. Delicate, it was etched with what were either designs or words in an alphabet he didn't know.

Clenching his jaw, he sat up and touched the ring. *Clary?*

The answer was immediate and clear. He nearly slid off the bed with relief. *Simon. Thank God.*

Can you talk?

No. He felt rather than heard a tense distraction in the voice of her mind. *I'm glad you spoke to me, but now isn't good. I'm not alone.*

But you're all right?

I'm fine. Nothing's happened yet. I'm trying to gather information. I promise I'll talk to you the moment I hear anything.

Okay. Take care of yourself.

You too.

And she was gone. Sliding his legs over the side of the mattress, Simon did his best to flatten his sleep-mussed hair, and went to see if anyone else was awake.

They were. Alec, Magnus, Jocelyn, and Isabelle sat around the table in Magnus's living room. While Alec and Magnus were in jeans, both Jocelyn and Isabelle wore gear, Isabelle with her whip wrapped around her right arm. She glanced up as he came in but didn't smile; her shoulders were tense, her mouth a thin line. They all had mugs of coffee in front of them.

"There's a reason the ritual of the Mortal Instruments was so complicated." Magnus made the sugar bowl float over to himself and dumped some of the white powder into his coffee. "Angels act at the behest of God, not human beings—not even Shadowhunters. Summon one, and you're likely to find yourself blasted with divine wrath. The whole point of the Mortal Instruments ritual wasn't that it allowed someone to summon Raziel. It was that it protected the summoner from the Angel's wrath once he *did* appear."

"Valentine—," Alec began.

"Yes, Valentine also summoned a very minor angel. And it never spoke to him, did it? Never gave him a sliver of help, though he harvested its blood. And even then he must have been using incredibly powerful spells just to bind it. My understanding is that he tied its life to the Wayland manor, so that when the angel died the manor collapsed to rubble." He tapped a blue-painted fingernail on his mug. "And he damned himself. Whether you believe in Heaven and Hell or not, he damned himself surely.

When he summoned Raziel, Raziel struck him down. Partly in revenge for what Valentine had done to his brother angel."

"Why are we talking about summoning angels?" Simon asked, perching himself on the end of the long table.

"Isabelle and Jocelyn went to see the Iron Sisters," said Alec. "Looking for a weapon that could be used on Sebastian that wouldn't affect Jace."

"And there isn't one?"

"Nothing in this world," said Isabelle. "A Heavenly weapon might do it, or something with a seriously demonic alliance. We were exploring the first option."

"Summoning up an angel to give you a weapon?"

"It's happened before," said Magnus. "Raziel gave the Mortal Sword to Jonathan Shadowhunter. In the old stories, the night before the battle of Jericho, an angel appeared and gave Joshua a sword."

"Huh," said Simon. "I would have thought angels would have been all about peace, not weapons."

Magnus snorted. "Angels are not just messengers. They are soldiers. Michael is said to have routed armies. They are not patient, angels. Certainly not with the vicissitudes of human beings. Anyone who tried to summon Raziel without the Mortal Instruments to protect them would probably be blasted to death on the spot. Demons are easier to summon. There are more of them, and many are weak. But then, a weak demon can help you only so much—"

"We can't summon a demon," said Jocelyn, aghast. "The Clave—"

"I thought you stopped caring what the Clave thought of you years ago," Magnus said.

"It's not just me," said Jocelyn. "The rest of you. Luke. My daughter. If the Clave knew—"

"Well, they won't know, will they?" said Alec, his usually gentle voice edged. "Unless you tell them."

Jocelyn looked from Isabelle's still face to Magnus's inquiring one, to Alec's stubborn blue eyes. "You're really considering this? Summoning a demon?"

"Well, not just any demon," said Magnus. "Azazel."

Jocelyn's eyes blazed. "*Azazel?*" Her eyes scanned the others, as if looking for support, but Izzy and Alec glanced down at their mugs, and Simon just shrugged.

"I don't know who Azazel is," he said. "Isn't he the cat from *The Smurfs?*" He cast about, but Isabelle just looked up and rolled her eyes at him. *Clary?* he thought.

Her voice came through, tinged with alarm. *What is it? What's happened? Did my mom find out I'm gone?*

Not yet, he thought back. *Is Azazel the cat from* The Smurfs?

There was a long pause. *That's Azrael, Simon. And no more using the magic rings for Smurf questions.*

And she was gone. Simon glanced up from his hand and saw Magnus looking at him quizzically. "He's not a cat, Sylvester," he said. "He's a Greater Demon. Lieutenant of Hell and Forger of Weapons. He was an angel who taught mankind how to make weapons, when before it had been knowledge only angels possessed. That caused him to fall, and now he is a demon. 'And the whole earth has been corrupted by the works that were taught by Azazel. To him ascribe all sin.'"

Alec looked at Magnus in amazement. "How did you know all that?"

"He's a friend of mine," said Magnus, and, noting their

expressions, sighed. "Okay, not really. But it is in the *Book of Enoch*."

"Seems dangerous." Alec frowned. "It sounds like he's beyond a Greater Demon, even. Like Lilith."

"Fortunately, he is already bound," said Magnus. "If you summon him, his spirit form will come to you but his corporeal self will remain bound to the jagged rocks of Duduael."

"The jagged rocks of . . . Oh, whatever," Isabelle said, winding her long dark hair into a bun. "He's the demon of weapons. Fine. I say we give it a go."

"I can't believe you're even considering this," said Jocelyn. "I learned from watching my husband what dabbling in raising demons can do. Clary—" She broke off then, as if sensing Simon's gaze on her, and turned. "Simon," she said, "do you know, is Clary awake yet? We've been letting her sleep, but it's almost eleven."

Simon hesitated. "I don't know." This, he reasoned, was true. Wherever Clary was, she *could* be asleep. Even though he had just talked to her.

Jocelyn looked puzzled. "But weren't you in the room with her?"

"No, I wasn't. I was—" Simon broke off, realizing the hole he'd just dug himself. There were three spare bedrooms. Jocelyn had been in one, Clary the other. Which would obviously mean he must have slept in the third room with—

"Isabelle?" said Alec, his eyebrows raised. "You slept in Isabelle's room?"

Isabelle waved a hand. "No need to worry, big brother. Nothing happened. Of course," she added as Alec's shoulders relaxed, "I was totally passed-out drunk, so he could really have done whatever he wanted and I wouldn't have woken up."

"Oh, please," said Simon. "All I did was tell you the entire plot of *Star Wars*."

"I don't think I remember that," said Isabelle, taking a cookie from the plate on the table.

"Oh, yeah? Who was Luke Skywalker's best childhood friend?"

"Biggs Darklighter," Isabelle said immediately, and then hit the table with the flat of her hand. "That is *so* cheating!" Still, she grinned at him around her cookie.

"Ah," said Magnus. "Nerd love. It is a beautiful thing, while also being an object of mockery and hilarity for those of us who are more sophisticated."

"All right, that's enough." Jocelyn stood up. "I'm going to get Clary. If you're going to raise a demon, I don't want to be here, and I don't want my daughter here either." She headed toward the hallway.

Simon blocked her way. "You can't do that," he said.

Jocelyn looked at him with a set face. "I know you're going to say that this is the safest place for us, Simon, but with a demon being raised, I just—"

"It's not that." Simon took a deep breath, which didn't help, since his blood no longer processed oxygen. He felt slightly sick. "You can't go wake her up because . . . because she isn't here."

10

The Wild Hunt

Jordan's old room at the Praetor House looked like any dormitory room at any college. There were two iron-framed beds, each set against a different wall. Through the window separating them green lawns were visible three floors down. Jordan's side of the room was fairly bare—it looked as if he had taken most of his photographs and books with him to Manhattan—though there were some tacked-up pictures of beaches and the ocean, and a surfboard leaning against one wall. A little jolt went through Maia as she saw that on the bedside table was a gold-framed photo of her with Jordan, taken at Ocean City, the boardwalk and the beach behind them.

Jordan looked at the photograph and then at her, and

blushed. He slung his bag onto his bed and stripped off his jacket, his back to her.

"When will your roommate be back?" she asked into the suddenly uncomfortable silence. She wasn't sure why they were both embarrassed. They certainly hadn't been when they'd been in the truck together, but now, here in Jordan's space, the years they had spent not speaking seemed to press them apart.

"Who knows? Nick's on assignment. They're dangerous. He might not come back." Jordan sounded resigned. He tossed his jacket over the back of a chair. "Why don't you lie down? I'm going to take a shower." He headed for the bathroom, which, Maia was relieved to see, was attached to his room. She didn't feel like dealing with one of those shared-bathroom-down-the-hall things.

"Jordan—," she began, but he'd already closed the bathroom door behind him. She could hear water running. With a sigh she kicked off her shoes and lay down on the absent Nick's bed. The blanket was dark blue plaid, and smelled like pinecones. She looked up and saw that the ceiling was wallpapered with photographs. The same laughing blond boy, who looked about seventeen, smiled down at her out of each picture. Nick, she guessed. He looked happy. Had Jordan been happy, here at the Praetor House?

She reached out and flipped the photograph of the two of them toward her. It had been taken years ago, when Jordan was skinny, with big hazel eyes that dominated his face. They had their arms around each other and looked sunburned and happy. Summer had darkened both their skins and put light streaks in Maia's hair, and Jordan had his head turned slightly toward her, as if he were going to say something or kiss her. She couldn't remember which. Not anymore.

She thought of the boy whose bed she was sitting on, the boy who might never come back. She thought of Luke, slowly dying, and of Alaric and Gretel and Justine and Theo and all the others of her pack who had lost their lives in the war against Valentine. She thought of Max, and of Jace, two Lightwoods lost—for, she had to admit in her heart, she didn't think they would ever get Jace back. And lastly and strangely she thought of Daniel, the brother she had never mourned for, and to her surprise she felt tears sting the backs of her eyes.

She sat up abruptly. She felt as if the world were tilting and she was clinging on helplessly, trying to keep from tumbling into a black abyss. She could feel the shadows closing in. With Jace lost and Sebastian out there, things could only get darker. There would only be more loss and more death. She had to admit, the most alive she'd felt in weeks had been those moments at dawn, kissing Jordan in his car.

As if she were in a dream, she found herself getting to her feet. She walked across the room and opened the door to the bathroom. The shower was a square of frosted glass; she could see Jordan's silhouette through it. She doubted he could hear her over the running water as she pulled off her sweater and shimmied out of her jeans and underwear. With a deep breath she crossed the room, slid the shower door open, and stepped inside.

Jordan spun around, pushing the wet hair out of his eyes. The shower was running hot, and his face was flushed, making his eyes shine as if the water had polished them. Or maybe it wasn't just the water making the blood rise under his skin as his eyes took her in—all of her. She looked back at him steadily, not embarrassed, watching the way the Praetor Lupus pendant shone in the wet hollow of his throat, and the slide of the soap suds over his shoulders and chest as he stared at her, blinking water out of his eyes. He was beautiful, but then she had always thought so.

"Maia?" he said unsteadily. "Are you . . . ?"

"Shh." She put her finger against his lips, drawing the shower door closed with her other hand. Then she stepped closer, wrapping both arms around him, letting the water wash both of them clean of the darkness. "Don't talk. Just kiss me."

So he did.

"What in the name of the Angel do you mean Clary isn't there?" Jocelyn demanded, white-faced. "How do you know that, if you just woke up? Where has she gone?"

Simon swallowed. He had grown up with Jocelyn as almost a second mother to him. He was used to her protectiveness of her daughter, but she had always seen him as an ally in that, someone who would stand between Clary and the dangers of the world. Now she was looking at him like the enemy. "She texted me last night . . . ," Simon began, then stopped as Magnus waved him over to the table.

"You might as well sit down," he said. Isabelle and Alec were watching wide-eyed from either side of Magnus, but the warlock didn't look particularly surprised. "Tell us all what's going on. I have a feeling this is going to take a while."

It did, though not as long as Simon might have hoped. When he was done explaining, hunched over on his chair and staring down at Magnus's scratched table, he lifted his head to see Jocelyn fixing him with a green stare as cold as arctic water. "You let my daughter go off . . . with *Jace* . . . to some unfindable, untraceable place where none of us can reach her?"

Simon looked down at his hands. "I can reach her," he said, holding up his right hand with the gold ring on the finger. "I told you. I heard from her this morning. She said she was fine."

"You never should have let her leave in the first place!"

"I didn't *let* her. She was going to go anyway. I thought she might as well have some kind of a lifeline, since it's not like I could stop her."

"To be fair," said Magnus, "I don't think anyone could. Clary does what she wants." He looked at Jocelyn. "You can't keep her in a cage."

"I *trusted* you," she snapped at Magnus. "How did she get out?"

"She made a Portal."

"But you said there were wards—"

"To keep threats out, not to keep guests in. Jocelyn, your daughter isn't stupid, and she does what she thinks is right. You can't stop her. No one can stop her. *She is a great deal like her mother.*"

Jocelyn looked at Magnus for a moment, her mouth slightly open, and Simon realized that of course Magnus must have known Clary's mother when she was young, when she betrayed Valentine and the Circle and nearly died in the Uprising. "She's a little girl," she said, and turned to Simon. "You've spoken to her? Using these—these rings? Since she left?"

"This morning," said Simon. "She said she was fine. That everything was fine."

Instead of seeming reassured, Jocelyn only looked angrier.

"I'm sure that's what she *said*. Simon, I can't believe you allowed her to do this. You should have restrained her—"

"What, tied her up?" Simon said in disbelief. "Handcuffed her to the diner table?"

"If that's what it took. You're stronger than she is. I'm disappointed in—"

Isabelle stood up. "Okay, that's enough." She glared at Jocelyn. "It is totally and completely unfair to yell at Simon over something Clary decided to do *on her own*. And if Simon had tied her up for you, then what? Were you planning on keeping her tied up forever? You'd have to let her go eventually, and then what? She wouldn't trust Simon anymore, and she already doesn't trust you because you stole her memories. And that, if I recall, was because you were trying to protect her. Maybe if you hadn't *protected* her so much, she would know more about what is dangerous and what isn't, and be a little less secretive—and less reckless!"

Everyone stared at Isabelle, and for a moment Simon was reminded of something that Clary had said to him once—that Izzy rarely made speeches, but when she did, she made them *count*. Jocelyn was white around the lips.

"I'm going to the station to be with Luke," she said. "Simon, I expect reports from you every twenty-four hours that my daughter is all right. If I don't hear from you every night, I'm going to the Clave."

And she stalked out of the apartment, slamming the door behind her so hard that a long crack appeared in the plaster beside it.

Isabelle sat back down, this time beside Simon. He said nothing to her but held out his hand, and she took it, slipping her fingers between his.

"So," Magnus said finally, breaking the silence. "Who's up for raising Azazel? Because we're going to need a whole lot of candles."

Jace and Clary spent the day wandering—through mazelike tiny streets that ran along canals whose water ranged from deep green to murky blue. They made their way among the tourists in Saint Mark's Square, and over the Bridge of Sighs, and drank small, powerful cups of espresso at Caffè Florian. The disorienting maze of streets reminded Clary a bit of Alicante, though Alicante lacked Venice's feeling of elegant decay. There were no roads here, no cars, only twisting little alleys, and bridges arching over canals whose water was as green as malachite. As the sky overhead darkened to the deep blue of late autumn twilight, lights began to go on—in tiny boutiques, in bars and restaurants that seemed to appear out of nowhere and disappear again into shadow as she and Jace passed, leaving light and laughter behind.

When Jace asked Clary if she was ready for dinner, she nodded firmly, yes. She had begun to feel guilty that she had gotten no information out of him and that she was, actually, enjoying herself. As they crossed over a bridge to the Dorsoduro, one of the quieter sections of the city, away from the tourist throng, she determined that she would get *something* out of him that night, something worth relaying to Simon.

Jace held her hand firmly as they went over a final bridge and the street opened out into a great square on the side of an enormous canal the size of a river. The basilica of a domed church rose on their right. Across the canal more of the city lit the evening, throwing illumination onto the water, which shifted and glimmered with light. Clary's hands itched for chalk and pencils, to draw the light as it faded out of the sky, the darkening water, the jagged outlines of the buildings, their reflections slowly dimming in the canal. Everything seemed washed with a steely blueness. Somewhere church bells were chiming.

She tightened her hand on Jace's. She felt very far away here from everything in her life, distant in a way that she had not felt in Idris. Venice shared with Alicante the sense of being a place out of time, torn from the past, as if she had stepped into a painting or the pages of a book. But it was also a *real* place, one she had grown up knowing about, wanting to visit. She looked sidelong at Jace, who was gazing down the canal. The steely blue light was on him, too, darkening his eyes, the shadows under his cheekbones, the lines of his mouth. When he caught her gaze on him, he looked over and smiled.

He led her around the church and down a flight of mossy steps to a path along the canal. Everything smelled of wet stone and water and dampness and years. As the sky darkened, something broke the surface of the canal water a few feet from Clary. She heard the splash and looked in time to see a green-haired woman rise from the water and grin at her; she had a beautiful face but sharklike teeth and a fish's yellow eyes. Pearls were wound through her hair. She sank again below the water, without a ripple.

"Mermaid," said Jace. "There are old families of them that have lived here in Venice a long, long time. They're a little odd. They do better in clean water, far out to sea, living on fish instead of garbage." He looked toward the sunset. "The whole city is sinking," he said. "It'll all be under water in a hundred years. Imagine swimming down into the ocean and touching the top of Saint Mark's Basilica." He pointed across the water.

Clary felt a flicker of sadness at the thought of all this beauty being lost. "Isn't there anything they can do?"

"To raise a whole city? Or hold back the ocean? Not much," Jace said. They had come to a set of stairs leading up. The wind came off the water and lifted his dark gold hair off his forehead, his neck. "All things tend toward entropy. The whole universe is moving outward, the stars pulling away from one another, God knows what falling through the cracks between them." He paused. "Okay, that sounded a little crazy."

"Maybe it was all the wine at lunch."

"I can hold my liquor." They turned a corner, and a fairy-land of lights gleamed out at them. Clary blinked, her eyes adjusting. It was a small restaurant with tables set outside and inside, heat lamps wound with Christmas lights like a forest of magical trees between the tables. Jace detached himself from her long enough to get them a table, and soon they were sitting by the side of the canal, listening to the splash of water against stone and the sound of small boats bobbing up and down with the tide.

Tiredness was beginning to wash over Clary in waves, like the lap of water against the sides of the canal. She told Jace what she wanted and let him order in Italian, relieved when the waiter went away so she could lean forward and rest her elbows on the table, her head on her hands.

"I think I have jet lag," she said. "Interdimensional jet lag."

"You know, time *is* a dimension," Jace said.

"Pedant." She flicked a bread crumb from the basket on the table at him.

He grinned. "I was trying to remember all the deadly sins the other day," he said. "Greed, envy, gluttony, irony, pedantry . . ."

"I'm pretty sure irony isn't a deadly sin."

"I'm pretty sure it is."

"Lust," she said. "Lust is a deadly sin."

"And spanking."

"I think that falls under lust."

"I think it should have its own category," said Jace. "Greed, envy, gluttony, irony, pedantry, lust, and spanking." The white Christmas lights were reflected in his eyes. He looked more beautiful than he ever had, Clary thought, and correspondingly more distant, more hard to touch. She thought of what he had said about the city sinking, and the spaces between the stars, and remembered the lines of a Leonard Cohen song that Simon's band used to cover, not very well. *"There is a crack in everything/That's how the light gets in."* There had to be a crack in Jace's calm, some way she could reach through to the real him she believed was still in there.

Jace's amber eyes studied her. He reached out to touch her hand, and it was only after a moment that Clary realized that his fingers were on her gold ring. "What's that?" he said. "I don't remember you having a faerie-work ring."

His tone was neutral, but her heart skipped a beat. Lying straight to Jace's face wasn't something she had a lot of practice with. "It was Isabelle's," she said with a shrug. "She was throwing out all the stuff that faerie ex-boyfriend of hers gave her—Meliorn—and I thought this was pretty, so she said I could have it."

"And the Morgenstern ring?"

This seemed like a place to tell the truth. "I gave it to Magnus so he could try to track you with it."

"*Magnus.*" Jace said the name as if it were a stranger's, and exhaled a breath. "Do you still feel like you made the right decision? Coming with me here?"

"Yes. I'm happy to be with you. And—well, I always wanted to see Italy. I've never traveled much. Never been out of the country—"

"You were in Alicante," he reminded her.

"Okay, other than visiting magical lands no one else can see, I haven't traveled much. Simon and I had plans. We were going to go backpacking around Europe after we graduated high school . . ." Clary's voice trailed off. "It sounds silly now."

"No, it doesn't." He reached out and pushed a strand of hair behind her ear. "Stay with me. We can see the whole world."

"I am with you. I'm not going anywhere."

"Is there anything special you want to see? Paris? Budapest? The Leaning Tower of Pisa?"

Only if it falls on Sebastian's head, she thought. "Can we travel to Idris? I mean, I guess, can the apartment travel there?"

"It can't get past the wards." His hand traced a path down her cheek. "You know, I really missed you."

"You mean you haven't been going on romantic dates with Sebastian while you've been away from me?"

"I tried," Jace said, "but no matter how liquored up you get him, he just won't put out."

Clary reached for her glass of wine. She was starting to get used to the taste of it. She could feel it burning a path down her throat, heating her veins, adding a dreamlike quality to the night. She was in Italy, with her beautiful boyfriend, on a beautiful night, eating delicious food that melted in her mouth. These were the kinds of moments that you remembered all your life. But it felt like touching only the edge of happiness; every time she looked at Jace, happiness slipped away from her. How could he be Jace and not-Jace, all at once? How could you be heartbroken and happy at the same time?

They lay in the narrow twin bed that was meant for only one person, wrapped together tightly under Jordan's flannel sheet. Maia lay with her head in the crook of his arm, the sun from the window warming her face and shoulders. Jordan was propped on his arm, leaning over her, his free hand running through her hair, pulling her curls out to their full length and letting them slide back through his fingers.

"I missed your hair," he said, and dropped a kiss onto her forehead.

Laughter bubbled up from somewhere deep inside her, that sort of laughter that came with the giddiness of infatuation. "Just my hair?"

"No." He was grinning, his hazel eyes lit with green, his brown hair thoroughly rumpled. "Your eyes." He kissed them, one after another. "Your mouth." He kissed that, too, and she hooked her fingers through the chain against his bare chest that held the Praetor Lupus pendant. "Everything about you."

She twisted the chain around her fingers. "Jordan . . . I'm sorry about before. About snapping at you about the money, and Stanford. It was just a lot to take in."

His eyes darkened, and he ducked his head. "It's not like I don't know how independent you are. I just . . . I wanted to do something nice for you."

"I know," she whispered. "I know you worry about me needing you, but I shouldn't be with you because I need you. I should be with you because I love you."

His eyes lit up—incredulous, hopeful. "You— I mean, you think it's possible you could feel that way about me again?"

"I never stopped loving you, Jordan," she said, and he caught her against him with a kiss so intense it was bruising. She moved closer to him, and things might have proceeded as they had in the shower if a sharp knock hadn't come at the door.

"Praetor Kyle!" a voice shouted through the door. "Wake up! Praetor Scott wishes to see you downstairs in his office."

Jordan, his arms around Maia, swore softly. Laughing, Maia ran her hand slowly up his back, tangling her fingers in his hair. "You think Praetor Scott can wait?" she whispered.

"I think he has a key to this room and he'll use it if he feels like it."

"That's all right," she said, brushing her lips against his ear. "We have lots of time, right? All the time we'll ever need."

Chairman Meow lay on the table in front of Simon, completely asleep, his four legs sticking straight into the air. This, Simon felt, was something of an achievement. Since he had become a vampire, animals tended not to like him; they avoided him if they could, and hissed or barked if he came too close. For Simon, who had always been an animal lover, it was a hard loss. But he supposed if you were already the pet of a warlock, perhaps you'd learned to accept weird creatures in your life.

Magnus, as it turned out, hadn't been joking about the candles. Simon was taking a moment to rest and drink some coffee; it stayed down well, and the caffeine took the edge off the beginning prickles of hunger. All afternoon, they had been helping Magnus set the scene for raising Azazel. They had raided local bodegas for tea lights and prayer candles, which they had placed in a careful circle. Isabelle and Alec were scattering the floorboards outside the circle with a mixture of salt and dried belladonna as Magnus instructed them, reading aloud from *Forbidden Rites, A Necromancer's Manual of the Fifteenth Century*.

"What have you done to my cat?" Magnus demanded, returning to the living room carrying a pot of coffee, with a circle of mugs floating around his head like a model of the planets rotating around the sun. "You drank his blood, didn't you? You *said* you weren't hungry!"

Simon was indignant. "I did not drink his blood. He's fine!" He poked the Chairman in the stomach. The cat yawned. "Second, you asked me if I was hungry when you were ordering pizza, so I said no, because I can't eat pizza. I was being polite."

"That doesn't give you the right to eat my cat."

"Your cat is fine!" Simon reached to pick up the tabby, who jumped indignantly to his feet and stalked off the table. "See?"

"Whatever." Magnus threw himself down in the seat at the head of the table; the mugs banged into place as Alec and Izzy straightened up, done with their task. Magnus clapped his hands. "Everyone! Gather around. It's time for a meeting. I'm going to teach you how to summon a demon."

Praetor Scott was waiting for them in the library, still in the same swivel chair, a small bronze box on the desk between them. Maia and Jordan sat down across from him, and Maia couldn't help wondering if it was written all over her face, what she and Jordan had been doing. Not that the Praetor was looking at them with much interest.

He pushed the box toward Jordan. "It's a salve," he said. "If applied to Garroway's wound, it should filter the poison from his blood and allow the demon steel to work its way free. He should heal in a few days."

Maia's heart leaped—finally some good news. She reached for the box before Jordan could, and opened it. It was indeed filled with a dark waxy salve that smelled sharply herbal, like crushed bay leaves.

"I—," Praetor Scott began, his eyes flicking to Jordan.

"She should take it," said Jordan. "She's close to Garroway and is part of the pack. They trust her."

"Are you saying they don't trust the Praetor?"

"Half of them think the Praetor is a fairy tale," Maia said, adding "sir" as an afterthought.

Praetor Scott looked annoyed, but before he could say anything, the phone on his desk rang. He seemed to hesitate, then lifted the receiver to his ear. "Scott here," he said, and then, after a moment, "Yes—yes, I think so." He hung up, his mouth curving into a not entirely pleasant smile. "Praetor Kyle," he said. "I'm glad you dropped in on us today of all days. Stay a moment. This matter somewhat concerns you."

Maia was startled at this pronouncement, but not as startled as she was a moment later when a corner of the room began to shimmer and a figure appeared, slowly developing—it was like watching images appear on film in a darkroom—and the figure of a young boy took shape. His hair was dark brown, short and straight, and a gold necklace gleamed against the brown skin of his throat. He looked slight and ethereal, like a choirboy, but there was something in his eyes that made him seem much older than that.

"Raphael," she said, recognizing him. He was ever so slightly transparent—a Projection, she realized. She'd heard of them but had never seen one up close.

Praetor Scott looked at her in surprise. "You know the head of the New York vampire clan?"

"We met once, in Brocelind Woods," said Raphael, looking her over without much interest. "She is a friend of the Daylighter, Simon."

"Your assignment," Praetor Scott said to Jordan, as if Jordan could have forgotten.

Jordan's forehead creased. "Has something happened to him?" he asked. "Is he all right?"

"This is not about him," said Raphael. "It is about the rogue vampire, Maureen Brown."

"Maureen?" Maia exclaimed. "But she's only, what, thirteen?"

"A rogue vampire is a rogue vampire," said Raphael. "And Maureen has been cutting quite a swath for herself through TriBeCa and the Lower East Side. Multiple injured and at least six kills. We've managed to cover them up, but . . ."

"She's Nick's assignment," said Praetor Scott with a frown. "But he hasn't been able to find a trace of her. We may need to send in someone with more experience."

"I urge you to do so," said Raphael. "If the Shadowhunters were not so concerned with their own . . . emergency at this juncture, they would surely have involved themselves by now.

And the last thing the clan needs after the affair with Camille is a censuring by the Shadowhunters."

"I take it Camille is still missing as well?" said Jordan. "Simon told us everything that happened the night Jace disappeared, and Maureen seemed to be doing Camille's bidding."

"Camille is not new-made and is therefore not our concern," said Scott.

"I know, but—find her, and you may find Maureen, that's all I'm saying," said Jordan.

"If she were with Camille, she would not be killing at the rate she is," said Raphael. "Camille would prevent her. She is bloodthirsty but she knows the Conclave, and the Law. She would keep Maureen and her activities out of their line of sight. No, Maureen's behavior has all the hallmarks of a vampire gone feral."

"Then, I think you're right." Jordan sat back. "Nick should have backup in dealing with her, or—"

"Or something might happen to him? If it does, perhaps it will help you focus more in future," said Praetor Scott. "On your *own* assignment."

Jordan's mouth opened. "Simon wasn't responsible for Turning Maureen," he said. "I told you—"

Praetor Scott waved away his words. "Yes, I know," he said, "or you would have been pulled from your assignment, Kyle. But your subject did bite her, and under your watch as well. And it was her association with the Daylighter, however distant, that led to her eventual Turning."

"The Daylighter is dangerous," said Raphael, his eyes shining. "It is what I have been saying all along."

"He is not dangerous," Maia said fiercely. "He has a good

heart." She saw Jordan glance at her a little, sidelong, so quickly that she wondered if she'd imagined it.

"Yap, yap, yap," said Raphael dismissively. "You werewolves cannot focus on the matter at hand. I trusted you, Praetor, for new-fledged Downworlders are your department. But allowing Maureen to run wild reflects badly on my clan. If you do not find her soon, I will call up every vampire at my disposal. After all"—he smiled, and his delicate incisors shone—"in the end she is ours to kill."

When the meal was over, Clary and Jace walked back to the apartment through a mist-shrouded evening. The streets were deserted and the canal water shone like glass. Rounding a corner, they found themselves beside a quiet canal, lined with shuttered houses. Boats bobbed gently on the curving water, each a half-moon of black.

Jace laughed softly and moved forward, his hand pulling out of Clary's. His eyes were wide and golden in the lamplight. He knelt by the side of the canal, and she saw a flash of white-silver—a stele—and then one of the boats sprang free of its mooring chain and began to drift toward the center of the canal. Jace slid the stele back into his belt and leaped, landing lightly on the wooden seat at the front of the boat. He held his hand out to Clary. "Come on."

She looked from him to the boat and shook her head. It was only a little bigger than a canoe, painted black, though the paint was damp and splintering. It looked as light and fragile as a toy. She imagined upending it and both of them being dumped into the ice-green canal. "I can't. I'll knock it over."

Jace shook his head impatiently. "You can do it," he said. "I trained you." To demonstrate he took a step back. Now he was standing on the thin edge of the boat, just beside the oarlock. He looked at her, his mouth crooked in a half smile. By all the laws of physics, she thought, the boat, unbalanced, ought to have been toppling sideways into the water. But Jace balanced lightly there, back straight, as if he were made of nothing more than smoke. Behind him was the backdrop of water and stone, canal and bridges, not a single modern edifice in sight. With his bright hair and the way he carried himself, he could have been some Renaissance prince.

He held out a hand to her again. "Remember. You're as light as you want to be."

She remembered. Hours of training in how to fall, to balance, how to land like Jace did, as if you were a piece of ash sifting gently downward. She sucked her breath in and leaped, the green water flying by beneath her. She alighted in the bow of the boat, wobbling on the wooden seat, but steady.

She let out her breath in a whoosh of relief and heard Jace laugh as he leaped down to the flat bottom of the boat. It was leaky. A thin layer of water covered the wood. He was also nine inches taller than she was, so that with her standing on the seat in the bow, their heads were on a level.

He put his hands on her waist. "So," he said. "Where do you want to go now?"

She looked around. They had drifted far away from the bank of the canal. "Are we stealing this boat?"

"'Stealing' is such an ugly word," he mused.

"What do you want to call it?"

He picked her up and swung her around before putting her down. "An extreme case of window-shopping."

He pulled her closer, and she stiffened. Her feet skidded out from under her, and the two of them slid to the curved floor of the boat, which was flat and damp and smelled like water and wet wood.

Clary found herself resting on top of Jace, her knees on either side of his hips. Water was soaking into his shirt, but he didn't seem to mind. He threw his hands behind his head, folding them, his shirt pulling up. "You literally knocked me down with the strength of your passion," he observed. "Nice work, Fray."

"You only fell because you wanted to. I know you," she said. The moon shone down on them like a spotlight, like they were the only people under it. "You never slip."

He touched her face. "I may not slip," he said, "but I fall."

Her heart pounded, and she had to swallow before she could reply lightly, as if he were joking. "That may be your worst line of all time."

"Who says it's a line?"

The boat rocked, and she leaned forward, balancing her hands on his chest. Her hips pressed against his, and she watched his eyes as they widened, going from wickedly sparkling gold to dark, the pupil swallowing the iris. She could see herself and the night sky in them.

He propped himself up on one elbow, and slipped a hand around the back of her neck. She felt him arch up against her, lips brushing hers, but she drew back, not quite allowing the kiss. She wanted him, wanted him so much she felt hollow on the inside, as if desire had burned her clean through. No matter what her mind said—that this was not Jace, not *her Jace*, still her body remembered him, the shape and feel of him, the scent of his skin and hair, and wanted him *back*.

She smiled against his mouth as if she were teasing him, and rolled to the side, curling next to him in the wet bottom of the boat. He didn't protest. His arm curved around her, and the rocking of the boat beneath them was gentle and lulling. She wanted to put her head on his shoulder, but didn't.

"We're drifting," she said.

"I know. There's something I want you to see." Jace was looking up at the sky. The moon was a great white billow, like a sail; Jace's chest rose and fell steadily. His fingers tangled in her hair. She lay still beside him, waiting and watching as the stars ticked by like an astrological clock, and she wondered what they were waiting for. At last she heard it, a long slow rushing noise, like water pouring through a broken dam. The sky darkened and churned as figures rushed across it. She could barely make them out through the clouds and the distance, but they seemed to be men, with long hair like cirrus clouds, riding horses whose hooves gleamed the color of blood. The sound of a hunting horn echoed across the night, and the stars shivered and the night folded in on itself as the men vanished behind the moon.

She let her breath out in a slow exhalation. "What was that?"

"The Wild Hunt," said Jace. His voice sounded distant and dreamlike. "Gabriel's Hounds. The Wild Host. They have many names. They are faeries who disdain the earthly Courts. They ride across the sky, pursuing an eternal hunt. On one night a year a mortal can join them—but once you've joined the Hunt, you can never leave it."

"Why would anyone want to do that?"

Jace rolled and was suddenly on top of Clary, pressing her down into the bottom of the boat. She hardly noticed the damp; she could feel heat rolling off him in waves, and his eyes burned. He had a way of propping himself over her so that she wasn't crushed but she could feel every part of him against her—the shape of his hips, the rivets in his jeans, the tracings of his scars. "There's something appealing about the idea," he said. "Of losing all your control. Don't you think?"

She opened her mouth to answer, but he was already kissing her. She had kissed him so many times—soft gentle kisses, hard and desperate ones, brief brushes of the lips that said good-bye, and kisses that seemed to go on for hours—and this was no different. The way the memory of someone who had once lived in a house might linger even after they were gone, like a sort of psychic imprint, her body *remembered* Jace. Remembered the way he tasted, the slant of his mouth over hers, his scars under her fingers, the shape of his body under her hands. She let go of her doubts and reached up to pull him toward her.

He rolled sideways, holding her, the boat rocking underneath them. Clary could hear the splash of water as his hands drifted down her side to her waist, his fingers lightly stroking the sensitive skin at the small of her back. She slid her hands into his hair and closed her eyes, wrapped in mist, the sound and smell of water. Endless ages went by, and there was only Jace's mouth on hers, the lulling motion of the boat, his hands on her skin. Finally, after what could have been hours or minutes, she heard the sound of someone shouting, an angry Italian voice, rising and cutting through the night.

Jace drew back, his look lazy and regretful. "We'd better go."

Clary looked up at him, dazed. "Why?"

"Because that's the guy whose boat we stole." Jace sat up, tugging his shirt down. "And he's about to call the police."

11

Ascribe All Sin

Magnus said that no electricity could be used during the summoning of Azazel, so the loft apartment was lit only by candlelight. The candles burned in a circle in the center of the room, all different heights and brightness, though they shared a similar blue-white flame.

Inside the circle, a pentagram had been drawn by Magnus, using a rowan stick that had burned the pattern of overlapping triangles into the floor. In between the spaces formed by the pentagram were symbols unlike anything Simon had seen before: not quite letters and not quite runes, they gave off a chilly sense of menace despite the heat of the candle flames.

It was dark outside the windows now, the sort of dark that came with the early sunsets of approaching winter. Isabelle,

Alec, Simon, and finally, Magnus—who was chanting aloud from *Forbidden Rites*—each stood at one cardinal point around the circle. Magnus's voice rose and fell, the Latin words like a prayer, but one that was inverted and sinister.

The flames rose higher and the symbols carved into the floor began to burn black. Chairman Meow, who had been watching from a corner of the room, hissed and fled into the shadows. The blue-white flames rose, and now Simon could hardly see Magnus through them. The room was getting hotter, the warlock chanting faster, his black hair curling in the humid heat, sweat gleaming on his cheekbones. *"Quod tumeraris: per Jehovam, Gehennam, et consecratam aquam quam nunc spargo, signumque crucis quod nunc facio, et per vota nostra, ipse nunc surgat nobis dicatus Azazel!"*

There was a burst of fire from the center of the pentagram, and a thick black wave of smoke rose, dissipating slowly through the room, making everyone but Simon cough and choke. It swirled like a whirlpool, coalescing slowly in the center of the pentagram into the figure of a man.

Simon blinked. He wasn't sure what he'd expected, but it wasn't this. A tall man with auburn hair, neither young nor old—an ageless face, inhuman and cold. Broad-shouldered, dressed in a well-cut black suit and shining black shoes. Around each wrist was a dark red groove, the marks of some sort of binding, rope or metal, that had cut into the skin over many years. In his eyes were leaping red flames.

He spoke. "Who summons Azazel?" His voice was like metal grinding on metal.

"I do." Magnus firmly shut the book he was holding. "Magnus Bane."

Azazel craned his head slowly toward Magnus. His head seemed to swivel unnaturally on his neck, like the head of a snake. "Warlock," he said. "I know who you are."

Magnus raised his eyebrows. "You do?"

"Summoner. Binder. Destroyer of the demon Marbas. Son of—"

"Now," said Magnus quickly. "There's no need to go into all of that."

"But there is." Azazel sounded reasonable, even amused. "If it is infernal assistance you require, why not summon your father?"

Alec was looking at Magnus with his mouth open. Simon felt for him. He didn't think any of them had ever assumed that Magnus even knew who his father was, beyond that he had been a demon who had tricked his mother into believing he was her husband. Alec clearly knew no more about it than the rest of them, which, Simon imagined, was probably something he wasn't too happy about.

"My father and I are not on the best of terms," said Magnus. "I would prefer not to involve him."

Azazel raised his hands. "As you say, *Master*. You hold me within the seal. What do you demand?"

Magnus said nothing, but it was clear from the expression on Azazel's face that the warlock was speaking to him silently, mind to mind. The flames leaped and danced in the demon's eyes, like eager children listening to a story. "Clever Lilith," the demon said at last. "To raise the boy from death, and secure his life by binding him to someone whom you cannot bear to kill. She was always better at manipulating human emotions than most of the rest of us. Perhaps because she was something close to human once."

"Is there a way?" Magnus sounded impatient. "To break the bond between them?"

Azazel shook his head. "Not without killing them both."

"Then, is there a way to harm Sebastian only, without hurting Jace?" It was Isabelle, eager; Magnus shot her a quelling look.

"Not with any weapon I might create, or have at my disposal," said Azazel. "I can craft only weapons whose alliance is demonic. A bolt of lightning from the hand of an angel, perhaps, might burn away what was evil in Valentine's son and either break their tie or cause it to become more benevolent in nature. If I might make a suggestion . . ."

"Oh," said Magnus, narrowing his cat's eyes, "please do."

"I can think of a simple solution that will separate the boys, keep yours alive, and neutralize the danger of the other one. And I will ask very little of you in return."

"You are *my* servant," Magnus said. "If you wish to leave this pentagram, you will do what I ask, and not demand favors in return."

Azazel hissed, and fire curled from his lips. "If I am not bound here, then I am bound there. It makes little difference to me."

"'For this is Hell, nor am I out of it,'" said Magnus, with the air of someone quoting an old saying.

Azazel showed a metallic smile. "You may not be proud like old Faustus, warlock, but you are impatient. I am sure my willingness to remain in this pentagram will outlast your desire to keep watch over me inside it."

"Oh, I don't know," Magnus said. "I've always been fairly bold where decorating is concerned, and having you here does add that little extra touch of something to the room."

"*Magnus*," Alec said, clearly not thrilled at the idea of an immortal demon taking up residence in his boyfriend's loft.

"Jealous, little Shadowhunter?" Azazel grinned at Alec. "Your warlock is not my type, and besides, I would hardly want to anger his—"

"Enough," Magnus said. "Tell us what the 'little' thing you want in return for your plan is."

Azazel templed his hands—hard workman's hands, the color of blood, topped with black nails. "One happy memory," he said. "From each of you. Something to amuse me while I am bound like Prometheus to his rock."

"A *memory*?" said Isabelle in astonishment. "You mean it would vanish out of our heads? We wouldn't be able to recall it anymore?"

Azazel squinted at her through the flames. "What are you, little one? A Nephilim? Yes, I would take your memory and it would become mine. You would no longer know that it had happened to you. Although, please do avoid giving me memories of demons you've slaughtered under the light of the moon. Not the sort of thing I enjoy. No, I want these memories to be . . . personal." He grinned, and his teeth gleamed like an iron portcullis.

"I'm old," Magnus said. "I have many memories. I would give one up, if needed. But I cannot speak for the rest of you. No one should be forced to give up something like this."

"I'll do it," Isabelle said immediately. "For Jace."

"I will too, of course," said Alec, and then it was Simon's turn. He thought suddenly of Jace, cutting his wrist and giving him his blood in the tiny room on Valentine's boat. Risking his own life for Simon's. It might have been for Clary's sake at its heart, but it was still a debt. "I'm in."

"Good," Magnus said. "All of you, try to think of happy memories. They must be genuinely happy. Something that gives you pleasure in the recollection." He shot a sour glance at the smug demon in the pentagram.

"I'm ready," Isabelle said. She was standing with her eyes closed, her back straight as if braced for pain. Magnus moved toward her and laid his fingers against her forehead, murmuring softly.

Alec watched Magnus with his sister, his mouth tight, then shut his eyes. Simon shut his own too, hastily, and tried to summon up a happy memory—something to do with Clary? But so many of his memories of her were tinged now with his worry over her well-being. Something from when they were very young? An image swam to the forefront of his mind—a hot summer day at Coney Island, him on his father's shoulders, Rebecca running behind them, trailing a handful of balloons. Looking up at the sky, trying to find shapes in the clouds, and the sound of his mother's laughter. *No,* he thought, *not that. I don't want to lose that—*

There was a cool touch on his forehead. He opened his eyes and saw Magnus lowering his hand. Simon blinked at him, his mind suddenly blank. "But I wasn't thinking of anything," he protested.

Magnus's cat eyes were sad. "Yes, you were."

Simon glanced around the room, feeling a little dizzy. The others looked the same, as if they were awakening from a strange dream; he caught Isabelle's eye, the dark flutter of her lashes, and wondered what she had thought about, what happiness she had given away.

A low rumble from the center of the pentagram drew his

gaze from Izzy. Azazel stood, as close to the edge of the pattern as he could, a slow growl of hunger coming from his throat. Magnus turned and looked at him, a look of disgust on his face. His hand was closed into a fist, and something seemed to be shining between his fingers as if he held a witchlight runestone. He turned and flung it, fast and sideways, into the center of the pentagram. Simon's vampire vision tracked it. It was a bead of light that expanded as it flew, expanded into a circle holding multiple images. Simon saw a piece of azure ocean, the corner of a satin dress that belled out as its wearer spun, a glimpse of Magnus's face, a boy with blue eyes—and then Azazel opened his arms and the circle of images vanished into his body, like a stray piece of trash sucked into the fuselage of a jet plane.

Azazel gasped. His eyes, which had been darting flickers of red flame, blazed like bonfires now, and his voice crackled when he spoke. "Ahhhh. Delicious."

Magnus spoke sharply. "Now for your side of the bargain."

The demon licked his lips. "The solution to your problem is this. You release me into the world, and I take Valentine's son and bring him living into Hell. He will not die, and therefore your Jace will live, but he will have left this world behind, and slowly their connection will burn away. You will have your friend back."

"And then what?" Magnus said slowly. "We release you into the world, and then you return and let yourself be bound again?"

Azazel laughed. "Of course not, foolish warlock. The price for the favor is my freedom."

"Freedom?" Alec spoke, sounding incredulous. "A Prince of

Hell, set free in the world? We already gave you our memories —"

"The memories were the price you paid to hear my plan," said Azazel. "My freedom is what you will pay to have my plan enacted."

"That is a cheat, and you know it," said Magnus. "You ask for the impossible."

"So do you," said Azazel. "By all rights your friend is lost to you forever. 'For if a man vow a vow unto the Lord, or swear an oath to bind his soul with a bond, he shall not break his word.' And by the terms of Lilith's spell, their souls are bound, and both agreed."

"Jace would never agree—," Alec began.

"He said the words," said Azazel. "Of his own will or under compunction, it does not matter. You are asking me to sever a bond only Heaven can sever. But Heaven will not help you; you know that as well as I. That is why men summon demons and not angels, is it not? This is the price you pay for my intervention. If you do not want to pay it, you must learn to accept what you've lost."

Magnus's face was pale and tight. "We will converse among ourselves and discuss whether your offer is acceptable. In the meantime *I banish you.*" He waved his hand, and Azazel vanished, leaving behind the smell of charred wood.

The four people in the room stared at one another incredulously. "What he is asking for," Alec said finally, "it isn't possible, is it?"

"Theoretically anything is possible," said Magnus, staring ahead as if into an abyss. "But to loose a Greater Demon on the world—not just a Greater Demon, a Prince of Hell, second only to Lucifer himself—the destruction he could wreak—"

"Isn't it possible," Isabelle said, "that Sebastian could wreak just as much destruction?"

"Like Magnus said," Simon put in bitterly, "anything's possible."

"There could be almost no greater crime in the eyes of the Clave," said Magnus. "Whoever loosed Azazel upon the world would be a wanted criminal."

"But if it were to destroy Sebastian . . ." Isabelle began.

"We don't have proof Sebastian's plotting anything," said Magnus. "For all we know, all he wants is to settle down in a nice country house in Idris."

"With Clary and Jace?" Alec said incredulously.

Magnus shrugged. "Who knows what he wants with them? Maybe he's just lonely."

"No way did he kidnap Jace off that roof because he's desperately in need of a bromance," said Isabelle. "He's *planning something*."

They all looked at Simon. "Clary's trying to find out what. She needs some time. And don't say 'We don't have time,'" he added. "She knows that."

Alec raked a hand through his dark hair. "Fine, but we just wasted a whole day. A day we didn't have. No more stupid ideas." His voice was uncharacteristically sharp.

"Alec," Magnus said. He put a hand on his boyfriend's shoulder; Alec was standing still, staring angrily at the floor. "Are you okay?"

Alec looked at him. "Who are you again?"

Magnus gave a little gasp; he looked—for the first time Simon could remember—actually unnerved. It lasted only a moment, but it was there. "*Alexander,*" he said.

"Too soon to joke about the happy memory thing, I take it," Alec said.

"You think?" Magnus's voice soared. Before he could say anything else, the door swung open and Maia and Jordan came in. Their cheeks were red from the cold, and—Simon saw with a small start—Maia was wearing Jordan's leather jacket.

"We just came from the station," she said excitedly. "Luke hasn't woken up yet, but it looks like he's going to be all right—" She broke off, looking around at the still-glimmering pentagram, the clouds of black smoke, and the scorched patches on the floor. "Okay, *what* have you guys been doing?"

With the help of a glamour and Jace's ability to swing himself one-armed up onto a curving old bridge, Clary and Jace escaped the Italian police without being arrested. Once they had stopped running, they collapsed against the side of a building, laughing, side by side, their hands interlinked. Clary felt a moment of pure sharp happiness and had to bury her head against Jace's shoulder, reminding herself, in a hard internal voice, that *this wasn't him*, before her laughter trailed off into silence.

Jace seemed to take her sudden quiet as a sign that she was tired. He held her hand lightly as they made their way back to the street they'd started out from, the narrow canal with bridges on both ends. In between them Clary recognized the blank, featureless townhouse they'd left. A shudder ran over her.

"Cold?" Jace pulled her toward him and kissed her; he was so much taller than she was that he either had to bend down or pick her up; in this case he did the latter, and she suppressed a gasp as he swung her up and *through* the wall of the house.

Setting her down, he kicked a door—which had appeared suddenly behind them—shut with a bang, and was about to shuck off his jacket when there was the sound of a stifled chuckle.

Clary pulled away from Jace as lights blazed up around them. Sebastian sat on the sofa, his feet up on the coffee table. His fair hair was tousled; his eyes were glossy black. He wasn't alone, either. There were two girls there, one on either side of him. One was fair, a little scantily dressed, in a glittering short skirt and spangled top. She had her hand splayed out across Sebastian's chest. The other was younger, softer-looking, with black hair cut short, a red velvet band around her head, and a lacy black dress.

Clary felt her nerves tighten. *Vampire*, she thought. She didn't know how she knew, but she did—whether it was the waxy white sheen of the dark-haired girl's skin or the bottomlessness of her eyes, or perhaps Clary was just learning to sense these things, the way Shadowhunters were supposed to. The girl knew she knew; Clary could tell. The girl grinned, showing her little pointed teeth, and then bent to run them over Sebastian's collarbone. His lids fluttered, fair eyelashes lowering over dark eyes. He looked up at Clary through them, ignoring Jace.

"Did you enjoy your little date?"

Clary wished she could say something rude, but instead she just nodded.

"Well, then, would you like to join us?" he said, indicating himself and the two girls. "For a drink?"

The dark-haired girl laughed and said something in Italian to Sebastian, her voice questioning.

"No," said Sebastian. *"Lei è mia sorella."*

The girl sat back, looking disappointed. Clary's mouth

was dry. Suddenly she felt Jace's hand against hers, his callused fingertips rough. "I don't think so," he said. "We're going upstairs. We'll see you in the morning."

Sebastian wiggled his fingers, and the Morgenstern ring on his hand caught the light, sparking like a signal fire. *"Ci vediamo."*

Jace led Clary out of the room and up the glass stairs; only when they were in the corridor did she feel like she had gotten her breath back. This different Jace was one thing. Sebastian was something else. The sense of menace that rose off him was like smoke off a fire. "What did he say?" she asked. "In Italian?"

"He said, 'No, she is my sister,'" said Jace. He did not say what the girl had asked Sebastian.

"Does he do this much?" she asked. They had stopped in front of Jace's room, on the threshold. "Bring girls back?"

Jace touched her face. "He does what he wants, and I don't ask," he said. "He could bring a six-foot tall pink rabbit in a bikini back home with him if he wanted to. It's not my business. But if you're asking *me* if I've brought any girls back here, the answer is no. I don't want anybody but you."

It hadn't been what she was asking, but she nodded anyway, as if reassured. "I don't want to go back downstairs."

"You can sleep in my room with me tonight." His gold eyes were luminous in the dark. "Or you can sleep in the master bedroom. You know I wouldn't ever ask you—"

"I want to be with you," she said, surprising herself with her own vehemence. Maybe it was just that the idea of sleeping in that bedroom, where Valentine had once slept, where he had hoped to live again with her mother, was too much. Or maybe it was that she was tired, and she had only ever spent one night in the same bed as Jace, and they had slept with only their hands touching, as if an unsheathed sword had lain between them.

"Give me a second to clean up the room. It's a mess."

"Yeah, when I was in there before, I think I might *actually have seen a fleck of dust on the windowsill.* You'd better get on that."

He tugged a lock of her hair, running it through his fingers. "Not to actively work against my own interests, but do you need something to sleep in? Pajamas, or . . ."

She thought of the wardrobe full of clothes in the master bedroom. She was going to have to get used to the idea. Might as well start now. "I'll get a nightgown."

Of course, she thought several moments later, standing over an open drawer, the sort of nightgowns men bought because they wanted the women in their lives to wear them were not *necessarily* the kind of thing you might buy for yourself. Clary usually slept in a tank top and pajama shorts, but everything here was silky or lacy or barely there, or all three. She settled finally on a pale green silk shift that hit her midthigh. She thought of the red nails of the girl downstairs, the one with her hand on Sebastian's chest. Her own nails were bitten, her toenails never decorated with much more than clear polish. She wondered what it would be like to be more like Isabelle, so aware of your own feminine power you could wield it as a weapon instead of gazing at it mystified, like someone presented with a housewarming gift they had no idea where to display.

She touched the gold ring on her finger for luck before heading into Jace's bedroom. He was sitting on the bed, shirtless in black pajama bottoms, reading a book in the small pool of yellow light from the bedside lamp. She stood for a moment, watching him. She could see the delicate play of muscles under his skin as he turned the pages—and could see Lilith's Mark, just over his heart. It didn't look like the black lacework of the rest of his Marks; it was silvery-red, like blood-tinged mercury. It seemed not to belong on him.

The door slipped closed behind her with a click, and Jace looked up. Clary saw his face change. She might not have been such a big fan of the nightgown, but he definitely was. The look on his face made a shiver run over her skin.

"Are you cold?" He threw the covers back; she crawled in with him as he tossed the book onto the nightstand, and they slid together under the blanket, until they were facing each other. They had lain in the boat for what had seemed like hours, kissing, but this was different. That had been out in public, under the gaze of the city and the stars. This was a sudden intimacy, just the two of them under the blanket, their breath and the heat of their bodies mingling. There was no one to watch them, no one to stop them, no *reason* to stop. When he reached out and laid his hand against her cheek, she thought the thunder of her own blood in her ears might deafen her.

Their eyes were so close together, she could see the pattern of gold and darker gold in his irises, like a mosaic opal. She had been cold for so long, and now she felt as if she were burning and melting at the same time, dissolving into him—and they were barely touching. She found her gaze drawn to the places he was most vulnerable—his temples, his eyes, the pulse at the base of his throat, wanting to kiss him there, to feel his heart-beat against her lips.

His scarred right hand moved down her cheek, across her shoulder and side, stroking her in a single long caress that ended at her hip. She could see why men liked silk nightclothes so much. There was no friction; it was like sliding your hands across glass. "Tell me what you want," he said in a whisper that couldn't quite disguise the hoarseness in his voice.

"I just want you to hold me," she said. "While I sleep. That's all I want right now."

His fingers, which had been stroking slow circles on her hip, stilled. "That's all?"

It wasn't what she wanted. What she wanted was to kiss him until she lost track of space and time and location, as she had in the boat—to kiss him until she forgot who she was and why she was here. She wanted to use him like a drug.

But that was a very bad idea.

He watched her, restless, and she remembered the first time she had seen him and how she had thought he seemed deadly as well as beautiful, like a lion. *This is a test,* she thought. And maybe a dangerous one. "That's all."

His chest rose and fell. Lilith's Mark seemed to pulse against the skin just over his heart. His hand tightened on her hip. She could hear her own breathing, as shallow as low tide.

He pulled her toward him, rolling her over until they lay tucked together like spoons, her back to him. She swallowed a gasp. His skin was hot against hers, as if he were slightly feverish. But his arms as they went around her were familiar. The two of them fit together, as always, her head under his chin, her spine against the hard muscles of his chest and stomach, her legs bent around his. "All right," he whispered, and the feel of his breath against the back of her neck raised goose bumps over her body. "So we'll sleep."

And that was all. Slowly her body relaxed, the thudding of her heart slowing. Jace's arms around her felt the way they always had. Comfortable. She closed her hands around his and shut her eyes, imagining their bed cut free of this strange prison, floating through space or on the surface of the ocean, just the two of them alone.

She slept like that, her head tucked under Jace's chin, her spine fitted to his body, their legs entwined. It was the best sleep she had had in weeks.

Simon sat on the edge of the bed in Magnus's spare room, staring down at the duffel bag in his lap.

He could hear voices from the living room. Magnus was explaining to Maia and Jordan what had happened that night, with Izzy occasionally interjecting a detail. Jordan was saying something about how they should order Chinese food so they wouldn't starve; Maia laughed and said as long as it wasn't from the Jade Wolf, that would be fine.

Starving, Simon thought. He was getting hungry—hungry enough to have begun to feel it, like a pull on all his veins. It was a different kind of hunger than human hunger. He felt scraped out, a hollow emptiness inside. If you struck him, he thought, he would ring like a bell.

"Simon." His door opened, and Isabelle slid inside. Her black hair was down and loose, almost reaching her waist. "Are you okay?"

"I'm fine."

She saw the duffel bag on his lap, and her shoulders tensed. "Are you leaving?"

"Well, I wasn't planning to stay forever," Simon said. "I mean, last night was—different. You asked . . ."

"Right," she said in an unnaturally bright voice. "Well, you can get a ride back with Jordan at least. Did you notice him and Maia, by the way?"

"Notice what about them?"

She lowered her voice. "Something *definitely* happened between them on their little road trip. They're all couply now."

"Well, that's good."

"Are you jealous?"

"Jealous?" he echoed, confused.

"Well, you and Maia . . ." She waved a hand, looking up at him through her lashes. "You were . . ."

"Oh. No. No, not at all. I'm glad for Jordan. This will make him really happy." He meant it too.

"Good." Isabelle looked up then, and he saw that her cheeks were rosy red, and not just from the cold. "Would you stay here tonight, Simon?"

"With you?"

She nodded, not looking at him. "Alec's going out to get some more of his clothes from the Institute. He asked if I wanted to go back with him, but I—I'd rather stay here with you." She raised her chin, looking at him directly. "I don't want to sleep by myself. If I stay here, will you stay with me?" He could tell how much she hated to ask.

"Of course," he said, as lightly as he possibly could, pushing the thought of his hunger out of his head, or trying to.

The last time he had tried to forget to drink, it had ended with Jordan pulling him off a semiconscious Maureen.

But that was when he hadn't eaten for days. This was different. He knew his limits. He was sure of it.

"Of course," he said again. "That would be great."

Camille smirked up at Alec from her divan. "So where does Magnus think you are now?"

Alec, who had put a plank of wood across two cinderblocks to form a sort of bench, stretched his long legs out and looked at his boots. "At the Institute, picking up clothes. I was going to go up to Spanish Harlem, but I came here instead."

Her eyes narrowed. "And why is that?"

"Because I can't do it. I can't kill Raphael."

Camille threw up her hands. "And why not? Have you some sort of personal bond with him?"

"I barely know him," Alec said. "But killing him is deliberately breaking Covenant Law. Not that I haven't broken Laws before, but there's a difference between breaking them for good reasons and breaking them for selfish ones."

"Oh, dear God." Camille began to pace. "Spare me from Nephilim with consciences."

"I'm sorry."

Her eyes narrowed. "Sorry? I'll *make* you—" She broke off. "Alexander," she went on in a more composed voice. "What of Magnus? If you continue as you have been, you will lose him."

Alec watched her as she moved, catlike and composed, her face blank of anything now but a curious sympathy. "Where was Magnus born?"

Camille laughed. "You don't even know that? My goodness.

Batavia, if you must know." She snorted at his look of incomprehension. "Indonesia. Of course, it was the Dutch East Indies then. His mother was a native, I believe; his father was some dull colonial. Well, not his *real* father." Her lips curved into a smile.

"Who was his real father?"

"Magnus's father? Why, a demon, of course."

"Yes, but *which* demon?"

"How could it possibly matter, Alexander?"

"I get the feeling," Alec went on stubbornly, "that he's a pretty powerful, high-up demon. But Magnus won't talk about him."

Camille collapsed back onto the divan with a sigh. "Well, of course he won't. One must preserve some mystery in one's relationship, Alec Lightwood. A book that one has not read yet is always more exciting than a book one has memorized."

"You mean I tell him too much?" Alec pounced on the morsel of advice. Somewhere here, inside this cold, beautiful shell of a woman, was someone who had shared a unique experience with him—of loving and being loved by Magnus. Surely she must know something, some secret, some key that would keep him from screwing everything up.

"Almost certainly. Although, you've been alive for such a short time that I can't imagine how much there could be to say. Certainly you must be out of anecdotes."

"Well, it seems clear to me that your policy of not telling him anything didn't work out either."

"I was not so invested in keeping him as you are."

"Well," Alec asked, knowing it was a bad idea but not being able to help it, "if you *had been* interested in keeping him, what would you have done differently?"

Camille sighed dramatically. "The thing that you are too young to understand is that we all hide things. We hide them from our lovers because we wish to present our best selves, but also because if it is real love, we expect our loved one to simply understand it, without needing to ask. In a true partnership, the kind that lasts through the ages, there is an unspoken communion."

"B-but," Alec stammered, "I would have thought he would have wanted me to open up. I mean, I have a hard time being open even with people I've known my whole life—like Isabelle, or Jace . . ."

Camille snorted. "That's another thing," she said. "You no longer need other people in your life once you have found your true love. No wonder Magnus feels he cannot open up to you, when you rely so heavily upon these other people. When love is true, you should meet each other's every desire, every need— Are you listening, young Alexander? For my advice is precious, and not given often . . ."

The room was filled with translucent dawn light. Clary sat up, watching Jace as he slept. He was on his side, his hair a pale brass color in the bluish air. His cheek was pillowed on his hand, like a child's. The star-shaped scar on his shoulder was revealed, and so were the patterns of old runes up and down his arms, back, and sides.

She wondered if other people would find the scars as beautiful as she did, or if she only saw them that way because she loved him and they were part of him. Each one told the story of a moment. Some had even saved his life.

He murmured in his sleep and turned over onto his back. His hand, the Voyance rune clear and black on the back of it, was splayed across his stomach, and above it was the one rune that Clary did not find beautiful: Lilith's rune, the one that bound him to Sebastian.

It seemed to pulse, like Isabelle's ruby necklace, like a second heart.

Silent as a cat, she moved up the bed and onto her knees. She reached up and pulled the Herondale dagger from the wall. The photograph of her and Jace together fluttered free, spinning in the air before landing face-down on the floor.

She swallowed and looked back at him. Even now, he was so alive, he seemed to glow from inside, as if lit by inner fire. The scar on his chest pulsed its steady beat.

She lifted the knife.

Clary came awake with a start, her heart slamming against her rib cage. The room swung around her like a carousel: it was still dark, and Jace's arm was around her, his breath warm on the back of her neck. She could feel his heartbeat against her spine. She closed her eyes, swallowing against the bitter taste in her mouth.

It was a dream. Just a dream.

But there was no way she was getting back to sleep now. She sat up carefully, gently moving Jace's arm away, and climbed off the bed.

The floor was icy cold, and she winced as her bare feet touched it. She found the knob of the bedroom door in the half-light, and swung it open. And froze.

Though there were no windows in the hallway outside, it was lit by pendant chandeliers. Puddles of something that looked sticky and dark marred the floor. Along one white-painted wall was the clear mark of a bloody handprint. Blood spattered the wall at intervals leading to the stairs, where there was a single long, dark smear.

Clary looked toward Sebastian's room. It was quiet, the door shut, no light showing beneath it. She thought of the blond girl in the spangled top, looking up at him. She looked at the bloody handprint again. It was like a message, a hand thrust out, saying *Stop*.

And then Sebastian's door opened.

He stepped out. He was wearing a thermal shirt over black jeans, and his silver-white hair was rumpled. He was yawning; he did a double take when he saw her, and a look of genuine surprise passed over his face. "What are you doing up?"

Clary sucked in a breath. The air tasted metallic. "What am I doing? What are *you* doing?"

"Going downstairs to get some towels to clean up this mess," he said matter-of-factly. "Vampires and their games . . ."

"This doesn't look like the outcome of a *game*," Clary said. "The girl—the human girl who was with you—what happened to her?"

"She got a little frightened at the sight of fangs. Sometimes they do." At the look on her face, he laughed. "She came around. Even wanted more. She's asleep in my bed now, if you want to check and make sure she's alive."

"No . . . That's not necessary." Clary dropped her eyes. She wished she'd worn something besides this silk nightgown to bed. She felt undressed. "What about you?"

"Are you asking if I'm all right?" She hadn't been, but Sebastian looked pleased. He pulled the collar of his shirt aside, and she could see two neat puncture wounds just at his collarbone. "I could use an *iratze*."

Clary said nothing.

"Come downstairs," he said, and gestured for her to follow him as he padded past her, barefoot, and down the glass staircase. After a moment she did as he'd asked. He flicked on the lights as he went, so by the time they reached the kitchen, it was glowing with warm light. "Wine?" he said to her, pulling the refrigerator door open.

She settled herself on one of the counter stools, smoothing down her nightgown. "Just water."

She watched him as he poured two glasses of mineral water—one for her, one for him. His smooth economical movements were like Jocelyn's, but the control with which he moved must have been instilled in him by Valentine. It reminded her of the way Jace moved, like a carefully trained dancer.

He pushed her water toward her with one hand, the other tipping his glass toward his lips. When he was done, he slammed the glass back down on the counter. "You probably know this, but fooling around with vampires certainly makes you thirsty."

"Why would I know that?" Her question came out sharper than intended.

He shrugged. "Figured you were playing some biting games with that Daylighter."

"Simon and I never played *biting games*," she said in a frozen tone. "In fact, I can't figure out why anyone would want vampires feeding on them on purpose. Don't you hate and despise Downworlders?"

"No," he said. "Don't mix me up with Valentine."

"Yeah," she muttered. "Tough mistake to make."

"It's not my fault I look exactly like him and you look like *her*." His mouth curled into an expression of distaste at the thought of Jocelyn. Clary scowled at him. "See, there you go. You're always looking at me like that."

"Like what?"

"Like I burn down animal shelters for fun and light my cigarettes with orphans." He poured another glass of water. As he turned his head from her, she saw that the puncture wounds at his throat were already beginning to heal over.

"You killed a child," she said sharply, knowing as she said it that she should be keeping her mouth shut, going along with the pretense that she didn't think Sebastian was a monster. But *Max*. He was alive in her head, talking to her about Naruto, or asleep on a sofa at the Institute with a book on his lap and his glasses askew on his small face. "That's not something you can be forgiven for, ever."

Sebastian drew in a breath. "So that's it," he said. "Cards on the table so soon, little sister?"

"What did you think?" Her voice sounded thin and tired to her own ears, but he flinched as if she'd snapped at him.

"Would you believe me if I told you it was an accident?" he said, setting his glass down on the counter. "I didn't mean to kill him. Just to knock him out, so he wouldn't tell—"

Clary silenced him with a look. She knew she couldn't hide the hatred in her eyes: knew she should, knew it was impossible.

"I mean it. I meant to knock him out, like I did Isabelle. I misjudged my own strength."

"And Sebastian Verlac? The real one? You killed him, didn't you?"

Sebastian looked at his own hands as if they were strange to him: there was a silver chain holding a flat metal plate, like an ID bracelet, around his right wrist—hiding the scar where

Isabelle had sliced his hand away. "He wasn't supposed to fight back—"

Disgusted, Clary started to slide off the stool, but Sebastian caught at her wrist, pulling her toward him. His skin was hot against hers and she remembered, in Idris, the time his touch had burned her. "Jonathan Morgenstern killed Max. But what if I'm not the same person? Haven't you noticed I won't even use the same name?"

"Let me go."

"You believe Jace is different," Sebastian said quietly. "You believe he isn't the same person, that my blood changed him. Don't you?"

She nodded without speaking.

"Then, why is it so hard to believe it might go the other way? Maybe his blood changed me. Maybe I'm not the same person I was."

"You stabbed Luke," she said. "Someone I care about. Someone I love—"

"He was about to blow me to pieces with a shotgun," said Sebastian. "You love him; I don't know him. I was saving my life, and Jace's. Do you really not understand that?"

"And maybe you're just saying whatever you think you need to say to get me to trust you."

"Would the person I used to be care if you trusted me?"

"If you wanted something."

"Maybe I just want a sister."

At that, her eyes flicked up to his—involuntary, disbelieving. "You don't know what a family is," she said. "Or what you'd do with a sister if you had one."

"I do have one." His voice was low. There were bloodstains

at the collar of his shirt, just where it touched his skin. "I'm giving you a chance. To see that what Jace and I are doing is the right thing. Can you give me a chance?"

She thought of the Sebastian she had known in Idris. She had heard him sound amused, friendly, detached, ironic, intense, and angry. She had never heard him sound pleading.

"Jace trusts you," he said. "But I don't. He believes you love him enough to throw over everything you've ever valued or believed in to come and be with him. No matter what."

Her jaw tightened. "And how do you know I wouldn't?"

He laughed. "Because you're *my* sister."

"We're nothing alike," she spat, and saw the slow smile on his face. She bit back the rest of her words, but it was already too late.

"That's what I would have said," he said. "But come on, Clary. You're here. You can't go back. You've thrown your lot in with Jace. You might as well do it wholeheartedly. Be a part of what's happening. Then you can make up your own mind about . . . me."

Not looking at him but down at the marble floor, she nodded, very slightly.

He reached up and brushed away the hair that had fallen into her eyes, and the kitchen lights sparked off the bracelet he wore, the one she had noticed before, with letters etched into it. *Acheronta movebo.* Boldly she put her hand on his wrist. "What does this mean?"

He looked at her hand where it touched the silver on his wrist. "It means 'Thus always to tyrants.' I wear it to remind me of the Clave. It's said this was shouted by the Romans who murdered Caesar before he could become a dictator."

"Traitors," said Clary, dropping her hand.

Sebastian's dark eyes flashed. "Or fighters for freedom. History gets written by the winners, little sis."

"And you intend to write this portion?"

He grinned at her, his dark eyes alight. "You bet I do."

12

The Stuff of Heaven

When Alec returned to Magnus's apartment, all the lights were off, but the living room was glowing with a blue-white flame. It took him several moments to realize it was coming from the pentagram.

He kicked his shoes off by the door and padded as quietly as he could into the master bedroom. The room was dark, a strand of multicolored Christmas lights wrapped around the window frame the only illumination. Magnus was asleep on his back, the covers pulled up to his waist, his hand flat against his belly-button-free stomach.

Alec quickly stripped down to his boxers and climbed into bed, hoping not to wake Magnus. Unfortunately, he hadn't counted on Chairman Meow, who had tucked himself under the covers. Alec's elbow came down squarely on the cat's tail, and the Chairman yowled and darted off the bed, causing Magnus to sit up, blinking.

"What's going on?"

"Nothing," Alec said, silently cursing all cats. "I couldn't sleep."

"So you went out?" Magnus rolled onto his side and touched Alec's bare shoulder. "Your skin's cold, and you smell like nighttime."

"I was walking around," Alec said, glad it was too dim in the room for Magnus to really see his face. He knew he was a terrible liar.

"Around where?"

One must preserve some mystery in one's relationship, Alec Lightwood.

"Places," Alec said airily. "You know. Mysterious places."

"Mysterious places?"

Alec nodded.

Magnus flopped back against the pillows. "I see you went to Crazytown," he muttered, closing his eyes. "Did you bring me anything back?"

Alec leaned over and kissed Magnus on the mouth. "Just that," he said softly, drawing back, but Magnus, who had started to smile, already had hold of his arms.

"Well, if you're going to wake me up," he said, "you might as well make it worth my time," and he pulled Alec down on top of him.

Considering they'd already spent one night in bed together, Simon hadn't expected his second night with Isabelle to be quite so awkward. But then again, this time Isabelle was sober, and awake, and obviously expecting something from him. The problem was, he wasn't sure exactly what.

He had given her a button-down shirt of his to wear, and he looked away politely while she climbed under the blanket and edged back against the wall, giving him plenty of space.

He didn't bother changing, just took off his shoes and socks and crawled in next to her in his T-shirt and jeans. They lay side by side for a moment, and then Isabelle rolled against him, draping an arm awkwardly across his side. Their knees bumped together. One of Isabelle's toenails scratched his ankle. He tried to move forward, and their foreheads knocked.

"Ouch!" Isabelle said indignantly. "Shouldn't you be better at this?"

Simon was bewildered. "Why?"

"All those nights you've spent in Clary's bed, wrapped in your beautiful platonic embraces," she said, pressing her face against his shoulder so her voice was muffled. "I figured . . ."

"We just *slept*," said Simon. He didn't want to say anything about how Clary fit perfectly against him, about how being in a bed with her was as natural as breathing, about the way the scent of her hair reminded him of childhood and sunshine and simplicity and grace. That, he had a feeling, would not be helpful.

"I know. But I don't just *sleep*," Isabelle said irritably. "With anybody. I don't stay the night usually at all. Like, ever."

"You said you wanted to—"

"Oh, shut up," she said, and kissed him. This was marginally more successful. He'd kissed Isabelle before. He loved the texture of her soft lips, the way his hands felt in her long, dark hair. But as she pressed herself against him, he also felt the warmth of her body, her long bare legs against him, the pulse of her blood—and the snap of his fang teeth as they came out.

He pulled back hastily.

"*Now* what is it? You don't want to kiss me?"

"I do," he tried to say, but his fangs were in the way. Isabelle's eyes widened.

"Oh, you're hungry," she said. "When was the last time you had any blood?"

"Yesterday," he managed to say, with some difficulty.

She lay back against his pillow. Her eyes were impossibly big and black and lustrous. "Maybe you should feed yourself," she said. "You know what happens if you don't."

"I don't have any blood with me. I'll have to go back to the apartment," Simon said. His fangs had already begun to retract.

Isabelle caught him by the arm. "You don't have to drink cold animal blood. I'm right here."

The shock of her words was like a pulse of energy zipping through his body, setting his nerves on fire. "You're not serious."

"Sure I am." She started to unbutton the shirt she was wearing, baring her throat, her collarbone, the tracery of faint veins visible beneath her pale skin. The shirt fell open. Her blue bra covered a lot more than many bikinis might, but Simon still felt his mouth go dry. Her ruby flashed like a red stoplight below her collarbone. *Isabelle.* As if reading his mind, she reached up and drew her hair back, draping it over one shoulder, leaving the side of her throat naked. "Don't you want . . . ?"

He caught her wrist. "Isabelle, don't," he said urgently. "I can't control myself, can't control it. I could hurt you, kill you."

Her eyes shone. "You won't. You can hold yourself back. You did with Jace."

"I'm not *attracted* to Jace."

"Not even a little?" she said hopefully. "Eensy bit? Because that would be kind of hot. Ah, well. Too bad. Look, attracted or not, you bit him when you were starving and dying, and you still held back."

"I didn't hold back with Maureen. Jordan had to pull me off."

"You would have." She took her finger and pressed it to his lips, then ran it down his throat, across his chest, coming to a stop where his heart had once beat. "I trust you."

"Maybe you shouldn't."

"I'm a Shadowhunter. I can fight you off if I have to."

"Jace didn't fight me off."

"Jace is in love with the idea of dying," said Isabelle. "I'm *not*." She slung her legs around his hips—she was amazingly flexible—and slid forward until she could brush her lips against his. He wanted to kiss her, wanted it so badly his whole body ached. He opened his mouth tentatively, touched his tongue to hers, and felt a sharp pain. His tongue had slid along the razor edge of his fang. He tasted his own blood and drew back abruptly, turning his face away from her.

"Isabelle, I *can't*." He closed his eyes. She was warm and soft in his lap, teasing, torturous. His fangs ached painfully; his whole body felt like sharp wires were twisting through his veins. *"I don't want you to see me like this."*

"Simon." Gently she touched his cheek, turning his face toward her. "This is who you are—"

His fangs had retracted, slowly, but they still ached. He hid his face in his hands and spoke between his fingers. "You can't possibly want this. You can't possibly want *me*. My own mother threw me out of the house. I bit Maureen—she was only a kid. I mean, look at me, look what I am, where I live, what I do. I'm *nothing*."

Isabelle stroked his hair lightly. He looked at her between his fingers. Up close he could see that her eyes weren't black but a very dark brown, flecked with gold. He was sure he could see pity in them. He didn't know what he expected her to say. Isabelle used boys and threw them away. Isabelle was beautiful and tough and perfect and didn't need anything. Least of all a vampire who wasn't even very good at being a vampire.

He could feel her breathing. She smelled sweet—blood, mortality, gardenias. "You're not nothing," she said. "Simon. Please. Let me see your face."

Reluctantly he lowered his hands. He could see her more clearly now. She looked soft and lovely in the moonlight, her skin pale and creamy, her hair like a black waterfall. She unlooped her hands from around his neck. "Look at these," she said, touching the white scars of healed Marks that snowflaked her silvery skin—on her throat, on her arms, on the curves of her breasts. "Ugly, aren't they?"

"Nothing about you is ugly, Izzy," said Simon, honestly shocked.

"Girls aren't supposed to be covered in scars," Isabelle said matter-of-factly. "But they don't bother you."

"They're part of you— No, of course they don't bother me."

She touched his lips with her fingers. "Being a vampire is part of *you*. I didn't ask you to come here last night because I couldn't think of anyone else to ask. I want to be with you, Simon. It scares the hell out of me, but I do."

Her eyes shimmered, and before he could wonder for more than a moment whether it was with tears, he had leaned forward and kissed her. This time it wasn't awkward. This time she leaned into him, and he was suddenly under her, rolling her on top of him. Her long black hair fell down around them both like a curtain. She whispered to him softly as he ran his hands up her back. He could feel her scars under his fingertips, and he wanted to tell her he thought of them as ornaments, testaments to her bravery that only made her more beautiful. But that would have meant stopping kissing her, and he didn't want to do that. She was moaning and moving in his arms; her fingers were in his hair as the two of them rolled sideways, and now she was under him, and his arms were full of the softness and warmth of her, and his mouth with the taste of her, and the scent of her skin, salt and perfume and . . . blood.

He stiffened again, all over, and Isabelle felt it. She caught hold of his shoulders. She was luminous in the darkness. "Go ahead," she whispered. He could feel her heart, slamming against his chest. "I want you to."

He closed his eyes, pressed his forehead to hers, tried to calm himself. His fangs were back, pushing into his lower lip, hard and painful. "No."

Her long, perfect legs wrapped around him, her ankles locking, holding him to her. "I want you to." Her breasts flattened against his chest as she arched up against him, baring her throat. The scent of her blood was everywhere, all over him, filling the room.

"Aren't you scared?" he whispered.

"Yes. But I still want you to."

"Isabelle—I can't—"

He bit her.

His teeth slid, razor-sharp, into the vein at her throat like a knife slicing into the skin of an apple. Blood exploded into his mouth. It was like nothing he had experienced before. With Jace he had been barely alive; with Maureen the guilt had crushed him even as he had drunk from her. He had certainly never had the sense that either of the people he had bitten had *liked* it.

But Isabelle gasped, her eyes flying open and her body arcing up against him. She purred like a cat, stroking his hair, his back, little urgent movement of her hands saying *Don't stop, Don't stop*. Heat poured out of her, into him, lighting his body; he had never felt, imagined, anything else like it. He could feel the strong, sure beat of her heat, pounding through her veins into his, and for that moment it was as if he lived again, and his heart contracted with pure elation—

He broke away. He wasn't sure how, but he broke away and rolled onto his back, his fingers digging hard into the mattress at his sides. He was still shuddering as his fangs retracted. The room shimmered all around him, the way things did in the few moments after he drank human, living blood.

"Izzy . . . ," he whispered. He was afraid to look at her, afraid that now that his teeth were no longer in her throat, she would stare at him with revulsion or horror.

"What?"

"You didn't stop me," he said. It was half accusation, half hope.

"I didn't want to." He looked at her. She was on her back, her chest rising and falling fast, as if she'd been running. There were two neat puncture wounds in the side of her throat, and two thin lines of blood that ran down her neck to her collarbone. Obeying an instinct that seemed to run deep under the skin, Simon leaned forward and licked the blood from her throat, tasting salt, tasting Isabelle. She shuddered, her fingers fluttering in his hair. "Simon . . ."

He drew back. She was looking at him with her big dark eyes, very serious, her cheeks flushed. "I . . ."

"What?" For a wild moment he thought she was going to say 'I love you,' but instead she shook her head, yawned, and hooked her finger through one of the belt loops on his jeans. Her fingers played with the bare skin at his waist.

Somewhere Simon had heard that yawning was a sign of blood loss. He panicked. "Are you okay? Did I drink too much? Do you feel tired? Are—"

She scooted closer to him. "I am *fine*. You made yourself stop. And I'm a Shadowhunter. We replace blood at triple the rate a normal human being does."

"Did you . . ." He could barely bring himself to ask. "Did you like it?"

"Yeah." Her voice was husky. "I liked it."

"Really?"

She giggled. "You couldn't tell?"

"I thought maybe you were faking it."

She raised herself up on one elbow and looked down at him with her glowing dark eyes—how could eyes be dark and bright at the same time? "I don't fake things, Simon," she said. "And I don't lie, and I don't pretend."

"You're a heartbreaker, Isabelle Lightwood," he said, as lightly as he could with her blood still running through him like fire. "Jace told Clary once you'd walk all over me in high-heeled boots."

"That was then. You're different now." She eyed him. "You're not scared of me."

He touched her face. "And you're not scared of anything."

"I don't know." Her hair fell forward. "Maybe you'll break *my* heart." Before he could say anything, she kissed him, and he wondered if she could taste her own blood. "Now shut up. I want to sleep," she said, and she curled up against his side and closed her eyes.

Somehow, now, they fit, where they hadn't before. Nothing was awkward, or poking into him, or banging against his leg. It didn't feel like childhood and sunlight and gentleness. It felt strange and heated and exciting and powerful and . . . different. Simon lay awake, his eyes on the ceiling, his hand stroking Isabelle's silky black hair absently. He felt like he'd been caught up in a tornado and deposited somewhere very far away, where nothing was familiar. Eventually he turned his head and kissed Izzy, very lightly, on the forehead; she stirred and murmured but didn't open her eyes.

When Clary woke in the morning, Jace was still asleep, curled on his side, his arm outstretched just enough to touch her shoulder. She kissed his cheek and got to her feet. She was about to pad into the bathroom to take a shower when she was overcome by curiosity. She went quietly to the bedroom door and peered out.

The blood on the hallway wall was gone, the plaster unmarked. It was so clean she wondered if the whole thing had been a dream—the blood, the conversation in the kitchen with Sebastian, all of it. She took a step across the corridor, placed her hand against the wall where the bloody handprint had been—

"Good morning."

She whirled. It was her brother. He had come out of his room soundlessly and was standing in the middle of the hall, regarding her with a crooked smile. He looked freshly showered; damp, his fair hair was the color of silver, almost metallic.

"You planning to wear that all the time?" he asked, eyeing her nightgown.

"No, I was just . . ." She didn't want to say she'd been checking to see if there was still blood in the hall. He just looked at her, amused and superior. Clary backed away. "I'm going to get dressed."

He said something after her, but she didn't pause to hear what it was, just darted into the master bedroom and closed the door behind her. A moment later she heard voices in the hallway—Sebastian's again, and a girl's, speaking musical Italian. The girl from last night, she thought. The one he'd said was asleep in his room. It was only then that she realized how much she'd suspected he was lying.

But he'd been telling the truth. *I'm giving you a chance,* he'd said. *Can you give me a chance?*

Could she? This was Sebastian they were talking about. She mulled it over feverishly while she showered and dressed carefully. The clothes in the wardrobe, having been selected for Jocelyn, were so far from her usual style that it was hard to choose what to wear. She found a pair of jeans—designer, from the price tag still attached—and a dotted silk shirt with a bow at the neck that had a vintage feel she liked. She threw her own velvet jacket on over it and headed back to Jace's room, but he was gone, and it wasn't hard to guess where. The rattle of dishes, the sound of laughter, and the smell of cooking floated up from downstairs.

She took the glass stairs two at a time, but paused on the bottom step, looking into the kitchen. Sebastian was leaning against the refrigerator, arms crossed, and Jace was making something in a pan that involved onions and eggs. He was barefoot, his hair messy, his shirt buttoned haphazardly, and the sight of him made her heart turn over. She had never seen him like this, first thing in the morning, still with that warm golden aura of sleep clinging to him, and she felt a piercing sadness that all these firsts were happening with a Jace who wasn't really *her* Jace.

Even if he did look happy, eyes shadow-free, laughing as he flipped the eggs in the pan and slid an omelet onto a plate. Sebastian said something to him, and Jace looked over at Clary and smiled. "Scrambled or fried?"

"Scrambled. I didn't know you could make eggs." She came down from the steps and over to the kitchen counter. Sun was streaming through the windows—despite the lack of clocks in the house, she guessed it was late morning—and the kitchen glittered in glass and chrome.

"Who can't make eggs?" Jace wondered aloud.

Clary raised her hand—and at the same time so did Sebastian. She couldn't help a little jerk of surprise, and put her arm down hastily, but not before Sebastian had seen and grinned. He was always grinning. She wished she could slap it off his face.

She looked away from him and busied herself putting together a breakfast plate from what was on the table—bread, fresh butter, jam, and sliced bacon—the chewy, round kind. There was juice, too, and tea. They ate pretty well here, she thought. Although, if Simon was anything to go by, teenage boys were always hungry. She glanced toward the window—

and did a double take. The view was no longer of a canal but of a hill rising in the distance, topped by a castle.

"Where are we now?" she asked.

"Prague," said Sebastian. "Jace and I have an errand to do here." He glanced out the window. "We should probably get going soon, in fact."

She smiled sweetly at him. "Can I come with you?"

Sebastian shook his head. "No."

"Why not?" Clary crossed her arms over her chest. "Is this some manly bonding thing I can't be a part of? Are you getting matching haircuts?"

Jace handed her a plate with scrambled eggs on it, but he was looking at Sebastian. "Maybe she could come," he said. "I mean, this particular errand—it's not dangerous."

Sebastian's eyes were like the woods in the Frost poem, dark and deep. They gave nothing away. "Anything can turn dangerous."

"Well, it's your decision." Jace shrugged, reached for a strawberry, popped it into his mouth, and sucked the juice off his fingers. Now that, Clary thought, was a clear and absolute difference between this Jace and hers. Her Jace had a ferocious and all-consuming curiosity about everything. He would never shrug and go along with someone else's plan. He was like the ocean ceaselessly throwing itself against a rocky shore, and this Jace was . . . a calm river, shining in the sun.

Because he's happy?

Clary's hand tensed on her fork, her knuckles whitening. She hated that little voice in her head. Like the Seelie Queen, it planted doubts where there shouldn't be doubts, asked questions that had no answer.

"I'm going to get my stuff." After grabbing another berry off the plate, Jace popped it into his mouth and shot upstairs. Clary craned her head up. The clear glass steps seemed invisible, making it look like he was flying upward, not running.

"You're not eating your eggs." It was Sebastian. He had come around the counter—still noiselessly, dammit—and was looking at her, his eyebrows raised. He had the faintest accent, a mixture of the accent of the people who lived in Idris and something more British. She wondered if he'd been hiding it before or if she just hadn't noticed.

"I don't actually like eggs," she confessed.

"But you didn't want to tell Jace that, because he seemed so pleased to be making you breakfast."

Since this was accurate, Clary said nothing.

"Funny, isn't it?" said Sebastian. "The lies good people tell. He'll probably make you eggs every day for the rest of your life now, and you'll choke them down because you can't tell him you don't like them."

Clary thought of the Seelie Queen. "Love makes liars of us all?"

"Exactly. Quick study, aren't you?" He took a step toward her, and an anxious tingle seared her nerves. He was wearing the same cologne Jace wore. She recognized the citrusy black-pepper scent, but on him it smelled different. Wrong, somehow."We have that in common," Sebastian said, and began to unbutton his shirt.

She stood up hastily. "What are you doing?"

"Easy there, little sis." He popped the last button, and his shirt hung open. He smiled lazily. "You're the magical rune girl, aren't you?"

Clary nodded slowly.

"I want a strength rune," he said. "And if you're the best, I want it from you. You wouldn't deny your big brother a rune, would you?" His dark eyes raked her. "Besides, you want me to give you a chance."

"And you want me to give *you* a chance," she said. "So I'll make you a deal. I'll give you a strength rune if you let me come with you on your errand."

He stripped the shirt the rest of the way off and dropped it onto the counter. "Deal."

"I don't have a stele." She didn't want to look at him, but it was hard not to. He seemed to be deliberately invading her personal space. His body was much like Jace's—hard, without any extra ounce of flesh anywhere, the muscles showing clearly under the skin. He was scarred like Jace too, though he was so pale that the white marks stood out less than they did against Jace's golden skin. On her brother they were like silver pen on white paper.

He drew a stele from his belt and handed it to her. "Use mine."

"All right," she said. "Turn around."

He did. And she swallowed back a gasp. His bare back was striped with ragged scars, one after the other, too even to be random accident.

Whip marks.

"Who did this to you?" she said.

"Who do you think? Our father," he said. "He used a whip made of demon metal, so no *iratze* could heal them. They're meant to remind me."

"Remind you of what?"

"Of the perils of obedience."

She touched one. It felt hot under her fingertips, as if newly made, and rough, where the skin around it was smooth. "Don't you mean 'disobedience'?"

"I mean what I said."

"Do they hurt?"

"All the time." Impatiently he glanced back over his shoulder. "What are you waiting for?"

"Nothing." She set the tip of the stele to his shoulder blade, trying to keep her hand steady. Part of her mind raced, thinking how easy it would be to Mark him with something that would damage him, sicken him, twist his insides—but what would happen to Jace if she did? Shaking her hair out of her face, she carefully drew the *Fortis* rune at the juncture of shoulder blade and back, just where, if he were an angel, he would have wings.

When she was done, he turned and took the stele from her, then shrugged his shirt back on. She didn't expect a thank-you—and didn't get one. He rolled his shoulders back as he buttoned the shirt, and grinned. "You *are* good," he said, but that was all.

A moment later the steps rattled, and Jace returned, shrugging on a suede jacket. He had clipped on his weapons belt too, and wore fingerless dark gloves.

Clary smiled at him with a warmth she didn't feel. "Sebastian says I can come with you."

Jace raised his eyebrows. "Matching haircuts for everyone?"

"I hope not," said Sebastian. "I look terrible with curls."

Clary glanced down at herself. "Do I need to change into gear?"

"Not really. This isn't the sort of errand where we're expecting to have to fight. But it's good to be prepared. I'll get you something from the weapons room," said Sebastian, and vanished upstairs. Clary cursed herself silently for not having found the weapons room while she was searching. Surely it had something inside that could provide some sort of clue as to what they were planning—

Jace touched the side of her face, and she jumped. She'd nearly forgotten he was there. "You sure you want to do this?"

"Absolutely. I'm going stir-crazy in the house. Besides, you taught me to fight. I figure you'd want me to use it."

His lips quirked into a devilish grin; he brushed her hair back and murmured something into her ear about using what she'd learned from him. He leaned away as Sebastian joined them, his own jacket on and a weapons belt in his hand. There was a dagger thrust through it, and a seraph blade. He reached out to draw Clary close to him and pulled the belt around her waist, double-looping it and settling it low on her hips. She was too surprised to push him away and he was done before she had the chance; turning away, he moved toward the wall, where the outline of a doorway had appeared, shimmering like a doorway in a dream.

They stepped through it.

A soft knock on the library door made Maryse raise her head. It was a cloudy day, dim outside the library windows, and the green-shaded lamps cast small pools of light in the circular room. She couldn't say how long she'd been sitting behind the desk. Empty coffee mugs littered the surface in front of her.

She rose to her feet. "Come in."

There was a soft click as the door opened, but no sound of

footsteps. A moment later a parchment-robed figure glided into the room, his hood raised, shadowing his face. *You called on us, Maryse Lightwood?*

Maryse rolled her shoulders back. She felt cramped and tired and old. "Brother Zachariah. I was expecting— Well. It doesn't matter."

Brother Enoch? He is senior to me, but I thought perhaps that your call might have something to do with the disappearance of your adoptive son. I have a particular interest in his well-being.

She looked at him curiously. Most Silent Brothers didn't editorialize, or speak of their personal feelings, if they had any. Smoothing her tangled hair back, she stepped out from behind the desk. "Very well. I want to show you something."

She had never really gotten used to the Silent Brothers, to the soundless way they moved, as if their feet didn't touch the ground. Zachariah seemed to hover beside her as she led him across the library to a map of the world tacked to the north wall. It was a Shadowhunter map. It showed Idris in the center of Europe and the ward around it as a border of gold.

On a shelf below the map were two objects. One was a shard of glass crusted with dried blood. The other was a worn leather cuff bracelet, decorated with the rune for angelic power.

"These are—"

Jace Herondale's cuff and Jonathan Morgenstern's blood. I understood attempts to track them were unsuccessful?

"It isn't tracking precisely." Maryse straightened her shoulders. "When I was in the Circle, there was a mechanism Valentine used by which he could locate us all. Unless we were in certain protected places, he knew where we were at all times. I thought there was a chance he might have done the same to

Jace when he was a child. He never seemed to have trouble finding him."

What kind of mechanism do you speak of?

"A mark. Not one from the Gray Book. We all had it. I had nearly forgotten about it; after all, there was no way to get rid of it."

If Jace had it, would he not know of it, and take steps to prevent you using it to find him?

Maryse shook her head. "It could be as small as a tiny, almost invisible white mark under his hair, as mine is. He would not have known he had it—Valentine wouldn't have wanted to tell him."

Brother Zachariah moved apart from her, examining the map. *And what has been the result of your experiment?*

"Jace has it," Maryse said, but she did not sound pleased or triumphant. "I've seen him on the map. When he appears, the map flares, like a spark of light, in the location where he is; and his cuff flares at the same time. So I know it is him, and not Jonathan Morgenstern. Jonathan never appears on the map."

And where is he? Where is Jace?

"I've seen him appear, just for a few seconds each time, in London, Rome, and Shanghai. Just a little while ago he flickered into existence in Venice, and then vanished again."

How is he traveling so quickly between cities?

"By Portal?" She shrugged. "I don't know. I just know that every time the map flickers, I know he's alive . . . for now. And it's like I can breathe again, just for a little while." She shut her mouth decidedly, lest the other words come pouring out—how she missed Alec and Isabelle but could not bear to call them back to the Institute, where Alec at least would be expected to take responsibility in the manhunt for his own brother. How she still thought of Max every day and it was like someone had emptied her lungs of air, and she would catch at her heart, afraid she was dying. She could not lose Jace, too.

I can understand that. Brother Zachariah folded his hands in front of him. His hands looked young, not gnarled or bent, his fingers slender. Maryse often wondered how the Brothers aged and how long they lived, but that information was secret to their order. *There is little more powerful than the love of family. But what I do not know is why you chose to show this to me.*

Maryse took a shuddering breath. "I know I should show it to the Clave," she said. "But the Clave knows of his bond with Jonathan now. They are hunting them both. They will kill Jace if they find him. And yet to keep it to myself is surely treason." She hung her head. "I decided that telling you, the Brothers, was something I could bear. Then it is your choice whether to show it to the Clave. I—I can't stand that it be mine."

Zachariah was silent a long moment. Then his voice, gentle in her head, said, *Your map tells you that your son is still alive. If you give it to the Clave, I do not think it will help them much, besides telling them that he is traveling fast and is impossible to track. They know that already. You keep the map. I will not speak of it for now.*

Maryse looked at him in astonishment. "But . . . you are a servant of the Clave . . ."

I was once a Shadowhunter like you. I lived like you do. And like you, there were those I loved enough to put their welfare before anything else—any oath, any debt.

"Did you . . ." Maryse hesitated. "Did you ever have children?"

No. No children.

"I'm sorry."

Do not be. And try not to let fear for Jace devour you. He is a Herondale, and they are survivors—

Something snapped inside Maryse. "He is not a Herondale. He is a Lightwood. Jace *Lightwood*. He's my son."

There was a long pause. Then, *I did not mean to imply otherwise*, said Brother Zachariah. He unclasped his thin hands and stepped back. *There is one thing you must be aware of. If Jace appears on the map for more than a few seconds at a time, you* will *have to tell the Clave. You should brace yourself for the possibility.*

"I don't think I can," she said. "They'll send hunters after him. Set a trap for him. He's just a boy."

He was never just *a boy*, said Zachariah, and he turned to glide from the room. Maryse did not watch him go. She had returned to staring at the map.

Simon?

Relief opened like a flower in his chest. Clary's voice, tentative but familiar, filled his head. He looked sideways. Isabelle was still sleeping. Midday light was visible around the edges of the curtains.

Are you awake?

He rolled onto his back, stared up at the ceiling. *Of course I'm awake.*

Well, I wasn't sure. You're what, six, seven hours behind where I am. It's twilight here.

Italy?

We're in Prague now. It's pretty. There's a big river and a lot of buildings with spires. Looks a little like Idris from a distance. It's cold here, though. Colder than at home.

Okay, enough with the weather report. Are you safe? Where are Sebastian and Jace?

They're with me. I wandered off a little, though. I said I wanted to commune with the view from the bridge.

So I'm the view from the bridge?

She laughed, or at least he felt something that was like laughter in his head—a soft, nervous laughter. *I can't take too long. Though, they don't really seem to suspect anything. Jace . . . Jace definitely doesn't. Sebastian is harder to read. I don't think he trusts me. I searched his room yesterday, but there's nothing—I mean, nothing—to indicate what they're planning. Last night . . .*

Last night?

Nothing. It was odd, how she could be inside his head and he could still sense that she was hiding something. *Sebastian has in his room the box my mom used to own. With his baby stuff in it. I can't figure out why.*

Don't waste your time trying to figure out Sebastian, Simon told her. *He's not worth it. Figure out what they're going to do.*

I'm trying. She sounded irritable. *Are you still at Magnus's?*

Yeah. We've moved to phase two of our plan.

Oh, yeah? What was phase one?

Phase one was sitting around the table, ordering pizza, and arguing.

What's phase two? Sitting around the table drinking coffee and arguing?

Not exactly. Simon took a deep breath. *We raised the demon Azazel.*

Azazel? Her mental voice spiked upward; Simon almost clutched at his ears. *So that's what the stupid Smurf question was about. Tell me you're kidding.*

I'm not. It's a long story. He filled her in as best he could, watching Isabelle breathe as he did, watching the light outside the window grow brighter. *We thought he could help us find a weapon that can hurt Sebastian without hurting Jace.*

Yeah, but—demon-raising? Clary didn't sound convinced. *And Azazel is no ordinary demon. I'm the one with Team Evil over here. You're Team Good. Keep it in mind.*

You know nothing's that *simple, Clary.*

It was as if he could feel her sigh, a breath of air that passed over his skin, raising the hairs on the back of his neck. *I know.*

Cities and rivers, Clary thought as she took her fingers from the gold ring on her right hand and turned away from the view off Charles Bridge, back to Jace and Sebastian. They were on the other side of the old stone bridge, pointing off at something she couldn't see. The water below was the color of metal, sliding soundlessly around the bridge's ancient struts; the sky was the same color, pocked with black clouds.

The wind whipped at her hair and coat as she walked over to join Sebastian and Jace. They all set off again, the two boys conversing softly; she could have joined the conversation if she'd wanted to, she supposed, but there was something about the still loveliness of the city, its spires rising into mist in the distance, that made her want to be quiet, to look and to think on her own.

The bridge emptied out into a twisting cobblestone street lined with tourist shops, shops selling blood-red garnets and big chunks of golden Polish amber, heavy Bohemian glass, and wooden toys. Even at this hour, touts stood outside nightclubs, holding free passes or cards that would give you discounts on drinks; Sebastian gestured them aside impatiently, snapping his annoyance in Czech. The press of people was relieved when the street widened into an old medieval square. Despite the cold weather, it was filled with milling pedestrians and kiosks were selling sausages and hot, spiced cider. The three of them stopped for food and ate around a tall rickety table while the huge astronomical clock in the square's center began to chime the hour. Clanking machinery started up, and a circle of dancing wooden figures appeared from doors on either side of the clock—the twelve apostles, Sebastian explained as the figures whirled around and around.

"There's a legend," he said, leaning forward with his hands cupped around a mug of hot cider, "that the king had the eyes of the clock maker put out after this clock was finished, so he could never build anything as beautiful again."

Clary shuddered and moved a little closer to Jace. He had been quiet since they'd left the bridge, as if lost in thought. People—girls, mainly—stopped to look at him as they passed, his hair bright and startling among the winter-dark colors of the Old Square. "That's sadistic," she said.

Sebastian ran his finger around the rim of his mug, and licked the cider off. "The past is another country."

"Foreign country," said Jace.

Sebastian looked at him with lazy eyes. "What?"

"'The past is a foreign country: they do things differently there,'" Jace said. "That's the whole quote."

Sebastian shrugged and pushed his mug away. You got a euro for returning them to the stand where you bought the cider, but Clary suspected Sebastian couldn't be bothered to fake good citizenship for a measly euro. "Let's go."

Clary wasn't finished with her cider, but she set it down anyway and followed as Sebastian led them away from the square, among a maze of narrow, twisting streets. Jace had corrected Sebastian, she thought. Certainly it had been over something minor, but wasn't Lilith's blood magic supposed to bind him to her brother in such a way that he thought everything Sebastian did was right? Could this be a sign—even a tiny sign—that the spell that connected them was starting to fade?

It was stupid to hope, she knew. But sometimes hope was all you had.

The streets grew narrower, darker. The clouds overhead had completely blocked out the lowering sun, and old-fashioned gas lamps burned here and there, illuminating the misty dimness. The streets had turned to cobblestones, and the sidewalks were narrowing, forcing them to walk in a line, as if they were picking their way across a narrow bridge. Only the sight of other pedestrians, appearing and disappearing out of the fog, made Clary feel that she had not stepped through some sort of warp in time into a dream city out of her own imagination.

Finally they reached an archway of stone that opened out into a small square. Most of the stores had turned off their lights, though across from them one was lit up. It said ANTIKVARIAT in gold letters, and the window was full of old display bottles of different substances, their peeling labels marked in Latin. Clary was surprised when Sebastian headed toward it. What use could they possibly have for old bottles?

She dismissed the thought when they stepped over the threshold. The store inside was dimly lit and smelled of mothballs, but it was stuffed, every cranny, with an incredible selection of junk—and not-junk. Beautiful celestial maps warred for space with salt and pepper shakers shaped like the figures from the clock in the Old Town Square. There were heaps of old tobacco and cigar tins, stamps mounted in glass, old cameras of East German and Russian design, a gorgeous cut-glass bowl in a deep emerald shade sitting side by side with a stack of water-stained old calendars. An antique Czech flag hung from a mounting pole overhead.

Sebastian moved forward through the stacks toward a counter in the back of the store, and Clary realized that what she had taken for a mannequin was in fact an old man with a face as creased and wrinkled as an old bedsheet, leaning back against the counter with his arms crossed. The counter itself was glass-fronted and held heaps of vintage jewelry and sparkling glass beads, small chain purses with gem clasps, and rows of cuff links.

Sebastian said something in Czech, and the man nodded and indicated Clary and Jace with a jerk of his chin and a suspicious look. His eyes were, Clary saw, a dark red color. She narrowed her own eyes, concentrating hard, and began to strip the glamour from him.

It wasn't easy; it seemed to stick to him like flypaper. In the end she managed to pull it away only enough to see in flashes the real creature standing in front of her—tall and human-shaped, with gray skin and ruby-red eyes, a mouth full of pointed teeth that jutted every which way, and long, serpentine arms that ended in heads like an eel's—narrow, evil-looking, and toothy.

"A Vetis demon," Jace muttered in her ear. "They're like dragons. They like to stockpile sparkly things. Junk, jewels, it's all the same to them."

Sebastian was looking back over his shoulder at Jace and Clary. "They're my brother and sister," he said after a moment. "They are entirely to be trusted, Mirek."

A faint shudder ran under Clary's skin. She didn't like the idea of posing as Jace's sister, even for a demon's benefit.

"I don't like this," the Vetis demon said. "You said we would be dealing only with you, Morgenstern. And while I know Valentine had a daughter"—his head dipped toward Clary—"I also know he had only one son."

"He's adopted," said Sebastian breezily, gesturing toward Jace.

"Adopted?"

"I think you'll find the definition of the modern family is really changing at an impressive pace these days," said Jace.

The demon—Mirek—didn't *look* impressed. "I don't like this," he said again.

"But you'll like *this*," said Sebastian, taking a pouch, tied at the top, from his pocket. He turned it upside down above the counter, and a clattering pile of bronze coins fell out, clinking together as they rolled across the glass. "Pennies from dead men's eyes. A hundred of them. Now, do you have what we agreed on?"

One toothed hand felt its way across the counter and bit gently at a coin. The demon's red eyes flickered over the pile. "That is all very well, but it is not enough to buy what you seek." He gestured with an undulating arm, and above it appeared what looked to Clary like a hunk of rock crystal—only it was more luminous, more sheer, silvery, and beautiful. She realized with a jolt that it was the stuff seraph blades were made from. "Pure *adamas*," Mirek said. "The stuff of Heaven. Priceless."

Anger crackled across Sebastian's face like lightning, and for a moment Clary saw the vicious boy underneath, the one who had laughed while Hodge lay dying. Then the look was gone. "But we agreed on a price."

"We also agreed you would come alone," said Mirek. His red eyes returned to Clary, and to Jace, who hadn't moved but whose aspect had taken on the controlled stillness of a crouching cat's. "I'll tell you what else you can give me," he said. "A lock of your sister's pretty hair."

"Fine," Clary said, stepping forward. "You want a snip of my hair—"

"No!" Jace moved to block her. "He's a dark magician, Clary. You have no idea what he could do with a lock of your hair or a bit of blood."

"Mirek," Sebastian said slowly, not looking at Clary. And in that moment she wondered, If Sebastian wanted to trade a lock of her hair for the *adamas*, what was to stop him? Jace had objected, but he was also compelled to do what Sebastian asked of him. In the crunch, what would win out? The compulsion or Jace's feelings for her? "Absolutely not."

The demon blinked a slow lizardlike blink. "Absolutely not?"

"You will not touch a hair on my sister's head," said Sebastian. "Nor will you renege on our bargain. No one cheats Valentine Morgenstern's son. The agreed upon price, or—"

"Or what?" Mirek snarled. "Or I'll be sorry? You are not Valentine, little boy. Now, that was a man who inspired loyalty—"

"No," said Sebastian, sliding a seraph blade from the belt at his waist. "I am not Valentine. I do not intend to deal with demons as Valentine did. If I cannot have your loyalty, I will have your fear. Know that I am more powerful than my father ever was, and if you do not deal fairly with me, I will take your life, and have what I have come for." He raised the blade he held. *"Dumah,"* he whispered, and the blade shot forth, shimmering like a column of fire.

The demon recoiled, snapping several words in a muddy-sounding language. Jace's hand already had a dagger in it. He called out to Clary, but not fast enough. Something struck her hard on the shoulder, and she fell forward, sprawling on the cluttered floor. She flipped over onto her back, fast, looked up—

And screamed. Looming over her was a massive snake—or at least it had a thick, scaled body and a head hooded like a cobra's, but its body was jointed, insectile, with a dozen skittering legs that ended in jagged claws. Clary fumbled for her weapons belt as the creature reared back, yellow venom dripping from its fangs, and struck.

Simon had fallen back asleep after "speaking" with Clary. When he awoke again, the lights were on, and Isabelle knelt on the edge of the bed, wearing jeans and a worn T-shirt she must have borrowed from Alec. It had holes in the sleeves, and the stitching around the hem was coming undone. She had the collar pulled away from her throat and was using the tip of a stele to trace a rune onto the skin of her chest, just below her collarbone.

He raised himself up on his elbows. "What are you doing?"

"Iratze," she said. "For this." She tucked her hair back behind her ear, and he saw the two puncture wounds he'd made in the side of her throat. As she finished the rune, they smoothed over, leaving only the faintest white flecks behind.

"Are you . . . all right?" His voice came out in a whisper. Smooth. He was trying to bite back the other questions he wanted to ask. *Did I hurt you? Do you think I'm a monster now? Have I creeped you out completely?*

"I'm fine. I slept a lot later than I normally ever do, but I think that's probably a good thing." Seeing his expression, Isabelle slid her stele into her belt. She crawled toward Simon with a cat-like grace and positioned herself over him, her hair falling down around them. They were so close their noses touched. She looked at him unblinklingly. "Why are you so crazy?" she said, and he could feel her breath against his face, as soft as a whisper.

He wanted to pull her down and kiss her—not bite her, just kiss her—but at that exact moment the apartment door buzzer sounded. A second later, someone knocked on the bedroom door—banged on it, really, making it shake on its hinges.

"Simon. Isabelle." It was Magnus. "Look, I don't care if you're asleep or doing unspeakable things to each other. Get dressed and come out to the living room. Now."

Simon locked gazes with Isabelle, who looked as puzzled as he did. "What's going on?"

"Just get out here," Magnus said, and the sound of his retreating feet was loud as he stalked away from their room.

Isabelle rolled off Simon, much to his disappointment, and sighed. "What do you think it is?"

"No idea," said Simon. "Emergency meeting of Team Good, I guess." He'd found the phrase amusing when Clary had used it. Isabelle, though, just shook her head and sighed.

"I'm not sure there is any such thing as Team Good these days," she said.

13
The Bone Chandelier

As the serpent's head drove down toward Clary, a shining blur slashed across it, almost blinding her. A seraph blade, its shimmering knife edge slicing the demon's head cleanly off. The head crumpled, spraying venom and ichor; Clary rolled to one side, but some of the toxic substance splattered onto her torso. The demon vanished before its two halves could strike the floor. Clary bit down on her cry of pain and moved to get to her feet. A hand was suddenly thrust into her field of vision—an offer to pull her to her feet. *Jace,* she thought, but as she looked up, she realized she was staring at her brother.

"Come on," said Sebastian, his hand still out. "There are more of them."

She grabbed his hand and let him lift her to her feet. He

was splattered with demon blood too—blackish-green stuff that burned where it touched, leaving scorched patches on his clothing. As she stared at him, one of the snake-headed things—Elapid demons, she realized belatedly, remembering an illustration in a book—reared up behind him, its neck flattening out like a cobra's. Without thinking, Clary grabbed his shoulder and shoved him out of the way, hard; he staggered back as the demon struck, and Clary rose to meet it with the dagger she had yanked from her belt. She turned her body aside as she drove the dagger home, avoiding the creature's fangs; its hiss turned to a gurgle as the blade sank in and she dragged it down, gutting the creature open the way someone might gut a fish. Burning demon blood exploded over her hand in a hot torrent. She screamed but kept her grip on the dagger as the Elapid winked out of existence.

She whirled around. Sebastian was fighting another of the Elapids by the door of the shop; Jace was fending off two next to a display of antique ceramics. Shards of pottery littered the floor. Clary swung her arm back and threw the dagger, as Jace had taught her to. It soared through the air and struck one of the creatures in the side, sending it jittering and squeaking away from Jace. Jace whirled around and, seeing her, winked before reaching up to scissor off the head of the remaining Elapid demon. Its body collapsed as it vanished and Jace, splattered in black blood, grinned.

A surge of something went through Clary—a sense of buzzing elation. Both Jace and Isabelle had spoken to her of the high of battle, but she'd never really experienced it before. Now she did. She felt all-powerful, her veins humming, strength uncoiling from the base of her spine. Everything seemed to have slowed down around her. She watched as the injured Elapid demon spun and turned on her, racing toward her on its insectile feet, lips already curling back from its fangs. She stepped back, yanked the antique flag from its mounting place on the wall, and slammed the end of it into the Elapid's open, gaping mouth. The pole punched out through the back of the creature's skull, and the Elapid disappeared, taking the flag with it.

Clary laughed out loud. Sebastian, who had just finished off another demon, swung around at the noise, and his eyes widened. "Clary! Stop him!" he shouted, and she spun around to see Mirek, his hands fumbling at a door set into the back of the shop.

She broke into a run, yanking the seraph blade from her belt as she went. "*Nakir!*" she cried, vaulting up onto the counter, and she flung herself from the top of it as her weapon exploded into brightness. She landed on the Vetis demon, knocking him to the ground. One of his eel-like arms snapped at her, and she sliced it off with a sawing motion of her blade. More black blood sprayed. The demon looked at her with red, frightened eyes.

"Stop," he wheezed. "I could give you whatever you want—"

"I *have* everything I want," she whispered, and drove her seraph blade down. It plunged into the demon's chest, and Mirek disappeared with a hollow cry. Clary thumped to her knees on the carpet.

A moment later two heads appeared over the side of the counter, staring down at her—one golden-blond and one silver-blond. Jace and Sebastian. Jace was wide-eyed; Sebastian looked pale. "Name of the Angel, Clary," he breathed. "The *adamas*—"

"Oh, that stuff you wanted? It's right here." It had rolled

partly under the counter. Clary held it up now, a luminous chunk of silver, smeared where her bloody hands had touched it.

Sebastian swore with relief and grabbed the *adamas* out of her hands as Jace vaulted over the counter in a single movement and landed beside Clary. He knelt down and pulled her close, running his hands over her, his eyes dark with concern. She caught at his wrists.

"I'm all right," she said. Her heart was pounding, her blood still singing in her veins. He opened his mouth to say something, but she leaned forward and put her hands on either side of his face, her nails digging in. "I feel *good*." She looked at him, rumpled and sweaty and bloody as he was, and wanted to kiss him. She wanted—

"All right, you two," said Sebastian. Clary pulled away from Jace and glanced up at her brother. He was grinning down at them, lazily spinning the *adamas* in one hand. "Tomorrow we use this," he said, nodding toward it. "But tonight—once we're cleaned up a little—we celebrate."

Simon padded barefoot out into the living room, Isabelle behind him, to find a surprising tableau. The circle and the pentagram in the center of the floor were shining with a bright silver light, like mercury. Smoke rose from the center of it, a tall black-red column, tipped with white. The whole room smelled of burning. Magnus and Alec stood outside the circle, and with them Jordan and Maia, who—given the coats and hats they were wearing—looked as if they had just arrived.

"What's going on?" Isabelle asked, stretching her long limbs with a yawn. "Why is everyone watching the Pentagram Channel?"

"Just hang on a second," Alec said grimly. "You'll see."

Isabelle shrugged and added her gaze to the others'. As everyone watched, the white smoke began to swirl, fast and then faster, a mini-tornado that tore across the center of the pentagram, leaving words behind it spelled out in scorch marks:

HAVE YOU MADE YOUR DECISION YET?

"Huh," Simon said. "Has it been doing that all morning?"

Magnus threw his arms up. He was wearing leather pants and a shirt with a zigzag metallic lightning bolt on it. "All night, too."

"Just asking the same question over and over?"

"No, it says different things. Sometimes it swears. Azazel appears to be having some fun."

"Can it hear us?" Jordan cocked his head to the side. "Hey, there, demon guy."

The fiery letters rearranged themselves. HELLO, WEREWOLF.

Jordan took a step back and looked at Magnus. "Is this . . . normal?"

Magnus seemed deeply unhappy. "It is most decidedly not normal. I have never called up a demon as powerful as Azazel, but even so—I've been through the literature, and I can't find an example of this happening before. It's getting out of control."

"Azazel must be sent back," Alec said. "Like, permanently sent back." He shook his head. "Maybe Jocelyn was right. No good can come from summoning demons."

"I'm pretty sure I came from someone summoning a demon," Magnus noted. "Alec, I've done this hundreds of times. I don't know why this time would be different."

"Azazel can't get out, can he?" said Isabelle. "Of the pentagram, I mean."

"No," said Magnus, "but he shouldn't be able to be doing any of the other things he's doing either."

Jordan leaned forward, his hands on his blue-jeaned knees. "What's it like being in Hell, dude?" he asked. "Hot or cold? I've heard both."

There was no reply.

"Good job, Jordan," said Maia. "I think you annoyed him."

Jordan poked at the edge of the pentagram. "Can it tell the future? So, pentagram, is our band going to make it big?"

"It's a demon from Hell, not a Magic Eight Ball, Jordan," said Magnus irritably. "And stay away from the borders of the pentagram. Summon a demon and trap it in a pentagram, and it can't get out to harm you. But step into the pentagram, and you've put yourself in the demon's range of power—"

At that moment the pillar of smoke began to coalesce. Magnus's head whipped up, and Alec stood, almost knocking over his chair, as the smoke took on the form of Azazel. His suit formed first—a gray and silver pinstripe, with elegant cuffs—and then he seemed to fill it out, his flame eyes the last thing to appear. He looked around him in evident pleasure. "The gang's all here, I see," he said. "So, have you come to a decision?"

"We have," said Magnus. "I don't believe we'll be requiring your services. Thanks anyway."

There was a silence.

"You can go now." Magnus wiggled his fingers in a goodbye wave. "Ta."

"I don't think so," Azazel said pleasantly, whipping out his handkerchief and buffing his nails with it. "I think I'll stay. I like it here."

Magnus sighed and said something to Alec, who went to the table and returned carrying a book, which he handed to the warlock. Magnus flipped it open and began to read. "*Damned spirit, begone. Return thou to the realm of smoke and flame, of ash and—*"

"That won't work on me," said the demon in a bored voice. "Go ahead and try, if you like. I'll still be here."

Magnus looked at him with eyes smoldering with rage. "You can't force us to bargain with you."

"I can try. It's hardly as if I have anything better to occupy—"

Azazel broke off as a familiar shape streaked through the room. It was Chairman Meow, hot on the heels of what looked like a mouse. As everyone watched in surprise and horror, the small cat dashed through the outline of the pentagram—and Simon, acting on instinct rather than rational thought, jumped into the pentagram after him and scooped him up into his arms.

"Simon!" He knew without turning around that it was Isabelle, her cry reflexive. He turned to look at her as she clapped her hand over her mouth and looked at him with wide eyes. They were all staring. Izzy's face was drained white with horror, and even Magnus looked unsettled.

Summon a demon and trap it in a pentagram, and it can't get out to harm you. But step into the pentagram, and you've put yourself in the demon's range of power.

Simon felt a tap on his shoulder. He dropped Chairman Meow as he turned, and the small cat streaked out of the pentagram and across the room to hide under a sofa. Simon looked up. The massive face of Azazel loomed over him. This close, he could see the cracks in the demon's skin, like cracks in marble, and the flames deep in Azazel's pitted eyes. When Azazel smiled, Simon saw that each of his teeth was tipped with a needle of iron.

Azazel exhaled. A cloud of hot sulfur spread around Simon. He was dimly aware of Magnus's voice, rising and falling in a chant, and Isabelle screaming something as the demon's hands clamped around his arms. Azazel lifted Simon off the ground so his feet were dangling in the air—and threw him.

Or tried to. His hands slipped off Simon; Simon dropped to the ground in a crouch as Azazel shot backward and seemed to hit an invisible barrier. There was a sound like stone shattering. Azazel slid to his knees, then painfully rose to his feet. He looked up with a roar, teeth flashing, and stalked toward Simon—who, realizing belatedly what was going on, reached up with a shaking hand and pushed the hair back from his forehead.

Azazel stopped in his tracks. His hands, the nails tipped with the same sharp iron as his teeth, curled in toward his sides. "Wanderer," he breathed. "Is it you?"

Simon stayed frozen. Magnus was still chanting softly in the background, but everyone else was silent. Simon was afraid to look around, to catch the eye of any of his friends. Clary and Jace, he thought, had already seen the work of the Mark, its blazing fire. No one else had. No wonder they were wordless.

"No," Azazel said, his fiery eyes narrowing. "No, you are too young, and the world too old. But who would dare place Heaven's mark on a vampire? And why?"

Simon lowered his hand. "Touch me again and find out," he said.

Azazel gave a rumbling sound—half laughter, half disgust. "I think not," he said. "If you have been dabbling in bending the will of Heaven, even my freedom is not worth gambling for by allying my fate with yours." He glanced around the room. "You are all madmen. Good luck, human children. You will need it."

And he vanished in a burst of flame, leaving searing black smoke—and the stink of sulfur—behind.

"Hold still," Jace said, taking the Herondale dagger in his hand and using the tip of it to slice Clary's shirt open from the collar to the hem. He took the two halves of it and pushed them gingerly off her shoulders, leaving her sitting on the edge of the sink in just her jeans and a camisole. Most of the ichor and venom had gotten on her jeans and coat, but the fragile silk shirt was trashed. Jace dropped it into the sink, where it sizzled in the water, and applied his stele to her shoulder, tracing the outlines of the healing rune lightly.

She closed her eyes, feeling the burn of the rune, and then a rush as the relief from pain spread up her arms and down her back. It was like Novocain, but without making her numb.

"Better?" Jace asked.

She opened her eyes. "Much." It wasn't perfect—the *iratze* didn't have much effect on burns caused by demon venom, but those tended to heal quickly on Shadowhunter skin. As it was, they stung only a little, and Clary, still feeling the high of the battle, barely noticed it. "Your turn?"

He grinned and offered her the stele. They were in the back of the antiques store. Sebastian had gone to lock up and dim the lights up front, lest they attract mundane attention. He was excited about "celebrating" and when he had left them, had been debating whether to go back to the apartment and change, or straight to the nightclub in the Malá Strana.

If there was a part of Clary that felt the wrongness of it, the idea of celebrating anything, it was lost in the humming of her blood. Amazing that it had taken fighting alongside *Sebastian* of all people to flip the switch inside her that seemed to turn her Shadowhunter instincts on. She wanted to leap tall buildings in a single bound, do a hundred flips, learn to scissor her blades the way Jace did. Instead she took the stele from him and said, "Take your shirt off, then."

He pulled it over his head, and she tried to look unaffected. He had a long cut along his side, angry purple-red along the edges, and the burns of demon blood across his collarbone and right shoulder. Still, he was the most beautiful person she had ever known. Pale gold skin, broad shoulders, narrow waist and hips, that thin line of golden hair that ran from his navel to the waistband of his jeans. She pulled her eyes away from him and set the stele to his shoulder, industriously carving into his skin what had to be the millionth healing rune he'd ever gotten.

"Good?" she asked when she was finished.

"Mmm-hmm." He leaned in, and she could smell the scent of him—blood and charcoal, sweat, and the cheap soap they'd found by the sink. "I liked that," he said. "Didn't you? Fighting together like that?"

"It was . . . intense." He was standing between her legs already; he moved closer, fingers looping into the waistband of her jeans. Her hands fluttered to his shoulders, and she saw the gleam of the gold leaf-ring on her finger. It sobered her slightly. *Don't get distracted; don't get lost in this. This isn't Jace, isn't Jace, isn't Jace.*

His lips brushed hers. "I thought it was incredible. *You* were incredible."

"Jace," she whispered, and then there was a banging on the door. Jace let go of her in surprise, and she slid backward, knocking into the faucet, which immediately turned on, spraying them both with water. She yelped with surprise, and Jace burst out laughing, turning to throw the door open as Clary twisted around to turn the faucet off.

It was Sebastian, of course. He looked remarkably clean, considering what they'd been through. He'd discarded his stained leather jacket in favor of an antique military coat, which, thrown over his T-shirt, lent him a look of thrift-store chic. He was carrying something in his hands, something black and shiny.

He raised his eyebrows.

"Is there a reason you just threw my sister into the sink?'"

"I was sweeping her off her feet," said Jace, bending down to grab his shirt. He yanked it back on. Like Sebastian's, his outerwear had sustained most of the damage, though there was a rip down the side of the shirt where a demon's claw had slashed through.

"I brought you something to wear," said Sebastian, handing the shiny black thing to Clary, who had wriggled out of the sink and was now standing, dripping soapy water onto the tiled floor. "It's vintage. It looks about your size."

Startled, Clary handed Jace back his stele and took the proffered garment. It was a dress—a slip, really—jet-black, with elaborately beaded straps and a lace hem. The straps were adjustable, and the fabric was stretchy enough that she suspected Sebastian was right, it probably *would* fit her. Part of her didn't like the idea of wearing something Sebastian had picked, but she couldn't exactly go out to a club in an unraveling camisole and a pair of soaking-wet jeans. "Thanks," she said finally. "All right, both of you get out of here while I change."

They left, closing the door behind them. She could hear them, raised boys' voices, and though she couldn't hear the words, she could tell they were joking with each other. Comfortably. Familiarly. It was so strange, she thought as she shucked off her jeans and cami and slipped the dress over her head. Jace, who hardly ever opened up to anyone, was laughing and joking around with Sebastian.

She turned to look at herself in the mirror. The black washed the color out of her skin, made her eyes look big and dark and her hair redder, her arms and legs long and thin and pale. Her eyes were smudged with dark shadow. The boots she had been wearing under her jeans added a certain toughness to the outfit. She wasn't sure if she looked pretty exactly, but she sure looked like she was someone who shouldn't be messed with.

She wondered if Isabelle would approve.

She unlocked the bathroom door and stepped out. She was in the dim back of the store, where all the junk that wasn't housed up front had been tossed carelessly. A velvet curtain separated it from the rest of the establishment. Jace and Sebastian were on the other side of the curtain, talking, though she still couldn't make out the words. She pulled the curtain aside and stepped out.

The lights were on, though the metal awning had been lowered over the glass front of the store, rendering the inside invisible to passersby. Sebastian was going through the stuff on the shelves, his long careful hands taking down object after object, subjecting them to a cursory inspection, and placing them back on the shelf.

Jace was the first one to see Clary. She saw his eyes spark, and remembered the first time he had seen her dressed up, wearing Isabelle's clothes, on her way to Magnus's party. As they had then, his eyes traveled slowly from the boots, up her legs, hips, waist, chest, and came to rest on her face. He smiled lazily.

"I could point out that that's not a dress, that's underwear," he said, "but I doubt it would be in my best interest."

"Need I remind you," said Sebastian, "that *that is my sister*?"

"Most brothers would be delighted to see such a clean-cut gentleman as myself squiring their sisters about town," said Jace, grabbing an army jacket off one of the racks and sliding his arms into it.

"Squiring?" Clary echoed. "Next you'll be telling me you're a rogue and a rake."

"And then it's pistols at dawn," said Sebastian, striding toward the velvet curtain. "I'll be right back. I've got to wash the blood out of my hair."

"Fussy, fussy," Jace called after him with a grin, then reached for Clary and pulled her against him. His voice dropped to a low whisper. "Remember when we went to Magnus's party? You came out into the lobby with Isabelle, and Simon almost had an apoplectic fit?"

"Funny, I was thinking about the same thing." She tipped her head back to look up at him. "I don't remember you saying anything at the time about the way I looked."

His fingers slid under the straps of her slip dress, the tips brushing her skin. "I didn't think you liked me much. And I didn't think a detailed description of all the things I wanted to do to you, delivered in front of an audience, would have been the thing to change your mind."

"You didn't think I liked *you*?" Her voice rose incredulously. "Jace, when has a girl ever not liked you?"

He shrugged. "Doubtless the lunatic asylums of the world are filled with unfortunate women who have failed to see my charms."

A question hovered on the tip of her tongue, one she had always wanted to ask him but never had. After all, what did it really matter what he'd done before he met her? As if he could read the expression on her face, his golden eyes softened slightly.

"I never cared what girls thought about me," he said. "Not before you."

Before you. Clary's voice shook a little. "Jace, I wondered—"

"Your verbal foreplay is boring and annoying," said Sebastian, reappearing around the velvet curtain, his silver hair damp and tousled. "Ready to go?"

Clary stepped free of Jace, blushing; Jace looked unruffled. "We're the ones who've been waiting for you."

"Looks like you found a way to pass the agonizing time. Now come on. Let's go. I'm telling you, you're going to *love* this place."

"I am never getting my security deposit back," said Magnus glumly. He sat on top of the table, among the pizza boxes and coffee mugs, watching as the rest of Team Good did their best to clean up the destruction left by Azazel's appearance—the smoking holes pocked into the walls, the sulfurous black goo dripping from the ceiling pipes, the ash and other grainy black substances ground into the floor. Chairman Meow was stretched across the warlock's lap, purring. Magnus was off cleaning duty because he'd allowed his apartment to be half-destroyed; Simon was off cleaning duty because after the pentagram incident no one seemed to know quite what to make of him. He'd tried to talk to Isabelle, but she'd only shaken her mop at him in a threatening manner.

"I have an idea," Simon said. He was sitting next to Magnus, his elbows on his knees. "But you're not going to like it."

"I have a feeling you're right, Sherwin."

"Simon. My name is Simon."

"Whatever." Magnus waved a slender hand. "What's your idea?"

"I've got the Mark of Cain," said Simon. "That means nothing can kill me, right?"

"You can kill yourself," Magnus said, somewhat unhelpfully. "As far as I know, inanimate objects can accidentally kill you. So if you were planning on teaching yourself the lambada on a greased platform over a pit full of knives, I wouldn't."

"There goes my Saturday."

"But nothing else can kill you," Magnus said. His eyes had drifted away from Simon, and he was watching Alec, who appeared to be battling a Swiffer. "Why?"

"What happened in the pentagram, with Azazel, made me think," said Simon. "You said summoning angels is more dangerous than summoning demons, because they might smite down the person who summoned them, or scorch them with heavenly fire. But if *I* did it . . ." His voice trailed off. "Well, I'd be safe, wouldn't I?"

That snapped Magnus's attention back. "You? Summon an angel?"

"You could show me how," said Simon. "I know I'm not a warlock, but Valentine did it. If he did it, shouldn't I be able to? I mean, there are humans who can do magic."

"I couldn't promise you'd live," Magnus said, but there was a spark of interest in his voice that belied the warning. "The Mark is Heaven's protection, but does it protect you against Heaven itself? I don't know the answer."

"I didn't think you did. But you agree that out of all of us I probably have the best chance, right?"

Magnus looked over at Maia, who was splashing dirty water at Jordan and laughing as he twisted away, yelping. She pushed her curling hair back, leaving a dark streak of dirt across her forehead. She looked young. "Yes," Magnus said reluctantly. "Probably you do."

"Who is your father?" asked Simon.

Magnus's eyes went back to Alec. They were gold-green, as unreadable as the eyes of the cat he held on his lap. "Not my favorite topic, Smedley."

"Simon," said Simon. "If I'm going to die for you all, the least you could do is remember my name."

"You're not dying for me," said Magnus. "If it weren't for Alec, I'd be . . ."

"You'd be where?"

"I had a dream," Magnus said, his eyes distant. "I saw a city all of blood, with towers made of bone, and blood ran in the streets like water. Maybe you can save Jace, Daylighter, but you can't save the world. The darkness is coming. 'A land of darkness, as darkness itself; and of the shadow of death, without any order, and where the light is as darkness.' If it weren't for Alec, I'd be gone from here."

"Where would you go?"

"Hide. Wait for it to blow over. I'm not a hero." Magnus picked up Chairman Meow and dumped him onto the floor.

"You love Alec enough to stick around," said Simon. "That's kind of heroic."

"You loved Clary enough to wreck your whole life for her," said Magnus with a bitterness that was not characteristic of him. "See where that got you." He raised his voice. "All right, everybody. Get over here. Sheldon's had an idea."

"Who's Sheldon?" said Isabelle.

The streets of Prague were cold and dark, and though Clary kept her ichor-burned coat wrapped around her shoulders, she found the icy air cutting into the buzzing hum in her veins, muting the leftover high from the battle. She bought a cup of hot wine to keep the buzz going, wrapping her hands around it for warmth as she, Jace, and Sebastian lost themselves in a twisting labyrinth of ever narrower, ever darker ancient streets. There were no street signs or names, and no other pedestrians; the only constant was the moon moving through thick clouds overhead. At last a shallow flight of stone steps took them down into a tiny square, one side of which was lit by a flashing neon sign that said KOSTI LUSTR. Below the sign was an open door, a blank spot in the wall that looked like a missing tooth.

"What does that mean, '*Kosti Lustr*'?" Clary asked.

"It means '*The Bone Chandelier.*' It's the name of the night-club," said Sebastian, sauntering forward. His pale hair reflected the changing neon colors of the sign: hot red, cold blue, metallic gold. "You coming?"

A wall of sound and light hit Clary the moment she entered the club. It was a big, tightly packed space that looked like it had once been the interior of a church. She could still see stained-glass windows high up in the walls. Darting colored spotlights picked out the blissed-out faces of dancers in the churning crowd, lighting them up one at a time: hot pink, neon green, burning violet. There was a DJ booth along one wall, and trance music blasted from the speakers. The music pounded up through her feet, into her blood, vibrating her bones. The room was hot with the press of bodies and the smell of sweat and smoke and beer.

She was about to turn and ask Jace if he wanted to dance, when she felt a hand on her back. It was Sebastian. She tensed but didn't pull away. "Come on," he said into her ear. "We're not staying up here with the hoi polloi."

His hand was like iron pressing against her spine. She let him propel her forward, through the dancers; the crowd seemed to part to let them through, people looking up to glance at Sebastian, then dropping their gazes, backing away. The heat increased, and Clary was almost gasping by the time they reached the far side of the room. There was an archway there that she hadn't noticed before. A set of worn stone steps led downward, curving away into darkness.

She glanced up as Sebastian took his hand away from her back. Light blazed around them. Jace had taken out his witch-light rune-stone. He grinned at her, his face all angles and shadows in the harsh, focused light.

"'Easy is the descent,'" he said.

Clary shivered. She knew the whole phrase. *Easy is the descent into Hell.*

"Come on." Sebastian jerked his head, and then he was moving downward, graceful and sure-footed, not worried about slipping on the age-smoothed stones. Clary followed a little more slowly. The air grew cooler as they went down, and the sound of the pounding music faded. She could hear their breathing, and see their shadows thrown, distorted and spindly, against the walls.

She heard the new music before they reached the bottom of the stairs. It had an even more insistent beat than the music in the club upstairs; it shot through her ears and into her veins and spun her around. She was almost dizzy by the time they reached the last of the stairs and stepped out into a massive room that stole her breath.

Everything was stone, the walls bumpy and uneven, the floor smooth beneath their feet. A massive statue of a black-winged angel rose along the far wall, its head lost in shadows far above, its wings dripping strings of garnets that looked like drops of blood. Explosions of color and light burst like cherry bombs throughout the room, nothing like the artificial light upstairs—these were beautiful, sparkling like fireworks, and every time one burst, it rained down a glittering shimmer onto the dancing crowd below. Huge marble fountains sprayed sparkling water; black rose petals drifted onto the surface. And far above everything, dangling down above the packed floor of dancers on a long golden cord, was a massive chandelier made of bones.

It was as intricate as it was gruesome. The main body of the chandelier was formed by spinal columns, fused together;

femurs and tibias dripped like decoration from the arms of the fixture, which swooped up to cradle human skulls, each holding a massive taper. Black wax dripped like demon blood to spatter on the dancers below, none of whom seemed to notice. And the dancers themselves—whirling and spinning and clapping—none of them were human.

"Werewolves and vampires," said Sebastian, answering Clary's unasked question. "In Prague they're allies. This is where they . . . relax." A hot breeze was blowing through the room, like desert wind; it lifted his silvery hair and blew it across his eyes, hiding their expression.

Clary wriggled out of her coat and held it pressed against her chest almost like a shield. She looked around with wide eyes. She could sense the nonhuman-ness of the others in the room, the vampires with their pallor and their swift and languid grace, the werewolves fierce and fast. Most were young, dancing close, writhing up and down each other's bodies. "But—won't they mind us being here? Nephilim?"

"They know me," said Sebastian. "And they'll know you're with me." He reached out and tugged the coat out of her grip. "I'll go get that hung up for you."

"Sebastian—," But he was gone, into the crowd.

She looked at Jace beside her. He had his thumbs hooked into his belt and was looking around with casual interest. "Vampire coat check?" she said.

"Why not?" Jace smiled. "You'll notice he didn't offer to take my coat. Chivalry is dead, I tell you." He tipped his head to the side at her quizzical expression. "Whatever. There's probably someone he has to talk to here."

"So this isn't just for fun?"

"Sebastian never does anything just for fun." Jace took her hands and pulled her toward him. "But I do."

To Simon's complete lack of surprise, no one was enthusiastic about his plan. There was a loud chorus of disapproval, followed by a clamor of voices trying to talk him out of it, and questions, mostly directed at Magnus, about the safety of the whole enterprise. Simon rested his elbows on his knees and waited it out.

Eventually he felt a soft touch on his arm. He turned, and to his surprise it was Isabelle. She gestured at him to follow her.

They wound up in the shadows near one of the pillars as the argument raged behind them. Since Isabelle had initially been one of the loudest dissenters, he braced himself for her to yell at him. However, she only looked at him with her mouth tight.

"Okay," he said finally, hating the silence. "I guess you're not pleased with me right now."

"You *guess*? I'd kick your butt, vampire, but I don't want to ruin my expensive new boots."

"Isabelle—"

"I'm not your girlfriend."

"Right," Simon said, though he couldn't help a twinge of disappointment. "I know that."

"And I've never begrudged you the time you've spent with Clary. I even encouraged it. I know how much you care about her. And how much she cares about you. But this—this is an insane risk you're talking about taking. Are you *sure*?"

Simon looked around—at Magnus's messy apartment, the small group in the corner arguing about his fate. "This isn't just about Clary."

"Well, it isn't about your mother, is it?" Isabelle said. "That she called you a monster? You don't have anything to prove, Simon. That's her problem, not yours."

"It's not like that. Jace saved my life. I owe him."

Isabelle looked surprised. "You're not doing this just to pay Jace back, are you? Because I think by now everyone's pretty even."

"No, not completely," he said. "Look, we all know the situation. Sebastian can't be running around loose. It isn't safe. The Clave is right about that much. But if he dies, Jace dies. And if Jace dies, Clary . . ."

"She'll survive," Isabelle said, her voice quick and hard. "She's tough and strong."

"She'll hurt. Maybe forever. I don't want her to hurt like that. I don't want *you* to hurt like that."

Isabelle crossed her arms. "Of course not. But do you think she won't be hurt, Simon, if something happens to *you*?"

Simon bit his lip. He actually hadn't thought about it. Not like that. "What about you?"

"What about me?"

"Will you be hurt if something happens to me?"

She kept looking at him, her back straight, her chin steady. But her eyes were shining. "Yes."

"But you want me to help Jace."

"Yes. I want that, too."

"You have to let me do this," he said. "It's not just for Jace, or for you and Clary, though you're all a big part of it. It's because I believe darkness is coming. I believe Magnus when he says it. I believe Raphael is truly afraid of a war. I believe we're seeing a small piece of Sebastian's plan, but I don't think it's any coincidence he took Jace with him when he went. Or that he and Jace are linked. He knows we need Jace to win a war. He knows what Jace is."

Isabelle didn't deny it. "You're just as brave as Jace."

"Maybe," said Simon. "But I'm not Nephilim. I can't do what he can do. And I don't mean as much to as many people."

"Special destinies and special torments," Isabelle whispered. "Simon—you mean a lot to me."

He reached out, and lightly cupped her cheek. "You're a warrior, Iz. It's what you do. It's what you are. But if you can't fight Sebastian because hurting him would hurt Jace, you can't fight the war. And if you have to kill Jace to win the war, I think it'll kill part of your soul. And I don't want to see that, not if I could do something to change it."

She swallowed. "It's not fair," she said. "That it has to be you—"

"This is my choice, to do this. Jace doesn't have a choice. If he dies, it's for something he didn't have anything to do with, not really."

Isabelle expelled a breath. She uncrossed her arms and took him by the elbow. "All right," she said. "Let's go."

She steered him back toward the group, who broke off their argument and stared when she cleared her throat, as if they hadn't quite realized the two of them had been missing until this moment.

"That's enough," she said. "Simon has made his decision, and it's his decision to make. He's going to summon Raziel. And we're going to help him in any way we can."

They danced. Clary tried to lose herself in the pounding beat of the music, the rush of blood in her veins, the way she had once been able to do at Pandemonium with Simon. Of course Simon had been a fairly terrible dancer, and Jace was an excellent dancer. She supposed it made sense. With all that trained fighting control and careful grace, there wasn't much he couldn't make his body do. When he flung his head back, his hair was dark with sweat, pasted to his temples, and the curve of his throat gleamed in the light of the bone chandelier.

She saw the way the other dancers looked at him—appreciation, speculation, predatory hunger. A possessiveness she couldn't name or control rose up inside her. She moved closer, sliding up his body the way she'd seen girls do on the dance floor before but had never had the nerve to try herself. She'd always been convinced she'd get her hair caught on someone's belt buckle, but things were different now. Her months of training didn't pay off just in a fight, but any time she had to use her body. She felt fluid, in control, in a way she never had before. She pressed her body against Jace's.

His eyes had been closed; he opened them just as an explosion of colored light lit up the darkness above them. Metallic drops rained down on them; droplets were caught in Jace's hair and shimmering on his skin like mercury. He touched his fingers to a drop of silver liquid on his collarbone and showed it to her, his lips curving. "Do you remember what I told you that first time at Taki's? About faerie food?"

"I remember you said you ran down Madison Avenue naked with antlers on your head," said Clary, blinking silver drops off her lashes.

"I don't think that was ever proved to have actually been me." Only Jace could talk while he danced and not make it look awkward. "Well, this stuff"—and he flicked at the silvery liquid that mixed with his hair and skin, painting him in metal—"is like that. It'll get you . . ."

"High?"

He watched her with darkened eyes. "It can be fun." Another of the drifting flower-things burst above their head; this spatter was silver-blue, like water. Jace licked a drop off the side of his hand, studying her.

High. Clary had never done drugs, didn't even drink. Maybe if you counted the bottle of Kahlúa she and Simon had smuggled out of his mom's liquor cabinet and drunk when they'd been thirteen. They'd been heartily sick afterward; Simon had, in fact, thrown up in a hedge. It hadn't been worth it, but she did remember the sensation of being dizzy and giggly and happy for no reason.

When Jace lowered his hand, his mouth was stained with silver. He was still watching her, gold eyes dark under his long lashes.

Happy for no reason.

She thought of the way they had been together in the time after the Mortal War before Lilith had begun to possess him. He had been the Jace in the photograph on his wall then: so happy. They both had been happy. There had been no nagging doubt when she looked at him, none of this feeling of tiny knives under her skin, eroding the closeness between them.

She leaned up then, and kissed him, slowly and definitively, on the lips.

Her mouth exploded with a sweet-sour taste, a mixture of wine and candy. More of the silvery liquid rained down on them as she pulled away from him, licking her mouth deliberately.

Jace was breathing hard; he reached for her, but she spun away, laughing.

She felt wild and free suddenly, and incredibly light. She knew there was something terribly important she was supposed to be doing, but she couldn't remember what it was, or why she had cared. The faces of the dancers around her no longer looked vulpine and faintly frightening, but darkly beautiful. She was in a great echoing cavern, and the shadows around her were painted with colors lovelier and brighter than any sunset. The angel statue that loomed above her seemed benevolent, a thousand times more so than Raziel and his cold white light, and a high singing note sounded from it, pure and clear and perfect. She spun, faster and faster, leaving behind grief, memories, loss, until she spun into a pair of arms that snaked around her from behind and held her tight. She looked down and saw scarred hands locked around her waist, slim beautiful fingers, the Voyance rune. Jace. She melted back against him, closing her eyes, letting her head fall into the curve of his shoulder. She could feel his heart beating against her spine.

No one else's heart beat like Jace's did, or ever could.

Her eyes flew open, and she spun around, her hands out to push him away. "Sebastian," she whispered. Her brother grinned down at her, silver and black like the Morgenstern ring.

"Clarissa," he said. "I want to show you something."

No. The word came and went, dissolving like sugar into liquid. She couldn't remember why she was supposed to say no to him. He was her brother; she should love him. He had brought her to this beautiful place. Perhaps he had done bad things, but that was a long time ago and she could no longer remember what they were.

"I can hear angels singing," she said to him.

He chuckled. "I see you found out that silvery stuff isn't just glitter." He reached forward and stroked his forefinger across her cheekbone; it was silver when it came away, as if he had caught a painted tear. "Come along, angel girl." He held out his hand.

"But Jace," she said. "I lost him in the crowd—"

"He'll find us." Sebastian's hand clamped around hers, surprisingly warm and comforting. She let him draw her toward one of the fountains in the middle of the room, and set her down on the wide marble edge. He sat down beside her, her hand still in his. "Look in the water," he said. "Tell me what you see."

She leaned over and looked into the smooth dark surface of the pool. She could see her own face reflected back at her, her eyes wide and wild, her eye makeup smudged like bruises, her hair tangled. And then Sebastian leaned over too, and she saw his face beside hers. The silver of his hair reflected in the water made her think of the moon on the river. She reached to touch its brilliance, and the water shivered apart, their reflections distorting, unrecognizable.

"What is it?" Sebastian said, and there was a low urgency in his voice.

Clary shook her head; he was being very silly. "I saw you and me," she said in a chiding tone. "What else?"

He put his hand under her chin and turned her face toward him. His eyes were black, night-black, with only a ring of silver separating the pupil from the iris. "Don't you see it? We're the same, you and me."

"The same?" She blinked at him. There was something very wrong with what he was saying, though she couldn't say quite what. "No . . ."

"You're my sister," he said. "We have the same blood."

"You have demon blood," she said. "Lilith's blood." For some reason this struck her as funny, and she giggled. "You're all dark, dark, dark. And Jace and I are light."

"You have a dark heart in you, Valentine's daughter," he said. "You just won't admit it. And if you want Jace, you had better accept it. Because he belongs to me now."

"Then, who do you belong to?"

Sebastian's lips parted; he said nothing. For the first time, Clary thought, he looked as if he had nothing to say. She was surprised; his words hadn't meant much to her, and she'd merely been idly curious. Before she could say anything else, a voice above them said:

"What's going on?" It was Jace. He looked from one of them to the other, his face unreadable. More of the shimmering stuff had gotten on him, silver drops clinging to the gold of his hair. "Clary." He sounded annoyed. She pulled away from Sebastian and hopped to her feet.

"Sorry," she said breathlessly. "I got lost in the crowd."

"I noticed," he said. "One second I was dancing with you, and the next you were gone and a very persistent werewolf was trying to get the buttons on my jeans undone."

Sebastian chuckled. "Girl or boy werewolf?"

"Not sure. Either way, they could have used a shave." He took Clary's hand, lightly ringing her wrist with his fingers. "Do you want to go home? Or dance some more?"

"Dance some more. Is that all right?"

"Go ahead." Sebastian leaned back, his hands braced behind him on the fountain's edge, his smile like the edge of a straight razor. "I don't mind watching."

Something flashed across Clary's vision: the memory of a bloody handprint. It was gone as soon as it had come, and she frowned. The night was too beautiful to think of ugly things. She looked back at her brother only for a moment before she let Jace lead her back through the crowd to its edge, near the shadows, where the press of bodies was lighter. Another ball of colored light burst above their heads as they went, scattering silver, and she tipped her head up, catching the salt-sweet drops on her tongue.

In the center of the room, beneath the bone chandelier, Jace stopped and she swung toward him. Her arms were around him, and she felt the silver liquid trickling down her face like tears. The fabric of his T-shirt was thin and she could feel the burn of his skin underneath. Her hands slid up under the hem, her nails scratching lightly over his ribs. Silver drops of liquid spangled his eyelashes as he lowered his glance to hers, leaned to whisper in her ear. His hands moved over her shoulders, down her arms. Neither of them were really dancing anymore: the hypnotic music went on around them, and the whirl of other dancers, but Clary barely noticed. A couple moving past laughed and made a derisive comment in Czech; Clary couldn't understand it, but suspected the gist was *Get a room.*

Jace made an impatient noise, and then he was moving through the crowd again, drawing her after him and into one of the shadowy alcoves that lined the walls.

There were dozens of these circular alcoves, each lined with a stone bench and provided with a velvet curtain that could be pulled closed to provide a modicum of privacy. Jace yanked the curtain shut and they crashed against each other like the sea against the shore. Their mouths collided and slid together; Jace lifted her up so she was pressed against him, his fingers twisting in the slippery material of her dress.

Clary was conscious of heat and softness, hands seeking and finding, yielding and pressure. Her hands under Jace's T-shirt, her fingernails clawing at his back, savagely pleased when he gasped. He bit down on her bottom lip and she tasted blood in her mouth, salt and hot. It was as if they wanted to cut each other apart, she thought, to climb inside each other's bodies and share their heartbeats, even if it killed them both.

It was dark in the alcove, so dark that Jace was only an outline of shadows and gold. His body pinned Clary's to the wall. His hands slid down along her body and reached the end of her dress, drawing it up along her legs.

"What are you doing?" she whispered. "Jace?"

He looked at her. The peculiar light in the club turned his eyes an array of fractured colors. His smile was wicked. "You can tell me to stop whenever you want," he said. "But you won't."

Sebastian drew aside the dusty velvet curtain that closed off the alcove, and smiled.

A bench ran around the inside of the small circular room, and a man sat there, leaning his elbows on a stone table. He had long black hair tied back, a scar or mark in the shape of a leaf on one cheek, and his eyes were as green as grass. He wore a white suit, and a handkerchief with green leaf embroidery peeked from one pocket.

"Jonathan Morgenstern," Meliorn said.

Sebastian did not correct him. Faeries took great stock in names, and would never call him by anything but the name his father had chosen for him. "I wasn't sure you would be here at the appointed time, Meliorn."

"May I remind you that the Fair Folk do not lie," said the knight. He reached up and twitched the curtain shut behind Sebastian. The pounding music outside was discreetly muffled, though by no means inaudible. "Come in, then, and seat yourself. Wine?"

Sebastian settled himself on the bench. "No, nothing." Wine, like the faerie liquor, would only cloud his thoughts, and faeries seemed to have a higher tolerance. "I admit I was surprised when I received the message that you wished to meet here."

"You above all should know that the Lady has a special interest in you. She knows of all your movements." Meliorn took a sip of wine. "There was a great demonic disturbance here in Prague tonight. The Queen was concerned."

Sebastian spread his arms out. "As you can see, I am unharmed."

"A disturbance so great will surely win the attention of the Nephilim. In fact, if I am not mistaken, several of them already disport themselves without."

"Without what?" Sebastian asked innocently.

Meliorn took another sip of wine and glared.

"Oh, right. I always forget the amusing way faeries talk. You mean there are Shadowhunters in the crowd outside, looking for me. I know that. I noticed them earlier. The Queen does not think much of me if she does not think I can handle a few Nephilim on my own." Sebastian drew a dagger from his belt and twirled it, the very little light in the alcove sparking off the blade.

"I shall tell her you said so," muttered Meliorn. "I must admit, I have no idea what attraction you hold for her. I have taken your measure and found it lacking, but I have not my lady's taste."

"Weighed in the balance and found wanting?" Amused,

Sebastian leaned forward. "Let me break it down for you, faerie knight. I'm young. I'm pretty. And I'm willing to burn the whole world to the ground to get what I want." His dagger traced a crack in the stone table. "Like myself, the Queen is content to play a long game. But what I desire to know is this: When the twilight of the Nephilim comes, will the Courts stand with or against me?"

Meliorn's face was blank. "The Lady says she stands with you."

Sebastian's mouth curled at the corner. "That is excellent news."

Meliorn snorted. "I always presumed the race of humans would end themselves," he said. "Through a thousand years I have prophesied that you would be your own deaths. But I did not expect the end to come like this."

Sebastian twirled the bright dagger between his fingers. "No one ever does."

"Jace," Clary whispered. "Jace, anyone could come in and see us."

His hands didn't stop what they were doing. "They won't." He trailed a path of kisses down her neck, effectively scattering her thoughts. It was hard to hold on to what was real, with his hands on her, and her mind and memories in a whirl, and her fingers were so tightly bunched in Jace's shirt that she was sure she was going to rip the material.

The stone wall was cold against her back, but Jace was kissing her shoulder, easing the strap of her dress down. She was hot and cold and shivering. The world had fractured into bits, like the bright pieces inside a kaleidoscope. She was going to come apart under his hands.

"Jace—" She clung to his shirt. It was sticky, viscous. She glanced down at her hands and for a moment didn't comprehend what she saw there. Silver fluid, mixed with red.

Blood.

She looked up. Hanging upside-down from the ceiling above them, like a grisly piñata, was a human body, rope binding its ankles. Blood dripped from its cut throat.

Clary screamed, but the scream made no sound. She pushed at Jace, who stumbled back; there was blood in his hair, on his shirt, on her bare skin. She pulled up the straps of her dress and stumbled to the curtain that hid the alcove, yanking it open.

The statue of the angel was no longer quite as it had been. The black wings were bat's wings, the lovely, benevolent face twisted into a sneer. Dangling from the ceiling on twisted ropes were the slaughtered bodies of men, women, animals—slashed open, their blood dripping down like rain. The fountains pulsed blood, and what floated on top of the liquid was not flowers but open severed hands. The writhing, clawing dancers on the floor were drenched in blood. As Clary watched, a couple spun by, the man tall and pale, the woman limp in his arms, her throat torn, obviously dead. The man licked his lips and bent down for another bite, but before he did, he glanced at Clary and grinned, and his face was streaked with blood and silver. She felt Jace's hand on her arm, tugging her back, but she fought free of him. She was staring at the glass tanks along the wall that she had thought held brilliant fish. The water was not clear but blackish and sludgy, and drowned human bodies floated in it, their hair spinning around them like the filaments of luminous jellyfish. She thought of Sebastian floating in his glass coffin. A scream rose in her throat, but she choked it back as silence and darkness overwhelmed her.

14

As Ashes

Clary came back to consciousness slowly, with the dizzy sensation she recalled from that first morning in the Institute, when she had woken with no idea of where she was. Her whole body ached, and her head felt as if someone had smashed an iron barbell into it. She was lying on her side, her head pillowed on something rough, and there was a weight around her shoulder. Glancing down, she saw a slim hand, pressed protectively against her sternum. She recognized the Marks, the faint white scars, even the blue mapping of veins across his forearm. The weight inside her chest eased, and she sat up carefully, slipping out from under Jace's arm.

They were in his bedroom. She recognized the incredible neatness, the carefully made bed with its hospital corners. It still wasn't disarranged. Jace was asleep, propped up against the headboard, still in the same clothes he'd worn the night before. He even had his shoes on. He had clearly fallen asleep holding her, though she had no recollection of it. He was still splattered with the odd silvery substance from the club.

He stirred slightly, as if sensing that she was gone, and wrapped his free arm around himself. He didn't look injured or hurt, she thought, just exhausted, his long dark gold eyelashes curled in the hollow of the shadows beneath his eyes. He looked vulnerable asleep—a little boy. He could have been *her* Jace.

But he wasn't. She remembered the nightclub, his hands on her in the dark, the bodies and blood. Her stomach churned, and she put a hand over her mouth, swallowing down nausea. She felt sickened by what she remembered, and underneath the sickness was a nagging prickle, the sense that she was missing something.

Something important.

"Clary."

She turned. Jace's eyes were half-open; he was looking at her through his lashes, the gold of his eyes dulled with exhaustion. "Why are you awake?" he said. "It's barely dawn."

Her hands bunched in the tangle of blankets. "Last night," she said, her voice uneven. "The bodies—the blood—"

"The what?"

"That's what I saw."

"I didn't." He shook his head. "Faerie drugs," he said. "You knew. . ."

"It seemed so real."

"I'm sorry." His eyes closed. "I wanted to have fun. It's

supposed to make you happy. Make you see pretty things. I thought we would have fun together."

"I saw blood," she said. "And dead people floating in tanks—"

He shook his head, his lashes fluttering down. "None of it was real . . ."

"Even what happened with you and me—?" Clary broke off, because his eyes were closed, his chest rising and falling steadily. He was asleep.

She rose to her feet, not looking at Jace, and went into the bathroom. She stood looking at herself in the mirror, numbness spreading through her bones. She was covered in smears of silvery residue. It reminded her of the time a metallic pen had burst inside her backpack, ruining everything in it. One of her bra straps had snapped, probably where Jace had yanked on it the night before. Her eyes were surrounded with smeared black stripes of mascara, and her skin and hair were sticky with silver.

Feeling faint and sick, she stripped off the slip dress and her underwear, tossing them into the wastebasket before crawling into the hot water.

She washed her hair over and over again, trying to get the dried silver gunk out. It was like trying to wash out oil paint. The scent of it lingered too, like the water from a vase after the flowers have rotted, faint and sweet and spoiled on her skin. No amount of soap seemed to be able to get rid of it.

Finally convinced she was as clean as she was going to get, she dried off and went to the master bedroom to get dressed. It was a relief to climb back into jeans and boots and slip on a comfortable cotton sweater. It was only then, as she pulled on her second boot, that the nagging feeling returned, the feeling that she was missing something. She froze.

Her ring. The gold ring that let her speak to Simon.

It was gone.

Frantically she searched for it, tearing through the wastebasket to see if the ring had gotten caught on her dress, then searching every inch of Jace's room while he slept peacefully on. She combed through the carpet, the bedclothes, checking the nightstand drawers.

At last she sat back, her heart slamming against her chest, a sick feeling in her stomach.

The ring was gone. Lost, somewhere, somehow. She tried to remember the last time she'd seen it. Surely it had flashed on her hand while she'd wielded that dagger against the Elapid demons. Had it fallen off in the junk store? In the nightclub?

She dug her nails into her blue-jeaned thighs until the pain made her gasp. *Focus,* she told herself. *Focus.*

Maybe the ring had fallen from her finger somewhere else in the apartment. Probably Jace had carried her upstairs at some point. It was a small chance, but every chance had to be explored.

She rose to her feet and went as soundlessly as she could out into the hallway. She moved toward Sebastian's room, and hesitated. She couldn't imagine why the ring would be in there, and waking him up would only be counterproductive. She turned around and made her way down the stairs instead, walking carefully to mask the sound of her boots.

Her mind was racing. With no way to contact Simon, what was she going to do? She needed to tell him about the antiques shop, the *adamas*. She should have talked to him sooner. She wanted to punch the wall, but she forced her mind to slow down, to consider her options. Sebastian and Jace were beginning to trust her; if she could get away from them briefly, on a busy city street, she could use a pay phone to *call* Simon. She could duck into an Internet café and e-mail him. She knew more about mundane technology than they did. Losing the ring didn't mean it was over.

She would *not* give up.

Her mind was so occupied with thoughts of what to do next that at first she didn't see Sebastian. Fortunately, he had his back to her. He stood in the living room, facing the wall.

Already at the bottom of the staircase, Clary froze, then darted across the floor and flattened herself against the half wall that separated the kitchen from the larger room. There was no reason to panic, she told herself. She lived here. If Sebastian saw her, she could say she had come downstairs for a glass of water.

But the chance to observe him without his knowledge was too tempting. She turned her body slightly, peering over and around the kitchen counter.

Sebastian still had his back to her. He had changed his clothes since the nightclub. The army jacket was gone; he wore a button-down shirt and jeans. As he turned, and his shirt lifted, she could see that his weapon belt was slung around his waist. As he raised his right hand, she saw that he held his stele—and there was something about the way he held it, just for a moment, with a careful thoughtfulness, that reminded her of the way her mother held a paintbrush.

She closed her eyes. It felt like fabric snagging on a hook, the jerk inside her heart when she recognized something in Sebastian that reminded her of her mother or herself. That reminded her that however much of his blood was poison, just as much was the same blood that ran in her own veins.

She opened her eyes again, in time to see a doorway form in front of Sebastian. He reached for a scarf that hung on a peg on the wall, and stepped out into darkness.

Clary had a split second to decide. Stay and search the rooms, or follow Sebastian and see where he was going. Her feet made the choice before her mind did. Spinning away from the wall, she darted through the dark opening of the door moments before it closed behind her.

The room Luke was lying in was lit only by the streetlights' glow, which came through the slatted windows. Jocelyn knew she could have asked for a light, but she preferred it like this. The darkness hid the extent of his injuries, the pallor of his face, the sunken crescents beneath his eyes.

In fact, in the dimness he looked very like the boy she had known in Idris before the Circle had been formed. She remembered him in the school yard, skinny and brown-haired, with blue eyes and nervous hands. He'd been Valentine's best friend, and because of that, no one had ever really looked at him. Even she hadn't, or she would not have been so enormously blind as to miss his feelings for her.

She remembered the day of her wedding to Valentine, the sun bright and clear through the crystal roof of the Accords Hall. She'd been nineteen and Valentine twenty, and she remembered how unhappy her parents had been that she'd chosen to marry so young. Their disapproval had seemed like nothing to her—they didn't understand. She'd been so sure there would never be anyone for her but Valentine.

Luke had been his best man. She remembered his face as she walked down the aisle—she had looked at him only briefly before turning her full attention to Valentine. She remembered thinking that he must not have been well, that he looked as if he were in pain. And later, in Angel Square, as the guests milled about—most of the members of the Circle were there, from Maryse and Robert Lightwood, already married, to barely fifteen Jeremy Pontmercy—and she stood with Luke and Valentine, someone made the old joke about how if the groom hadn't showed up, the bride would have had to marry the best man. Luke had been wearing evening clothes, with the gold runes for good luck in marriage on them, and he had looked very handsome, but while everyone else had laughed, he'd gone terribly white. *He must really hate the idea of marrying me*, she'd thought. She remembered touching his shoulder with a laugh.

"Don't look like that," she'd teased. "I know we've known each other forever, but I promise you'll never have to marry me!"

And then Amatis had come up, dragging a laughing Stephen with her, and Jocelyn had forgotten all about Luke, the way he had looked at her—and the odd way Valentine had looked at *him*.

She glanced over at Luke now and started in her chair. His eyes were open, for the first time in days, and fixed on her.

"Luke," she breathed.

He looked puzzled. "How long—have I been asleep?"

She wanted to throw herself onto him, but the thick bandages still wrapped around his chest held her back. She caught at his hand instead and put it against her cheek, her fingers interlocking with his. She closed her eyes and, as she did, felt tears slip from under her lids. "About three days."

"Jocelyn," he said, sounding really alarmed now. "Why are we at the station? Where's Clary? I really don't remember—"

She lowered their interlaced hands and, in as steady a voice as she could manage, told him what had happened—about Sebastian and Jace, and the demon metal embedded in his side, and the help of the Praetor Lupus.

"Clary," he said immediately, when she was finished. "We have to go after her."

Drawing his hand from hers, he started to struggle into a sitting position. Even in the dim light she could see his pallor deepen as he winced with pain.

"That's not possible. Luke, lie back down, please. Don't you think if there were any way to go after her, I would have?"

He swung his legs over the side of the bed so he was sitting up; then, with a gasp, he leaned back on his hands. He looked awful. "But the danger—"

"Do you think I haven't thought about the danger?" Jocelyn put her hands on his shoulders and pushed him gently back against the pillows. "Simon's been in contact with me every night. She's all right. She is. And you're in no shape to do anything about it. Killing yourself won't help her. Please trust me, Luke."

"Jocelyn, I can't just lie here."

"You can," she said, standing up. "And you will, if I have to sit on you myself. What on earth is wrong with you, Lucian? Are you out of your mind? I'm terrified about Clary, and I've been terrified about you, too. Please don't do this—don't do this to me. If anything happened to you—"

He looked at her with surprise. There was already a red stain on the white bandages that wrapped his chest, where his movements had pulled his wound open. "I . . ."

"*What?*"

"I'm not used to you loving me," he said.

There was a meekness to his words that she didn't associate with Luke, and she stared at him for a moment before she said, "Luke. Lie back down, please."

As a sort of compromise he leaned further back against the pillows. He was breathing hard. Jocelyn darted to the nightstand, poured him a glass of water, and, returning, thrust it into his hand. "Drink it," she said. "Please."

Luke took the glass, his blue eyes following her as she sat back down in the chair beside his bed, from which she had barely moved for so many hours that she was surprised she and the chair hadn't become one. "You know what I was thinking about?" she asked. "Just before you woke up?"

He took a sip of the water. "You looked very far away."

"I was thinking about the day I married Valentine."

Luke lowered the glass. "The worst day of my life."

"Worse than the day you got bitten?" she asked, folding her legs up under her.

"Worse."

"I didn't know," she said. "I didn't know how you felt. I wish I had. I think things would have been different."

He looked at her incredulously. "How?"

"I wouldn't have married Valentine," she said. "Not if I'd known."

"You would—"

"I wouldn't," she said sharply. "I was too stupid to realize how you felt, but I was also too stupid to realize how *I* felt. I've always loved you. Even if I didn't know it." She leaned forward and kissed him gently, not wanting to hurt him; then she put her cheek against his. "Promise me you won't put yourself in danger. Promise."

She felt his free hand in her hair. "I promise."

She leaned back, partly satisfied. "I wish I could go back in time. Fix everything. Marry the right guy."

"But then we wouldn't have Clary," he reminded her. She loved the way he said "we," so casually, as if there were no doubt at all in his mind that Clary was his daughter.

"If you'd been there more while she was growing up . . ." Jocelyn sighed. "I just feel like I did everything wrong. I was so focused on protecting her that I think I protected her too much. She rushes headlong into danger without thinking. When we were growing up, we saw our friends die in battle. She never has. And I wouldn't want that for her, but sometimes I worry that she doesn't believe she *can* die."

"Jocelyn." Luke's voice was soft. "You raised her to be a good person. Someone with values, who believes in good and evil and strives to be good. Like you always have. You can't raise a child to believe the opposite of what you do. I don't think she doesn't believe she can die. I think, just like you always did, she believes there are things worth dying *for*."

Clary crept after Sebastian through a network of narrow streets, keeping to the shadows close beside the buildings. They were no longer in Prague—that much was immediately clear. The roads were dark, the sky above was the hollow blue of very early morning, and the signs hung above the shops and stores she passed were all in French. As were the street signs: RUE DE LA SEINE, RUE JACOB, RUE DE L'ABBAYE.

As they moved through the city, people passed her like ghosts. The occasional car rumbled by, trucks backed up to stores, making early-morning deliveries. The air smelled like river water and trash. She was fairly sure where they were already, but then a turn and an alley took them to a wide avenue, and a signpost loomed up out of the misty darkness. Arrows pointed in different directions, showing the way to the Bastille, to Notre Dame, and to the Latin Quarter.

Paris, Clary thought, slipping behind a parked car as Sebastian crossed the street. *We're in Paris.*

It was ironic. She'd always wanted to go to Paris with someone who knew the city. Had always wanted to walk its streets, to see the river, to paint the buildings. She'd never imagined this. Never imagined creeping after Sebastian, across the Boulevard Saint Germain, past a bright yellow *bureau de poste*, up an avenue where the bars were closed but the gutters were full of beer bottles and cigarette butts, and down a narrow street lined with houses. Sebastian stopped before one, and Clary froze as well, flat against a wall.

She watched as he raised a hand and punched a code into a box set beside the door, her eyes following the movements of his fingers. There was a click; the door opened and he slipped through. The moment it closed, she darted after him, pausing to key in the same code—X235—and waiting to hear the soft sound that meant the door was unlocked. When the sound came, she wasn't sure if she was more relieved or surprised. *It shouldn't be this easy.*

A moment later she stood inside a courtyard. It was square, surrounded on all sides by ordinary-looking buildings. Three staircases were viewable through open doors. Sebastian, however, had disappeared.

So it wasn't going to be that easy.

She moved forward into the courtyard, conscious as she did so that she was bringing herself out of sheltering shadow and into the open, where she could be seen. The sky was lightening with every passing moment. The knowledge that she was visible prickled the back of her neck, and she ducked into the shadow of the first stairwell she encountered.

It was plain, with wooden stairs leading up and down, and a cheap mirror on the wall in which she could see her own pale face. There was a distinct smell of rotting garbage, and she wondered for a moment if she were near where the trash bins were stored, before her tired mind clicked over and she realized: The stink was the presence of demons.

Her tired muscles started to shake, but she tightened her hands into fists. She was painfully conscious of her lack of weaponry. She took a deep breath of the stinking air and began to make her way down the steps.

The smell grew stronger and the air darker as she made her way downstairs, and she wished for a stele and a night-vision rune. But there was nothing to be done about it. She kept going as the staircase curved around and around, and she was suddenly grateful for the lack of light as she stepped in a patch of something sticky. She clutched for the banister and tried to breathe through her mouth. The darkness thickened, until she was walking blind, her heart pounding so loudly she was sure it must be announcing her presence. The streets of Paris, the ordinary world, seemed eons away. There was only the darkness and herself, going down and down and down.

And then—light flared in the distance, a tiny point, like the tip of a match bursting into flame. She moved closer to the banister, almost crouching, as the light grew. She could see her own hand now, and the outline of the steps below her. There were only a few more. She reached the bottom of the stairs and glanced around.

Any resemblance to an ordinary apartment building was gone. Somewhere along the way the wooden stairs had turned into stone, and she stood now in a small, stone-walled room lit by a torch that gave off a sickly greenish light. The floor was rock, polished smooth, and carved with multiple strange symbols. She edged around them as she crossed the room to the only other exit, a curved stone arch, at the apex of which was set a human skull between the *V* of two enormous ornamental crossed axes.

Through the archway she could hear voices. They were too distant for her to make out what they were saying, but they were voices nonetheless. *This way*, they seemed to say. *Follow us.*

She stared up at the skull, and its empty eyes gazed back at her mockingly. She wondered where she was—if Paris was still above her or if she had stepped into another world entirely, the way one did when one entered the Silent City. She thought of Jace, whom she had left sleeping in what now seemed like another life.

She was doing this for him, she reminded herself. To get him back. She stepped through the arch into the corridor beyond, instinctively flattening herself against the wall. Soundlessly she crept along, the voices growing louder and louder. It was dim in the hall but not lightless. Every few feet another greenish torch burned, giving off a charred odor.

A door opened suddenly in the wall to her left, and the voices grew louder.

"*. . . not like his father,*" one said, the words as raspy as sandpaper. *"Valentine would not deal with us at all. He would make slaves of us. This one will give us this world."*

Very slowly Clary peered around the edge of the doorway.

The room was bare, smooth-walled, and empty of all furniture. Inside it was a group of demons. They were lizardlike, with hard green-brown skin, but each had a set of six octopus-like legs that made a dry, skittering sound as they moved. Their heads were bulbous, alien, set with faceted black eyes.

She swallowed bile. She was reminded of the Ravener that had been one of the first demons she'd ever seen. Something about the grotesque combination of lizard, insect, and alien made her stomach turn. She pressed closer to the wall, listening hard.

"That is, if you trust him." It was hard to tell which of them was talking. Their legs clenched and unclenched as they moved, raising and lowering their bulbous bodies. They didn't seem to have mouths but clusters of small tentacles that vibrated as they spoke.

"The Great Mother trusted him. He is her child."

Sebastian. Of course they were talking about Sebastian.

"He is also Nephilim. They are our great enemies."

"They are his enemies as well. He bears the blood of Lilith."

"But the one he calls his companion bears the blood of our enemies. He is of the angels." The word was spat with such hate that Clary felt it like a slap.

"Lilith's child assures us he has him well in hand, and indeed he seems obedient."

A dry, insectile chuckle.*"You young ones are too consumed with worry. The Nephilim have long kept this world from us. Its riches are great. We will drink it dry and leave it as ashes. As for the angel boy, he will be the last of his kind to die. We will burn him on a pyre until he is only golden bones."*

Rage rose in Clary. She sucked in a breath—a tiny sound, but a sound. The demon nearest her jerked its head up. For a moment Clary froze, trapped in the glare of its mirrored black eyes.

Then she turned and ran. Ran, back toward the entryway and the stairs and their path up into darkness. She could hear commotion behind her, the creatures screaming, and then the slithering, skittering noise of them coming after her. She cast one glance over her shoulder and realized she wasn't going to make it. Despite her head start, they were almost on her.

She could hear her own harsh breathing, sawing in and out, as she reached the archway, spun, and leaped to catch hold of it with her hands. She swung herself forward with all her force, her booted feet driving into the first of the demons, knocking it backward as it shrilled loudly. Still dangling, she caught at the handle of one of the crossed axes below the skull and yanked.

Stuck fast, it didn't move.

She closed her eyes, gripped it tighter, and with all her strength, *pulled.*

The axe came away from the wall with a rending sound, showering down rocks and mortar. Unbalanced, Clary fell, and landed in a crouch, the axe held out in front of her. It was heavy, but she barely felt it. It was happening again, what had happened in the junk shop. The slowing of time, the increased intensity of sensation. She could feel every whisper of the air against her skin, every unevenness of the ground under her feet. She braced herself as the first of the demons scuttled through the doorway and reared back like a tarantula, its legs pawing the air above her. Beneath the tentacles on its face were a pair of long, dripping fangs.

The axe in her hand seemed to swing forward of its own accord, sinking deep into the creature's chest. She immediately remembered Jace telling her not to go for the chest wound but for the decapitation. Not all demons had hearts. But in this case she was lucky. She had struck either the heart or some other vital organ. The creature thrashed and squealed; blood bubbled up around the wound, and then it vanished, leaving her to reel back a step, her ichor-slicked weapon in her hand. The demon's blood was black and stinking, like tar.

As the next one lunged for her, she ducked low, swinging out with the axe and slicing through several of its legs. Howling, it tipped sideways like a broken chair; already the next demon was trampling over its body, trying to get to her. She swung again, her axe burying itself in the creature's face. Ichor sprayed and she darted backward, pressing herself up against the stairwell. If one of them got around behind her, she was dead.

Maddened, the demon whose face she'd slashed open lurched at her again; she swung out with her axe, severing one of its legs, but another leg wrapped itself around her wrist. Hot agony shot up her arm. She screamed and tried to wrench her hand back, but the demon's grip was too strong. It felt as if thousands of hot needles were stabbing into her skin. Still screaming, she drove out with her left arm, slamming her fist into the creature's face, where her axe had already sliced it. The demon gave a hiss and loosed its grip fractionally; she wrenched her hand free just as it reared back—

And out of nowhere a shimmering blade drove down, burying itself in the demon's skull. As she stared, the demon vanished, and she saw her brother, a blazing seraph blade in his hand, ichor splattered across his white shirtfront. Behind him the room was empty save for the body of one of the demons, still twitching, but with black fluid pouring from its severed leg stumps like oil from a smashed car.

Sebastian. She stared at him in amazement. Had he just saved her life?

"Get away from me, Sebastian," she hissed.

He didn't seem to hear her. "Your arm."

She glanced down at her right wrist, still throbbing in agony. A thick band of saucer-shaped wounds encircled it where the demon's suckers had fastened themselves to her skin. Already the wounds were darkening, turning a sickening blue-black.

She looked back up at her brother. His white hair looked like a halo in the darkness. Or it might have been the fact that her vision was going. Light was haloing around the green torch on the wall too, and around the seraph blade burning in Sebastian's hand. He was talking, but his words were blurred, indistinct, as if he were speaking underwater.

". . . deadly poison," he was saying. "What the hell were you thinking, Clarissa?" His voice faded out, and back in again. She struggled to focus. ". . . to fight off six Dahak demons with an ornamental axe—"

"Poison," she repeated, and for a moment his face came clear again, the lines of strain around his mouth and eyes pronounced and startling. "So I guess you didn't save my life after all, did you?"

Her hand spasmed, and the axe slid out of her grip, clattering to the ground. She felt her sweater catch on the rough wall as she began to slide down it, wanting nothing more than to lie on the floor. But Sebastian wouldn't let her rest. His arms were under hers, lifting her up, and then he was carrying her, her good arm slung around his neck. She wanted to struggle away from him, but her energy had deserted her. She felt a stinging pain on the inside of her elbow, a burn—the touch of a stele. Numbness spread through her veins. The last thing she saw before she closed her eyes was the face of the skull in the archway. She could have sworn its hollow eyes were full of laughter.

15
MAGDALENA

Nausea and pain came and went in ever-tightening whirl-pools. Clary could see only a blur of colors around her: she was conscious that her brother was carrying her, every one of his steps slamming into her skull like an ice pick. She was aware that she was clinging to him and the strength of his arms a comfort—that it was bizarre that anything about Sebastian would be a comfort, and that he seemed to be taking care not to jostle her too much as he walked. Very distantly, she knew that she was gasping for breath, and she heard her brother say her name.

Then everything went silent. For a moment she thought that was the end of it: she had died, died battling demons, the way most Shadowhunters did. Then she felt another pricking burn on the inside of her arm, and a surge of what felt like ice spilling through her veins. She squeezed her eyes shut against the pain, but the cold of whatever Sebastian had done to her was like having a glass of water dashed in her face. Slowly, the world ceased its spinning, the whirlpools of nausea and pain lessening until they were only ripples in the tide of her blood. She could breathe again.

With a gasp, she opened her eyes.

Blue sky.

She was lying on her back, staring up at an endlessly blue sky, touched with cottony clouds, like the painted sky on the ceiling of the infirmary in the Institute. She stretched out her aching arms. The right one still bore the marks of her bracelet of injuries, though they were fading to a light pink. On her left arm was an *iratze*, paling to invisibility, and there was a *mendelin* for pain in the crook of her elbow.

She took a deep breath. Autumn air, tinged with the smell of leaves. She could see the tops of trees, hear the murmur of traffic, and—

Sebastian. She heard a low chuckle and realized she wasn't just lying down, she was lying propped against her brother. Sebastian, who was warm and breathing, and whose arm cradled her head. The rest of her was stretched out along a slightly damp wooden bench.

She jerked upright. Sebastian laughed again; he was sitting at the end of a park bench with elaborate iron armrests. His scarf was folded up in his lap, where she'd been lying, and the arm that hadn't been cradling her head was stretched out along the back of the bench. He had unbuttoned his white shirt to hide the ichor stains. Beneath it he wore a plain gray T-shirt.

The silver bracelet glittered on his wrist. His black eyes studied her with amusement as she scooted as far away from him on the bench as she could get.

"Good thing you're so short," he said. "If you were much taller, carrying you would have been extremely inconvenient."

She kept her voice steady with an effort. "Where are we?"

"The *Jardin du Luxembourg*," he said. "The Luxembourg Gardens. It's a very nice park. I had to take you somewhere you could lie down, and the middle of the street didn't seem like a good idea."

"Yeah, there's a word for leaving someone to die in the middle of the street. Vehicular manslaughter."

"That's two words, and I think it's only vehicular manslaughter, technically, if you run them over yourself." He rubbed his hands together as if to warm them. "Anyway, why would I leave you to die in the middle of the street after I went through all that effort to save your life?"

She swallowed, and looked down at her arm. The wounds were even more faded now. If she hadn't known to look for them, she probably wouldn't have noticed them at all. "Why did you?"

"Why did I what?"

"Save my life."

"You're my sister."

She swallowed. In the morning light his face had some color in it. There were faint burns along his neck where demon ichor had splashed him. "You never cared that I was your sister before."

"Didn't I?" His black eyes flicked up and down her. She remembered when Jace had come into her house after she'd fought the Ravener demon and she'd been dying of the poison. He'd cured her just as Sebastian had, and carried her out the same way. Maybe they were more alike than she had ever wanted to think, even before the spell that had bound them.

"Our father's dead," he said. "There are no other relatives. You and I, we are the last. The last of the Morgensterns. You are my only chance for someone whose blood runs in my veins too. Someone like me."

"You knew I was following you," she said.

"Of course I did."

"And you let me."

"I wanted to see what you would do. And I admit I didn't think you would follow me down there. You're braver than I thought." He picked up the scarf from his lap and drew it around his neck. The park was beginning to fill up, with tourists clutching maps, parents with children in hand, old men sitting on other benches like this one, smoking pipes. "You would never have won that fight."

"I might have."

He grinned, a quick sideways grin, as if he couldn't help it. "Maybe."

She scuffed her boots in the grass, which was wet with dew. She wasn't going to thank Sebastian. Not for anything. "Why are you dealing with demons?" she demanded. "I listened to them talking about you. I know what you're doing—"

"No, you don't." The grin was gone, the superior tone back. "First, those weren't the demons I was dealing with. Those were their guards. That's why they were in a separate room and why I wasn't there. Dahak demons aren't that smart, though they are mean and tough and defensive. So it's not like they were really informed about what was going on. They were just repeating gossip they'd heard from their masters. Greater Demons. *That* was who I was meeting with."

"And that's supposed to make me feel better?"

He leaned toward her across the bench. "I'm not trying to make you feel better. I'm trying to tell you the truth."

"No wonder you look like you're having an allergy attack," she said, though it wasn't precisely true. Sebastian looked annoyingly tranquil, though the set of his jaw and the pulse in his temple told her he wasn't as calm as he pretended. "The Dahak said you were going to give this world to the demons."

"Now, does that sound like something I'd do?"

She just looked at him.

"I thought you said you were going to give me a chance," he said. "I'm not who I was when you met me in Alicante." His gaze was clear. "Besides, I'm not the only person you've ever met who believed in Valentine. He was my father. Our father. It's not easy to doubt the things you've grown up believing."

Clary crossed her arms over her chest; the air was fresh but cold, with a wintery snap in it. "Well, that's true."

"Valentine was wrong," he said. "He was so obsessed with the wrongs he believed the Clave had done to him that he could see nothing past proving himself right to them. He wanted the Angel to rise and tell them that he was Jonathan Shadowhunter returned, that he was their leader and his way was the right way."

"It didn't exactly happen like that."

"I know what happened. Lilith spoke to me of it." He said this offhandedly, as if conversations with the mother of all warlocks were something everyone had every once in a while.

"Do not fool yourself into thinking that what happened was because the Angel has great compassion, Clary. Angels are as cold as icicles. Raziel was angered because Valentine had forgotten the mission of all Shadowhunters."

"Which is?"

"To kill demons. That is our mandate. Surely you must have heard that more and more demons have been spilling into our world in recent years? That we have no idea how to keep them out?"

An echo of words came back to her, something Jace had said to her what seemed like a lifetime ago, the first time they had ever visited the Silent City. *We might be able to block them from coming here, but nobody's even been able to figure out how to do that. In fact, more and more of them are coming through. There used to be only small demon invasions into this world, easily contained. But even in my lifetime more and more of them have spilled in through the wardings. The Clave is always having to dispatch Shadowhunters, and a lot of times they don't come back.*

"A great war with demons is coming, and the Clave is woefully unprepared," said Sebastian. "That much my father was correct about. They are too set in their ways to hear warnings or to change. I do not wish the destruction of Downworlders as Valentine did, but I worry that the Clave's blindness will doom this world that Shadowhunters protect."

"You want me to believe you care if this world is destroyed?"

"Well, I do live here," Sebastian said, more mildly than she would have expected. "And sometimes extreme situations call for extreme measures. To destroy the enemy it can be necessary to understand him, even to treat with him. If I can make those Greater Demons trust me, then I can lure them here, where they can be destroyed, and their followers as well. That ought to turn back the tide. Demons will know that this world is not as easy pickings as they imagined it."

Clary shook her head. "And you're going to do this with what, just you and Jace? You're pretty impressive, don't get me wrong, but even the two of you—"

Sebastian stood up. "You really don't imagine I could have thought this through, do you?" He looked down at her, the fall wind blowing his white hair across his face. "Come with me. I want to show you something."

She hesitated. "Jace—"

"Is still asleep. Trust me, I know." He held out his hand. "Come with me, Clary. If I can't make you believe I have a plan, maybe I can prove it to you."

She stared at him. Images tumbled through her mind like shaken confetti: the junk shop in Prague, her gold leaf-ring falling away into darkness, Jace holding her in the alcove in the club, the glass tanks of dead bodies. Sebastian with a seraph blade in his grip.

Prove it to you.

She took his hand and let him pull her to her feet.

It was decided, though not without a great deal of arguing, that in order for the summoning of Raziel to take place, Team Good would need to find a fairly secluded location. "We can't summon a sixty-foot angel in the middle of Central Park," Magnus observed dryly. "People might notice, even in New York."

"Raziel's sixty feet tall?" Isabelle said. She was slumped down in an armchair she had pulled up to the table. There were rings under her dark eyes; she—like Alec, Magnus, and

Simon—was exhausted. They had all been awake for hours, poring through books of Magnus's so old that their pages were as thin as onionskin. Both Isabelle and Alec could read Greek and Latin, and Alec had a better knowledge of demon languages than Izzy did, but there were still many only Magnus could understand. Maia and Jordan, realizing they could be more help elsewhere, had left for the police station to check on Luke. Meanwhile, Simon had tried to make himself useful in other ways—getting food and coffee, copying down symbols as Magnus instructed, fetching more paper and pencils, and even feeding Chairman Meow, who had thanked him by coughing up a hair ball on the floor of Magnus's kitchen.

"Actually, he's only fifty-nine feet tall, but he likes to exaggerate," said Magnus. Tiredness was not improving his temper. His hair was sticking straight up, and there were smudges of glitter on the backs of his hands where he had rubbed his eyes. "He's an angel, Isabelle. Haven't you ever studied *anything*?"

Isabelle clicked her tongue in annoyance. "Valentine raised an angel in his cellar. I don't see why you need all this space—"

"Because Valentine is just WAY MORE AWESOME than me," snapped Magnus, dropping his pen. "Look—"

"Don't shout at my sister," said Alec. He said it quietly, but with force behind the words. Magnus looked at him in surprise. Alec continued, "Isabelle, the size of angels, when they appear in the earthly dimension, varies depending on their power. The angel Valentine summoned was of a lower rank than Raziel. And if you were to summon an angel of an even higher rank, Michael, or Gabriel—"

"I couldn't make a spell that would bind them, even momentarily," said Magnus in a subdued voice. "We're summoning Raziel in part because we're hoping that as the creator of Shadowhunters, he will have a special compassion—or, really, any compassion—for your situation. He's also of about the right rank. A less powerful angel might not be able to help us, but a more powerful angel . . . well, if something went wrong . . ."

"It might not just be me who dies," said Simon.

Magnus looked pained, and Alec glanced down at the papers strewn across the table. Isabelle put her hand on top of Simon's. "I can't believe we're actually sitting here talking about summoning an angel," she said. "My whole life we've sworn on the Angel's name. We know our power comes from angels. But the idea of seeing one . . . I can't really imagine it. When I try to think about it, it's too big an idea."

A silence fell across the table. There was a darkness in Magnus's eyes that made Simon wonder if he had ever seen an angel. He wondered whether he ought to ask, but was saved deciding by the buzzing of his cell phone.

"One second," he muttered, and got to his feet. He flipped the phone open and leaned against one of the loft's pillars. It was a text—several—from Maia.

GOOD NEWS! LUKE IS AWAKE AND TALKING. IT LOOKS LIKE HE'S GOING TO BE OKAY.

Relief poured over Simon in a wave. Finally, good news. He flipped the phone shut and reached for the ring on his hand. *Clary?*

Nothing.

He swallowed his nerves. She was probably asleep. He looked up to find all three of the people at the table staring at him.

"Who called?" Isabelle asked.

"It was Maia. She says Luke's up and talking. That he's going to be okay." There was a chatter of relieved voices, but Simon was still staring down at the ring on his hand. "She gave me an idea."

Isabelle had been on her feet, heading toward him; at that, she paused, looking worried. Simon supposed he didn't blame her. His ideas had been downright suicidal of late. "What is it?" she said.

"What do we need to summon Raziel? How much space?" Simon asked.

Magnus paused over a book. "A mile around at least. Water would be good. Like Lake Lyn—"

"Luke's farm," Simon said. "Upstate. An hour or two away. It should be shut up now, but I know how to get there. And there's a lake. Not as big as Lyn, but . . ."

Magnus closed the book he was holding. "That's not a bad idea, Seamus."

"A few hours?" Isabelle said, looking up at the clock. "We could be there by—"

"Oh, no," said Magnus. He pushed the book away from him. "While your enthusiasm is boundless and impressive, Isabelle, I'm too exhausted to properly cast the summoning spell at the moment. And this isn't something I want to take risks with. I think we can all agree."

"So when?" Alec asked.

"We need a few hours sleep at least," Magnus said. "I say we leave early afternoon. Sherlock—sorry, *Simon*—call and see if you can borrow Jordan's truck in the meantime. And now . . ." He pushed his papers to the side. "I'm going to sleep. Isabelle,

Simon, you're more than welcome to use the spare room again if you like."

"Different spare rooms would be better," Alec muttered.

Isabelle looked at Simon with questioning dark eyes, but he was already reaching into his pocket for his phone. "Okay," he said. "I'll be back by noon, but for now there's something important I have to do."

In the daylight Paris was a city of narrow, curving streets that opened out into wide avenues, mellow golden buildings with slate-colored roofs, and a glittering river that sliced across it like a dueling scar. Sebastian, despite his claim that he was going to prove to Clary that he had a plan, didn't say much as they made their way up a street lined with art galleries and stores selling dusty old books, to reach the Quai des Grands Augustins by the river's edge.

There was a cool wind coming off the Seine, and she shivered. Sebastian unwound the scarf from around his neck and handed it to her. It was a heathery black and white tweed, still warm from being wrapped around his neck.

"Don't be stupid," he said. "You're cold. Put it on."

Clary wound it around her neck. "Thanks," she said reflexively, and winced.

There. She had thanked Sebastian. She waited for a bolt of lightning to shoot out of the clouds and strike her dead. But nothing happened.

He gave her an odd look. "You all right? You look like you're going to sneeze."

"I'm fine." The scarf smelled like citrusy cologne and boy. She wasn't sure what she'd thought it would smell like. They started to walk again. This time Sebastian slowed his pace, walking alongside her, pausing to explain that neighborhoods in Paris were numbered, and they were crossing from the sixth into the fifth, the Latin Quarter, and that the bridge they could see spanning the river in the distance was the Pont Saint-Michel. There were a lot of young people walking past them, Clary noticed; girls her age or older, impossibly stylish in tight-fitting pants and sky-high heels, long hair blowing in the wind off the Seine. Quite a few of them stopped to give Sebastian appreciative glances, which he didn't seem to notice.

Jace, she thought, would have noticed. Sebastian *was* striking, with his icy white hair and black eyes. She had thought he was handsome the first time she'd met him, and he'd had his hair dyed black then; it hadn't suited him, really. He looked better like this. The pallor of his hair gave his skin some color, drew your eyes to the flush along his high cheekbones, the graceful shape of his face. His eyelashes were incredibly long, a shade darker than his hair, and curled slightly, just like Jocelyn's—*so* unfair. Why hadn't she gotten the curling lashes in the family? And why didn't he have a single freckle? "So," she said abruptly, cutting him off in the middle of a sentence, "what are we?"

He gave her a sidelong look. "What do you mean, 'What are we?'"

"You said we're the last of the Morgensterns. Morgenstern is a German name," said Clary. "So, what are we, German? What's the story? Why aren't there any more but us?"

"You don't know anything about Valentine's family?" Incredulity tinged Sebastian's voice. He had stopped next to the wall that ran along the Seine, beside the pavement. "Didn't your mother ever tell you anything?"

"She's your mother too, and no, she didn't. Valentine's not her favorite topic."

"Shadowhunter names are compounded," said Sebastian slowly, and he climbed up on top of the wall. He reached a hand down, and after a moment she let him take hers and pull her up onto the wall beside him. The Seine ran gray-green below them, fly-speck tourist boats chugging by at a leisurely pace. "Fair-child, Light-wood, White-law. 'Morgenstern' means 'morning star.' It's a German name, but the family was Swiss."

"Was?"

"Valentine was an only child," Sebastian said. "His father—our grandfather—was killed by Downworlders, and our great-uncle died in a battle. He didn't have any children. This"—he reached out and touched her hair—"is from the Fairchild side. There's English blood there. I look more like the Swiss side. Like Valentine."

"Do you know anything about our grandparents?" Clary asked, fascinated despite herself.

Sebastian dropped his hand and leaped down off the wall. He held his hand up for her, and she took it, balancing as she leaped down. For a moment she collided with his chest, hard and warm beneath his shirt. A passing girl shot her an amused, jealous look, and Clary pulled back hastily. She wanted to shout after the girl that Sebastian was her brother, and that she hated him anyway. She didn't.

"I know nothing about our maternal grandparents," he said. "How could I?" His smile was crooked. "Come. I want to show you a favorite place of mine."

Clary hung back. "I thought you were going to prove to me that you had a plan."

"All in due time." Sebastian started to walk, and after a moment she followed him. *Find out his plan. Make nice until you do.* "Valentine's father was a lot like him," Sebastian went on. "He put his faith in strength. 'We are God's chosen warriors.' That's what he believed. Pain made you strong. Loss made you powerful. When he died . . ."

"Valentine changed," Clary said. "Luke told me."

"He loved his father and he hated him. Something you might understand from knowing Jace. Valentine raised us as his father had raised him. You always return to what you know."

"But Jace," Clary said. "Valentine taught him more than just fighting. He taught him languages, and how to play the piano—"

"That was Jocelyn's influence." Sebastian said her name unwillingly, as if he hated the sound of it. "She thought Valentine ought to be able to talk about books, art, music—not just killing things. He passed that on to Jace."

A wrought iron blue gate rose to their left. Sebastian ducked under it and beckoned Clary to follow him. She didn't have to duck but went after him, her hands stuffed into her pockets. "What about you?" she asked.

He held up his hands. They were unmistakably her mother's hands—dexterous, long-fingered, meant for holding a brush or a pen. "I learned to play the instruments of war," he said, "and paint in blood. I am not like Jace."

They were in a narrow alley between two rows of buildings made of the same golden stone as many of the other buildings of Paris, their roofs sparkling copper-green in the sunlight. The street underfoot was cobblestone, and there were no cars or motorcycles. To her left was a café, a wooden sign dangling from a wrought iron pole the only clue that there was any commercial business on this winding street.

"I like it here," Sebastian said, following her gaze, "because it's as if you were in a past century. No noise of cars, no neon lights. Just—peaceful."

Clary stared at him. *He's lying,* she thought. *Sebastian doesn't have thoughts like this. Sebastian, who tried to burn Alicante to the ground, doesn't care about "peaceful."*

She thought then of where he'd grown up. She'd never seen it, but Jace had described it to her. A small house—a cottage, really—in a valley outside Alicante. The nights would have been silent there and the sky full of stars at night. But would he miss that? *Could* he? Was that the sort of emotion you could have when you weren't really even human?

It doesn't bother you? she wanted to say. *Being in the place the real Sebastian Verlac grew up and lived, until you ended his life? Walking these streets, bearing his name, knowing that somewhere, his aunt is grieving for him? And what did you mean when you said he wasn't supposed to fight back?*

His black eyes regarded her thoughtfully. He had a sense of humor, she knew; there was a streak of mordant wit in him that was sometimes not unlike Jace's. But he didn't smile.

"Come on," he said then, breaking off her reverie. "This place has the best hot chocolate in Paris."

Clary wasn't sure how she'd know if this were true or not, given that this was the first time she'd ever been to Paris, but once they sat down, she had to admit the hot chocolate was excellent. They made it at your table—which was small and wooden, as were the old-fashioned high-backed chairs—in a blue ceramic pot, using cream, chocolate powder, and sugar.

The result was a cocoa so thick your spoon could stand up in it. They had croissants, too, and dunked them into the chocolate.

"You know, if you want another croissant, they'll bring you one," said Sebastian, leaning back in his chair. They were the youngest people in the place by decades, Clary noticed. "You're attacking that one like a wolverine."

"I'm hungry." She shrugged. "Look, if you want to talk to me, talk. Convince me."

He leaned forward, his elbows on the table. She was reminded of looking into his eyes the night before, of noticing the silver ring around the iris of his eye. "I was thinking about what you said last night."

"I was hallucinating last night. I don't remember what I said to you."

"You asked me who I belonged to," said Sebastian.

Clary paused with her cup of chocolate halfway to her mouth. "I did?"

"Yeah." His eyes studied her face intently. "And I don't have an answer."

She set her cup down, feeling suddenly, intensely uncomfortable. "You don't have to belong to anyone," she said. "It's just a figure of speech."

"Well, let me ask you something now," Sebastian said. "Do you think you can forgive me? I mean, do you think forgiveness is possible for someone like me?"

"I don't know." Clary gripped the edge of the table. "I—I mean, I don't know much about forgiveness as a religious concept, just your garden-variety kind of forgiving people." She took a deep breath, knowing she was babbling. It was something in the steadiness of Sebastian's dark gaze on her, as if he actually expected her to give him the answers to questions no one else could answer. "I know you have to do things, to earn forgiveness. Change yourself. Confess, repent—and make amends."

"Amends," Sebastian echoed.

"To make up for what you've done." She looked down at her mug. There was no making up for the things Sebastian had done, not in any way that made sense.

"*Ave atque vale*," Sebastian said, looking down at his mug of chocolate.

Clary recognized the traditional words Shadowhunters spoke over their dead. "Why are you saying that? I'm not dying."

"You know it's from a poem," he said. "By Catullus. '*Frater, ave atque vale.*' 'Hail and farewell, my brother.' He speaks of ashes, of the rites of the dead, and his own grief for his brother. I was taught the poem young, but I didn't *feel* it—either his grief, or his loss, or even the wondering what it would be like to die and to have no one grieve you." He looked up at her sharply. "What do you think it would have been like if Valentine had brought you up along with me? Would you have loved me?"

Clary was very glad she had put her cup down, because if she hadn't, she would have dropped it. Sebastian was looking at her not with any shyness or the sort of natural awkwardness that might be attendant on such a bizarre question, but as if she were a curious, foreign life-form.

"Well," she said. "You're my brother. I would have loved you. I would have . . . had to."

He kept looking at her with the same still, intent gaze. She wondered if she should ask him if he thought that meant he would have loved her, too. Like a sister. But she had a feeling he had no idea what that meant.

"But Valentine didn't bring me up," she said. "In fact, I killed him."

She wasn't sure why she said it. Maybe she wanted to see if it was possible to upset him. After all, Jace had told her once that he thought Valentine might have been the only thing Sebastian had ever cared about.

But he didn't blanch. "Actually," he said, "the Angel killed him. Though it was because of you." His fingers traced patterns on the worn tabletop. "You know, when I first met you, in Idris, I had hopes—I had thought you would be like me. And when you were nothing like me, I hated you. And then, when I was brought back, and Jace told me what you did, I realized that I had been wrong. You *are* like me."

"You said that last night," Clary said. "But I'm not—"

"You killed our father," he said. His voice was soft. "And *you don't care*. Never given it a second thought, have you? Valentine beat Jace bloody for the first ten years of his life, and Jace still misses him. Grieved for him, though they share no blood at all. But he was your father and you killed him and you've never missed a night of sleep over it."

Clary stared at him with her mouth open. It was unfair. So unfair. Valentine had never been a father to her—hadn't loved her—had been a monster who'd had to die. She had killed him because she'd had no choice.

Unbidden in her mind rose the image of Valentine, driving his blade into Jace's chest, then holding him as he died. Valentine had wept over the son he'd murdered. But she had never cried for her father. Had never even considered it.

"I'm right, aren't I?" said Sebastian. "Tell me I'm wrong. Tell me you're not like me."

Clary stared down at her cup of chocolate, now cold. She felt like a vortex had opened up inside her head and was sucking away her thoughts and words. "I thought you thought *Jace* was like you," she said finally in a choked voice. "I thought that's why you wanted him with you."

"I need Jace," said Sebastian. "But in his heart he's not like me. You are." He stood up. He must have paid the bill at some point; Clary couldn't remember. "Come with me."

He held his hand out. She stood up without taking it and retied his scarf mechanically; the chocolate she had drunk felt like acid churning in her stomach. She followed Sebastian out of the café and into the alley, where he stood looking up at the blue sky overhead.

"I'm not like Valentine," Clary said, stopping next to him. "Our mother—"

"*Your* mother," he said, "hated me. Hates me. You saw her. She tried to kill me. You want to tell me you take after your mother, fine. Jocelyn Fairchild is ruthless. She always has been. She pretended to love our father for months, years maybe, so she could gather enough information on him to betray him. She engineered the Uprising and watched all her husband's friends *slaughtered.* She stole your memories. Have you forgiven her? And when she ran from Idris, do you honestly think she ever planned to take me with her? She must have been relieved at the thought that I was dead—"

"She wasn't!" Clary snapped. "She had a box that had your baby things in it. She used to take it out and cry over it. Every year on your birthday. I know you have it in your room."

Sebastian's thin, elegant lips twisted. He turned away from her and started walking down the alley. "Sebastian!" Clary called after him. "Sebastian, *wait.*" She wasn't sure why she wanted him to come back. Admittedly, she had no idea where she was or how to find her way back to the apartment, but it was more than that. She wanted to stand and fight, to prove she wasn't what he said she was. She raised her voice to a shout: *"Jonathan Christopher Morgenstern!"*

He stopped and turned slowly, looking back over his shoulder at her.

She walked toward him, and he watched her walk, his head cocked to the side, his black eyes narrow. "I bet you don't even know my middle name," she said.

"Adele." There was a musicality to the way he said it, a familiarity that made her uncomfortable. "Clarissa Adele."

She reached his side. "Why Adele? I never knew."

"I don't know myself," he said. "I know Valentine never would have wanted you to be called Clarissa Adele. He told me he always hoped to name a daughter Seraphina, after his mother. Our grandmother." He turned around and started walking again, and this time she kept pace. "After our grandfather was killed, she died—heart attack. Died of grief, Valentine always said."

Clary thought of Amatis, who had never gotten over her first love, Stephen; of Stephen's father, who had died of grief; of the Inquisitor, her whole life dedicated to revenge. Of Jace's mother, cutting her wrists when her husband died. "Before I met the Nephilim, I would have said it was impossible to die of grief."

Sebastian chuckled dryly. "We don't form attachments like

mundanes do," he said. "Well, sometimes, surely. Not everyone is the same. But the bonds between us tend to be intense and unbreakable. That's why we do so badly with others not of our kind. Downworlders, mundanes—"

"My mother's marrying a Downworlder," Clary said, stung. They had paused in front of a square stone building with blue painted shutters, almost at the end of the alley.

"He was Nephilim once," said Sebastian. "And look at our father. Your mother betrayed him and left him, and he still spent the rest of his life waiting to find her again and convince her to come back to him. That whole closet full of clothes—" He shook his head.

"But Valentine told Jace that love is a weakness," said Clary. "That it would destroy you."

"Wouldn't you think that, if you spent half your life chasing a woman even though she hated your guts, because you couldn't forget about her? If you had to remember that the person you loved best in the world stabbed you in the back and twisted the knife?" He leaned in for a moment, close enough that when he spoke, his breath stirred her hair. "Maybe you are more like your mother than our father. But what difference does it make? You have ruthlessness in your bones and ice in your heart, Clarissa. Don't tell me any differently."

He spun away before she could answer him, and mounted the front step of the blue-shuttered house. A strip of electric buzzers ran down the side of the wall beside the door, each with a name hand-scrawled on a placard beside it. He pressed the button beside the name Magdalena, and waited. Eventually a scratchy voice came through the speaker:

"Qui est là?"

"C'est le fils et la fille de Valentine," he said. *"Nous avions rendez-vous?"*

There was a pause, and then the buzzer sounded. Sebastian yanked the door open—and held it open, politely letting Clary go before him. The stairs were wooden, as worn and smooth as the side of a ship. They trudged up them in silence to the top floor, where the door was propped slightly open onto the landing. Sebastian went through first, and Clary followed.

She found herself in a large, airy light space. The walls were white, as were the curtains. Through one window she could see the street beyond, lined with restaurants and boutiques. Cars whizzed by, but the sound of them didn't seem to penetrate inside the apartment. The floor was polished wood, the furniture white-painted wood or upholstered couches with colorful throw pillows. A section of the apartment was set up as a sort of studio. Light poured down from a skylight onto a long wooden table. There were easels, cloths tossed over them to obscure their contents. A paint-stained smock hung from a hook on the wall.

Standing by the table was a woman. Clary would have guessed her age at about Jocelyn's, if there had not been several factors obscuring her age. She wore a shapeless black smock that hid her body; only her white hands and her face and throat were visible. On each of her cheeks was carved a thick black rune, running from the outside corner of her eye to her lips. Clary had not seen the runes before, but she could sense their meaning—power, skill, workmanship. The woman had thick long auburn hair, falling in waves to her waist, and her eyes, when she raised them, were a peculiar flat orange color, like a dying flame.

The woman clasped her hands in front of her smock loosely. In a nervous, melodic voice, she said, *"Tu dois être Jonathan Morgenstern. Et elle, c'est ta sœur? Je pensais que—"*

"I am Jonathan Morgenstern," Sebastian said. "And this is my sister, yes. Clarissa. Please speak English in front of her. She doesn't understand French."

The woman cleared her throat. "My English is rusty. It has been years since I used it."

"It seems good enough to me. Clarissa, this is Sister Magdalena. Of the Iron Sisters."

Clary was startled into speech. "But I thought the Iron Sisters never left their fortress—"

"They don't," said Sebastian. "Unless they are disgraced by having their part in the Uprising discovered. Who do you think armed the Circle?" He smiled at Magdalena mirthlessly. "The Iron Sisters are Makers, not fighters. But Magdalena fled the Fortress before her part in the Uprising could be discovered."

"I had not seen another Nephilim in fifteen years until your brother contacted me," said Magdalena. It was hard to tell who she was looking at while she spoke; her featureless eyes seemed to wander, but she was clearly not blind. "Is it true? Do you have the . . . material?"

Sebastian reached into a pouch hanging from his weapons belt and took from it a chunk of what looked like quartz. He set it down on the long table, and a stray shaft of sunlight, passing across the skylight, lit it seemingly from within. Clary caught her breath. It was the *adamas* from the junk shop in Prague.

Magdalena drew in a hissing breath.

"Pure *adamas*," said Sebastian. "No rune has ever touched it."

The Iron Sister came around the table and laid her hands

upon the *adamas*. Her hands, also scarred with multiple runes, trembled. "*Adamas pur,*" she whispered. "It has been years since I touched the holy material."

"It is all yours to craft with," said Sebastian. "When you are done, I shall pay you in more of it. That is, if you believe you can create what I asked for."

Magdalena drew herself up. "Am I not an Iron Sister? Did I not take the vows? Do my hands not shape the stuff of Heaven? I can deliver what I promised, Valentine's son. Never doubt it."

"Good to hear." There was a trace of humor in Sebastian's voice. "I will return tonight, then. You know how to summon me if you need to."

Magdalena shook her head. All her attention was back on the glassine substance, the *adamas*. She stroked it with her fingers. "Yes. You may go."

Sebastian nodded and took a step back. Clary hesitated. She wanted to seize the woman, ask her what Sebastian had demanded she do, ask her why she would ever have broken Covenant Law to work beside Valentine. Magdalena, as if sensing her hesitation, looked up and smiled thinly.

"The two of you," she said, and for a moment Clary thought she was going to say that she did not understand why they were together, that she had heard that they hated each other, that Jocelyn's daughter was a Shadowhunter while Valentine's son was a criminal. But she only shook her head. "*Mon Dieu,*" she said, "but you look just like your parents."

16

Brothers and Sisters

When Clary and Sebastian returned to the apartment, the living room was empty, but there were dishes in the sink where there hadn't been before.

"I thought you said Jace was asleep," she said to Sebastian, a note of accusation in her voice.

Sebastian shrugged. "He was when I said it." There was light mockery in his voice but no serious unkindness. They had walked back from Magdalena's together mostly in silence, but not a bad sort of silence. Clary had let her mind wander, only jerked back to reality on occasion by the realization that it was Sebastian she was walking beside. "I'm pretty sure I know where he is."

"In his room?" Clary started for the stairs.

"No." He moved in front of her. "Come on. I'll show you."

He headed up the stairs at a rapid pace and into the master bedroom, Clary on his heels. As she watched in puzzlement, he tapped the side of the wardrobe. It slid away, revealing a set of stairs behind it. Sebastian cast a smirk over his shoulder at her as she came up behind him. "You're kidding," she said. "Secret stairs?"

"Don't tell me that's the strangest thing you've seen today." He took the stairs two at a time, and Clary, though bone-weary, followed him. The stairs curved around and opened out into a wide room with a polished wooden floor and high walls. All manner of weapons hung from the walls, just as they did in the training room in the Institute—*kindjals* and *chakhrams*, maces and swords and daggers, crossbows and brass knuckles, throwing stars and axes and samurai swords.

Training circles were neatly painted on the floor. In the center of them stood Jace, his back to the door. He was shirtless and barefoot, in black warm-up pants, a knife in each of his hands. An image flashed in her head: Sebastian's bare back, scarred with unmistakeable whip stripes. Jace's was smooth, pale gold skin over muscle, marked only with the typical scars of a Shadowhunter—and the scratches her own nails had made last night. She felt herself flush, but her mind was still on the question: why would Valentine have whipped one boy to the point of scarring but not the other?

"Jace," she said.

He turned. He was clean. The silvery fluid was gone, and his gold hair was almost bronze-dark, pasted damply to his head. His skin glistened with sweat. The expression on his face was guarded. "Where were you?"

Sebastian went to the wall and began to examine the weapons there, running his bare hand along the blades. "I thought Clary might want to see Paris."

"You could have left me a note," said Jace. "It isn't as if our situation is the safest, Jonathan. I'd rather not have to worry about Clary—"

"I followed him," Clary said.

Jace turned and looked at her, and for a moment she caught a glimpse, in his eyes, of the boy in Idris who had shouted at her for spoiling all his careful plans to keep her safe. But this Jace was different. His hands didn't shake when he looked at her, and the pulse in his throat stayed steady. "You did what?"

"I followed Sebastian," she said. "I was awake and I wanted to see where he was going." She put her hands into her jeans pockets and looked at him defiantly. His eyes took her in, from her wind-mussed hair to her boots, and she felt the blood rise up in her face. Sweat shone along his collarbones, and the ridges of his stomach muscles. His workout pants were folded over at the waist, showing the *V* of his hip bones. She remembered what it had felt like to have his arms around her, to be pressed close enough against him that she could feel every detail of his bones and muscles against her body—

She felt a wave of embarrassment so acute, it was dizzying. What made it worse was that Jace didn't seem in the least bit awkward, or as if the previous night had affected him as much as it had her. He seemed only . . . annoyed. Annoyed, and sweaty, and hot.

"Yeah, well," he said, "the next time you decide to sneak out of our magically warded apartment through a door that shouldn't really exist, leave a note."

She raised her eyebrows. "Are you being sarcastic?"

He threw one of his knives into the air and caught it. "Possibly."

"I took Clary to see Magdalena," Sebastian said. He had taken a throwing star down from the wall and was examining it. "We brought the *adamas*."

Jace had tossed the second knife into the air; he missed catching it this time, and it stuck point-down into the floor. "You did?"

"I did," Sebastian said. "And I told Clary the plan. I told her that we were planning to lure Greater Demons here so we could destroy them."

"But not how you planned to accomplish that," Clary said. "You never told me *that* part."

"I thought it would be better to tell you with Jace here," said Sebastian. He snapped his wrist forward suddenly, and the throwing star flew toward Jace, who blocked it with a swift flick of his knife. It clattered to the ground. Sebastian whistled. "Fast," he commented.

Clary whirled on her brother. "You could have hurt him—"

"Anything that injures him injures me," said Sebastian. "I was showing you how much I trust him. Now I want you to trust *us*." His black eyes bored into her. "*Adamas*," he said. "The stuff I brought to the Iron Sister today. Do you know what's made out of it?"

"Of course. Seraph blades. The demon towers of Alicante. Steles . . ."

"And the Mortal Cup."

Clary shook her head. "The Mortal Cup is gold. I've seen it."

"*Adamas* dipped in gold. The Mortal Sword, too, has a hilt

of the stuff. They say it's the material the palaces of Heaven are built from. And it isn't easy to get hold of. Only the Iron Sisters can work the stuff, and only they're supposed to have access to it."

"So why did you give some to Magdalena?"

"So she could make a second Cup," said Jace.

"A second Mortal Cup?" Clary looked from one of them to the other, incredulous. "But you can't just do that. Just make another Mortal Cup. If you could, the Clave wouldn't have panicked so much when the original Mortal Cup went missing. Valentine wouldn't have needed it so badly—"

"It's a cup," said Jace. "However crafted, it will always be a cup until the Angel voluntarily pours his blood into it. That's what makes it what it is."

"And you think you can get Raziel to voluntarily pour his blood into a second cup for you?" Clary couldn't keep the razor edge of disbelief from her voice. "Good luck."

"It's a trick, Clary," said Sebastian. "You know how everything has an alliance? Seraphic or demonic? What the demons believe is that we want the demonic equivalent of Raziel. A demon great in power who will mix his blood with ours and create a new race of Shadowhunters. Ones not bound by the Law, or the Covenant, or the rules of the Clave."

"You told them you want to make . . . backward Shadowhunters?"

"Something like that." Sebastian laughed, raking fingers through his fair hair. "Jace, do you want to help me explain?"

"Valentine was a zealot," said Jace. "He was wrong about a lot of things. He was wrong to consider killing Shadowhunters. He was wrong about Downworlders. But he wasn't wrong about the Clave or the Council. Every Inquisitor we've had has been corrupt. The Laws handed down by the Angel are arbitrary and nonsensical, and their punishments are worse. 'The Law is hard, but it is the Law.' How many times have you heard that? How many times have we had to duck and avoid the Clave and its Laws even when we were trying to save them? Who put me in prison?—the Inquisitor. Who put *Simon* in prison? The Clave. Who would have let him burn?"

Clary's heart had started to pound. Jace's voice, so familiar, saying these words, made her bones feel weak. He was right and also wrong. As Valentine had been. But she wanted to believe him in a way she hadn't wanted to believe Valentine.

"Fine," she said. "I understand the Clave is corrupt. But I don't see what that has to do with making deals with demons."

"Our mandate is to destroy demons," said Sebastian. "But the Clave has been pouring all its energy into other tasks. The wards have been weakening, and more and more demons have been spilling into earth, but the Clave turns a blind eye. We have opened a gate in the far north, on Wrangel Island, and we will lure demons through it with the promise of this Cup. Only, when they pour their blood into it, they will be destroyed. I have made deals like this with several Greater Demons. When Jace and I have killed them, the Clave will see we are a power to be reckoned with. They will have to listen to us."

Clary stared. "Killing Greater Demons isn't that easy."

"I did it earlier today," said Sebastian. "Which is incidentally why neither of us is going to get in trouble for killing all those bodyguard demons. I killed their master."

Clary looked from Jace to Sebastian and back again. Jace's eyes were cool, interested; Sebastian's gaze was more intense.

It was as if he were trying to see into her head. "Well," she said slowly. "That's a lot to take in. And I don't like the idea of you putting yourselves in that kind of danger. But I'm glad you trusted me enough to tell me."

"I told you," Jace said. "I told you she'd understand."

"I never said she wouldn't." Sebastian didn't take his eyes off Clary's face.

She swallowed hard. "I didn't sleep much last night," she said. "I need to rest."

"Too bad," said Sebastian. "I was going to ask if you wanted to climb the Eiffel Tower." His eyes were dark, unreadable; she couldn't tell if he was joking or not. Before she could say anything in reply, Jace's hand slid into hers.

"I'll go with you," he said. "I didn't sleep that well myself." He nodded at Sebastian. "See you for dinner."

Sebastian made no reply. They were nearly to the steps when Sebastian called out: "Clary."

She turned around, drawing her hand out of Jace's. "What?"

"My scarf." He held out his hand for it.

"Oh. Right." Taking a few steps toward him, she tugged with nervous fingers at the knotted cloth around her throat. After a moment of watching her, Sebastian made an impatient noise and stalked across the room toward her, his long legs covering the space between them quickly. She stiffened as he put his hand to her throat and deftly undid the knot with a few motions, then unwrapped the scarf. She thought for a moment that he lingered before unwrapping it fully, his fingers brushing her throat—

She remembered him kissing her on the hill by the burned remains of the Fairchild manor, and how she had felt as if she were falling, into a dark and abandoned place, lost and terrified. She backed up hastily, and the scarf fell away from her neck as she turned. "Thanks for lending it to me," she said, and darted back to follow Jace down the stairs, not looking behind to see her brother watch her go, holding the scarf, a quizzical expression on his face.

Simon stood among the dead leaves and looked up the path; once more the human impulse to take a deep breath came on him. He was in Central Park, near the Shakespeare Garden. The trees had lost the last of their autumn luster, the gold and green and red turning to brown and black. Most of the branches were bare.

He touched the ring on his finger again. *Clary?*

Again there was no reply. His muscles felt as tense as strung wires. It had been too long since he had been able to raise her using the ring. He told himself over and over that she could be sleeping, but nothing could untie the terrible knot of tension in his stomach. The ring was his only connection to her, and right now it felt like nothing more than a hunk of dead metal.

He dropped his hands to his sides and moved forward, up the path, past the statues and the benches inscribed with verses from Shakespeare's plays. The path turned a curving right, and suddenly he could see her, sitting up ahead on a bench, looking away from him, her dark hair in a long braid down her back. She was very still, waiting. Waiting for him.

Simon straightened his back and walked toward her, even though every step felt as if it were weighted with lead.

She heard him as he approached and turned around, her

pale face going even paler as he sat down beside her. "Simon," she said on an exhale of breath. "I wasn't sure you'd come."

"Hi, Rebecca," he said.

She held out her hand, and he took it, silently thanking the forethought that had made him put on gloves that morning, so that if he touched her she wouldn't feel the chill of his skin. It hadn't been that long since he'd seen her last—maybe four months—but already she seemed like the photograph of someone he'd known a long time ago, even though everything about her was familiar—her dark hair; her brown eyes, the same shape and color as his own; the spatter of freckles across her nose. She wore jeans, a bright yellow parka, and a green scarf with big yellow cotton flowers. Clary called Becky's style "hippie-chic"; about half her clothes came from vintage stores, and the other half she sewed herself.

As he squeezed her hand, her dark eyes filled with tears. "Si," she said, and put her arms around him and hugged him. He let her, patting her arms, her back, clumsily. When she pulled back, wiping at her eyes, she frowned. "God, your face is cold," she said. "You should wear a scarf." She looked at him accusingly. "Anyway, where have you *been?*"

"I told you," he said. "I was staying with a friend."

She gave a short bark of laughter. "Okay, Simon, that so doesn't cut it," she said. "What the hell is going on?"

"Becks . . ."

"I called home about Thanksgiving," Rebecca said, staring straight ahead at the trees. "You know, what train I should take, that sort of thing. And you know what Mom said? She said not to come home, there wasn't going to be any Thanksgiving. So I called you. *You* didn't pick up. I called Mom to find out where you were. She hung up on me. Just—hung up on me. So I came home. That's when I saw the religious weirdness all over the door. I freaked out on Mom, and she told me you were *dead*. Dead. My own brother. She said you were dead and a monster took your place."

"What did you do?"

"I got the hell out of there," said Rebecca. Simon could tell she was trying to sound tough, but there was a thin, frightened edge to her voice. "It was pretty clear Mom had lost it."

"Oh," Simon said. Rebecca and his mother had always shared a fraught relationship. Rebecca liked to refer to his mother as "nuts" or "the crazy lady." But it was the first time he'd had the sense she really meant it.

"Damn right, *oh*," Rebecca snapped. "I was frantic. I texted you every five minutes. Finally I get that crap text from you about staying with a friend. Now you want to meet me here. What the hell, Simon? How long has this been going on?"

"How long has what been going on?"

"What do you think? Mom being totally mental." Rebecca's small fingers picked at her scarf. "We have to do something. Talk to someone. Doctors. Get her on meds or something. I didn't know what to *do*. Not without you. You're my brother."

"I can't," Simon said. "I mean, I can't help you."

Her voice softened. "I know it sucks and you're just in high school, but, Simon, we have to make these decisions together."

"I mean I can't help you get her on meds," he said. "Or take her to the doctor. Because she's right. I am a monster."

Rebecca's mouth dropped open. "Has she brainwashed you?"

"No—"

Her voice wobbled. "You know, I thought maybe she'd *hurt* you—the way she was talking—but then I thought, *No, she'd never do that, no matter what.* But if she did—if she laid a finger on you, Simon, so help me—"

Simon couldn't take it anymore. He stripped off his glove and held his hand out to his sister. His sister, who'd held his hand on the beach when he was too small to toddle into the ocean unassisted. Who'd mopped blood off him after soccer practice, and tears off him after their father had died and their mother was a zombie lying in her room staring at the ceiling. Who'd read to him in his race-car-shaped bed when he still wore footie pajamas. *I am the Lorax. I speak for the trees.* Who once accidentally shrunk all his clothes in the wash so they were doll-size, when she was trying to be domestic. Who packed his lunch when their mother didn't have time. *Rebecca,* he thought. The last tie he had to cut.

"Take my hand," he said.

She took it, and winced. "You're so cold. Have you been sick?"

"You could say that." He looked at her, willing her to sense something wrong with him, *really* wrong, but she only looked back at him with trusting brown eyes. He bit back a flare of impatience. It wasn't her fault. She didn't know. "Take my pulse," he said.

"I don't know how to take someone's pulse, Simon. I'm an art history major."

He reached over and moved her fingers up to his wrist. "Press down. Do you feel anything?"

For a moment she was still, her bangs swinging over her forehead. "No. Am I supposed to?"

"Becky—" He pulled his wrist back in frustration. There

was nothing else for it. There was only one way. "Look at me," he said, and when her eyes swung up to his face, he let his fangs snap out.

She screamed.

She screamed, and fell off the bench onto the hard-packed dirt and leaves. Several passersby looked at them curiously, but it was New York, and they didn't stop or stare, just kept moving.

Simon felt wretched. This was what he'd wanted, but it was different actually looking at her crouching there, so pale that her freckles stood out like ink blots, her hand over her mouth. Just like it had been with his mother. He remembered telling Clary there was no worse feeling than not trusting the people you loved; he'd been wrong. Having the people you loved be afraid of you was worse. "Rebecca," he said, and his voice broke. "Becky—"

She shook her head, her hand still over her mouth. She was sitting in the dirt, her scarf trailing in the leaves. Under other circumstances it might have been funny.

Simon got down off the bench and knelt down next to her. His fangs were gone, but she was looking at him as if they were still there. Very hesitantly he reached out and touched her on the shoulder. "Becks," he said. "I would never hurt you. I would never hurt Mom, either. I just wanted to see you one last time to tell you I'm going away and you won't need to see me again. I'll leave you both alone. You can have Thanksgiving. I won't show up. I won't try to stay in touch. I won't—"

"Simon." She grabbed his arm, and then she was pulling him toward her, like a fish on a line. He half-fell against her, and she hugged him, her arms around him, and the last time she'd hugged him like this was the day of their father's funeral, when he'd cried in that way one cried when it didn't seem like it was ever going to stop. "I don't want to never see you again."

"Oh," Simon said. He sat back in the dirt, so surprised that his mind had gone blank. Rebecca put her arms around him again, and he let himself lean against her, even though she was slighter than he was. She had held him up when they'd been children, and she could do it again. "I thought you wouldn't."

"Why?" she said.

"I'm a vampire," he said. It was weird, hearing it like that, out loud.

"So there are vampires?"

"And werewolves. And other, weirder stuff. This just—happened. I mean, I got attacked. I didn't choose it, but it doesn't matter. This is me now."

"Do you . . ." Rebecca hesitated, and Simon sensed that this was the big question, the one that really mattered. "Bite people?"

He thought about Isabelle, then pushed the mental image hastily away. *And I bit a thirteen-year-old girl. And a dude. It's not as weird as it sounds.* No. Some things were not his sister's business. "I drink blood out of bottles. Animal blood. I don't hurt people."

"Okay." She took a deep breath. "Okay."

"Is it? Okay, I mean?"

"Yeah. I love you," she said. She rubbed his back awkwardly. He felt something damp on his hand and looked down. She was crying. One of her tears had splashed onto his fingers. Another one followed, and he closed his hand around it. He was shivering, but not from cold; still, she pulled off her scarf and wrapped it around them both. "We'll figure it out," she said. "You're my little brother, you dumb idiot. I love you no matter what."

They sat together, shoulder to shoulder, looking off into the shadowy spaces between the trees.

It was bright in Jace's bedroom, midday sunlight pouring through the open windows. The moment Clary walked in, the heels of her boots clicking on the hardwood floor, Jace closed the door and locked it behind her. There was a clatter as he dropped the knives onto his bedside table. She began to turn, to ask him if he was all right, when he caught her around the waist and pulled her against him.

The boots gave her extra height, but he still had to bend down to kiss her. His hands, on her waist, lifted her up and against him—a second later his mouth was on hers and she forgot all issues of height and awkwardness. He tasted like salt and fire. She tried to shut out everything but sensation—the familiar smell of his skin and sweat, the chill of his damp hair against her cheek, the shape of his shoulders and back under her hands, the way her body fit to his.

He pulled her sweater over her head. Her T-shirt was short-sleeved, and she felt the heat coming off him against her skin. His lips parted hers, and she felt herself coming apart as his hand slid down to the top button on her jeans.

It took all the self-control she had to catch at his wrist with her hand, and hold it still. "Jace," she said. "Don't."

He drew away, enough for her to see his face. His eyes were glassy, unfocused. His heart pounded against hers. "Why?"

She squeezed her eyes shut. "Last night—if we hadn't—if I hadn't fainted, then I don't know what would have happened, and we were in the middle of a room full of people. Do you really think I want my first time with you—or *any* time with you—to be in front of a bunch of strangers?"

"That wasn't our fault," he said, pushing his fingers softly through her hair. The scarred palm of his hand scratched her cheek lightly. "That silver stuff was faerie drugs, I told you. We were high. But I'm sober now, and you're sober now . . ."

"And Sebastian's upstairs, and I'm exhausted, and . . ." *And this would be a terrible, terrible idea that both of us would regret.* "And I don't feel like it," she lied.

"You don't feel like it?" Disbelief colored his voice.

"I'm sorry if no one's ever said that to you before, Jace, but, no. I don't feel like it." She looked pointedly down at his hand, still at the waistband of her jeans. "And now I feel like it even less."

He raised both eyebrows, but instead of saying anything he simply let go of her.

"Jace . . ."

"I'm going to go take a cold shower," he said, backing away from her. His face was blank, unreadable. When the bathroom door slammed shut behind him, she walked over to the bed—neatly made up, no residual silver on the coverlet—and sank down, putting her head in her hands. It wasn't as if she and Jace never fought; she'd always thought they argued about as much as normal couples did, usually good-naturedly, and they'd never been angry with each other in any significant way. But there was something about the coldness at the back of this Jace's eyes that shook her, something far off and unreachable that made it harder than ever to push away the question always at the back of her mind: *Is any of the real Jace still in there? Is there anything left to save?*

***

Now this is the Law of the Jungle,
as old and as true as the sky,
And the Wolf that shall keep it may prosper,
but the Wolf that shall break it must die.
As the creeper that girdles the tree trunk,
the Law runneth forward and back;
For the strength of the Pack is the Wolf,
and the strength of the Wolf is the Pack.

Jordan stared blindly at the poem tacked to the wall of his bedroom. It was an old print that he'd found in a used-book store, the words surrounded by an elaborate border of leaves. The poem was by Rudyard Kipling, and it so neatly encapsulated the rules by which werewolves lived, the Law that bound their actions, that he wondered if Kipling hadn't been a Downworlder himself, or at least known about the Accords. Jordan had felt compelled to buy the print and stick it up on his wall, though he'd never been one for poetry.

He'd been pacing his apartment for the last hour, sometimes taking his phone out to see if Maia had texted, in between bouts of opening the refrigerator and staring into it to see if anything worth eating had appeared. It hadn't, but he didn't want to go out to get food in case she came to the apartment while he was out. He also took a shower, cleaned up the kitchen, tried to watch TV and failed, and started the process of organizing all his DVDs by color.

He was restless. Restless in the way he sometimes got before the full moon, knowing the Change was coming, feeling the pull of the tides in his blood. But the moon was waning, not waxing, and it wasn't the Change making him feel like crawling out of his skin. It was Maia. It was being without her, after almost two solid days in her company, never more than a few feet away from her.

She'd gone without him to the police station, saying that now wasn't the time to upset the pack with a nonmember, even though Luke was healing. There was no need for Jordan to come, she'd argued, since all she had to do was ask Luke if it was all right for Simon and Magnus to visit the farm tomorrow, and then she'd call up to the farm and warn any of the pack who might be staying up there to clear off the property. She was right, Jordan knew. There *was* no reason for him to go with her, but the moment she was gone, the restlessness kicked up inside him. Was she leaving because she was sick of being with him? Had she rethought and decided she'd been right about him before? And what was going on between them? Were they dating? *Maybe you should have asked her before you slept together, genius*, he told himself, and realized he was standing in front of the refrigerator again. Its contents hadn't changed—bottles of blood, a defrosting pound of ground beef, and a dented apple.

The key turned in the front door lock, and he jumped away from the refrigerator, spinning around. He looked down at himself. He was barefoot, in jeans and an old T-shirt. Why hadn't he taken the time while she'd been away to shave, look better, put on some cologne or *something*? He ran his hands quickly through his hair as Maia came into the living room, dropping his spare set of keys onto the coffee table. She had changed clothes, into a soft pink sweater and jeans. Her cheeks were pink from the cold, her lips red and her eyes bright. He wanted to kiss her so badly it hurt.

Instead he swallowed. "So—how did it go?"

"Fine. Magnus can use the farm. I already texted him." She strolled over to him and leaned her elbows on the counter. "I also told Luke what Raphael said about Maureen. I hope that's okay."

Jordan was puzzled. "Why'd you think he needed to know?"

She seemed to deflate. "Oh, God. Don't tell me I was supposed to keep it a secret."

"No—I was just wondering—"

"Well, if there really is a rogue vampire cutting her way through Lower Manhattan, the pack should know. It's their territory. Besides, I wanted his advice about whether we should tell Simon or not."

"What about *my* advice?" He was playing at sounding hurt, but there was a little part of him that meant it. They'd discussed it before, whether Jordan should tell his assignment that Maureen was out there and killing, or whether it would just be another burden to add to everything Simon was dealing with now. Jordan had come down on the side of not telling him—what could he do about it, anyway?—but Maia hadn't been so sure.

She jumped up on top of the counter and swung around to face him. Even sitting down, she was taller than him this way, her brown eyes sparkling down into his. "I wanted *grown-up* advice."

He grabbed hold of her swinging legs and ran his hands up the seams of her jeans. "I'm eighteen—not grown-up enough for you?"

She put her hands on his shoulders and flexed them, as if testing his muscles. "Well, you've definitely *grown* . . ."

He pulled her down from the counter, catching her around the waist and kissing her. Fire sizzled up and down his veins as she kissed him back, her body melting against his. He slid his hands up into her hair, knocking her knitted cap off and letting her curls spring free. He kissed her neck as she pulled his shirt up over his head and ran her hands all over him—shoulders, back, arms, purring in her throat like a cat. He felt like a helium balloon—high from kissing her, and light with relief. So she wasn't done with him after all.

"Jordy," she said. "Wait."

She almost never called him that, unless it was serious. His heartbeat, already wild, speeded up further. "What's wrong?"

"It's just—if every time we see each other, we fall into bed—and I know I started it, I'm not blaming you or anything— It's just that maybe we should *talk*."

He stared at her, at her big dark eyes, the fluttery pulse in her throat, the flush on her cheeks. With an effort he spoke evenly. "Okay. What do you want to talk about?"

She just looked at him. After a moment she shook her head and said, "Nothing." She locked her hands behind his head and pulled him close, kissing him hard, fitting her body against his. "Nothing at all."

Clary didn't know how long it was before Jace came out of the bathroom, toweling off his wet hair. She looked up at him from where she was still sitting on the edge of the bed. He was sliding a blue cotton T-shirt on over smooth golden skin marked with white scars.

She darted her eyes away as he came across the room and sat down next to her on the bed, smelling strongly of soap.

"I'm sorry," he said.

Now she did look at him, in surprise. She had wondered if he were capable of being sorry, in his current state. His expression was grave, a little curious, but not insincere.

"Wow," she said. "That cold shower must have been brutal."

His lips quirked up at the side, but his expression grew serious again almost immediately. He put his hand under her chin. "I shouldn't have pushed you. It's just—ten weeks ago, just holding each other would have been unthinkable."

"I know."

He cupped her face in his hands, his long fingers cool against her cheeks, tilting her face up. He was looking down at her, and everything about him was so familiar—the pale gold irises of his eyes, the scar on his cheek, the full lower lip, the slight chip in his tooth that saved his looks from being so perfect that they were annoying—and yet somehow it was like coming back to a house she had lived in as a child, and knowing that though the exterior might look the same, a different family lived there now. "I never cared," he said. "I wanted you anyway. I always wanted you. Nothing mattered to me but you. Not ever."

Clary swallowed. Her stomach fluttered, not just with the usual butterflies she felt around Jace but with real uneasiness. "But Jace. That's not true. You cared about your family. And—I always thought you were proud of being Nephilim. One of the angels."

"Proud?" he said. "To be half angel, half human—you're always conscious of your own inadequacy. You're not an angel. You're not beloved of Heaven. Raziel doesn't care about us. We can't even pray to him. We pray to nothing. We pray *for* nothing.

Remember when I told you I thought I had demon blood, because it explained why I felt the way I did about you? It was a relief in a way, thinking that. I've never been an angel, never even close. Well," he added. "Maybe the fallen kind."

"Fallen angels are demons."

"I don't want to be Nephilim," said Jace. "I want to be something else. Stronger, faster, better than human. But different. Not subservient to the Laws of an angel who couldn't care less about us. Free." He ran his hand through a curl of her hair. "I'm happy now, Clary. Doesn't that make a difference?"

"I thought we were happy together," Clary said.

"I've always been happy with you," he said. "But I never thought I deserved it."

"And now you do?"

"And now that feeling's gone," he said. "All I know is that I love you. And for the first time, that's good enough."

She closed her eyes. A moment later he was kissing her again, very softly this time, his mouth tracing the shape of hers. She felt herself go pliant under his hands. She sensed it as his breathing quickened and her own pulse jumped. His hands stroked down through her hair, over her back, to her waist. His touch was comforting—the feel of his heartbeat against hers like familiar music—and if the key was slightly different, with her eyes closed, she couldn't tell. Their blood was the same, under the skin, she thought, as the Seelie Queen had said; her heart raced when his did, had nearly stopped when his had. If she had to do it all again, she thought, under the pitiless gaze of Raziel, she would have done the same thing.

This time he drew back, letting his fingers linger on her

cheek, her lips. "I want what you want," he said. "Whenever you want it."

Clary felt a shudder go down her spine. The words were simple, but there was a dangerous and seductive invitation to the fall of his voice: *Whatever you want, whenever you want it.* His hand smoothed down her hair, to her back, lingering at her waist. She swallowed. There was only so much that she was going to be able to hold back.

"Read to me," she said suddenly.

He blinked down at her. "What?"

She was looking past him, at the books on his nightstand. "It's a lot to process," she said. "What Sebastian said, what happened last night, everything. I need to sleep, but I'm too keyed up. When I was young and I couldn't sleep, my mother used to read to me to relax me."

"And I remind you of your mother now? I have got to look into a manlier cologne."

"No, it's just— I thought it would be nice."

He scooted back against the pillows, reaching for the stack of books by the bed. "Anything particular you want to hear?" With a flourish he picked up the book on top of the stack. It looked old, leather-bound, the title stamped in gold on the front. *A Tale of Two Cities*. "Dickens is always promising . . ."

"I've read that before. For school," Clary recalled. She scooted up on the pillows beside Jace. "But I don't remember any of it, so I wouldn't mind hearing it again."

"Excellent. I've been told I have a lovely, melodic reading voice." He flipped the book open to the front page, where the title was printed in ornate script. Across from it was a long dedication, the ink faded now and barely legible, though Clary could make out the signature: *With hope at last, William Herondale.*

"Some ancestor of yours," Clary said, brushing her finger against the page.

"Yes. Odd that Valentine had it. My father must have given it to him." Jace opened to a random page and began to read:

"He unshaded his face after a little while, and spoke steadily. 'Don't be afraid to hear me. Don't shrink from anything I say. I am like one who died young. All my life might have been.'

"'No, Mr. Carton. I am sure that the best part of it might still be; I am sure that you might be much, much worthier of yourself.'"

"Oh, I do remember this story now," Clary said. "Love triangle. She picks the boring guy."

Jace chuckled softly. "Boring to you. Who can say what got Victorian ladies hot beneath the petticoats?"

"It's true, you know."

"What, about the petticoats?"

"No. That you have a lovely reading voice." Clary turned her face against his shoulder. It was times like this, more than when he was kissing her, that hurt—times when he could have been her Jace. As long as she kept her eyes closed.

"All that, and abs of steel," Jace said, turning another page. "What more could you ask for?"

17

Valediction

As I strolled down along the quay
All in the lateness of the day
I heard a lovely maiden say:
"Alack, for I can get no play."
A minstrel boy heard what she said
And straight he rushed to her aid . . .

"Do we have to keep listening to this wail-ey music?" Isabelle demanded, her booted foot tapping against the dashboard of Jordan's truck.

"I happen to like this wail-ey music, my girl, and since I'm driving, *I* get to choose," Magnus said loftily. He was indeed driving. Simon had been surprised that he knew how, though he wasn't sure why. Magnus had been alive for ages. Surely he had found time to squeeze in a few weeks of driver's ed. Although Simon couldn't help wondering what birth date was on his license.

Isabelle rolled her eyes, probably because there wasn't enough room to do much else in the cab of the truck, with all four of them crammed together on the bench seat. Simon honestly hadn't expected her to come. He hadn't expected anyone to come to the farm with him but Magnus, though Alec had insisted on coming as well (much to Magnus's annoyance, as he considered the whole enterprise "too dangerous"), and then, just as Magnus had revved up the engine on the truck, Isabelle had come banging down the stairs of his apartment building and thrown herself through the front door, panting and out of breath. "I'm coming too," she'd announced.

And that was that. No one could budge or dissuade her. She wouldn't look at Simon as she insisted, or explain why she wanted to come, but she did, and here she was. She was wearing jeans and a purple suede jacket she must have stolen out of Magnus's closet. Her weapons belt was slung around her slim hips. She was mashed up against Simon, whose other side was crushed against the car door. A strand of her hair was flying free and tickling his face.

"What is this, anyway?" Alec said, frowning at the CD player, which was playing music, although without a CD in it. Magnus had simply tapped the sound system with a blue-flashing finger, and it had started playing. "Some faerie band?"

Magnus didn't answer, but the music swelled louder.

To mirror went she straightaway
And did her ebon hair array

And for her gown she much did pay.
Then down she walked along the street,
A handsome lad she chanced to meet,
And sore by dawn were her dainty feet,
But all the boys were gay.

Isabelle snorted. "All the boys *are* gay. In this truck, anyway. Well, not you, Simon."

"You noticed," said Simon.

"I think of myself as a freewheeling bisexual," added Magnus.

"Please never say those words in front of my parents," said Alec. "Especially my father."

"I thought your parents were okay with you, you know, coming out," Simon said, leaning around Isabelle to look at Alec, who was—as he often was—scowling, and pushing his floppy dark hair out of his eyes. Aside from the occasional exchange, Simon had never talked to Alec much. He wasn't an easy person to get to know. But, Simon admitted to himself, his own recent estrangement from his mother made him more curious about Alec's answer than he would have been otherwise.

"My mother seems to have accepted it," Alec said. "But my father—no, not really. Once he asked me what I thought had turned me gay."

Simon felt Isabelle tense next to him. "*Turned* you gay?" She sounded incredulous. "Alec, you didn't tell me that."

"I hope you told him you were bitten by a gay spider," said Simon.

Magnus snorted; Isabelle looked confused. "I've read Magnus's stash of comics," said Alec, "so I actually know what you're talking about." A small smile played around his mouth. "So would that give me the proportional gayness of a spider?"

"Only if it was a *really* gay spider," said Magnus, and he yelled as Alec punched him in the arm. "Ow, okay, never mind."

"Well, whatever," said Isabelle, obviously annoyed not to get the joke. "It's not like Dad's ever coming back from Idris, anyway."

Alec sighed. "Sorry to wreck your vision of our happy family. I know you want to think Dad's fine with me being gay, but he's not."

"But if you don't *tell* me when people say things like that to you, or do things to hurt you, then how can I help you?" Simon could feel Isabelle's agitation vibrating through her body. "How can I—"

"Iz," Alec said tiredly. "It's not like it's one big bad thing. It's a lot of little invisible things. When Magnus and I were traveling, and I'd call from the road, Dad never asked how he was. When I get up to talk in Clave meetings, no one listens, and I don't know if that's because I'm young or if it's because of something else. I saw Mom talking to a friend about her grandchildren and the second I walked into the room they shut up. Irina Cartwright told me it was a pity no one would ever inherit my blue eyes now." He shrugged and looked toward Magnus, who took a hand off the wheel for a moment to place it on Alec's. "It's not like a stab wound you can protect me from. It's a million little paper cuts every day."

"Alec," Isabelle began, but before she could say anything more, the sign for the turnoff loomed up ahead: a wooden placard in the shape of an arrow with the words THREE ARROWS FARM painted on it in block lettering. Simon remembered Luke kneeling on the farmhouse floor, painstakingly spelling out the words in black paint, while Clary added the—now weather-faded and almost invisible—pattern of flowers along the bottom.

"Turn left," he said, flinging his arm out and nearly hitting Alec. "Magnus, we're here."

It had taken several chapters of Dickens before Clary had finally succumbed to exhaustion and fallen asleep against Jace's shoulder. Half in dream and half in reality, she recalled him carrying her downstairs and laying her down in the bedroom she'd woken up in her first day in the apartment. He had drawn the curtains and closed the door after him as he left, shutting the room into darkness, and she had fallen asleep to the sound of his voice in the hallway, calling for Sebastian.

She dreamed of the frozen lake again, and of Simon crying out for her, and of a city like Alicante, but the demon towers were made of human bones and the canals ran with blood. She woke twisted in her sheets, her hair a mass of tangles. At first she thought that the voices outside her door were part of the dream, but as they grew louder, she raised her head to listen, still groggy and half-tangled in the webbing of sleep.

"Hey, little brother." It was Sebastian's voice, floating under her door from the living room. "Is it done?"

There was a long silence. Then Jace's voice, oddly flat and colorless. "It's done."

Sebastian's breath drew in sharply. "And the old lady—she did as we asked? Made the Cup?"

"Yes."

"Show it to me."

A rustle. Silence. Jace said, "Look, take it if you want it."

"No." There was a curious thoughtfulness in Sebastian's tone. "You hold on to it for the moment. You did the work of getting it back, after all. Didn't you?"

"But it was your plan." There was something in Jace's voice, something that made Clary lean forward and press her ear to the wall, suddenly desperate to hear more. "And I executed it, just as you wanted. Now, if you don't mind—"

"I do mind." There was a rustle. Clary imagined Sebastian standing up, looking down at Jace from the inch or so that divided them in height. "There's something wrong. I can tell. I can read you, you know."

"I'm tired. And there was a lot of blood. Look, I just need to clean myself off, and to sleep. And . . ." Jace's voice died.

"And to see my sister."

"I'd like to see her, yes."

"She's asleep. Has been for hours."

"Do I need to ask your permission?" There was a razored edge to Jace's voice, something that reminded Clary of the way he had once spoken to Valentine. Something she had not heard in the way he spoke to Sebastian in a long time.

"No." Sebastian sounded surprised, almost caught off guard. "I suppose if you want to barge in there and gaze wistfully at her sleeping face, go right ahead. I'll never understand why—"

"No," Jace said. "You never will."

There was silence. Clary could so clearly picture Sebastian staring after Jace, a quizzical look on his face, that it took her a moment before she realized that Jace must be coming to her room. She had only time to throw herself flat on the bed and shut her eyes before the door opened, letting in a slice of yellow-white light that momentarily blinded her. She made what she hoped was a realistic waking-up noise and rolled over, her hand over her face. "What . . . ?"

The door shut. The room was in darkness again. She could see Jace only as a shape that moved slowly toward her bed, until he was standing over her, and she couldn't help remembering another night when he had come to her room while she slept. *Jace standing by the head of her bed, still wearing his white mourning clothes, and there was nothing light or sarcastic or distant in the way he was looking down at her. "I've been wandering around all night—I couldn't sleep—and I kept finding myself walking here. To you."*

He was only an outline now, an outline with bright hair that shone in the faint light that filtered from beneath the door. "Clary," he whispered. There was a thump, and she realized he had fallen to his knees by the side of her bed. She didn't move, but her body tightened. His voice was a whisper. "Clary, it's me. It's *me*."

Her eyelids fluttered open, wide, and their gazes met. She was staring at Jace. Kneeling beside her bed, his eyes were level with hers. He wore a long dark woolen coat, buttoned all the way to the throat, where she could see black Marks—Soundless, Agility, Accuracy—like a sort of necklace against his skin. His eyes were very gold and very wide, and as if she could see through them, she saw *Jace*—her Jace. The Jace who had lifted her in his arms when she was dying of Ravener poison; the Jace who had watched her hold Simon against the rising daylight over the East River; the Jace who had told her about a little boy and the falcon his father had killed. The Jace she loved.

Her heart seemed to stop altogether. She couldn't even gasp.

His eyes were full of urgency and pain. "Please," he murmured. "Please believe me."

She believed him. They carried the same blood, loved the same way; this was *her* Jace, as much as her hands were her own hands, her heart her own heart. But—"*How?*"

"Clary, shh—"

She began to struggle into a sitting position, but he reached out and pushed her back against the bed by her shoulders. "We can't talk now. I have to go."

She grabbed for his sleeve, felt him wince. "*Don't leave me.*"

He dropped his head for just a moment; when he looked up again, his eyes were dry but the expression in them silenced her. "Wait a few moments after I go," he whispered. "Then slip out and up to my room. Sebastian can't know we're together. Not tonight." He dragged himself to his feet, his eyes pleading. "Don't let him hear you."

She sat up. "Your stele. Leave me your stele."

Doubt flickered in his eyes; she held his gaze steadily, then put her hand out. After a moment he reached into his pocket and took out the dully glowing implement; he laid it in her palm. For a moment their skin touched, and she shuddered—just a brush of the hand from this Jace was almost as powerful as all the kissing and tearing at each other they had done in the club the other night. She knew he felt it too, for he jerked his hand away and began to back toward the door. She could hear his breath, ragged and swift. He fumbled behind himself for the knob and let himself out, his eyes on her face until the very last moment, when the door closed between them with a decided *click*.

Clary sat in the darkness, stunned. Her blood felt as if it had thickened in her veins and her heart was having to work double time to keep beating. *Jace. My Jace.*

Her hand tightened on the stele. Something about it, its cold hardness, seemed to focus and sharpen her thoughts. She looked down at herself. She was wearing a tank top and pajama shorts; there were goose bumps on her arms, but not because it was cold. She set the tip of the stele to her inner arm and drew it slowly down the skin, watching as a Soundless rune spiraled across her pale, blue-veined skin.

She opened the door just a crack. Sebastian was gone, off to sleep most likely. There was music playing faintly from the television set—something classical, the sort of piano music Jace liked. She wondered if Sebastian appreciated music, or any sort of art. It seemed such a *human* capacity.

Despite her concern about where he'd gone, her feet were carrying her toward the passage that led to the kitchen—and then she was through the living room and dashing up the glass steps, her feet making no noise as she reached the top and sprinted down the hall to Jace's room. Then she was jerking open the door and sliding inside, the door clicking shut behind her.

The windows were open, and through them she could see rooftops and a curving slice of moon, a perfect Paris night. Jace's witchlight rune-stone sat on the nightstand beside his bed. It glowed with a dull energy that cast further illumination through the room. It was enough light for Clary to see Jace, standing between the two long windows. He had shrugged off the long black coat, which lay in a crumpled heap at his feet. She realized immediately why he had not taken it off when he'd come into the house, why he had kept it buttoned all the way to his throat. Because beneath it he wore only a gray button-down shirt, and jeans—and they were sticky and soaked with blood. Parts of the shirt were in ribbons, as if they had been slashed with a very sharp blade. His left sleeve was rolled up, and there was a white bandage wrapped around his forearm—he must have just done it—already darkening at the edges with blood. His feet were bare, his shoes kicked off, and the floor where he stood was splattered with blood, like scarlet tears. She set the stele down on his bedside table with a click.

"Jace," she said softly.

It suddenly seemed insane that there was this much space between them, that she was standing across the room from Jace, and that they weren't touching. She started toward him, but he held up a hand to ward her off.

"Don't." His voice cracked.Then his fingers went to the buttons on his shirt, undoing them, one by one. He shrugged the bloodstained garment off his shoulders and let it fall to the ground.

Clary stared. Lilith's rune was still in place, over his heart, but instead of shimmering red-silver it looked as if the hot tip of a poker had been dragged across the skin, charring it. She put her hand up to her own chest involuntarily, her fingers splaying over her heart. She could feel its beating, hard and fast. "Oh."

"Yeah. Oh," Jace said flatly. "This won't last, Clary. Me being myself again, I mean. Only as long as this hasn't healed."

"I—I wondered," Clary stammered. "Before—while you were sleeping—I thought about cutting the rune like I did when we fought Lilith. But I was afraid Sebastian would feel it."

"He would have." Jace's golden eyes were as flat as his voice. "He didn't feel this because it was made with a *pugio*—a dagger seethed in angel blood. They're incredibly rare; I've never even seen one in real life before." He ran his fingers through his hair. "The blade turned to hot ash after it touched me, but it did the damage it needed to do."

"You were in a fight. Was it a demon? Why didn't Sebastian go with—"

"Clary." Jace's voice was barely a whisper. "This—it'll take longer than an ordinary cut to heal . . . but not forever. And then I'll be *him* again."

"How much time? Before you go back to the way you were?"

"I don't know. I just don't know. But I wanted—I *needed* to be with you, like this, like myself, for as long as I could." He held out a hand to her stiffly, as if unsure of its reception. "Do you think you could—"

She was already running across the room to him. She threw her arms around his neck. He caught her and swung her up, burying his face in the crook of her neck. She breathed him in like air. He smelled of blood and sweat and ashes and Marks.

"It's you," she whispered. "It's really you."

He drew back to look at her. With his free hand he traced her cheekbone gently. She had missed that, his gentleness. It was one of the things that had made her fall in love with him in the first place—realizing that this scarred, sarcastic boy was gentle with the things he loved.

"I missed you," she said. "I missed you so much."

He closed his eyes as if the words hurt. She put her hand to his cheek. He leaned his head into her palm, his hair tickling her knuckles, and she realized his face was wet too.

The boy never cried again.

"It's not your fault," she said. She kissed his cheek with the same tenderness he had showed her. She tasted salt—blood and tears. He still hadn't spoken, but she could feel the wild beat of his heart against her chest. His arms were tight around her, as if he never meant to let go. She kissed his cheekbone, his jaw, and finally his mouth, a light press of lips on lips.

There was none of the frenzy there had been in the nightclub. It was a kiss meant to give solace, to say everything there was no time to say. He kissed her back, hesitant at first, then with greater urgency, his hand stealing up into her hair, winding the tresses between his fingers. Their kisses deepened slowly, softly, the intensity growing between them as it always did, like a blaze that started with a single match and flared into wildfire.

She knew how strong he was, but she still felt a shock as he carried her to the bed and laid her down gently among the scattered pillows, sliding his body over hers, one smooth gesture that reminded her what all those Marks on his body were *for*. Strength. Grace. Lightness of touch. She breathed his breath as they kissed, each kiss drawn out now, lingering, exploratory. Her hands drifted over him, his shoulders, the muscles of his arms, his back. His bare skin felt like hot silk under her palms.

When his hands found the hem of her tank top, she stretched her arms out, arching her back, wanting every barrier between them gone. The moment it was off, she pulled him back against her, their kisses fiercer now, as if they were struggling to reach some hidden place inside each other. She wouldn't have thought they could get any closer, but somehow as they kissed, they wound themselves into each other like intricate thread, each kiss hungrier, deeper than the last.

Their hands moved quickly over each other, and then more slowly, uncovering and unhurried. She dug her fingers into his shoulders when he kissed her throat, her collarbones, the star-shaped mark on her shoulder. She grazed his scar too, with the backs of her knuckles, and kissed the wounded Mark Lilith had made on his chest. She felt him shudder, wanting her, and she knew she was on the very brink of where there was no going back, and she didn't care. She knew what it was like to lose him now. She knew the black empty days that came after. And she knew that if she lost him again, she wanted this to remember. To hold on to. That she had been as close to him once as you could be to another person. She locked her ankles around the small of his back, and he groaned against her mouth, a soft, low, helpless sound. His fingers dug into her hips.

"Clary." He pulled away. He was shaking. "I can't . . . If we don't stop now, we won't be able to."

"Don't you want to?" She looked up at him in surprise. He was flushed, tousled, his fair hair a darker gold where sweat had pasted it to his forehead and temples. She could feel his heart stuttering inside his chest.

"Yes, it's just I've never—"

"You haven't?" She was surprised. "Done this before?"

He took a deep breath. "I have." His eyes searched her face, as if he were looking for judgment, disapprobation, even disgust. Clary looked back at him evenly. It was what she had assumed, anyway. "But not when it mattered." He touched her cheek with his fingers, feather-light. "I don't even know how . . ."

Clary laughed softly. "I think it's just been established that you do."

"That's not what I meant." He caught her hand and brought it to his face. "I want you," he said, "more than I have ever wanted anything in my life. But I . . ." He swallowed. "Name of the Angel. I'm going to kick myself for this later."

"Don't say you're trying to protect me," she said fiercely. "Because I—"

"It's not that," he said. "I'm not being self-sacrificing. I'm . . . jealous."

"You're—jealous? Of who?"

"Myself." His face twisted. "I hate the thought of him being with you. *Him.* That other me. The one Sebastian controls."

She felt her face start to burn. "At the club . . . last night . . ."

He dropped his head to her shoulder. A little bewildered, she stroked his back, feeling the scratches where her fingernails had torn his skin at the nightclub. The specific memory made her blush even harder. So did the knowledge that he could have gotten rid of the scratches with an *iratze* if he'd wanted to. But he hadn't. "I remember *everything* about last night," he said. "And it makes me crazy, because it was me but it wasn't. When we're together, I want it to be the real you. The real me."

"Isn't that what we are now?"

"Yes." He raised his head, kissed her mouth. "But for how long? I could turn back into *him* any minute. I couldn't do that to you. To us." His voice was bitter. "I don't even know how you can stand it, being around this *thing* that isn't me—"

"Even if you go back to being that in five minutes," she said, "it would have been worth it, just to be with you like this again. Not to have it end on that rooftop. Because this is you, and even that other you—there's pieces of the real you in there. It's like I'm looking through a blurred window at you, but it's *not* the real you. And at least I know now."

"What do you mean?" His hands tightened on her shoulders. "What do you mean at least you know?"

She took a deep breath. "Jace, when we were first together, like really *together*, you were so happy for that first month. And everything we did together was funny and fun and amazing. And then it was like it just started draining out of you, all that happiness. You didn't want to be with me or look at me—"

"I was afraid I was going to *hurt* you. I thought I was losing my mind."

"You didn't smile or laugh or joke. And I'm not blaming you. Lilith was creeping into your mind, controlling you. Changing you. But you have to remember—I know how stupid this sounds—I never had a boyfriend before. I thought maybe it was normal. That maybe you were just getting tired of me."

"I couldn't—"

"I'm not asking for reassurance," she said. "I'm telling you. When you're—like you are, controlled—you seem *happy*. I came here because I wanted to save you." Her voice dropped. "But I started to wonder what I was saving you from. How I could bring you back to a life you seemed so unhappy with."

"Unhappy?" He shook his head. "I was lucky. So, so lucky. And I couldn't see it." His eyes met hers. "I love you," he said. "And you make me happier than I ever thought I could be. And now that I know what it's like to be someone else—to lose myself—I want my life back. My family. You. All of it." His eyes darkened. "I want it *back*."

His mouth came down on hers, with bruising pressure, their lips open, hot and hungry, and his hands gripped her waist—and then the sheets on either side of her, almost tearing them. He pulled back, panting. "We *can't*—"

"Then quit kissing me!" she gasped. "In fact—" She ducked

out from under his grip, grabbing for her tank top. "I'll be right back."

She pushed past him and darted into the bathroom, locking the door behind her. She flicked on the light, and stared at herself in the mirror. She looked wild-eyed, her hair tangled, her lips swollen from kisses. She blushed and pulled her top back on, splashing cold water on her face, twisting her hair back into a knot. When she had convinced herself she no longer looked like the ravished maiden from the cover of a romance novel, she went for the hand towels—nothing romantic about *that*—grabbing one and wetting it down, then rubbing it with soap.

She came back out into the bedroom. Jace was sitting on the edge of the bed, in jeans and a clean, unbuttoned shirt, his tousled hair outlined by moonlight. He looked like a statue of an angel. Only, angels weren't usually streaked with blood.

She moved to stand in front of him. "All right," she said. "Take off your shirt."

Jace raised his eyebrows.

"I'm not going to attack you," she said impatiently. "I can take the sight of your naked chest without swooning."

"Are you sure?" he asked, obediently sliding the shirt off his shoulders. "Because viewing my naked chest has caused many women to seriously injure themselves stampeding to get to me."

"Yeah, well, I don't see anyone here but me. And I just want to clean the blood off you." He leaned back obediently on his hands. Blood had soaked through the shirt he'd been wearing and streaked his chest and the flat planes of his stomach, but as she ran her fingers carefully over him, she could feel that most of his cuts were shallow. If he had used an *iratze*, they'd probably already have faded.

He turned his face up to her, eyes shut, as she ran the damp washcloth over his skin, blood pinking the white cotton. She scrubbed at the dried streaks on his neck, wrung out the cloth, dunked it in the glass of water on the nightstand, and went to work on his chest. He sat with his head tilted back, watching her as the cloth glided over the muscles of his shoulders, the smooth line of arms, forearms, hard chest scarred with white lines, the black of permanent Marks.

"Clary," he said.

"Yes?"

The humor had gone from his voice. "I won't remember this," he said. "When I'm back—like I was, under *his* control, I won't remember being myself. I won't remember being with you, or talking to you like this. So just tell me—are they all right? My family? Do they know—"

"What's happened to you? A little. And no, they're not all right." His eyes closed. "I could lie to you," she said. "But you should know. They love you so much, and they want you back."

"Not like this," he said.

She touched his shoulder. "Are you going to tell me what happened? How you got these cuts?"

He took a deep breath, and the scar on his chest stood out, livid and dark. "I killed someone."

She felt the shock of his words go through her body like the recoil of a gun. She dropped the bloody towel, then bent down to retrieve it. When she looked up, he was staring down at her. In the moonlight the lines of his face were fine and sharp and sad. "Who?" she asked.

"You met her," Jace went on, each word like a weight. "The woman you went to visit with Sebastian. The Iron Sister. Magdalena." He twisted away from her and reached back to retrieve something tangled among the blankets of the bed. The muscles in his arms and back moved under the skin as he took hold of it and turned back to Clary, the object gleaming in his hand.

It was a clear, glassine chalice—an exact replica of the Mortal Cup, except that instead of being gold, it was carved of silvery-white *adamas*.

"Sebastian sent me—sent *him*—to get this from her tonight," Jace said. "And he also gave me the order to kill her. She wasn't expecting it. She wasn't expecting any violence, just payment and exchange. She thought we were on the same side. I let her hand me the Cup, and then I took my dagger and I—" He inhaled sharply, as if the memory hurt. "I stabbed her. I meant it to be through the heart, but she turned and I missed by inches. She staggered back and grabbed for her worktable—there was powdered *adamas* on it—she threw it at me. I think she meant to blind me. I turned my head away, and when I looked back she had an *aegis* in her hand. I think I knew what it was. The light of it seared my eyes. I cried out as she drove it toward my chest—I felt a searing pain in the Mark, and then the blade shattered." He looked down and gave a mirthless laugh. "The funny thing is, if I'd been wearing gear, this wouldn't have happened. I didn't because I didn't think it was worth the bother. I didn't think she could hurt me. But the *aegis* burned the Mark—Lilith's Mark—and suddenly I was back in myself, standing there over this dead woman with a bloody dagger in my hand and the Cup in the other."

"I don't understand. Why did Sebastian tell you to kill her? She was going to *give* the Cup to you. To Sebastian. She said—"

Jace expelled a ragged breath. "Do you remember what Sebastian said about that clock in Old Town Square? In Prague?"

"That the king had the clock maker's eyes put out after he made it, so he could never make anything as beautiful again," Clary said. "But I don't see—"

"Sebastian wanted Magdalena dead so she could never make anything like this again," said Jace. "And so she could never tell."

"Tell what?" She put her hand up, took hold of Jace's chin, and drew his face down so that he was looking at her. "Jace, *what is Sebastian really planning on doing*? The story he told in the training room, about wanting to raise demons so he could destroy them—"

"Sebastian wants to raise demons all right." Jace's voice was grim. "One demon in particular. Lilith."

"But Lilith's dead. Simon destroyed her."

"Greater Demons don't die. Not really. Greater Demons inhabit the spaces between worlds, the great Void, the emptiness. What Simon did was shatter her power, send her in shreds back to the nothingness she came from. But she'll slowly reform there. Be reborn. It would take centuries, but not if Sebastian helps her."

A cold feeling was growing in the pit of Clary's stomach. "Helps her how?"

"By summoning her back to this world. He wants to mix her blood and his in a cup and create an army of dark Nephilim. He wants to be Jonathan Shadowhunter reincarnated, but on the side of the demons, not the angels."

"An army of dark Nephilim? The two of you are tough, but you're not exactly an army."

"There are about forty or fifty Nephilim who either were once loyal to Valentine, or hate the current direction of the Clave and are open to hearing what Sebastian has to say. He's been in contact with them. When he raises Lilith, they'll be there." Jace took a deep breath. "And after that? With the power of Lilith behind him? Who knows who else will join his cause? He *wants* a war. He's convinced he'll win it, and I'm not sure he won't. For every dark Nephilim he makes, he will grow in power. Add that to the demons he's already made allegiances with, and I don't know if the Clave is prepared to withstand him."

Clary dropped her hand. "Sebastian never changed. Your blood never changed him. He's exactly like he always was." Her eyes flicked up to Jace's. "But you. You lied to me, too."

"*He* lied to you."

Her mind was whirling. "I know. I know that Jace isn't you—"

"*He* thinks it's for your good and you'll be happier in the end, but he did lie to you. And I would never do that."

"The *aegis*," Clary said. "If it can hurt you but Sebastian can't feel it, could it kill him but not hurt you?"

Jace shook his head. "I don't think so. If I had an *aegis*, I might be willing to try, but—no. Our life forces are tied together. An injury is one thing. If he were to die . . ." His voice hardened. "You know the easiest way to end this. Put a dagger in my heart. I'm surprised you didn't do it while I was sleeping."

"Could you? If it were me?" Her voice shook. "I believed there was a way to make this right. I still believe it. Give me your stele, and I'll make a Portal."

"You can't make a Portal from inside here," said Jace. "It won't work. The only way in and out of this apartment is through the wall downstairs, by the kitchen. It's the only place you can move the apartment from, too."

"Can you move us to the Silent City? If we go back, the Silent Brothers can figure out a way to separate you from Sebastian. We'll tell the Clave his plan so they'll be prepared—"

"I could move us to one of the entrances," Jace said. "And I will. I'll go. We'll go together. But just so there won't be any untruth between us, Clary, you have to know that they'll kill me. After I tell them what I know, they'll kill me."

"Kill you? No, they wouldn't—"

"Clary." His voice was gentle. "As a good Shadowhunter I ought to *volunteer* to die to stop what Sebastian is going to do. As a good Shadowhunter, I would."

"But none of this is your fault." Her voice rose, and she forced it back down, not wanting Sebastian, downstairs, to hear. "You can't help what's been done to you. You're a victim in this. It's not *you*, Jace; it's someone else, someone wearing your face. You shouldn't be punished—"

"It's not a matter of punishment. It's practicality. Kill me, Sebastian dies. It's no different from sacrificing myself in battle. It's all well and good to say I didn't choose this. It has happened. And what I am now, myself, will be gone again soon enough. And, Clary, I know it doesn't make sense, but I remember it—I remember all of it. I remember walking with you in Venice, and that night at the club, and sleeping in this bed with you, and don't you get it? I *wanted this.* This is all I *ever* wanted, to live with you like this, be with you like this. What am I supposed to think, when the worst thing that has ever happened to me gives me exactly what I want? Maybe Jace Lightwood can see all the ways this is wrong and messed-up, but Jace Wayland, Valentine's son . . . loves this life." His eyes were wide and gold as he looked at her, and she was reminded of Raziel, of his gaze that seemed to hold all the wisdom and all the sadness in the world. "And that's why I have to go," he said. "Before this wears off. Before I'm *him* again."

"Go where?"

"To the Silent City. I have to turn myself in—and the Cup, too."

Part Three
All Is Changed

All changed, changed utterly:
A terrible beauty is born.
—William Butler Yeats, "Easter, 1916"

18

RAZIEL

"Clary?"

Simon sat on the back porch steps of the farmhouse, looking down the path that led through the apple orchard and down to the lake. Isabelle and Magnus were on the path, Magnus glancing toward the lake and then up at the low mountains ringing the area. He was making notes in a small book with a pen whose end glowed a sparkling blue-green. Alec stood a little distance away, looking up at the trees lining the ridge of hills that separated the farmhouse from the road. He seemed to be standing as far from Magnus as he could while remaining in earshot. It seemed to Simon—the first to admit that he was not that observant about these things—that despite the joking around in the car, a perceptible distance had come between Magnus and Alec recently, one he couldn't quite put a finger on, but he knew it was there.

Simon's right hand was cradled in his left, his fingers circling the gold ring on his finger.

Clary, please.

He'd been trying to reach her every hour since he'd gotten the message from Maia about Luke. He'd gotten nothing. Not a flicker of response.

Clary, I'm at the farmhouse. I'm remembering you here, with me.

It was an unseasonably warm day, and a faint wind rustled the last of the leaves in the tree branches. After spending too long wondering what sort of clothes you were supposed to wear to meet angels in—a suit seemed excessive, even if he did have one left over from Jocelyn and Luke's engagement party—he was in jeans and a T-shirt, his arms bare in the sunlight. He had so many happy sunlit memories attached to this place, this house. He and Clary had come up here with Jocelyn almost every summer for as long as he could remember. They would swim in thc lake. Simon would tan brown, and Clary's fair skin would burn over and over. She'd get a million more freckles on her shoulders and arms. They'd play "apple baseball" in the orchard, which was messy and fun, and Scrabble and poker in the farmhouse, which Luke always won.

Clary, I'm about to do something stupid and dangerous and maybe suicidal. Is it so bad I want to talk to you one last time? I'm doing this to keep you safe, and I don't even know if you're alive for me to help you. But if you were dead, I'd know, wouldn't I? I'd feel it.

"All right. Let's go," Magnus said, appearing at the foot of the steps. He eyed the ring on Simon's hand, but made no comment.

Simon stood up and brushed off his jeans, then led the way down the wandering path through the orchard. The lake sparkled up ahead like a cold blue coin. As they neared it, Simon could see the old dock sticking out into the water, where once they had tied up kayaks before a big piece of the dock had broken off and drifted away. He thought he could almost hear the lazy hum of bees and feel the weight of summer on his shoulders. As they reached the lake's edge, he twisted around and looked up at the farmhouse, white-painted clapboard with green shutters and an old covered sunporch with tired white wicker furniture on it.

"You really liked it here, huh?" Isabelle said. Her black hair snapped like a banner in the breeze off the lake.

"How can you tell?"

"Your expression," she said. "Like you're remembering something good."

"It was good," Simon said. He reached up to push his glasses up his nose, remembered he no longer wore them, and lowered his hand. "I was lucky."

She looked down at the lake. She was wearing small gold hoop earrings; one was tangled in a bit of her hair, and Simon wanted to reach over and free it, to touch the side of her face with his fingers. "And now you're not?"

He shrugged. He was watching Magnus, who was holding what looked like a long, flexible rod and drawing in the wet sand at the lake's edge. He had the spell book open and was chanting as he drew. Alec was watching him, with the expression of someone watching a stranger.

"Are you scared?" Isabelle asked, moving slightly closer to Simon. He could feel the warmth of her arm against his.

"I don't know. So much of being scared is the physical feeling of it. Your heart speeding up, sweating, your pulse racing. I don't get any of that."

"That's too bad," Isabelle murmured, looking at the water. "Guys getting all sweaty is hot."

He shot her a half smile; it was harder than he thought it would be. Maybe he was scared. "That's enough of your sass and back talk, missy."

Isabelle's lip quivered as if she were about to smile. Then she sighed. "You know what it never even crossed my mind I wanted?" she said. "A guy who could make me laugh."

Simon turned toward her, reaching for her hand, not caring for the moment that her brother was watching. "Izzy . . ."

"All right," Magnus called out. "I'm done. Simon, over here."

They turned. Magnus was standing inside the circle, which was glowing with a faint white light. It was really two circles, a slightly smaller one inside a larger one, and in the space between the circles, dozens of symbols had been scrawled. They, too, glowed, a steely blue-white like the reflection off the lake.

Simon heard Isabelle's soft intake of breath, and he stepped away before he could look at her. It would just make it all harder. He moved forward, over the border of the circle, into its center, beside Magnus. Looking out from the center of the circle was like looking through water. The rest of the world seemed wavering and indistinct.

"Here." Magnus shoved the book into his hands. The paper was thin, covered in scrawled runes, but Magnus had taped a printout of the words, spelled out phonetically, over the incantation itself. "Just sound these out," he muttered. "It should work."

Holding the book against his chest, Simon slipped off the

gold ring that connected him to Clary, and handed it to Magnus. "If it doesn't," he said, wondering where his strange calm was coming from, "someone should take this. It's our only link to Clary, and what she knows."

Magnus nodded and slid the ring onto his finger. "Ready, Simon?"

"Hey," said Simon. "You remembered my name."

Magnus shot him an unreadable glance from his green-gold eyes, and stepped outside the circle. Immediately he was blurry and indistinct too. Alec joined him on one side, Isabelle on the other; Isabelle was hugging her elbows, and even through the wavering air Simon could tell how unhappy she looked.

Simon cleared his throat. "I guess you guys had better go."

But they didn't move. They seemed to be waiting for him to say something else.

"Thanks for coming here with me," he said finally, having racked his brain for something meaningful to say; they seemed to be expecting it. He wasn't the sort who made big farewell speeches or bid people dramatic good-byes. He looked at Alec first. "Um, Alec. I always liked you better than I liked Jace." He turned to Magnus. "Magnus, I wish I had the nerve to wear the kind of pants you do."

And last, Izzy. He could see her watching him through the haze, her eyes as black as obsidian.

"Isabelle," Simon said. He looked at her. He saw the question in her eyes, but there seemed nothing he could say in front of Alec and Magnus, nothing that would encompass what he felt. He moved back, toward the center of the circle, bowing his head. "Good-bye, I guess."

He thought they spoke back to him, but the wavering haze

between them blurred their words. He watched as they turned, retreating up the path through the orchard, back toward the house, until they had become dark specks. Until he could no longer see them at all.

He couldn't quite fathom not talking to Clary one last time before he died—he couldn't even remember the last words they'd exchanged. And yet if he closed his eyes, he could hear her laughter drifting over the orchard; he could remember what it had been like, before they had grown up and everything had changed. If he died here, perhaps it would be appropriate. Some of his best memories were here, after all. If the Angel struck him down with fire, his ashes could sift through the apple orchard and over the lake. Something about the idea seemed peaceful.

He thought of Isabelle. Then of his family—his mother, his father, and Becky. *Clary,* he thought lastly. *Wherever you are, you're my best friend. You'll always be my best friend.*

He raised the spell book and began to chant.

"No!" Clary stood up, dropping the wet towel. "Jace, you can't. They'll kill you."

He reached for a fresh shirt and shrugged it on, not looking at her as he did up the buttons. "They'll try to separate me from Sebastian first," he said, though he didn't sound as if he quite believed it. "If that doesn't work, *then* they'll kill me."

"Not good enough." She reached for him, but he turned away from her, jamming his feet into boots. When he turned back, his expression was grim.

"I don't have a choice, Clary. This is the right thing to do."

"It's insane. You're safe here. You can't throw away your life—"

"Saving myself is treason. It's putting a weapon into the hands of the enemy."

"Who cares about treason? Or the Law?" she demanded. "I care about *you*. We'll figure this out together—"

"*We* can't figure this out." Jace pocketed the stele on the nightstand, then caught up the Mortal Cup. "Because I'm only going to be *me* for a little while longer. I love you, Clary." He tilted her face up and kissed her, lingeringly. "Do this for me," he whispered.

"I absolutely will not," she said. "I will not try to help you get yourself killed."

But he was already striding toward the door. He drew her with him, and they stumbled down the corridor, speaking in whispers.

"This is crazy," Clary hissed. "Putting yourself in the path of danger—"

He blew out an exasperated breath. "As if you don't."

"Right, and it makes you *furious*," she whispered as she raced after him down the staircase. "Remember what you said to me in Alicante—"

They had reached the kitchen. He put the Cup down on the counter, reaching for his stele. "I had no right to say that," he told her. "Clary, this is what we *are*. We're Shadowhunters. This is what we do. There are risks we take that aren't just the risks you find in battle."

Clary shook her head, clutching both his wrists. "I won't let you."

A look of pain crossed his face. "Clarissa—"

She drew a deep breath, barely able to believe what she was about to do. But in her mind was the image of the morgue in the Silent City, of Shadowhunter bodies stretched out on marble slabs, and she could not bear for Jace to be one of them. Everything she had done—coming here, enduring everything she had endured, had been to save his life, and not just for herself. She thought of Alec and Isabelle, who had helped her, and Maryse, who loved him, and almost without knowing she was about to do it, she raised her voice and called out:

"Jonathan!" she screamed. *"Jonathan Christopher Morgenstern!"*

Jace's eyes widened into circles. "*Clary*—" he began, but it was too late already. She had let go of him and was backing away. Sebastian might already be coming; there was no way to tell Jace that it wasn't that she trusted Sebastian but that Sebastian was the only weapon she had at her disposal that could possibly make him stay.

There was a flash of movement, and Sebastian was there. He hadn't bothered with running down the stairs, just flipped himself over the side and landed between them. His hair was sleep-mussed; he wore a dark T-shirt and black pants, and Clary wondered distractedly if he slept in his clothes. He glanced between Clary and Jace, his black eyes taking in the situation. "Lovers' spat?" he inquired. Something glinted in his hand. A knife?

Clary's voice shook. "His rune's damaged. Here." She put her hand over her heart. "He's trying to go back, to give himself up to the Clave—"

Sebastian's hand shot out and grabbed the Cup out of Jace's hand. He slammed it down on the kitchen counter. Jace, still white with shock, watched him; he didn't move a muscle as Sebastian stepped close and took Jace by the front of the shirt. The top buttons on the shirt popped open, baring his collar, and Sebastian slashed the point of his stele across it, gashing an *iratze* into the skin. Jace bit down on his lip, his eyes full of hatred as Sebastian released him and took a step back, stele in hand.

"Honestly, Jace," he said. "The idea that you thought you could get away with something like this just knocks me out."

Jace's hands tightened into fists as the *iratze*, black as charcoal, began to sink into his skin. His words were eked out, breathless: "Next time . . . you want to be knocked out . . . I'd be happy to help you. Maybe with a brick."

Sebastian made a *tsk* noise. "You'll thank me later. Even you have to admit this death wish of yours is a little extreme."

Clary expected Jace to snap back at him again. But he didn't. His gaze traveled slowly across Sebastian's face. For that moment there was only the two of them in the room, and when Jace spoke, his words came cold and clear. "I won't remember this later," he said. "But you will. That person who acts like your friend—" He took a step forward, closing the space between himself and Sebastian. "That person who acts like they *like* you. That person isn't real. This is real. This is me. And I hate you. I will always hate you. And there is no magic and no spell in this world or any other that will ever change that."

For a moment the grin on Sebastian's face wavered. But Jace didn't. Instead, he tore his gaze from Sebastian and looked at Clary. "I need you to know," he said, "the truth—I didn't tell you all the truth."

"The truth is dangerous," said Sebastian, holding the stele before him like a knife. "Be careful what you say."

Jace winced. His chest was rising and falling rapidly; it was clear that the healing of the rune on his chest was causing him physical pain. "The plan," he said. "To raise Lilith, to make a new Cup, to create a dark army—that wasn't Sebastian's plan. *It was mine.*"

Clary froze. "What?"

"Sebastian knew what he wanted," said Jace. "But I figured out how he could do it. A new Mortal Cup—I gave him that idea." He jerked in pain; she could imagine what was happening under the cloth of his shirt: the skin knitting together, healing, Lilith's rune whole and shining once again. "Or, should I say, *he* did. That thing that looks like me but isn't? He'll burn down the world if Sebastian wants him to, and laugh while he's doing it. That's what you're saving, Clary. *That*. Don't you understand? I'd rather be dead—"

His voice choked off as he doubled over. The muscles in his shoulders tightened as ripples of what looked like pain went through him. Clary remembered holding him in the Silent City as the Brothers rooted through his mind for answers— Now he looked up, his expression bewildered.

His eyes shifted first not to her but to Sebastian. She felt her heart plummet, though she knew this was only her own doing.

"What's going on?" Jace said.

Sebastian grinned at him. "Welcome back."

Jace blinked, looking momentarily confused—and then his gaze seemed to slide inward, the way it did whenever Clary tried to bring up something that he couldn't process—Max's murder, the war in Alicante, the pain he was causing his family.

"Is it time?" he said.

Sebastian made a show of looking at his watch. "Just about. Why don't you go on ahead and we'll follow? You can start getting things ready."

Jace glanced around. "The Cup—where is it?"

Sebastian took it off the kitchen counter. "Right here. Feeling a little absentminded?"

Jace's mouth curled at the corner, and he grabbed the Cup back. Good-naturedly. There was no sign of the boy who had stood in front of Sebastian moments ago and told him he hated him. "All right. I'll meet you there." He turned to Clary, who was still frozen in shock, and kissed her cheek. "And you."

He drew back and winked at her. There was affection in his eyes, but it didn't matter. This was not her Jace, very clearly not her Jace, and she watched numbly as he crossed the room. His stele flashed, and a door opened in the wall; she caught a glimpse of sky and rocky plain, and then he stepped through it and was gone.

She dug her nails into her palms.

That thing that looks like me but isn't? He'll burn down the world if Sebastian wants him to, and laugh while he's doing it. That's what you're saving, Clary. That. Don't you understand? I'd rather be dead.

Tears burned at the back of her throat, and it was all she could do to hold them off as her brother turned to her, his black eyes very bright. "You called for me," he said.

"He wanted to give himself up to the Clave," she whispered, not sure who she was defending herself to. She had done what she'd had to, used the only weapon at hand, even if it was one she despised. "They would have killed him."

"You called for *me*," he said again, and took a step toward her. He reached out and lifted a long lock of her hair away from her face, tucking it back behind her ear. "He told you, then? The plan? All of it?"

She fought back a shiver of revulsion. "Not all of it. I

don't know what's happening tonight. What did Jace mean 'It's time'?"

He leaned down and kissed her forehead; she felt the kiss burn, like a brand between her eyes. "You'll find out," he said. "You've earned the right to be there, Clarissa. You can watch it all from your place at my side, tonight, at the Seventh Sacred Site. *Both* of Valentine's children, together . . . at last."

Simon kept his eyes on the paper, chanting out the words Magnus had written for him. They had a rhythm to them that was like music, light and sharp and fine. He was reminded of reading aloud his haftarah portion during his bar mitzvah, though he had known what the words meant then, and now he didn't.

As the chant went on, he felt a tightening around him, as if the air were becoming denser and heavier. It pressed down on his chest and shoulders. The air was growing warmer as well. If he were human, the heat might have been unbearable. As it was, he could feel the burn of it on his skin, singeing his eyelashes, his shirt. He kept his eyes fixed on the paper in front of him as a bead of blood ran from his hairline to drip onto the paper.

And then he was done. The last of the words—"Raziel"—was spoken, and he lifted his head. He could feel blood running down his face. The haze around him had cleared, and in front of him he saw the water of the lake, blue and sparkling, as untroubled as glass.

And then it exploded.

The center of the lake turned gold, then black. Water rushed away from it, pouring toward the edges of the lake, flying into the air until Simon was staring at a ring of water, like a circle of unbroken waterfalls, all shimmering and pouring upward and downward, the effect bizarre and strangely beautiful. Water droplets shivered down onto him, cooling his burning skin. He tipped his head back, just as the sky went black—all the blue of it gone, eaten up in a sudden shock of darkness and clamoring gray clouds. The water splashed back down into the lake, and from its center, the greatest density of its silver, rose a figure all of gold.

Simon's mouth went dry. He had seen countless paintings of angels, believed in them, had heard Magnus's warning. And still he felt as if he had been struck through with a spear as before him a pair of wings unfolded. They seemed to span the sky. They were vast, white and gold and silver, the feathers of them set with burning golden eyes. The eyes regarded him with scorn. Then the wings lifted, scattering clouds before them, and folded back, and a man—or the shape of a man, towering and many stories tall, unfolded itself and rose.

Simon's teeth had started to chatter. He wasn't sure why. But waves of power, of something more than power—of the elemental force of the universe—seemed to roll off the Angel as he rose to his full height. Simon's first and rather bizarre thought was that it looked as if someone had taken Jace and blown him up to the size of a billboard. Only he didn't quite look like Jace at all. He was gold all over, from his wings to his skin to his eyes, which had no whites at all, only a sheen of gold like a membrane. His hair was gold and looked cut from pieces of metal that curled like wrought ironwork. He was alien and terrifying. Too much of anything could destroy you, Simon thought. Too much darkness could kill, but too much light could blind.

Who dares to summon me? The Angel spoke in Simon's mind, in a voice like great bells sounding.

Tricky question, Simon thought. If he were Jace, he could say "one of the Nephilim," and if he were Magnus, he could say he was one of Lilith's children and a High Warlock. Clary and the Angel had already met, so he supposed they'd just chum it up. But he was Simon, without any titles to his name or any great deeds in his past. "Simon Lewis," he said finally, setting the spell book down and straightening up. "Night's Child, and . . . your servant."

My servant? Raziel's voice was frozen with icy disapproval. *You summon me like a dog and dare to call yourself my servant? You shall be blasted from this world, that your fate may serve as a warning to others not to do likewise. It is forbidden for my own Nephilim to summon me. Why should it be different for you, Daylighter?*

Simon supposed he should not be shocked that the Angel knew what he was, but it was startling nevertheless, as startling as the Angel's size. Somehow he had thought Raziel would be more human. "I—"

Do you think because you carry the blood of one of my descendants, I must show you mercy? If so, you have gambled and lost. The mercy of Heaven is for the deserving. Not for those who break our Covenant Laws.

The Angel raised a hand, his finger pointed directly at Simon.

Simon braced himself. This time he did not try to say the words, only thought them. *Hear, O Israel! The Lord is our God, the Lord is one—*

What Mark is that? Raziel's voice was confounded. *On your forehead, child.*

"It is the Mark," Simon stammered. "The first Mark. The Mark of Cain."

Raziel's great arm lowered slowly. *I would kill you, but the Mark prevents it. That Mark was meant to be set between your brows by Heaven's hand, yet I know it was not. How can this be?*

The Angel's obvious bafflement emboldened Simon. "One of your children, the Nephilim," he said. "One especially gifted. She set it there, to protect me." He took a step closer to the edge of the circle. "Raziel, I came to ask a favor of you, in the name of those Nephilim. They face a grave danger. One of their own has—has been turned to darkness, and he threatens all the rest. They need your help."

I do not intervene.

"But you did intervene," Simon said. "When Jace was dead, you brought him back. Not that we're not all really happy about that, but if you hadn't, none of this would be happening. So in a way it rests on you to set it right."

I may not be able to kill you, Raziel mused. *But there is no reason I should give you what you want.*

"I haven't even said what I want," said Simon.

You want a weapon. Something that can sever Jonathan Morgenstern from Jonathan Herondale. You would kill the one and preserve the other. Easiest of course to simply kill both. Your Jonathan was dead, and perhaps death longs for him still, and he for it. Has that ever crossed your mind?

"No," said Simon. "I know we're not much compared to you, but we don't kill our friends. We try to save them. If Heaven didn't want it that way, we ought never have been given the ability to love." He shoved his hair back, baring the Mark more fully. "No, you don't need to help me. But if you don't, there's nothing stopping me from calling you up again and again, now that I know you can't kill me. Think of it as me leaning against your Heavenly doorbell . . . forever."

Raziel, incredibly, seemed to chuckle at that. *You are stubborn,* he said. *A veritable warrior of your people, like him whose name you bear, Simon Maccabeus. And as he gave everything for his brother Jonathan, so shall you give everything for your Jonathan. Or are you not willing?*

"It's not just for him," said Simon, a little dazed. "But, yes, whatever you want. I will give it to you."

If I give you what you want, will you also vow never to bother me again?

"I don't think," said Simon, "that that will be a problem."

Very well, said the Angel. *I will tell you what I desire. I desire that blasphemous Mark on your forehead. I would take the Mark of Cain from you, for it was never your place to carry it.*

"I—but if you take the Mark, then you can kill me," Simon said. "Isn't it the only thing standing between me and your Heavenly wrath?"

The Angel paused to consider for a moment. *I shall swear not to harm you. Whether you bear the Mark or not.*

Simon hesitated. The Angel's expression turned thunderous. *The vow of an Angel of Heaven is the most sacred there is. Do you dare to distrust me, Downworlder?*

"I . . ." Simon paused for an excruciating moment. His eyes were filled with the memory of Clary standing on her tiptoes as she pressed the stele to his forehead; the first time he had seen the Mark work, when he had felt like the conductor for a lightning bolt, sheer energy passing through him with deadly force. It was a curse, one that had terrified him and made him an object of desire and fear. He had hated it. And yet now, faced with giving it up, the thing that made him special . . .

He swallowed hard. "Fine. Yes. I agree."

The Angel smiled, and his smile was terrible, like looking directly into the sun. *Then I swear not to harm you, Simon Maccabeus.*

"Lewis," Simon said. "My last name is Lewis."

But you are of the blood and faith of the Maccabees. Some say the Maccabees were Marked by the hand of God. In either case you are a warrior of Heaven, Daylighter, whether you like it or not.

The Angel moved. Simon's eyes watered, for Raziel seemed to draw the sky with him like a cloth, in swirls of black and silver and cloud-white. The air around him shuddered. Something flashed overhead like the glint of light off metal, and an object struck the sand and rocks beside Simon with a metallic clatter.

It was a sword—nothing special to look at either, a beaten-up-looking old iron sword with a blackened hilt. The edges were ragged, as if acid had eaten at them, though the tip was sharp. It looked like something that an archeological dig might have turned up, that hadn't been properly cleaned yet.

The Angel spoke. *Once when Joshua was near Jericho, he looked up and saw a man standing before him with a drawn sword in his hand. Joshua went to him and said, "Are you one of us, or one of our adversaries?" He replied, "Neither, but as commander of the army of the Lord, I have now come."*

Simon glanced down at the unprepossesing object at his feet. "And that's *this* sword?"

It is the sword of the Archangel Michael, commander of the armies of Heaven. It possesses the power of Heaven's fire. Strike your enemy with this, and it will burn the evil out of him. If he is more evil than good, more Hell's than Heaven's, it will also burn the life from him. It will most certainly sever his bond with your friend—and it can harm only one of them at a time.

Simon bent down and picked the sword up. It sent a shock through his hand, up his arm, into his motionless heart. Instinctively he raised it, and the clouds above seemed to part for a moment, a ray of light arcing down to strike the dull metal of the sword and make it sing.

The Angel looked down upon him with cold eyes. *The name of the sword cannot be spoken by your meager human tongue. You may call it Glorious.*

"I . . . ," Simon began. "Thank you."

Do not thank me. I would have killed you, Daylighter, but your Mark, and now my vow, prevent it. The Mark of Cain was meant to be placed upon you by God, and it was not. It shall be wiped from your brow, its protection removed. And if you call upon me again, I will not help you.

Instantly the beam of light shining down from the clouds intensified, striking the sword like a whip of fire, surrounding Simon in a cage of brilliant light and heat. The sword burned; he cried out and fell to the ground, pain lancing through his head. It felt as if someone were jabbing a red hot needle between his eyes. He covered his face, burying his head in his arms, letting the pain wash over him. It was the worst agony he had felt since the night he had died.

It faded slowly, ebbing like the tide. He rolled onto his back, staring up, his head still aching. The black clouds were beginning to roll back, showing a widening strip of blue; the Angel was gone, the lake surging under the growing light as if the water were boiling.

Simon began to sit up slowly, his eyes squinted painfully against the sun. He could see someone racing down the path from the farmhouse to the lake. Someone with long black hair, and a purple jacket that flew out behind her like wings. She hit the end of the path and leaped onto the lakeside, her boots kicking up puffs of sand behind her. She reached him and threw herself down, wrapping her arms around him. "Simon," she whispered.

He could feel the strong, steady beat of Isabelle's heart.

"I thought you were dead," she went on. "I saw you fall down, and—I thought you were dead."

Simon let her hold him, propping himself up on his hands. He realized he was listing like a ship with a hole in the side, and tried not to move. He was afraid that if he did, he would fall over. "I *am* dead."

"I *know*," Izzy snapped. "I mean more dead than usual."

"Iz." He raised his face to hers. She was kneeling over him, her legs around his, her arms around his neck. It looked uncomfortable. He let himself fall back into the sand, taking her with him. He thumped down onto his back in the cold sand with her on top of him and stared up into her black eyes. They seemed to take up the whole sky.

She touched his forehead in wonder. "Your Mark's gone."

"Raziel took it away. In exchange for the sword." He gestured toward the blade. Up at the farmhouse, he could see two dark specks standing in front of the sunporch, watching them. Alec and Magnus. "It's the Archangel Michael's sword. It's called Glorious."

"Simon . . ." She kissed his cheek. "You did it. You got the Angel. You got the sword."

Magnus and Alec had started down the path to the lake. Simon closed his eyes, exhausted. Isabelle leaned over him, her hair brushing the sides of his face. "Don't try to talk." She smelled like tears. "You're not cursed anymore," she whispered. "You're not cursed."

Simon linked his fingers with hers. He felt as if he were floating on a dark river, the shadows closing in around him. Only her hand anchored him to earth. "I know."

19

Love and Blood

Methodically and carefully Clary was tearing Jace's room apart. She was still in her tank top, though she'd pulled on a pair of jeans; her hair was scraped behind her head in a messy bun, and her nails were powdered with dust. She had searched under his bed, in all the drawers and cabinets, crawled under the wardrobe and desk, and looked in the pockets of all his clothes for a second stele, but she had found nothing.

She had told Sebastian she was exhausted, that she needed to go upstairs and lie down; he had seemed distracted and had waved her away. Images of Jace's face kept flashing behind her eyelids every time she shut her eyes—the way he had looked at her, betrayed, as if he didn't know her anymore.

But there was no point dwelling on that. She could sit on

the edge of the bed and cry into her hands, thinking about what she had done, but it would do no one any good. She owed it to Jace, to herself, to keep moving. Searching. If she could just find a stele—

She was lifting the mattress off the bed, searching the space between it and the box springs, when a knock came on the door.

She dropped the mattress, though not before discerning that there was nothing under it. She tightened her hands into fists, took a deep breath, stalked to the door and threw it open.

Sebastian stood on the threshold. For the first time he was wearing something other than black and white. The same black trousers and boots, admittedly, but he also wore a scarlet leather tunic, intricately worked with gold and silver runes, and held together by a row of metal clasps across the front. There were hammered silver bracelets on each of his wrists, and he wore the Morgenstern ring.

She blinked at him. "Red?"

"Ceremonial," he replied. "Colors mean different things to Shadowhunters than they do to humans." He said the word "humans" with contempt. "You know the old Nephilim children's rhyme, don't you?

Black for hunting through the night
For death and sorrow, the color's white.
Gold for a bride in her wedding gown,
And red to call enchantment down."

"Shadowhunters get married in gold?" Clary said. Not that she cared particularly, but she was trying to wedge her body into the gap between the door and the frame so that he couldn't look behind her and see the mess she'd made out of Jace's normally neat room.

"Sorry to crush your dreams of a white wedding." He grinned at her. "Speaking of which, I brought you something to wear."

He drew his hand out from behind his back. He was holding a folded item of clothing. She took it from him and let it unroll. It was a long, drifting column of scarlet fabric with an odd golden sheen to the material, like the edge of a flame. The straps were gold.

"Our mother used to wear this to Circle ceremonies before she betrayed our father," he said. "Put it on. I want you to wear it tonight."

"Tonight?"

"Well, you can hardly go to the ceremony in what you're wearing now." His eyes raked her, from her bare feet to the tank top clinging to her body with sweat, to her dusty jeans. "How you look tonight—the impression you make on our new acolytes—is important. Put it on."

Her mind was whirling. *The ceremony tonight. Our new acolytes.* "How much time do I have—to get ready?" she asked.

"An hour perhaps," he said. "We should be at the sacred site by midnight. The others will be gathering there. It wouldn't do to be late."

An hour. Heart hammering, Clary threw the garment across the bed, where it glimmered like chain mail. When she turned back, he was still in the doorway, a half smile on his face, as if he intended to wait there while she changed.

She moved to shut the door. He caught her wrist. "Tonight,"

he said, "you call me Jonathan. Jonathan Morgenstern. Your brother."

A shudder ran over her whole body, and she dropped her eyes, hoping he couldn't see the hatred in them. "Whatever you say."

The moment he was gone she reached for one of Jace's leather jackets. She slipped it on, taking comfort in the warmth and the familiar smell of him. She slid her feet into shoes and crept out into the hallway, wishing for a stele and a new Soundless rune. She could hear water running downstairs and Sebastian's off-key whistling, but her own footsteps still sounded like cannon explosions in her ears. She crept along, keeping close to the wall, until she reached Sebastian's door and slid inside.

It was dim, the only illumination the ambient city light coming from the windows, whose curtains were pulled back. It was a mess, just as it had been the first time she'd been in it. She started with his closet, stuffed full of expensive clothes—silk shirts, leather jackets, Armani suits, Bruno Magli shoes. On the floor of the closet was a white shirt, wadded up and stained with blood—blood old enough to have dried to brown. Clary looked at it for a long moment and shut the closet door.

She set herself to the desk next, pulling out drawers, rifling through papers. She'd rather hoped for something simple, like a lined piece of notebook paper with MY EVIL PLAN written across the top, but no luck. There were dozens of papers with complex numerical and alchemical figuring on them, and even a piece of stationery that began *My beautiful one* in Sebastian's cramped handwriting. She spared a moment to wonder who on earth Sebastian's beautiful one could be—she hadn't thought of him as someone who ever had romantic feelings about anyone—before turning to the nightstand by his bed.

She pulled open the drawer. Inside was a stack of notes. On top of them, something glimmered. Something circular and metallic.

Her faerie ring.

Isabelle sat with her arm around Simon as they drove back toward Brooklyn. He was exhausted, his head throbbing, his body pierced with aches. Though Magnus had given him back his ring at the lake, he had been unable to reach Clary with it. Worst of all, he was hungry. He liked how close Isabelle was sitting to him, the way she rested her hand just above the crook of his elbow, tracing patterns there, sometimes sliding her fingers down to his wrist. But the scent of her—perfume and blood—made his stomach growl.

It was starting to grow dark outside, the late-autumn sunset coming soon on the heels of the day, dimming the interior of the truck's cab. Alec's and Magnus's voices were murmurs in the shadows. Simon let his eyes flutter closed, seeing the Angel printed against the back of his lids, a burst of white light.

Simon! Clary's voice exploded inside his head, jerking him instantly awake. *Are you there?*

A sharp gasp escaped his lips. *Clary? I was so worried—*

Sebastian took my ring away from me. Simon, there may not be much time. I have to tell you. They have a second Mortal Cup. They plan to raise Lilith and create an army of dark Shadowhunters—ones with the same power as the Nephilim but allied to the demon world.

"You're kidding me," Simon said. It took him a moment to realize he'd spoken aloud; Isabelle stirred against him, and Magnus looked over curiously.

"You all right there, vampire?"

"It's Clary," Simon said. All three of them looked at him with identical astonished expressions. "She's trying to talk to me." He slapped his hands over his ears, slumping down in his seat and trying to concentrate on her words. *When are they going to do it?*

Tonight. Soon. I don't know where we are exactly—but it's about ten p.m. here.

Then you're about five hours ahead of us. Are you in Europe?

I can't even guess. Sebastian mentioned something called the Seventh Sacred Site. I don't know what that is, but I've found some of his notes and apparently it's an ancient tomb. It looks like a sort of doorway, and demons can be summoned through it.

Clary, I've never heard of anything like that—

But Magnus or the others might. Please, Simon. Tell them as quickly as you can. Sebastian's going to ressurrect Lilith. He wants war, a total war with the Shadowhunters. He has about forty or fifty Nephilim ready to follow him. They'll be there. Simon, he wants to burn the world down. We have to do anything we can to stop him.

If things are that dangerous, you need to get yourself out of there.

She sounded tired. *I'm trying. But it might be too late.*

Simon was dimly aware that everyone else in the truck was staring at him, concern on their faces. He didn't care. Clary's voice in his mind was like a rope tossed over a chasm, and if he could grip his end of it, maybe he could pull her to safety, or at least keep her from slipping away.

Clary, listen. I can't tell you how, it's too long a story, but we have a weapon. It can be used on either Jace or Sebastian without hurting the other, and according to the . . . person who gave it to us, it might be able to cut them apart.

Cut them apart? How?

He said it would burn all the evil out of the one we used it on. So if we used it on Sebastian, I'm guessing, it would burn away the bond between them because the bond is evil. Simon felt his head throb, and hoped he sounded more confident than he did. *I'm not sure. It's very powerful, anyway. It's called Glorious.*

And you'd use it on Sebastian? It would burn them apart without killing them?

Well, that's the idea. I mean, there is some chance it would destroy Sebastian. It would depend on if there's any good left in him. "If he's more Hell's than Heaven's" I think is what the Angel said—

The Angel? Her alarm was palpable. *Simon, what have you—*

Her voice broke off, and Simon was suddenly filled with a clamor of emotion—surprise, anger, terror. Pain. He cried out, sitting bolt upright.

Clary?

But there was only silence, ringing in his head.

Clary! he cried out, and then, aloud, he said: "Damn. She's gone again."

"What happened?" Isabelle demanded. "Is she all right? What's going on?"

"I think we have a lot less time than we thought," Simon said in a voice much calmer than he felt. "Magnus, pull the truck over. We have to talk."

"So," Sebastian said, filling the doorway as he looked down at Clary. "Would it be déjà vu if I asked you what you were doing in my room, little sister?"

Clary swallowed against her suddenly dry throat. The light in the hallway was bright behind Sebastian, turning him into a silhouette. She couldn't see the expression on his face. "Looking for you?" she hazarded.

"You're sitting on my bed," he said. "Did you think I was under it?"

"I . . ."

He walked into the room—sauntered, really, as if he knew something she didn't. Something no one else knew. "So why were you looking for me? And why haven't you changed for the ceremony?"

"The dress," she said. "It—doesn't fit."

"Of course it fits," he said, sitting down on the bed beside her. He turned to face her, his back to the headboard. "Everything else in that room fits you. This should fit you too."

"It's silk and chiffon. It doesn't stretch."

"You're a skinny little thing. It shouldn't have to." He took her right wrist, and she curled her fingers in, desperately trying to hide the ring. "Look, my fingers go right around your wrist."

His skin felt hot against hers, sending sharp prickles through her nerves. She remembered the way, in Idris, his touch had burned her like acid. "The Seventh Sacred Site," she said, not looking at him. "Is that where Jace went?"

"Yes. I sent him ahead. He's readying things for our arrival. We'll meet him there."

Her heart dived inside her chest. "He's not coming back?"

"Not before the ceremony." She caught the curling edge of Sebastian's smile. "Which is good, because he'd be so disappointed when I told him about *this*." He slid his hand swiftly over hers, uncurling her fingers. The gold ring blazed there, like a signal fire. "Did you think I wouldn't recognize faerie work?

Do you think the Queen is such a fool that she would send you off to retrieve these for her without knowing you would keep them for yourself? She *wanted* you to bring this here, where I would find it." He jerked the ring off her finger with a smirk.

"You've been in contact with the Queen?" Clary demanded. "How?"

"With this ring," Sebastian purred, and Clary remembered the Queen saying in her high sweet voice, *Jonathan Morgenstern could be a powerful ally. The Fair Folk are an old people; we do not make hasty decisions but wait to see in what direction the wind blows first.* "Do you really think she'd let you get your hands on something that would let you communicate with your little friends without her being able to listen in? Since I took it from you, I've spoken to her, she's spoken to me—you were a fool to trust her, little sister. She likes to be on the winning side of things, the Seelie Queen. And that side will be ours, Clary. *Ours*." His voice was low and soft. "Forget them, your Shadowhunter friends. Your place is with us. With *me*. Your blood cries out for power, like mine does. Whatever your mother may have done to twist your conscience, you know who you are." His hand caught at her wrist again, pulling her toward him. "Jocelyn made all the wrong decisions. She sided with the Clave against her family. This is your chance to rectify her mistake."

She tried to pull her arm back. "Let me go, Sebastian. I mean it."

His hand slid up from her wrist, encircling her upper arm with his fingers. "You're such a little thing. Who'd think you were such a spitfire? Especially in bed."

She leaped to her feet, jerking away from him. "*What* did you just say?"

He rose as well, his lips curving up at the corners. He was so much taller than she was, almost exactly as much taller as Jace was. He leaned in close to her when he spoke, and his voice was low and rough. "Everything that marks Jace, marks me," he said. "Down to your fingernails." He was grinning. "Eight parallel scratches on my back, little sister. Are you saying you didn't put them there?"

A soft explosion went off in her head, like a dull firework of rage. She looked at his laughing face, and she thought of Jace, and of Simon, and the words they'd just exchanged. If the Queen really could eavesdrop on her conversations, then she might know about Glorious already. But Sebastian didn't know. Couldn't know.

She snatched the ring from his hand, and threw it to the ground. She heard him give a shout, but she'd already brought her foot down on it, feeling it give way, the gold smashing to powder.

He looked at her incredulously as she drew her foot back. "You—"

She drew back her right hand, the strongest one, and drove her fist into his stomach.

He was taller, broader, and stronger than she was, but she had the element of surprise. He doubled over, choking, and she snatched the stele from his weapons belt. Then she ran.

Magnus jerked the wheel to the side so fast that the tires screeched. Isabelle shrieked. They bumped up onto the shoulder of the road, under the shadow of a copse of partly leafless trees.

The next thing Simon knew, the doors were open and everyone was tumbling out onto the blacktop. The sun was going down, and the headlights of the truck were on, lighting them all with an eerie glow.

"All right, vampire boy," said Magnus, shaking his head hard enough to shed glitter. "What the *hell* is going on?"

Alec leaned against the truck as Simon explained, repeating the conversation with Clary as accurately as he could before the whole thing flew out of his head.

"Did she say anything about getting her and Jace out of there?" Isabelle asked when he was done, her face pale in the yellowish glow from the headlights.

"No," said Simon. "And Iz—I don't think Jace wants to get out. He wants to be where he is."

Isabelle crossed her arms and looked down at her boots, her black hair sweeping across her face.

"What's this Seventh Sacred Site business?" said Alec. "I know about the seven wonders of the world, but seven sacred sites?"

"They're more in the interest of warlocks than Nephilim," said Magnus. "Each is a place where ley lines converge, forming a matrix—a sort of net within which magical spells are amplified. The seventh is a stone tomb in Ireland, at Poll na mBrón; the name means 'the cavern of sorrows.' It's in a very bleak, uninhabited area called the Burren. A good place to raise a demon, if it's a big one." He tugged at a spike of hair. "This is bad. Really bad."

"You think he could do it? Make—dark Shadowhunters?" Simon asked.

"Everything has an alliance, Simon. The alliance of the Nephilim is seraphic, but if it were demonic, they'd still be as strong, as powerful as they are now. But they would be dedicated to the eradication of mankind instead of its salvation."

"We have to get there," Isabelle said. "We have to stop them."

"'Him,' you mean," said Alec. "We have to stop him. Sebastian."

"Jace is his ally now. You have to accept that, Alec," Magnus said. A light misty drizzle had begun to fall. The drops gleamed like gold in the headlights' glow. "Ireland is five hours ahead. They're doing the ceremony at midnight. It's five o'clock here. We have an hour and a half—two hours, at most—to stop them."

"Then, we shouldn't be waiting. We should be going," Isabelle said, a tinge of panic in her voice. "If we're going to stop him—"

"Iz, there are only four of us," Alec said. "We don't even know what kind of numbers we're up against—"

Simon glanced at Magnus, who was watching Alec and Isabelle argue with a peculiarly detached expression. "Magnus," Simon said. "Why didn't we just Portal to the farm? You Portaled half of Idris to Brocelind Plain."

"I wanted to give you enough time to change your mind," said Magnus, not taking his eyes off his boyfriend.

"But we can Portal from here," Simon said. "I mean, you could do that for us."

"Yeah," Magnus said. "But like Alec says, we don't know what we're up against in terms of numbers. I'm a pretty powerful warlock, but Jonathan Morgenstern is no ordinary Shadowhunter, and neither is Jace, for that matter. And if they succeed in raising Lilith—she'll be a lot weaker than she was, but she's still Lilith."

"But she's dead," said Isabelle. "Simon killed her."

"Greater Demons don't die," said Magnus. "Simon . . . scattered her between worlds. It will take a long time for her to re-form and she will be weak for years. Unless Sebastian calls her up again." He pushed a hand through his wet, spiked hair.

"We have the sword," Isabelle said. "We can take out Sebastian. We have Magnus, and Simon—"

"We don't even know if the sword will work," said Alec. "And it won't do us much good if we can't get to Sebastian. And Simon isn't even Mr. Indestructible anymore. He can be killed just like the rest of us."

They all looked at Simon. "We have to try," he said. "Look—we don't know how many are going to be there, no. We have a little time. Not a lot, but enough—if we Portal—to grab some reinforcements."

"Reinforcements from where?" Isabelle demanded.

"I'll go to Maia and Jordan back at the apartment," said Simon, his mind quickly ticking over possibilities. "See if Jordan can get any assistance from the Praetor Lupus. Magnus, go to the downtown police station, see about enlisting whatever members of the pack are around. Isabelle and Alec—"

"You're splitting us up?" Isabelle demanded, her voice rising. "What about fire-messages, or—"

"No one's going to trust a fire-message about something like this," said Magnus. "And besides, fire-messages are for Shadowhunters. Do you really want to communicate this information to the Clave via fire-message instead of going to the Institute yourself?"

"Fine." Isabelle stalked around to the side of the car. She yanked the door open, but didn't get inside: instead she reached in, and drew out Glorious. It shone in the dim light like a bolt of dark lightning, the words carved on the blade flickering in the car light: *Quis ut Deus?*

The rain was starting to paste Isabelle's black hair to her neck. She looked formidable as she walked back to rejoin the group. "Then we leave the car here. We split up, but we meet back at the Institute in an hour. That's when we leave, whoever we have with us." She met each of her companion's eyes, one by one, daring them to challenge her. "Simon, take this."

She held out Glorious to him, hilt-forward.

"Me?" Simon was startled. "But I don't—I haven't really used a sword before."

"You called it down," Isabelle said, her dark eyes glossy in the rain. "The Angel gave it to you, Simon, and you will be the one who carries it."

Clary dashed down the hallway and hit the steps with a clatter, racing for the downstairs and for the spot on the wall that Jace had told her was the only entrance and exit from the apartment.

She had no illusions that she could escape. She needed only a few moments to do what had to be done. She heard Sebastian's boots loud on the glass staircase behind her, and put on a burst of speed, almost slamming into the wall. She jammed the stele into it point-first, drawing frantically: *a pattern as simple as a cross, new to the world—*

Sebastian's fist closed on the back of her jacket, jerking her backward, the stele flying out of her hand. She gasped as he swung her up off her feet and slammed her into the wall, knocking the breath out of her. He glanced at the mark she had made on the wall, and his lips curled into a sneer.

"The Opening rune?" he said. He leaned forward and hissed into her ear. "And you didn't even finish it. Not that it matters. Do you really think there's a place on this earth you could go where I couldn't find you?"

Clary responded with an epithet that would have gotten her kicked out of class at St. Xavier's. Just as he started to laugh, she raised her hand and slapped him across the face so hard, her fingers stung. In his surprise he loosened his grip on her, and she jerked away from him and flipped herself over the table, making for the downstairs bedroom, which at least had a lock on the door—

And he was in front of her, grabbing the lapels of her jacket and swinging her around. Her feet went out from under her, and she would have fallen if he hadn't pinned her to the wall with his body, his arms to either side, making a cage around her.

His grin was diabolical. Gone was the stylish boy who'd strolled by the Seine with her and drunk hot chocolate and talked about belonging. His eyes were all black, no pupil, like tunnels. "What's wrong, little sis? You look upset."

She could barely catch her breath. "Cracked . . . my . . . nail polish slapping your . . . worthless face. See?" She showed him her finger—just one of them.

"Cute." He snorted. "You know how I knew you'd betray us? How I knew you wouldn't be able to help it? Because you're too much like me."

He pressed her back harder against the wall. She could feel his chest rise and fall against hers. She was at eye level with the straight, sharp line of his collarbone. His body felt like a prison around hers, pinning her in place. "I'm nothing like you. Let me go—"

"You're everything like me," he growled into her ear. "You infiltrated us. You faked friendship, faked caring."

"I never had to fake caring about *Jace*."

She saw something flash in his eyes then, a dark jealousy, and she wasn't even sure who he was jealous of. He put his lips against her cheek, close enough that she felt them move against her skin when he spoke. "You screwed us over," he murmured. His hand was around her left arm like a vise; slowly he began to move it down. "Probably literally screwed Jace over—"

She couldn't help it, she flinched. She felt him inhale sharply. "You did," he said. "You slept with him." He sounded almost betrayed.

"It's none of your business."

He caught at her face, turning her to look at him, fingers digging into her chin. "You can't *screw* someone into being good. Nicely heartless move, though." His lovely mouth curved into a cold smile. "You know he doesn't remember any of it, right? Did he show you a good time, at least? Because I would have."

She tasted bile in her throat. "You're my brother."

"Those words don't mean anything where we're concerned. We aren't human. Their rules don't apply to us. Stupid laws about what DNA can be mixed with what. Hypocritical, really, considering. We're already experiments. The rulers of ancient Egypt used to marry their siblings, you know. Cleopatra married her brother. Strengthens the bloodline."

She looked at him with loathing. "I knew you were crazy," she said. "But I didn't realize you were absolutely, spectacularly out of your goddamned mind."

"Oh, I don't think there's anything crazy about it. Who do we belong with but each other?"

"Jace," she said. "I belong with Jace."

He made a dismissive noise. "You can have Jace."

"I thought you needed him."

"I do. But not for what you need him for." His hands were suddenly on her waist. "We can share him. I don't care what you do. As long as you know you belong to me."

She raised her hands, meaning to shove him away. "I don't belong to you. I belong to *me*."

The look in his eyes froze her in place. "I think you know better than that," he said, and brought his mouth down on hers, hard.

For a moment she was back in Idris, standing in front of the burned Fairchild manor, and Sebastian was kissing her, and she felt as if she were falling into darkness, into a tunnel that had no end. At the time she'd thought there was something wrong with her. That she couldn't kiss anyone but Jace. That she was broken.

Now she knew better. Sebastian's mouth moved on hers, as hard and cold as a razor-slice in the dark, and she raised herself up on the tips of her toes, and bit down hard on his lip.

He yelled and spun away from her, his hand to his mouth. She could taste his blood, bitter copper; it dripped down his chin as he stared at her with incredulous eyes. "You—"

She whirled and kicked him, hard, in the stomach, hoping it was still sore from where she'd punched him before. As he doubled up, she shot by him, running for the stairs. She was halfway there when she felt him grab her by the back of her collar. He swung her around as if he were swinging a baseball bat, and flung her at the wall. She hit it hard and sank to her knees, the breath knocked out of her.

Sebastian started toward her, his hands flexing at his sides, his eyes shimmering black like a shark's. He looked terrifying; Clary knew she ought to be frightened, but a cold, glassy detachment had come over her. Time seemed to have slowed. She remembered the fight in the junk shop in Prague, how she had disappeared into her own world where each movement was as precise as the movement of a watch. Sebastian reached down toward her, and she pushed up, off the ground, sweeping her legs sideways, knocking his feet out from under him.

He fell forward, and she rolled out of the way, bouncing to her feet. She didn't bother trying to run this time. Instead she grabbed the porcelain vase off the table and, as Sebastian rose to his feet, swung it at his head. It shattered, spraying water and leaves, and he staggered back, blood blooming against his white-silver hair.

He snarled and sprang at her. It was like being slammed by a wrecking ball. Clary flew backward, smashing through the glass tabletop, and hit the ground in an explosion of shards and agony. She screamed as Sebastian landed on top of her, driving her body down into the shattered glass, his lips drawn back in a snarl. He brought his arm down backhanded and cracked her across the face. Blood blinded her; she choked on the taste of it in her mouth, and its salt stung her eyes. She jerked up her knee, catching him in the stomach, but it was like kicking a wall. He grabbed her hands, forcing them down by her sides.

"Clary, Clary, Clary," he said. He was gasping. At least she'd winded him. Blood ran in a slow trickle from a gash on the side of his head, staining his hair scarlet. "Not bad. You weren't much of a fighter back in Idris."

"Get off me—"

He moved his face close to hers. His tongue darted out. She tried to jerk away but couldn't move fast enough as he licked the blood off the side of her face, and grinned. The grin split his lip, and more blood ran in a trickle down his chin. "You asked me who I belong to," he whispered. "I belong to *you.* Your blood is my blood, your bones my bones. The first time you saw me, I looked familiar, didn't I? Just like you looked familiar to me."

She gaped at him. "You're out of your mind."

"It's in the Bible," he said. "The Song of Solomon. 'Thou hast ravished my heart, my sister, my spouse; thou hast ravished my heart with one of thine eyes, with one chain of thy neck.'" His fingers brushed her throat, looping into the chain there, the chain that had held the Morgenstern ring. She wondered if he would crush her windpipe. "'I sleep, but my heart waketh: it is the voice of my beloved that knocketh, saying, Open to me, my sister, my love.'" His blood dripped onto her face. She held herself still, her body humming with the effort, as his hand slipped from her throat, along her side, to her waist. His fingers slid inside the waistband of her jeans. His skin was hot, burning; she could feel that he wanted her.

"You don't love me," she said. Her voice was thin; he was crushing the air from her lungs. She remembered what her mother had said, that every emotion Sebastian showed was a pretense. Her thoughts were clear as crystal; she silently thanked the battle euphoria for doing what it had to do and keeping her focused while Sebastian sickened her with his touch.

"And you don't care that I'm your brother," he said. "I know how you felt about Jace, even when you thought he was your brother. You can't lie to me."

"Jace is better than you."

"No one's better than me." He grinned, all white teeth and blood. "'A garden enclosed is my sister,'" he said. "'A spring shut up, a fountain sealed.' But not anymore, right? Jace took care of that." He fumbled at the button on her jeans, and she took advantage of his distraction to seize up a good-size triangular piece of glass from the ground and slam the jagged edge of it into his shoulder.

The glass slid along her fingers, slicing them open. He yelled, jerking back, but more in surprise than pain; the gear protected him. She slashed the glass down harder, this time into his thigh, and when he reared back, she drove her other elbow into his throat. He went sideways, choking, and she rolled, pinning him under her as she yanked the bloody glass free of his leg. She drove the shard down toward the pulsing vein in his neck—and stopped.

He was laughing. He lay under her, and he was laughing, his laughter vibrating up through her own body. His skin was spattered with blood—her blood, dripping down on him, his own blood where she had cut him, his silver-white hair matted with it. He let his arms fall to either side of him, outstretched like wings, a broken angel, fallen out of the sky.

He said, "Kill me, little sister. Kill me, and you kill Jace, too."

She brought the glass shard down.

20

A Door into the Dark

Clary screamed aloud in pure frustration as the shard of glass embedded itself in the wooden floor, inches from Sebastian's throat.

She felt him laugh underneath her. "You can't do it," he said. "You can't kill me."

"To hell with you," she snarled. "I can't kill *Jace*."

"Same thing," he said, and, sitting up so fast she barely saw him move, he belted her across the face with enough force to send her skidding across the glass-strewn floor. Her slide was arrested when she hit the wall, gagged, and coughed blood. She buried her head against her forearm, the taste and smell of her own blood everywhere, sickening and metallic. A moment later Sebastian's hand was fisted in her jacket and he was hauling her to her feet.

She didn't fight him. What was the point? Why fight someone when they were willing to kill you and they knew you weren't willing to kill, or even seriously wound, them? They'd always win. She stood still as he examined her. "Could be worse," he said. "Looks like the jacket kept you from any real damage."

Real damage? Her body felt like it had been sliced all over with thin knives. She glared at him through her eyelashes as he swung her up into his arms. It was like it had been in Paris, when he'd carried her away from the Dahak demons, but then she had been—if not grateful, at least confused, and now she was filled with a boiling hatred. She kept her body tense while he carried her upstairs, his boots ringing on the glass. She was trying to forget she was touching him, that his arm was under her thighs, his hands possessive on her back.

I will kill him, she thought. *I will find a way, and I will kill him.*

He walked into Jace's room and dumped her onto the floor. She staggered back a step. He caught her and ripped the jacket off her. Underneath she was wearing only a T-shirt. It was shredded as if she'd run a cheese grater over it, and stained everywhere with blood.

Sebastian whistled.

"You're a mess, little sister," he said. "Better get in the bathroom and wash some of that blood off."

"No," she said. "Let them see me like this. Let them see what you had to do to get me to come with you."

His hand shot out and grabbed her under the chin, forcing her face up to his. Their faces were inches apart. She wanted to close her eyes but refused to give him the satisfaction; she stared back at him, at the loops of silver in his black eyes, the blood on his lip where she'd bitten him. "You belong to me," he said again. "And I will have you by my side, however I have to force you to be there."

"Why?" she demanded, rage as bitter on her tongue as the taste of blood. "What do you care? I know you can't kill Jace, but you could kill me. Why don't you just *do* it?"

Just for a moment, his eyes went distant, glassy, as if he were seeing something invisible to her. "This world will be consumed by hellfire," he said. "But I will bring you and Jace safely through the flames if you only do what I ask. It is a grace I extend to no one else. Do you not see how foolish you are to reject it?"

"Jonathan," she said. "Don't you see how impossible it is to ask me to fight by your side when you want to *burn down the world?*"

His eyes refocused on her face. "But why?" It was almost plaintive. "Why is this world so precious to you? You *know* that there are others." His own blood was very red against his stark white skin. "Tell me you love me. Tell me you love me and will fight with me."

"I'll never love you. You were wrong when you said we have the same blood. Your blood is poison. Demon poison." She spat the last words.

He only smiled, his eyes glowing darkly. She felt something burn on her upper arm, and she jumped before she realized it was a stele; he was tracing an *iratze* on her skin. She hated him even as the pain faded. His bracelet clanked on his wrist as he moved his hand skillfully, completing the rune.

"I knew you lied," she said to him suddenly.

"I tell so many lies, sweetheart," he said. "Which one specifically?"

"Your bracelet," she said. "'*Acheronta movebo.*' It doesn't mean 'Thus always to tyrants.' That's '*sic semper tyrannis.*' This is from Virgil. '*Flectere si nequeo superos, Acheronta movebo.*' 'If I cannot move Heaven, I will raise Hell.'"

"Your Latin's better that I thought."

"I learn fast."

"Not fast enough." He released his grip on her chin. "Now get into the bathroom and clean yourself up," he said, shoving her backward. He grabbed her mother's ceremonial dress off the bed and dumped it into her arms. "Time grows short, and my patience wears thin. If you're not out in ten minutes, I'll come in after you. And trust me, you won't like that."

"I'm starving," Maia said. "I feel like I haven't eaten in days." She pulled the refrigerator door open and peered in. "Oh, yuck."

Jordan pulled her back, wrapping his arms around her, and nuzzled the back of her neck. "We can order food. Pizza, Thai, Mexican, whatever you want. As long as it doesn't cost more than twenty-five dollars."

She turned around in his arms, laughing. She was wearing one of his shirts; it was a little too big on him, and on her it hung nearly to her knees. Her hair was pulled up in a knot at the back of her neck. "Big spender," she said.

"For you, anything." He lifted her up by the waist and set her on one of the counter stools. "You can have a taco." He kissed her. His lips were sweet, slightly minty from toothpaste. She felt the buzz in her body that came from touching him, that started at the base of her spine and shot through all her nerves.

She giggled against his mouth, wrapping her arms around his neck. A sharp ringing cut through the humming in her blood as Jordan pulled away, frowning. "My phone." Hanging on to her with one hand, he fumbled behind himself on the counter until he found it. It had stopped ringing, but he lifted it anyway, frowning. "It's the Praetor."

The Praetor never called, or at least rarely. Only when something was of deadly importance. Maia sighed and leaned back. "Take it."

He nodded, already lifting the phone to his ear. His voice was a soft murmur in the back of her consciousness as she jumped down from the counter and went to the refrigerator, where the take-out menus were pinned. She riffled through them until she found the menu for the local Thai place she liked, and turned around with it in her hand.

Jordan was now standing in the middle of the living room, white-faced, with his phone forgotten in his hand. Maia could hear a tinny, distant voice coming from it, saying his name.

Maia dropped the menu and hurried across the room to him. She took the phone out of his hand, disconnected the call, and set it on the counter. "Jordan? What happened?"

"My roommate—Nick—you remember?" he said, disbelief in his hazel eyes. "You never met him but—"

"I saw the photos of him," she said. "Has something happened?"

"He's dead."

"How?"

"Throat torn out, all his blood gone. They think he tracked his assignment down and she killed him."

"Maureen?" Maia was shocked. "But she was just a little girl."

"She's a vampire now." He took a ragged breath. "Maia . . ."

She stared at him. His eyes were glassy, his hair tousled. A sudden panic rose inside her. Kissing and cuddling and even sex were one thing. Comforting someone when they were stricken with loss was something else. It meant commitment. It meant caring. It meant you wanted to ease their pain, and at the same time you were thanking God that whatever the bad thing was that had happened, it hadn't happened to *them*.

"Jordan," she said softly, and reaching up on her toes, she put her arms around him. "I'm sorry."

Jordan's heart beat hard against hers. "Nick was only seventeen."

"He was a Praetor, like you," she said softly. "He knew it was dangerous. *You're* only eighteen." He tightened his grip on her but said nothing. "Jordan," she said. "I love you. I love you and I'm sorry."

She felt him freeze. It was the first time she'd said the words since a few weeks before she'd been bitten. He seemed to be holding his breath. Finally he let it out with a gasp.

"Maia," he croaked. And then, unbelievably, before he could say another word—her phone rang.

"Never mind," she said. "I'll ignore it."

He let her go, his face soft, bemused with grief and amazement. "No," he said. "No, it could be important. You go ahead."

She sighed and went to the counter. It had stopped ringing by the time she reached it, but there was a text message blinking on the screen. She felt her stomach muscles tighten.

"What is it?" Jordan asked, as if he had sensed her sudden tension. Maybe he had.

"A 911. An emergency." She turned to him, holding the

phone. "A call to battle. It went out to everyone in the pack. From Luke—and Magnus. We have to leave right away."

Clary sat on the floor of Jace's bathroom, her back against the tile of the tub, her legs stretched out in front of her. She had cleaned the blood from her face and body, and rinsed her bloody hair in the sink. She was wearing her mother's ceremonial dress, rucked up to her thighs, and the tiled floor was cold against her bare feet and calves.

She looked down at her hands. They ought to look different, she thought. But they were the same hands she'd always had, thin fingers, squared-off nails—you didn't want long nails when you were an artist—and freckles on the backs of the knuckles. Her face looked the same too. All of her seemed the same, but she wasn't. These past few days had changed her in ways she couldn't quite yet fully comprehend.

She stood up and looked at herself in the mirror. She was pale, between the flame colors of her hair and the dress. Bruises decorated her shoulders and throat.

"Admiring yourself?" She hadn't heard Sebastian open the door, but there he was, smirking intolerably as always, propped against the frame of the doorway. He was wearing a kind of gear she had never seen before: the usual tough material, but in a scarlet color like fresh blood. He had also added an accessory to his outfit—a recurved crossbow. He held it casually in one hand, though it must have been heavy. "You look lovely, sister. A fitting companion for me."

She bit back her words with the taste of blood that still lingered in her mouth, and walked toward him. He caught at her arm as she tried to squeeze past him in the doorway. His hand ran over her bare shoulder. "Good," he said. "You're not Marked here. I hate it when women ruin their skin with scars. Keep the Marks on your arms and legs."

"I'd rather you didn't touch me."

He snorted, and swung the crossbow up. A bolt was fitted to it, ready to fire. "Walk," he said. "I'll be right behind you."

It took every ounce of effort she had not to flinch away from him. She turned and walked toward the door, feeling a burning between her shoulder blades where she imagined the arrow of the crossbow was trained. They moved like that down the glass stairs and through the kitchen and living room. He grunted at the sight of Clary's scrawled rune on the wall, reached around her, and under his hand a doorway appeared. The door itself swung open onto a square of darkness.

The crossbow jabbed Clary hard in the back. "Move."

Taking a deep breath, she stepped out into the shadows.

Alec slammed his hand against the button in the small cage elevator, and slumped back against the wall. "How much time do we have?"

Isabelle checked the glowing screen of her mobile phone. "About forty minutes."

The elevator lurched upward. Isabelle cast a covert glance at her brother. He looked tired—dark circles were under his eyes. Despite his height and strength, Alec, with his blue eyes and soft black hair almost to his collar, looked more delicate than he was. "I'm fine," he said, answering her unspoken question. "You're the one who's going to be in trouble for staying away from home. I'm over eighteen. I can do what I want."

"I texted Mom every night and told her I was with you and Magnus," Isabelle said as the elevator came to a stop. "It's not like she didn't know where I was. And speaking of Magnus . . ."

Alec reached across her and pulled the elevator's inside cage door open. "What?"

"Are you two okay? I mean, getting along all right?"

Alec shot her an incredulous look as he stepped out into the entryway. "Everything's going to hell in a handbasket, and you want to know about my relationship with Magnus?"

"I've always wondered about that expression," Isabelle said thoughtfully as she hurried after her brother down the hallway. Alec had long, long legs and, though she was fast, it was hard to keep up with him when he wanted it to be. "Why a handbasket? What *is* a handbasket, and why is it a particularly good form of transportation?"

Alec, who had been Jace's *parabatai* long enough to have learned to ignore conversational tangents, said, "Magnus and I are okay, I guess."

"Uh-oh," Isabelle said. "Okay, you guess? I know what it means when you say that. What happened? Did you have a fight?"

Alec was tapping his fingers against the wall as they raced along, a sure sign that he was uncomfortable. "Quit trying to meddle around in my love life, Iz. What about you? Why aren't you and Simon a couple? You obviously like him."

Isabelle let out a squawk. "I am *not* obvious."

"You are, actually," Alec said, sounding as if it surprised him, too, now that he thought about it. "Gazing at him all moony-eyed. The way you freaked out at the lake when the Angel appeared—"

"I thought Simon was dead!"

"What, *more* dead?" said Alec unkindly. Seeing the expression on his sister's face, he shrugged. "Look, if you like him, fine. I just don't see why you're not dating."

"Because he doesn't like *me*."

"Of course he does. Guys always like you."

"Forgive me if I think your opinion is biased."

"Isabelle," Alec said, and now there was kindness in his voice, the tone she associated with her brother—love and exasperation mixed together. "You know you're gorgeous. Guys have chased you since . . . forever. Why would Simon be different?"

She shrugged. "I don't know. But he is. I figure the ball is in his court. He knows how I feel. But I don't think he's rushing to do anything about it."

"To be fair, it's not like he doesn't have anything else going on."

"I know, but—he's always been like this. Clary—"

"You think he's still in love with Clary?"

Isabelle chewed her lip. "I—not exactly. I think she's the one thing he still has from his human life, and he can't let her go. And as long as he doesn't let her go, I don't know if there's room for me."

They had almost reached the library. Alec looked sideways at Isabelle through his lashes. "But if they're just friends—"

"Alec." She held up her hand, indicating that he should be quiet. Voices were coming from the library, the first one strident and immediately recognizable as their mother's:

"What do you mean she's missing?"

"No one's seen her in two days," said another voice—soft, female, and slightly apologetic. "She lives alone, so people weren't sure—but we thought, since you know her brother—"

Without a pause Alec straight-armed the door of the library open. Isabelle ducked past him to see her mother sitting behind the massive mahogany desk in the center of the room. In front of her stood two familiar figures: Aline Penhallow, dressed in gear, and beside her Helen Blackthorn, her curly hair in disarray. Both of them turned, looking surprised, as the door opened. Helen, beneath her freckles, was pale; she was also in gear, which drained the color out of her skin even more.

"Isabelle," said Maryse, rising to her feet. "Alexander. What's happened?"

Aline reached for Helen's hand. Silver rings flashed on both their fingers. The Penhallow ring, with its design of mountains, glinted on Helen's finger, while the intertwined thorn pattern of the Blackthorn family ring adorned Aline's. Isabelle felt her eyebrows go up; exchanging family rings was serious business. "If we're intruding, we can go—" Aline began.

"No, stay," said Izzy, striding forward. "We might need you."

Maryse settled back into her chair. "So," she said. "My children grace me with their presence. Where have you two been?"

"I told you," Isabelle said. "We were at Magnus's."

"Why?" Maryse demanded. "And I'm not asking you, Alexander. I'm asking my daughter."

"Because the Clave stopped looking for Jace," said Isabelle. "But we didn't."

"And Magnus was willing to help," Alec added. "He's been up all these nights, searching through spell books, trying to figure out where Jace might be. He even raised the—"

"No." Maryse put up a hand to silence him. "Don't tell me. I don't want to know." The black phone on her desk started to ring. They all stared at it. A black phone call was a call from Idris. No one moved to answer it, and in a moment it was silent.

"Why are you here?" Maryse demanded, turning her attention back to her offspring.

"We were looking for Jace—," Isabelle began again.

"It's the Clave's job to do that," Maryse snapped. She looked tired, Isabelle noticed, the skin stretched thin under her eyes. Lines at the corners of her mouth drew her lips into a frown. She was thin enough that the bones of her wrists seemed to protrude. "Not yours."

Alec slammed his hand down on the desk, hard enough to make the drawers rattle. "Would you *listen* to us? The Clave didn't find Jace, but we did. And Sebastian right along with him. And now we know what they're planning, and we have"—he glanced at the clock on the wall—"barely any time to stop them. Are you going to help or not?"

The black phone rang again. Again Maryse didn't even move to answer it. She was looking at Alec, her face white with shock. "You did what?"

"We know where Jace is, Mom," said Isabelle. "Or at least, where he's going to be. And what he's going to do. We know Sebastian's plan, and he has to be stopped. Oh, and we know how we can kill Sebastian but not Jace—"

"Stop." Maryse shook her head. "Alexander, explain. Concisely, and without hysteria. Thank you."

Alec launched into the story—leaving out, Isabelle thought, all the *good* parts, which was how he managed to summarize things so neatly. As abbreviated as his rendition was, both Aline and Helen were gaping by the end of it. Maryse stood very still, her features immobile. When Alec was done, she said in a hushed voice:

"Why have you done these things?"

Alec looked taken aback.

"For Jace," Isabelle said. "To get him back."

"You realize that by putting me in this position, you give me no choice but to notify the Clave," said Maryse, her hand resting on the black phone. "I wish you hadn't come here."

Isabelle's mouth went dry. "Are you seriously mad at us for finally telling you what's going on?"

"If I notify the Clave, they will send all their reinforcements. Jia will have no choice but to give them instructions to kill Jace on sight. Do you have any idea how many Shadowhunters Valentine's son has following him?

Alec shook his head. "Maybe forty, it sounds like."

"Say we brought twice as many as that. We could be fairly confident of defeating his forces, but what kind of chance would Jace have? There's almost no certainty he'd make it through alive. They'll kill him just to be sure."

"Then, we can't tell them," said Isabelle. "We'll go ourselves. We'll do this without the Clave."

But Maryse, looking at her, was shaking her head. "The Law says we have to tell them."

"I don't care about the Law—," Isabelle began angrily. She caught sight of Aline looking at her, and slammed her mouth shut.

"Don't worry," Aline said. "I'm not going to say anything to my mother. I owe you guys. Especially you, Isabelle." She tightened her jaw, and Isabelle remembered the darkness under a bridge in Idris, and her whip tearing into a demon, its claws locked onto Aline. "And besides, Sebastian killed my cousin. The *real* Sebastian Verlac. I have my own reasons to hate him, you know."

"Regardless," said Maryse. "If we do not tell them, we will be breaking the Law. We could be sanctioned, or worse."

"Worse?" said Alec. "What are we talking about here? Exile?"

"I don't know, Alexander," said his mother. "It would be up to Jia Penhallow, and whoever wins the Inquisitor's position, to decide our punishment."

"Maybe it'll be Dad," muttered Izzy. "Maybe he'll go easy on us."

"If we fail to notify them of this situation, Isabelle, there is no chance your father will make Inquisitor. None," said Maryse.

Isabelle took a deep breath. "Could we get our Marks stripped?" she said. "Could we . . . lose the Institute?"

"Isabelle," said Maryse. "We could lose *everything*."

Clary blinked, her eyes adjusting to the darkness. She stood on a rocky plain, whipped by wind, with nothing to break the force of the gale. Patches of grass grew up between slabs of gray rock. In the far distance bleak, scree-covered karst hills rose, black and iron against the night sky. There were lights up ahead. Clary recognized the bobbing white glare of witchlight as the door of the apartment swung shut behind them.

There was the sound of a dull explosion. Clary whirled around to see that the door had vanished; there was a charred patch of dirt and grass, still smoldering, where it had been. Sebastian was staring at it in absolute astonishment. "What—"

She laughed. A dark glee rose in her at the look on his face.

She had never seen him shocked like that, his pretenses gone, his expression naked and horrified.

He swung the crossbow back up, inches from her chest. If he fired it at this distance, the bolt would tear through her heart, killing her instantly. "What have you done?"

Clary gazed at him with dark triumph. "That rune. The one you thought was an unfinished Opening rune. It wasn't. It just wasn't anything you'd ever seen before. It was a rune I created."

"A rune for *what?*"

She remembered putting the stele to the wall, the shape of the rune she had invented on the night when Jace had come to her at Luke's house. "Destroying the apartment the second someone opened the door. The apartment's gone. You can't use it again. No one can."

"Gone?" The crossbow shook; Sebastian's lips were twitching, his eyes wild. "You *bitch*. You little—"

"Kill me," she said. "Go ahead. And explain it to Jace afterward. *I dare you.*"

He looked at her, his chest heaving up and down, his fingers trembling on the trigger. Slowly he slid his hand away from it. His eyes were small and furious. "There are worse things than dying," he said. "And I will do them all to you, little sister, once you've drunk from the Cup. *And you will like it.*"

She spat at him. He jabbed her hard, agonizingly, in the chest with the tip of the bow. "Turn around," he snarled, and she did, dizzy with a mixture of terror and triumph as he prodded her down a rocky slope. She was wearing thin slippers, and she felt every pebble and crack in the rocks. As they neared the witchlight, Clary saw the scene laid out before them.

In front of her, the ground rose to a low hill. Atop the hill, facing north, was a massive ancient stone tomb. It reminded her slightly of Stonehenge: there were two narrow standing stones that held up a flat capstone, making the whole assemblage resemble a doorway. In front of the tomb a flat sill stone, like the floor of a stage, stretched across the shale and grass. Grouped before the flat stone was a half-circle of about forty Nephilim, robed in red, carrying witchlight torches. Within their half-circle, against the dark ground, blazed a blue-white pentagram.

Atop the flat stone stood Jace. He wore scarlet gear like Sebastian; they had never looked so alike.

Clary could see the brightness of his hair even from a distance. He was pacing the edge of the flat sill stone, and as they grew closer, Clary driven ahead by Sebastian, she could hear what he was saying.

". . . gratitude for your loyalty, even over these last difficult years, and grateful for your belief in our father, and now in his sons. And his daughter."

A murmur ran around the square. Sebastian shoved Clary forward, and they moved through the shadows, and then climbed up onto the stone behind Jace. Jace saw them and inclined his head before turning back to the crowd; he was smiling. "You are the ones who will be saved," he said. "A thousand years ago the Angel gave us his blood, to make us special, to make us warriors. But it was not enough. A thousand years have passed, and still we hide in the shadows. We protect mundanes we do not love from forces of which they remain ignorant, and an ancient, ossified Law prevents us from revealing ourselves as their saviors. We die in our hundreds, unthanked, unmourned but by our own kind, and without recourse to the Angel who created us." He moved closer to the edge of the rock platform. The Shadowhunters before it were standing in a half-circle. His hair looked like pale fire. "Yes. I dare to say it. The Angel who created us will not aid us, and we are alone. More alone even than the mundanes, for as one of their great scientists once said, they are like children playing with pebbles on the seashore, while all around them the great ocean of truth lies undiscovered. But we know the truth. We are the saviors of this earth, *and we should be ruling it*."

Jace was a good speaker, Clary thought with a sort of pain at her heart, in the same way that Valentine had been. She and Sebastian were behind him now, facing the plain and the crowd on it; she could feel the stares of the gathered Shadowhunters on both of them.

"Yes. Ruling it." He smiled, a lovely easy smile, full of charm, edged with darkness. "Raziel is cruel and indifferent to our sufferings. It is time to turn from him. Turn to Lilith, Great Mother, who will give us power without punishment, leadership without the Law. Our birthright is power. It is time to claim it."

He looked sideways with a smile as Sebastian moved forward. "And now I'll let you hear the rest of it from Jonathan, whose dream this is," said Jace smoothly, and he retreated, letting Sebastian slide easily into his place. He took another step back, and now he was beside Clary, his hand reaching down to twine with hers.

"Good speech," she muttered. Sebastian was speaking; she ignored him, focusing on Jace. "Very convincing."

"You think? I was going to start off 'Friends, Romans, evildoers . . .' but I didn't think they'd see the humor."

"You think they're evildoers?"

He shrugged. "The Clave would." He looked away from Sebastian, down at her. "You look beautiful," he said, but his voice was oddly flat. "What happened?"

She was caught off guard. "What do you mean?"

He opened his jacket. Underneath he was wearing a white shirt. It was stained at the side and the sleeve with red. She noticed he was careful to turn away from the crowd as he showed her the blood. "I feel what he feels," he said. "Or did you forget? I had to *iratze* myself without anyone noticing. It felt like someone was slicing my skin with a razor blade."

Clary met his gaze. There was no point lying, was there? There was no going back, literally or figuratively. "Sebastian and I had a fight."

His eyes searched her face. "Well," he said, letting his jacket fall closed, "I hope you've worked it out, whatever it was."

"Jace . . . ," she began, but he had given his attention to Sebastian now. His profile was cold and clear in the moonlight, like a silhouette cut out of dark paper. In front of them Sebastian, who had set down his crossbow, raised his arms. "Are you with me?" he cried.

A murmur ran around the square, and Clary tensed. One of the group of Nephilim, an older man, threw his hood back and scowled. "Your father made us many promises. None were fulfilled. Why should we trust you?"

"Because I will bring you the fulfillment of my promises now. Tonight," Sebastian said, and from his tunic he drew the imitation Mortal Cup. It glowed softly white under the moon.

The murmuring was louder now. Under its cover Jace said, "I hope this goes smoothly. I feel like I didn't sleep last night at all."

He was facing the crowd and the pentagram, a look of keen interest on his face. His face was delicately angular in the witchlight. She could see the scar on his cheek, the hollows at his temples, the lovely shape of his mouth. *I won't remember this,* he had said. *When I'm back—like I was, under his control, I won't remember being myself.* And it was true. He had forgotten every detail. Somehow, though she had known it, had seen him forget, the pain of the reality was acute.

Sebastian stepped down off the rock and moved toward the pentagram. At the edge of it he began to chant. "*Abyssum invoco. Lilith invoco. Mater mea, invoco.*"

He drew a thin dagger from his belt. Tucking the Cup into the curve of his arm, he used the edge of the blade to slice into his palm. Blood welled, black in the moonlight. He slid the knife back into his belt and held his bleeding hand over the Cup, still chanting in Latin.

It was now or never. "Jace," Clary whispered. "I know this isn't really you. I know there's a part of you that can't be all right with this. Try to remember who you are, Jace Lightwood."

His head whipped around, and he looked at her in astonishment. "What are you talking about?"

"Please try to remember, Jace. I love you. You love me—"

"I do love you, Clary," he said, an edge to his voice. "But you said you understood. This is it. The culmination of everything we've worked toward."

Sebastian flung the contents of the Cup into the center of the pentagram. "*Hic est enim calix sanguinis mei.*"

"Not *we,*" Clary whispered. "I'm not part of this. Neither are you—"

Jace inhaled sharply. For a moment Clary thought it was

because of what she'd said—that maybe, somehow, she was breaking through his shell—but she followed his gaze and saw that a spinning ball of fire had appeared in the center of the pentagram. It was about the size of a baseball, but as she gazed, it grew, elongating and shaping itself, until at last it was the outline of a woman, made all of flames.

"Lilith," Sebastian said in a ringing voice. "As you called me forth, now I call you. As you gave me life, so I give life to you."

Slowly the flames darkened. She stood before them all now, Lilith, half again the height of an ordinary human, stripped naked with her black hair waterfalling down her back to her ankles. Her body was as gray as ash, fissured with black lines like volcanic lava. She turned her eyes to Sebastian, and they were writhing black snakes.

"My child," she breathed.

Sebastian seemed to glow, like witchlight himself—pale skin, pale hair, and his clothes looked black in the moonlight. "Mother, I have called you up as you wished of me. Tonight you will not just be my mother but mother to a new race." He indicated the waiting Shadowhunters, who were motionless, probably with shock. It was one thing to know a Greater Demon was going to be called, another to see one in the flesh. "The Cup," he said, and held it out to her, its pale white rim stained with his blood.

Lilith chuckled. It sounded like massive stones grinding against one another. She took the Cup and, as casually as one might pick an insect off a leaf, tore a gash in her ashy gray wrist with her teeth. Very slowly, sludgy black blood trickled forth, spattering into the Cup, which seemed to change, darkening under her touch, its clear translucence turning to mud. "As the

Mortal Cup has been to the Shadowhunters, both a talisman and a means of transformation, so shall this Infernal Cup be to you," she said in her charred, windblown voice. She knelt, holding out the Cup to Sebastian. "Take of my blood and drink."

Sebastian took the Cup from her hands. It had turned black now, a shimmering black like hematite.

"As your army grows, so shall my strength," Lilith hissed. "Soon I will be strong enough to truly return—and we shall share the fire of power, my son."

Sebastian inclined his head. "We proclaim you Death, my mother, and profess your resurrection."

Lilith laughed, raising her arms. Fire licked up her body, and she launched herself into the air, exploding into a dozen spinning particles of light that faded like the embers of a dying fire. When they were gone completely, Sebastian kicked at the pentagram, breaking its continuity, and raised his head. There was an awful smile on his face.

"Cartwright," he said. "Bring forth the first."

The crowd parted, and a robed man pushed forward, a stumbling woman at his side. A chain bound her to his arm, and long, tangled hair hid her face from view. Clary tensed all over. "Jace, what is this? What's going on?"

"Nothing," he said, looking ahead absently. "No one's going to be hurt. Just changed. Watch."

Cartwright, whose name Clary dimly remembered from her time in Idris, put his hand on his captive's head and forced her to their knees. Then he bent and took hold of her hair, jerking her head up. She looked up at Sebastian, blinking in terror and defiance, her face clearly outlined by the moon.

Clary sucked in her breath. "*Amatis.*"

21
Raising Hell

Luke's sister looked up, her blue eyes, so much like Luke's, fastening on Clary. She seemed dizzied, shocked, her expression a little unfocused as if she'd been drugged. She tried to start to her feet, but Cartwright shoved her back down. Sebastian started toward them, the Cup in his hand.

Clary scrambled forward, but Jace caught her by the arm, pulling her back. She kicked at him, but he'd already swung her up into his arms, his hand over her mouth. Sebastian was speaking to Amatis in a low, hypnotic voice. She shook her head violently, but Cartwright caught her by her long hair and jerked her head back. Clary heard her cry out, a thin sound over the wind.

Clary thought of the night she'd stayed up watching Jace's

chest rise and fall, thinking how she could end all this with a single knife blow. But *all this* hadn't had a face, a voice, a plan. Now that it wore Luke's sister's face, now that Clary knew the plan, it was too late.

Sebastian had one hand fisted in the back of Amatis's hair, the Cup jammed against her mouth. As he forced the contents down her throat, she retched and coughed, black fluid dripping down her chin.

Sebastian yanked the Cup back, but it had done its work. Amatis made an awful hacking sound, her body jerking upright. Her eyes bulged, turning as dark as Sebastian's. She slapped her hands over her face, a wail escaping her, and Clary saw in astonishment that the Voyance rune was fading from her hand—fading to pallor—and then it was gone.

Amatis dropped her hands. Her expression had smoothed and her eyes were blue again. They fastened on Sebastian.

"Release her," Clary's brother said to Cartwright, his gaze on Amatis. "Let her come to me."

Cartwright snapped the chain binding him to Amatis and stepped back, a curious mixture of apprehension and fascination on his face.

Amatis remained still a moment, her hands lolling at her sides. Then she stood and walked over to Sebastian. She knelt before him, her hair brushing the dirt. "Master," she said. "How may I serve you?"

"Rise," Sebastian said, and Amatis rose from the ground gracefully. She seemed to have a new way of moving, all of a sudden. All Shadowhunters were adroit, but she moved now with a silent grace that Clary found oddly chilling. She stood straight in front of Sebastian. For the first time Clary saw that what she had taken for a long white dress was a nightgown, as if she had been awakened and spirited out of bed. What a nightmare, to wake up here, among these hooded figures, in this bitter, abandoned place. "Come here to me," Sebastian beckoned, and Amatis stepped toward him. She was a head shorter than him at least, and she craned her head up as he whispered to her. A cold smile split her face.

Sebastian raised his hand. "Would you like to fight Cartwright?"

Cartwright dropped the chain he had been holding, his hand going to his weapons belt through the gap in his cloak. He was a young man, with fairish hair, and a wide, square-jawed face. "But I—"

"Surely some demonstration of her power is in order," said Sebastian. "Come, Cartwright, she is a woman, and older than you are. Are you afraid?"

Cartwright looked bewildered, but he drew a long dagger from his belt. "Jonathan—"

Sebastian's eyes flashed. "Fight him, Amatis."

Her lips curved. "I would be delighted to," she said, and sprang. Her speed was astonishing. She leaped into the air and swung her foot forward, knocking the dagger from his grip. Clary watched in astonishment as she darted up his body, driving her knee into his stomach. He staggered back, and she slammed her head into his, spinning around his body to jerk him hard by the back of his robes, yanking him to the ground. He landed at her feet with a sickening crack, and groaned in pain.

"And *that's* for dragging me out of my bed in the middle of the night," Amatis said, and wiped the back of her hand across her lip, which was bleeding slightly. A faint murmur of strained laughter went around the crowd.

"And there you see it," said Sebastian. "Even a Shadowhunter of no particular skill or strength—your pardon, Amatis—can become stronger, swifter, than their seraphically allied counterparts." He slammed one fist into the opposite palm. "Power. *Real* power. Who is ready for it?"

There was a moment of hesitation, and then Cartwright stumbled to his feet, one hand curved protectively over his stomach. "I am," he said, shooting a venomous look at Amatis, who only smiled.

Sebastian held up the Infernal Cup. "Then, come forward."

Cartwright moved toward Sebastian, and as he did, the other Shadowhunters broke formation, surging toward the place where Sebastian stood, forming a ragged line. Amatis stood serenely to the side, her hands folded. Clary stared at her, willing the older woman to look at her. It was Luke's sister. If things had gone as planned, she would have been Clary's step-aunt now.

Amatis. Clary thought of her small canal house in Idris, the way she had been so kind, the way she had loved Jace's father so much. *Please look at me,* she thought. *Please show me you're still yourself.* As if Amatis had heard her silent prayer, she raised her head and looked directly at Clary.

And smiled. Not a kind smile or a reassuring smile. Her smile was dark and cold and quietly amused. It was the smile of someone who would watch you drown, Clary thought, and not lift a finger to help. It was not Amatis's smile. It was not Amatis at all. Amatis was gone.

Jace had taken his hand from her mouth, but she felt no

desire to scream. No one here would help her, and the person standing with his arms around her, prisoning her with his body, wasn't Jace. The way that clothes retained the shape of their owner even if they had not been worn for years, or a pillow kept the outline of the head of the person who had once slept there even if they were long dead, that was all he was. An empty shell she had filled with her wishes and love and dreams.

And in doing so she had done the real Jace a terrible wrong. In her quest to save him, she had almost forgotten who she was saving. And she remembered what he had said to her during those few moments when he had been himself. *I hate the thought of him being with you.* Him. *That other me.* Jace had known they were two different people—that himself with the soul scraped out wasn't himself at all.

He had tried to turn himself over to the Clave, and she hadn't let him. She hadn't listened to what he'd wanted. She had made the choice for him—in a moment of flight and panic, but she had made it—not realizing that her Jace would rather die than be like this, and that she'd been not so much saving his life as damning him to an existence he would despise.

She sagged against him, and Jace, taking her sudden shift as an indicator that she wasn't fighting him anymore, loosened his grip on her. The last of the Shadowhunters was in front of Sebastian, reaching eagerly for the Infernal Cup as he held it out. "Clary—," Jace began.

She never found out what he would have said. There was a cry, and the Shadowhunter reaching for the Cup staggered back, an arrow in his throat. In disbelief Clary whipped her head around and saw, standing on top of the stone dolmen,

Alec, in gear, holding his bow. He grinned in satisfaction and reached back over his shoulder for another arrow.

And then, coming from behind him, the rest of them poured out onto the plain. A pack of wolves, running low to the ground, their brindled fur shining in the variegated light. Maia and Jordan were among them, she guessed. Behind them walked familiar Shadowhunters in an unbroken line: Isabelle and Maryse Lightwood, Helen Blackthorn and Aline Penhallow, and Jocelyn, her red hair visible even at a distance. With them was Simon, the hilt of a silver sword protruding over the curve of his shoulder, and Magnus, hands crackling with blue fire.

Her heart leaped in her chest. "I'm here!" she called out to them. *"I'm here!"*

"Can you see her?" Jocelyn demanded. "Is she there?"

Simon tried to focus on the milling darkness ahead of him, his vampire senses sharpening at the distinct scent of blood. Different kinds of blood, mixing together—Shadowhunter blood, demon blood, and the bitterness of Sebastian's blood. "I see her," he said. "Jace has hold of her. He's pulling her behind that line of Shadowhunters there."

"If they're loyal to Jonathan like the Circle was to Valentine, they'll make a wall of bodies to protect him, and Clary and Jace along with him." Jocelyn was all cold maternal fury, her green eyes burning. "We're going to have to break through it to get to them."

"What we need to get to is Sebastian," said Isabelle. "Simon, we'll hack a path for you. You get to Sebastian and run him through with Glorious. Once he falls—"

"The others will probably scatter," said Magnus. "Or,

depending on how tied they are to Sebastian, they might die or collapse along with him. We can hope, at least." He craned his head back. "Speaking of hope, did you see that shot Alec got off with his bow? That's my boyfriend." He beamed and wiggled his fingers; blue sparks shot from them. He shone all over. Only Magnus, Simon thought resignedly, would have access to sequined battle armor.

Isabelle uncurled her whip from around her wrist. It shot out in front of her, a lick of golden fire. "Okay, Simon," she said. "Are you ready?"

Simon's shoulders tightened. They were still some distance from the line of the opposing army—he didn't know how else to think of them—who were holding their line in their red robes and gear, their hands bristling with weapons. Some of them were exclaiming out loud in confusion. He couldn't hold back a grin.

"Name of the Angel, Simon," said Izzy. "What's there to smile about?"

"Their seraph blades don't work anymore," said Simon. "They're trying to figure out why. Sebastian just shouted at them to use other weapons." A cry came up from the line as another arrow swooped down from the tomb and buried itself in the back of a burly red-robed Shadowhunter, who collapsed forward. The line jerked and opened slightly, like a fracture in a wall. Simon, seeing his chance, dashed forward, and the others rushed with him.

It was like diving into a black ocean at night, an ocean filled with sharks and viciously toothed sea creatures colliding against one another. It was not the first battle Simon had ever been in, but during the Mortal War he had been newly

Marked with the Mark of Cain. It hadn't quite begun working yet, though many demons had reeled back upon seeing it. He had never thought he would miss it, but he missed it now, as he tried to shove forward through the tightly packed Shadowhunters, who hacked at him with blades. Isabelle was on one side of him, Magnus on the other, protecting him—protecting Glorious. Isabelle's whip sang out strong and sure, and Magnus's hands spat fire, red and green and blue. Lashes of colored fire struck the dark Nephilim, burning them where they stood. Other Shadowhunters screamed as Luke's wolves slunk among them, nipping and biting, leaping for their throats.

A dagger shot out with astonishing speed and sliced at Simon's side. He cried out but kept going, knowing the wound would knit itself together in seconds. He pushed forward—

And froze. A familiar face was before him. Luke's sister, Amatis. As her eyes settled on him, he saw the recognition in them. What was she doing here? Had she come to fight alongside them? But—

She lunged at him, a darkly gleaming dagger in her hand. She was *fast*—but not so fast that his vampire reflexes couldn't have saved him, if he hadn't been too astonished to move. Amatis was Luke's sister; he knew her; and that moment of disbelief might have been the end of him if Magnus hadn't jumped in front of him, shoving him backward. Blue fire shot from Magnus's hand, but Amatis was faster than the warlock, too. She spun away from the blaze and under Magnus's arm, and Simon caught the flash of moonlight off the blade of her knife. Magnus's eyes widened in shock as her midnight-colored blade drove downward, slicing through his armor. She jerked it back, the blade now slick with reflective blood; Isabelle screamed as Magnus collapsed to his knees. Simon tried to turn toward him, but the surge and pressure of the fighting crowd was carrying him away. He cried out Magnus's name as Amatis bent over the fallen warlock and raised the dagger a second time, aiming for his heart.

"Let go of me!" Clary shouted, writhing and kicking as she did her best to wrench herself out of Jace's grip. She could see almost nothing above the surging crowd of red-clad Shadowhunters that stood in front of her, Jace, and Sebastian, blocking her family and friends. The three of them were a few feet behind the line of battle; Jace was holding her tightly as she struggled, and Sebastian, to the side of them, was watching events unfold with a look of dark fury on his face. His lips were moving. She couldn't tell if he was swearing, praying, or chanting the words of a spell. "Let go of me, you—"

Sebastian turned, a frightening expression on his face, somewhere between a grin and a snarl. "Shut her up, Jace."

Jace, still gripping Clary, said, "Are we just going to stand back here and let them protect us?" He jerked his chin toward the line of Shadowhunters.

"Yes," Sebastian said. "We are too important to risk getting hurt, you and I."

Jace shook his head. "I don't like it. There are too many on the other side." He craned his neck to look out over the crowd. "What about Lilith? Can you summon her back, have her help us?"

"What, right here?" There was contempt in Sebastian's tone. "No. Besides, she's too weak now to be of much help. Once she could have smote down an army, but that piece of scum Downworlder with his Mark of Cain scattered her essence through the voids between the worlds. It was all she could do to appear and give us her blood."

"Coward," Clary spat at him. "You turned all these people into your slaves and you won't even fight to protect them—"

Sebastian raised his hand as if he meant to backhand her across the face. Clary wished he would, wished Jace could be there to see it happen when he did, but a smirk flashed across Sebastian's mouth instead. He lowered his hand. "And if Jace let you go, I suppose you'd fight?"

"Of course I would—"

"On what side?" Sebastian took a quick step toward her, raising the Infernal Cup. She could see what was inside it. Though many had drunk from it, the blood had remained at the same level. "Lift her head up, Jace."

"No!" She redoubled her efforts to get away. Jace's hand slipped beneath her chin, but she thought she felt hesitation in his touch.

"Sebastian," he said. "Not—"

"Now," Sebastian said. "There's no need for us to remain here. *We* are the important ones, not these cannon fodder. We've proved the Infernal Cup works. That's what matters." He seized the front of Clary's dress. "But it will be much easier to escape," he said, "without this one kicking and screaming and punching every step of the way."

"We can make her drink later—"

"No," Sebastian snarled. "Hold her still." And he raised the Cup and jammed it against Clary's lips, trying to pry open her mouth. She fought him, gritting her teeth. "Drink," Sebastian said in a vicious whisper, so low she doubted Jace could hear it. "I told you by the end of this night you would do whatever

I wanted. *Drink*." His black eyes darkened, and he dug the Cup in, slicing her bottom lip.

She tasted blood as she reached behind her, grabbing Jace's shoulders, using his body to push off against as she kicked out with her legs. She felt the seam rip on her dress as it split up the side and her feet slammed solidly against Sebastian's rib cage. He staggered back with the wind knocked out of him, just as she jerked her head back, hearing the solid *crack* as her skull connected with Jace's face. He yelled and loosened his grip on her enough for her to tear free. She ripped away from him and plunged into the battle without looking back.

Maia raced along the rocky ground, starlight raking its cool fingers through her coat, the strong scents of battle assailing her sensitive nose—blood, sweat, and the burned-rubber stench of dark magic.

The pack had spread out widely over the field, leaping and killing with deadly teeth and claws. Maia kept close to Jordan's side, not because she needed his protection but because she had discovered that side by side they fought better and more effectively. She had been in only one battle before, on Brocelind Plain, and that had been a chaotic whirl of demons and Downworlders. There were many fewer combatants here on the Burren, but the dark Shadowhunters were formidable, swinging their swords and daggers with a swift, frightening force. Maia had seen one slender man use a short-bladed dagger to whip the head off a wolf who'd been in midleap; what had collapsed to the ground was a headless human body, bloody and unrecognizable.

Even as she thought it, one of the scarlet-robed Nephilim

loomed up in front of them, a double-edged sword gripped in his hands. The blade was stained red-black under the moonlight. Jordan, beside Maia, snarled, but she was the one who launched herself at the man. He ducked away, slashing out with his sword. She felt a sharp pain in her shoulder and hit the ground on all four paws, pain stabbing through her. There was a clatter, and she knew she had knocked the man's sword from his hand. She growled in satisfaction and spun around, but Jordan was already leaping for the Nephilim's throat—

And the man caught him by the neck, out of the air, as if he were catching hold of a rebellious puppy. "Downworlder scum," he spat, and though it wasn't the first time Maia had heard such insults, something about the icy hatred of his tone made her shudder. "You should be a coat. I should be *wearing* you."

Maia sank her teeth into his leg. Coppery blood exploded into her mouth as the man shouted in pain and staggered back, kicking at her, his hold on Jordan slipping. Maia gripped him tight as Jordan lunged again, and this time the Shadowhunter's shout of rage was cut short as the werewolf's claws tore his throat open.

Amatis drove the knife toward Magnus's heart—just as an arrow whistled through the air and thumped into her shoulder, knocking her aside with such force that she spun halfway around and fell face-forward to the rocky ground. She was screaming, a noise quickly drowned out by the clash of weapons all around them. Isabelle knelt down by Magnus's side; Simon, glancing up, saw Alec on the stone tomb, standing frozen with the bow in his hands. He was probably too far away to see Magnus clearly; Isabelle had her hands against the warlock's chest, but Magnus—Magnus, who was always so kinetic, so bursting with energy—was utterly still under Isabelle's ministrations. She looked up and saw Simon staring at them; her hands were red with blood, but she shook her head at him violently.

"Keep going!" she shouted. *"Find Sebastian!"*

With a wrench Simon turned himself around and plunged back into the battle. The tight line of red-clad Shadowhunters had started to come undone. The wolves were darting here and there, herding the Shadowhunters away from one another. Jocelyn was sword to sword with a snarling man whose free arm dripped blood—and Simon realized something bizarre as he staggered forward, pushing his way through the narrow gaps between skirmishes: *None of the red-clad Nephilim were Marked.* Their skin was bare of decoration.

They were also, he realized—seeing out of the corner of his eye one of the enemy Shadowhunters lunging for Aline with a swinging mace, only to be gutted by Helen, darting in from the side—much faster than any Nephilim he had seen before, other than Jace and Sebastian. They moved with the swiftness of vampires, he thought, as one of them slashed at a leaping wolf, slitting its belly open. The dead werewolf crashed to the ground, now the corpse of a stocky man with curling fair hair. *Not Maia or Jordan.* Relief swamped him, and then guilt; he staggered forward, the smell of blood thick around him, and again he missed the Mark of Cain. If he had still borne it, he thought, he could have burned all these enemy Nephilim to the ground where they stood—

One of the dark Nephilim rose up in front of him, swinging a single-edged broadsword. Simon ducked, but he didn't need to. The man was barely halfway through the swing when an arrow caught him in the neck and he went down, gurgling blood. Simon's head jerked up, and he saw Alec, still atop the tomb; his face was a stony mask, and he was firing off arrows with machinelike precision, his hand reaching back mechanically to grasp one, fit it to the bow, and let fly. Each one struck a target, but Alec barely seemed to notice. By the time the arrow was flying, he was reaching for another one. Simon heard another one whistle by him and slam into a body as he darted forward, making for a cleared section of the battlefield—

He froze. There she was. Clary, a tiny figure fighting her way through the crowd bare-handed, kicking and pushing to get past. She wore a torn red dress, and her hair was a tangled mass and when she saw him, a look of incredulous amazement crossed her face. Her lips shaped his name.

Just behind her was Jace. His face was bloody. The crowd parted as he plunged through it, letting him by. Behind him, in the gap left by his passing, Simon could see a shimmer of red and silver—a familiar figure, topped now with white-gilt hair like Valentine's.

Sebastian. Still hiding behind the last line of defense of dark Shadowhunters. Seeing him, Simon reached over his shoulder and hauled Glorious from its sheath. A moment later a surge in the crowd hurled Clary toward him. Her eyes were nearly black with adrenaline, but her joy at seeing him was plain. Relief spilled through Simon, and he realized he'd been wondering if she was still herself, or changed, as Amatis had been.

"Give me the sword!" she cried, her voice almost drowned out by the clang of metal on metal. She thrust her arm forward to take it, and in that moment she was no longer Clary, his friend

since childhood, but a Shadowhunter, an avenging angel who belonged with that sword in her hand.

He held it out to her, hilt first.

Battle was like a whirlpool, Jocelyn thought, cutting her way through the pressing crowd, slashing out with Luke's *kindjal* at any spot of red that she saw. Things came at you and then surged away so quickly that all one was really aware of was a sense of uncontrollable danger, the struggle to stay alive and not drown.

Her eyes flicked frantically through the mass of fighters, searching for her daughter, for a glimpse of red hair—or even for a sight of Jace, because where he was, Clary would be too. There were boulders strewn across the plain, like icebergs in an unmoving sea. She scrambled up the rough edge of one, trying to get a better view of the battlefield, but she could make out only close-pressed bodies, the flash of weapons, and the dark, low-running shapes of wolves among the fighters.

She turned to scramble back down the boulder—

Only to find someone waiting for her at the bottom. Jocelyn came up short, staring.

He wore scarlet robes, and there was a livid scar along one of his cheeks, a relic of some battle unknown to her. His face was pinched and no longer young, but there was no mistaking him. "Jeremy," she said slowly, her voice barely audible over the clamor of the fighting. "Jeremy Pontmercy."

The man who had once been the youngest member of the Circle looked at her out of bloodshot eyes. "Jocelyn Morgenstern. Have you come to join us?"

"Join you? Jeremy, no—"

"You were in the Circle once," he said, stepping closer to her. A long dagger with an edge like a straight razor hung from his right hand. "You were one of us. And now we follow your son."

"I broke with you when you followed my husband," said Jocelyn. "Why do you think I'd follow you now that my son leads you?"

"Either you stand with us or against us, Jocelyn." His face hardened. "You cannot stand against your own son."

"Jonathan," she said softly. "He is the greatest evil Valentine ever committed. I could never stand with him. In the end, I never stood with Valentine. So what hope do you have of convincing me now?"

He shook his head. "You misunderstand me," he said. "I mean you cannot stand against him. Against us. The Clave cannot. They are not prepared. Not for what we can do. Are *willing* to do. Blood will run in the streets of every city. The world will burn. Everything you know will be destroyed. And we will rise from the ashes of your defeat, the phoenix triumphant. This is your only chance. I doubt your son will give you another."

"Jeremy," she said. "You were so young when Valentine recruited you. You could come back, come back even to the Clave. They would be lenient—"

"I can never come back to the Clave," he said with a hard satisfaction. "Don't you understand? Those of us who stand with your son, we are Nephilim no longer."

Nephilim no longer. Jocelyn began to reply, but before she could speak, blood burst from his mouth. He crumpled, and as he did, Jocelyn saw, standing behind him bearing a broadsword, Maryse.

The two women looked at each other for a moment over Jeremy's body. Then Maryse turned and walked back toward the battle.

The moment Clary's fingers closed around the hilt, the sword exploded with a golden light. Fire blazed down the blade from the tip, illuminating words carved blackly into the side—*Quis ut Deus?*—and making the hilt shine as if it contained the light of the sun. She nearly dropped it, thinking it had caught on fire, but the flame seemed contained inside the sword, and the metal was cool beneath her palms.

Everything after that seemed to happen very slowly. She turned, the sword blazing in her grip. Her eyes searched the crowd desperately for Sebastian. She couldn't see him, but she knew he was behind the tight knot of Shadowhunters she had punched through to get here. Gripping the sword, she moved toward them, only to find her way blocked.

By Jace.

"Clary," he said. It seemed impossible that she could hear him; the sounds around them were deafening: screams and growls, the clatter of metal on metal. But the sea of fighting figures seemed to have fallen away from them on either side like the Red Sea parting, leaving a clear space around her and Jace.

The sword burned, slippery in her grip. "Jace. Get out of the way."

She heard Simon, behind her, shout something; Jace was shaking his head. His golden eyes were flat, unreadable. His face was bloody; she had cracked her head against his cheekbone, and the skin was swelling and darkening. "Give me the sword, Clary."

"No." She shook her head, backing up a step. Glorious lit the space they stood in, lit the trampled, blood-smeared grass around her, and lit Jace as he moved toward her. "Jace. I can separate you from Sebastian. I can kill him without hurting you—"

His face twisted. His eyes were the same color as the fire in the sword, or they were reflecting it back, she wasn't sure which, and as she looked at him she realized it didn't matter. She was seeing Jace and not-Jace: her memories of him, the beautiful boy she'd met first, reckless with himself and others, learning to care and be careful. She remembered the night they had spent together in Idris, holding hands across the narrow bed, and the bloodstained boy who had looked at her with haunted eyes and confessed to being a murderer in Paris. "*Kill* him?" Jace-who-wasn't-Jace demanded now. "Are you out of your mind?"

And she remembered that night by Lake Lyn, Valentine driving the sword into him, and the way her own life had seemed to bleed out with his blood.

She had watched him die, there on the beach in Idris. And afterward, when she had brought him back, he had crawled to her and looked down at her with those eyes that burned like the Sword, like the incandescent blood of an angel.

I was in the dark, he had said. *There was nothing there but shadows, and I was a shadow. And then I heard your voice.*

But that voice blurred into another, more recent one: Jace facing down Sebastian in the living room of Valentine's apartment, telling her that he would rather die than live like this. She could hear him now, speaking, telling her to give him the sword, that if she didn't, he would take it from her. His voice was harsh, impatient, the voice of someone talking to a child. And she knew in that moment that just as he wasn't Jace, the Clary he loved wasn't her. It was a memory of her, blurred and distorted: the image of someone docile, obedient; someone who didn't understand that love given without free will or truthfulness wasn't love at all.

"Give me the sword." His hand was out, his chin raised, his tone imperious. "Give it to me, Clary."

"You want it?"

She raised Glorious, the way he had taught her to, balancing the weight of it, though it felt heavy in her hand. The flame in it grew brighter, until it seemed to reach upward and touch the stars. Jace was only the sword's length away from her, his golden eyes incredulous. Even now he couldn't believe she might hurt him, really hurt him. Even now.

She took a deep breath. "Take it."

She saw his eyes blaze up the way they had that day by the lake, and then she drove the sword into him, just as Valentine had done. She understood now that this was the way it had to be. He had died like this, and she had ripped him back from death. And now it had come again.

You cannot cheat death. In the end it will have its own.

Glorious sank into his chest, and she felt her bloody hand slide on the hilt as the blade ground against the bones of his rib cage, driving through him until her fist thumped against his body and she froze. He hadn't moved, and she was pressed up against him now, gripping Glorious as blood began to spill from the wound in his chest.

There was a scream—a sound of rage and pain and terror, the sound of someone being brutally torn apart. *Sebastian,*

Clary thought. Sebastian, screaming as his bond with Jace was severed.

But Jace. Jace didn't make a sound. Despite everything, his face was calm and peaceful, the face of a statue. He looked down at Clary, and his eyes shone, as if he were filling with light.

And then he began to burn.

Alec didn't remember scrambling down from the top of the stone tomb, or pushing his way across the stony plain among the litter of fallen bodies: dark Shadowhunters, dead and wounded werewolves. His eyes were seeking out only one person. He stumbled and nearly fell; when he looked up, his gaze scanning the field in front of him, he saw Isabelle, kneeling beside Magnus on the stony ground.

It felt like there was no air in his lungs. He had never seen Magnus so pale, or so still. There was blood on his leather armor, and blood on the ground beneath him. But it was impossible. Magnus had lived so long. He was permanent. A fixture. In no world Alec's imagination could conjure did Magnus die before he did.

"Alec." It was Izzy's voice, swimming up toward him as if through water. "Alec, he's breathing."

Alec let his own breath out in a shaking gasp. He held a hand out to his sister. "Dagger."

She handed him one silently. She had never paid as much attention as he had in field first aid classes; she had always said runes would do the job. He slit open the front of Magnus's leather armor and then the shirt beneath it, his teeth gritted. It could be that the armor was all that was holding him together.

He peeled back the sides gingerly, surprised at the steadiness of his own hands. There was a good deal of blood, and a wide stab wound under the right side of Magnus's ribs. But from the rhythm of Magnus's breathing, it was clear his lungs hadn't been punctured. Alec yanked off his jacket, wadded it up, and pressed it against the still-bleeding wound.

Magnus's eyes fluttered open. "Ouch," he said feebly. "Quit leaning on me."

"*Raziel*," Alec breathed thankfully. "You're all right." He slipped his free hand under Magnus's head, his thumb stroking Magnus's bloody cheek. "I thought . . ."

He looked up to glance at his sister before he said anything too embarassing, but she had slipped quietly away.

"I saw you fall," Alec said quietly. He bent down and kissed Magnus lightly on the mouth, not wanting to hurt him. "I thought you were dead."

Magnus smiled crookedly. "What, from that scratch?" He glanced down at the reddening jacket in Alec's hand. "Okay, a deep scratch. Like, from a really, really big cat."

"Are you delirious?" Alec said.

"No." Magnus's eyebrows drew together. "Amatis was aiming for my heart, but she didn't get anything vital. The problem is that the blood loss is sapping my energy and my ability to heal myself." He took a deep breath that ended in a cough. "Here, give me your hand." He raised his hand, and Alec twined their fingers together, Magnus's palm hard against his. "Do you remember, the night of the battle on Valentine's ship, when I needed some of your strength?"

"Do you need it again now?" Alec said. "Because you can have it."

"I always need your strength, Alec," Magnus said, and

closed his eyes as their intertwined fingers began to shine, as if between them they held the light of a star.

Fire exploded up through the hilt of the angel's sword and along the blade. The flame shot through Clary's arm like a bolt of electricity, knocking her to the ground. Heat lightning sizzled up and down her veins, and she curled up in agony, clutching herself as if she could keep her body from blowing to pieces.

Jace fell to his knees. The sword still pierced him, but it was burning now, with a white-gold flame, and the fire was filling his body like colored water filling a clear glass pitcher. Golden flame shot through him, turning his skin translucent. His hair was bronze; his bones were hard, shining tinder visible through his skin. Glorious itself was burning away, dissolving in liquid drops like gold melting in a crucible. Jace's head was thrown back, his body arched like a bow as the conflagration raged through him. Clary tried to pull herself toward him across the rocky ground, but the heat radiating from his body was too much. His hands clutched at his chest, and a river of golden blood slipped through his fingers. The stone on which he knelt was blackening, cracking, turning to ash. And then Glorious burned up like the last of a bonfire, in a shower of sparks, and Jace collapsed forward, onto the stones.

Clary tried to stand, but her legs buckled under her. Her veins still felt as if fire were shooting through them, and pain was darting across the surface of her skin like the touch of hot pokers. She pulled herself forward, bloodying her fingers, hearing her ceremonial dress rip, until she reached Jace.

He was lying on his side with his head pillowed on one

arm, the other arm flung out wide. She crumpled beside him. Heat radiated from his body as if he were a dying bed of coals, but she didn't care. She could see the rip in the back of his gear where Glorious had torn through it. There were ashes from the burned rocks mixed in with the gold of his hair, and blood.

Moving slowly, every movement hurting as if she were old, as if she had aged a year for every second Jace had burned, she pulled him toward her, so he was on his back on the blood-stained and blackened stone. She looked at his face, no longer gold but still, and still beautiful.

Clary laid her hand against his chest, where the red of his blood stood out against the darker red of his gear. She had felt the edges of the blade grind against the bones of his ribs. She had seen his blood spill through his fingers, so much blood that it had stained the rocks beneath him black and had stiffened the edges of his hair.

And yet. *Not if he's more Heaven's than Hell's.*

"Jace," she whispered. All around them were running feet. The shattered remains of Sebastian's small army was fleeing across the Burren, dropping their weapons as they went. She ignored them. "*Jace.*"

He didn't move. His face was still, peaceful under the moonlight. His eyelashes threw dark, spidering shadows against the tops of his cheekbones.

"Please," she said, and her voice felt as if it were scraping out of her throat. When she breathed, her lungs burned. "Look at me."

Clary closed her eyes. When she opened them again, her mother was kneeling down beside her, touching her shoulder.

Tears were running down Jocelyn's face. But that couldn't be— Why would her mother be crying?

"Clary," her mother whispered. "Let him go. He's dead."

In the distance Clary saw Alec kneeling beside Magnus. "No," Clary said. "The sword—it burns away what's evil. He could still live."

Her mother ran a hand down her back, her fingers tangling in Clary's filthy curls. "Clary, no . . ."

Jace, Clary thought fiercely, her hands curling around his arms. *You're stronger than this. If this is you, really you, you'll open your eyes and look at me.*

Suddenly Simon was there, kneeling on the other side of Jace, his face smeared with blood and grime. He reached for Clary. She whipped her head up to glare at him, at him and her mother, and saw Isabelle coming up behind them, her eyes wide, moving slowly. The front of her gear was stained with blood. Unable to face Izzy, Clary turned away, her eyes on the gold of Jace's hair.

"Sebastian," Clary said, or tried to say. Her voice came out as a croak. "Someone should go after him." *And leave me alone.*

"They're looking for him now." Her mother leaned in, anxious, her eyes wide. "Clary, let him go. Clary, baby . . ."

"Let her be," Clary heard Isabelle say sharply. She heard her mother's protest, but everything they were doing seemed to be going on at a great distance, as if Clary were watching a play from the last row. Nothing mattered but Jace. Jace, burning. Tears scalded the backs of her eyes. "Jace, goddamit," she said, her voice ragged. "*You are not dead.*"

"Clary," Simon said gently. "It was a chance . . ."

Come away from him. That was what Simon was asking, but

she couldn't. She wouldn't. "Jace," she whispered. It was like a mantra, the way he had once held her at Renwick's and chanted her name over and over. "Jace *Lightwood* . . ."

She froze. There. A movement so tiny, it was hardly a movement at all. The flutter of an eyelash. She leaned forward, almost overbalancing, and pressed her hand against the torn scarlet material over his chest, as if she could heal the wound she had made. She felt instead—so wonderful that for a moment it made no sense to her, could not possibly be—under her fingertips, the rhythm of his heart.

Epilogue

At first, Jace was conscious of nothing. Then there was darkness, and within the darkness, a burning pain. It was as if he'd swallowed fire, and it choked him and burned his throat. He gasped desperately for air, for a breath that would cool the fire, and his eyes flew open.

He saw darkness and shadows—a dimly lit room, known and unknown, with rows of beds and a window letting in hollow blue light, and he was in one of the beds, blankets and sheets pulled down and tangled around his body like ropes. His chest hurt as if a dead weight lay on it, and his hand scrabbled to find what it was, encountering only a thick bandage wrapped around his bare skin. He gasped again, another cooling breath.

"Jace." The voice was familiar to him as his own, and then

there was a hand gripping his, fingers interlacing with his own. With a reflex born out of years of love and familiarity, he gripped back.

"Alec," he said, and he was almost shocked at the sound of his own voice in his ears. It hadn't changed. He felt as if he had been scorched, melted, and recreated like gold in a crucible—but as what? Could he really be himself again? He looked up at Alec's anxious blue eyes, and knew where he was. The infirmary at the Institute. Home. "I'm sorry . . ."

A slim, callused hand stroked his cheek, and a second familiar voice said, "Don't apologize. You have nothing to apologize for."

He half-closed his eyes. The weight on his chest was still there: half a wound and half guilt. "Izzy."

Her breath caught. "It really is you, right?"

"Isabelle," Alec began, as if to warn her not to upset Jace, but Jace touched her hand. He could see Izzy's dark eyes shining in the dawn light, her face full of hopeful expectancy. This was the Izzy only her family knew, loving and worried.

"It's me," he said, and cleared his throat. "I could understand if you didn't believe me, but I swear on the Angel, Iz, it's me."

Alec said nothing, but his grip on Jace's hand tightened. "You don't need to swear," he said, and with his free hand touched the *parabatai* rune near his collarbone. "I know. I can feel it. I don't feel like I'm missing a part of me anymore."

"I felt it too." Jace took a ragged breath. "Something missing. I felt it, even with Sebastian, but I didn't know what it was I was missing. But it was you. My *parabatai*." He looked at Izzy. "And you. My sister. And . . ." His eyelids burned suddenly with a scorching light: the wound on his chest throbbed, and he saw *her* face, lit by the blaze of the sword. A strange burning spread through his veins, like white fire. "Clary. Please tell me—"

"She's completely all right," Isabelle said hastily. There was something else in her voice—surprise, unease.

"You swear. You're not just telling me that because you don't want to upset me."

"*She* stabbed *you*," Isabelle pointed out.

Jace gave a strangled laugh; it hurt. "She saved me."

"She did," Alec agreed.

"When can I see her?" Jace tried not to sound too eager.

"It really *is* you," Isabelle said, her voice amused.

"The Silent Brothers have been in and out, checking on you," said Alec. "On this"—he touched the bandage on Jace's chest—"and to see if you were awake yet. When they find out you are, they'll probably want to talk to you before they let you see Clary."

"How long have I been out cold?"

"About two days," said Alec. "Since we got you back from the Burren and were pretty sure you weren't going to die. Turns out it's not that easy to completely heal a wound made by an archangel's blade."

"So what you're saying is that I'm going to have a scar."

"A big ugly one," said Isabelle. "Right across your chest."

"Well, damn," said Jace. "And I was relying on that money from the topless underwear modeling gig I had lined up, too." He spoke wryly, but he was thinking that it was right, somehow, that he have a scar: that he *should* be marked by what had happened to him, physically as well as mentally. He had almost lost his soul, and the scar would serve to remind him of the fragility of will, and the difficulty of goodness.

And of darker things. Of what lay ahead, and what he could not allow to happen. His strength was returning; he could feel it, and he would bend all of it against Sebastian. Knowing that, he felt suddenly lighter, a little of the weight gone from his chest. He turned his head, enough to look into Alec's eyes.

"I never thought I'd fight on the opposite side of a battle from you," he said hoarsely. "Never."

"And you never will again," Alec said, his jaw set.

"Jace," Isabelle said. "Try to stay calm, all right? It's just . . ."

Now what? "Is something else wrong?"

"Well, you're glowing a bit," Isabelle said. "I mean, just a smidge. Of the glowing."

"Glowing?"

Alec raised the hand that held Jace's. Jace could see, in the darkness, a faint shimmer across his forearm that seemed to trace the lines of his veins like a map. "We think it's a leftover effect from the archangel's sword," he said. "It'll probably fade soon, but the Silent Brothers are curious. Of course."

Jace sighed and let his head fall back against the pillow. He was too exhausted to muster up much interest in his new, illuminated state. "Does that mean you have to go?" he asked. "Do you have to get the Brothers?"

"They instructed us to get them when you woke," said Alec, but he was shaking his head, even as he spoke. "But not if you don't want us to."

"I feel tired," Jace confessed. "If I could sleep a few more hours . . ."

"Of course. Of course you can." Isabelle's fingers pushed his hair back, out of his eyes. Her tone was firm, absolute: fierce as a mother bear protecting her cub.

Jace's eyes began to close. "And you won't leave me?"

"No," Alec said. "No, we won't ever leave you. You know that."

"Never." Isabelle took his hand, the one Alec wasn't holding, and pressed it fiercely. "Lightwoods, all together," she whispered. Jace's hand was suddenly damp where she was holding it, and he realized she was crying, her tears splashing down—crying for him, because she loved him; even after everything that had happened, she still loved him.

They both did.

He fell asleep like that, with Isabelle on one side of him and Alec on the other, as the sun came up with the dawn.

"What do you mean, I still can't see him?" demanded Clary. She was sitting on the edge of the couch in Luke's living room, the cord of the phone wrapped so tightly around her fingers that the tips had turned white.

"It's been only three days, and he was unconscious for two of them," said Isabelle. There were voices behind her, and Clary strained her ears to hear who was talking. She thought she could pick out Maryse's voice, but was she talking to Jace? Alec? "The Silent Brothers are still examining him. They still say no visitors."

"Screw the Silent Brothers."

"No thanks. There's strong and silent, and then there's just freaky."

"Isabelle!" Clary sat back against the squashy pillows. It was a bright fall day, and sunlight streamed in through the living room windows, though it did nothing to lighten her mood. "I just want to know that he's all right. That he isn't injured permanently, and he hasn't swollen up like a melon—"

"Of course he hasn't swollen up like a melon, don't be ridiculous."

"I wouldn't know. I wouldn't know because no one will tell me anything."

"He's all right," Isabelle said, though there was something in her voice that told Clary she was holding something back. "Alec's been sleeping in the bed next to his, and Mom and I have been taking turns staying with him all day. The Silent Brothers haven't been *torturing* him. They just need to know what he knows. About Sebastian, the apartment, everything."

"But I can't believe Jace wouldn't call me if he could. Not unless this is because he doesn't want to see me."

"Maybe he doesn't," Isabelle said. "It could have been that whole thing where you stabbed him."

"Isabelle—"

"I was just kidding, believe it or not. Name of the Angel, Clary, can't you show some patience?" Isabelle sighed. "Never mind. I forgot who I was talking to. Look, Jace said—not that I'm supposed to repeat this, mind you—that he needed to talk to you in person. If you could just wait—"

"That's all I have been doing," Clary said. "Waiting." It was true. She'd spent the past two nights lying in her room at Luke's house, waiting for news about Jace and reliving the last week of her life over and over in excruciating detail. The Wild Hunt; the antiques store in Prague; fountains full of blood; the tunnels of Sebastian's eyes; Jace's body against hers; Sebastian jamming the Infernal Cup against her lips, trying to pry them apart; the bitter stench of demon ichor. Glorious blazing up her arm, spearing through Jace like a bolt of fire, the beat of his heart under her fingertips. He hadn't even opened his eyes, but Clary had screamed that he was alive, that his heart was beating, and his family had descended on them, even Alec, half-holding up an exceptionally pale Magnus. "All I do is go around and around inside my own head. It's making me crazy."

"And that's where we're in agreement. You know what, Clary?"

"What?"

There was a pause. "You don't need *my* permission to come here and see Jace," Isabelle said. "You don't need anyone's permission to do anything. You're Clary Fray. You go charging into every situation without knowing how the hell it's going to turn out, and then you get through it on sheer guts and craziness."

"Not where my personal life is concerned, Iz."

"Huh," said Isabelle. "Well, maybe you should." And she put the phone down.

Clary stared at her receiver, hearing the distant tinny buzz of the dial tone. Then, with a sigh, she hung up and headed into her bedroom.

Simon was sprawled on the bed, his feet on her pillows, his chin propped on his hands. His laptop was propped open at the foot of the bed, frozen on a scene from *The Matrix*. He looked up as she came in. "Any luck?"

"Not exactly." Clary went over to her closet. She'd already dressed for the possibility that she might see Jace today, in jeans and a soft blue sweater she knew he liked. She pulled a corduroy jacket on and sat down on the bed beside Simon, sliding her feet into boots. "Isabelle won't tell me anything. The Silent Brothers don't want Jace to have visitors, but whatever. I'm going over anyway."

Simon closed the laptop and rolled over onto his back. "That's my brave little stalker."

"Shut up," she said. "Do you want to come with me? See Isabelle?"

"I'm meeting Becky," he said. "At the apartment."

"Good. Give her my love." She finished lacing her boots and reached forward to brush Simon's hair away from his forehead. "First I had to get used to you with that Mark on you. Now I have to get used to you without it."

His dark brown eyes traced her face. "With or without it, I'm still just me."

"Simon, do you remember what was written on the blade of the sword? Of Glorious?"

"*Quis ut Deus.*"

"It's Latin," she said. "I looked it up. It means *Who is like God?* It's a trick question. The answer is no one—no one is like God. Don't you see?"

He looked at her. "See what?"

"You said it. *Deus*. God."

Simon opened his mouth, and then closed it again. "I . . ."

"I know Camille told you that she could say God's name because she didn't believe in God, but I think it has to do with what you believe about yourself. If you believe you're damned, then you are. But if you don't . . ."

She touched his hand; he squeezed her fingers briefly and released them, his face troubled. "I need some time to think about this."

"Whatever you need. But I'm here if you need to talk."

"And I'm here if *you* do. Whatever happens with you and Jace at the Institute . . . you know you can always come over to my place if you want to talk."

"How's Jordan?"

"Pretty good," said Simon. "He and Maia are definitely together now. They're in that ooky stage where I feel like I should be giving them space all the time." He crinkled up his nose. "When she's not there, he frets about how he feels insecure because she's dated a bunch of dudes and he's spent the past three years doing military-style training for the Praetor and pretending he was asexual."

"Oh, come on. I doubt she cares about that."

"You know men. We have delicate egos."

"I wouldn't describe Jace's ego as delicate."

"No, Jace's is sort of the antiaircraft artillery tank of male egos," Simon admitted. He was lying with his right hand splayed across his stomach, and the gold faerie ring glittered on his finger. Since the other had been destroyed, it no longer seemed to have any powers, but Simon wore it anyway. Impulsively Clary bent down and kissed his forehead.

"You're the best friend anyone could ever have, you know that?" she said.

"I did know that, but it's always nice to hear it again."

Clary laughed and stood up. "Well, we might as well walk to the subway together. Unless you want to hang around here with the 'rents instead of in your cool downtown bachelor pad."

"Right. With my lovelorn roommate and my sister." He slid off the bed and followed her as she walked out into the living room. "You're not just going to Portal?"

She shrugged. "I don't know. It seems . . . wasteful." She crossed the hall and, after knocking quickly, stuck her head into the master bedroom. "Luke?"

"Come on in."

She went in, Simon beside her. Luke was sitting up in bed.

The bulk of the bandage that wrapped his chest was visible as an outline beneath his flannel shirt. There was a stack of magazines on the bed in front of him. Simon picked one up. "*Sparkle Like an Ice Princess: The Winter Bride*," he read out loud. "I don't know, man. I'm not sure a tiara of snowflakes would be the best look for you."

Luke glanced around the bed and sighed. "Jocelyn thought wedding planning might be good for us. Return to normalcy and all that." There were shadows under his blue eyes. Jocelyn had been the one to break the news to him about Amatis, while he was still at the police station. Though Clary had greeted him with hugs when he'd come home, he hadn't mentioned his sister once, and neither had she. "If it was up to me, I would elope to Vegas and have a fifty-dollar pirate-themed wedding with Elvis presiding."

"I could be the wench of honor," Clary suggested. She looked at Simon expectantly. "And you could be . . ."

"Oh, no," he said. "I am a hipster. I am too cool for themed weddings."

"You play D and D. You're a geek," she corrected him fondly.

"Geek is chic," Simon declared. "Ladies love nerds."

Luke cleared his throat. "I assume you came in here to tell me something?"

"I'm heading over to the Institute to see Jace," Clary said. "Do you want me to bring you anything back?"

He shook his head. "Your mother's at the store, stocking up." He leaned over to ruffle her hair, and winced. He was healing, but slowly. "Have fun."

Clary thought of what she was probably facing at the

Institute—an angry Maryse, a wearied Isabelle, an absent Alec, and a Jace who didn't want to see her—and sighed. "You bet."

The subway tunnel smelled like the winter that had finally come to the city—cold metal, dank, wet dirt, and a faint hint of smoke. Alec, walking along the tracks, saw his breath puff out in front of his face in white clouds, and he jammed his free hand into the pocket of his blue peacoat to keep it warm. The witchlight he held in his other hand illuminated the tunnel—green and cream-colored tiles, discolored with age, and sprung wiring, dangling like spiderwebs from the walls. It had been a long time since this tunnel had seen a moving train.

Alec had gotten up before Magnus had woken, again. Magnus had been sleeping late; he was resting from the battle at the Burren. He had used a great deal of energy to heal himself, but he wasn't entirely well yet. Warlocks were immortal but not invulnerable, and "a few inches higher and that would have been it for me," Magnus had said ruefully, examining the knife wound. "It would have stopped my heart."

There had been a few moments—minutes, even—when Alec had truly thought Magnus was dead. And after so much time spent worrying that he would grow old and die before Magnus did. What a bitter irony it would have been. The sort of thing he deserved, for seriously contemplating the offer Camille had made him, even for a second.

He could see light up ahead—the City Hall station, lit by chandeliers and skylights. He was about to douse his witchlight when he heard a familiar voice behind him.

"Alec," it said. "Alexander Gideon Lightwood."

Alec felt his heart lurch. He turned around slowly. "Magnus?"

Magnus moved forward, into the circle of illumination cast by Alec's witchlight. He looked uncharacteristically somber, his eyes shadowed. His spiky hair was rumpled. He wore only a suit jacket over a T-shirt, and Alec couldn't help wondering if he was cold.

"Magnus," Alec said again. "I thought you were asleep."

"Evidently," Magnus said.

Alec swallowed hard. He had never seen Magnus angry, not really. Not like this. Magnus's cat eyes were remote, impossible to read. "Did you follow me?" Alec asked.

"You could say that. It helped that I knew where you were going." Moving stiffly, Magnus took a folded square of paper from his pocket. In the dim light, all Alec could see was that it was covered with a careful, flourishing handwriting. "You know, when she told me you'd been here—told me about the bargain she'd struck with you—I didn't believe her. I didn't *want* to believe her. But here you are."

"Camille *told* you—"

Magnus held up a hand to cut him off. "Just stop," he said wearily. "Of course she told me. I warned you she was a master at manipulation and politics, but you didn't listen to me. Who do you think she'd rather have on her side—me or you? You're eighteen years old, Alexander. You're not exactly a powerful ally."

"I already told her," Alec said. "I wouldn't kill Raphael. I came here and told her the bargain was off, I wouldn't do it—"

"You had to come all the way here, to this abandoned subway station, to deliver that message?" Magnus raised his eyebrows. "You don't think you could have delivered essentially the same message by, perhaps, staying away?"

"It was—"

"And even if you did come here—unnecessarily—and tell her the deal was off," Magnus went on in a deadly calm voice, "why are you here *now*? Social call? Just visiting? Explain it to me, Alexander, if there's something I'm missing."

Alec swallowed. Surely there must be a way to explain. That he had been coming down here, visiting Camille, because she was the only person he could talk to about Magnus. The only person who knew Magnus, as he did, not just as the High Warlock of Brooklyn but as someone who could love and be loved back, who had human frailties and peculiarities and odd, irregular currents of mood that Alec had no idea how to navigate without advice. "Magnus—" Alec took a step toward his boyfriend, and for the first time that he remembered, Magnus moved away from him. His posture was stiff and unfriendly. He was looking at Alec the way he'd look at a stranger, a stranger he didn't like very much.

"I'm so sorry," Alec said. His voice sounded scratchy and uneven to his own ears. "I never meant—"

"I was thinking about it, you know," Magnus said. "That's part of why I wanted the Book of the White. Immortality can be a burden. You think of the days that stretch out before you, when you have been everywhere, seen everything. The one thing I hadn't experienced was growing old with someone—someone I loved. I thought perhaps it would be you. But that does not give you the right to make the length of my life *your choice* and not mine."

"I know." Alec's heart raced. "I know, and I wasn't going to do it—"

"I'll be out all day," Magnus said. "Come and get your things out of the apartment. Leave your key on the dining room table." His eyes searched Alec's face. "It's over. I don't want to see you again, Alec. Or any of your friends. I'm tired of being their pet warlock."

Alec's hands had begun to shake, hard enough that he dropped his witchlight. The light winked out, and he fell to his knees, scrabbling on the ground among the trash and the dirt. At last something lit up before his eyes, and he rose to see Magnus standing before him, the witchlight in his hand. It shone and flickered with a strangely colored light.

"It shouldn't light up like that," Alec said automatically. "For anyone but a Shadowhunter."

Magnus held it out. The heart of the witchlight was glowing a dark red, like the coal of a fire.

"Is it because of your father?" Alec asked.

Magnus didn't reply, only tipped the rune-stone into Alec's palm. As their hands touched, Magnus's face changed. "You're freezing cold."

"I am?"

"Alexander . . ." Magnus pulled him close, and the witchlight flickered between them, its color changing rapidly. Alec had never seen a witchlight rune-stone do that before. He put his head against Magnus's shoulder and let Magnus hold him. Magnus's heart didn't beat like human hearts did. It was slower, but steady. Sometimes Alec thought it was the steadiest thing in his life.

"Kiss me," Alec said.

Magnus put his hand to the side of Alec's face and gently, almost absently, ran his thumb along Alec's cheekbone. When he bent to kiss him, he smelled like sandalwood. Alec clutched the sleeve of Magnus's jacket, and the witchlight, held between their bodies, flared up in colors of rose and blue and green.

It was a slow kiss, and a sad one. When Magnus drew away, Alec found that somehow he was holding the witchlight alone; Magnus's hand was gone. The light was a soft white.

Softly, Magnus said, "*Aku cinta kamu.*"

"What does that mean?"

Magnus disentangled himself from Alec's grip. "It means I love you. Not that that changes anything."

"But if you love me—"

"Of course I do. More than I thought I would. But we're still done," Magnus said. "It doesn't change what you did."

"But it was just a mistake," Alec whispered. "One mistake—"

Magnus laughed sharply. "One mistake? That's like calling the maiden voyage of the *Titanic* a minor boating accident. Alec, you tried to shorten my life."

"It was just— She offered, but I thought about it and I couldn't go through with it—I couldn't do that to you."

"But you had to think about it. And you never mentioned it to me." Magnus shook his head. "You didn't trust me. You never have."

"I do," Alec said. "I will—I'll try. Give me another chance—"

"No," Magnus said. "And if I might give you a piece of advice: Avoid Camille. There is a war coming, Alexander, and you don't want your loyalties to be in question. Do you?"

And with that he turned and walked away, his hands in his pockets—walking slowly, as if he were injured, and not just from the cut in his side. But he was walking away just the same. Alec watched him until he moved beyond the glow of the witchlight and out of sight.

***

The inside of the Institute had been cool in the summer, but now, with winter well and truly here, Clary thought, it was warm. The nave was bright with rows of candelabras, and the stained-glass windows glowed softly. She let the front door swing shut behind her and headed for the elevator. She was halfway up the center aisle when she heard someone laughing.

She turned. Isabelle was sitting in one of the old pews, her long legs slung over the back of the seats in front of her. She wore boots that hit her midthigh, slim jeans, and a red sweater that left one shoulder bare. Her skin was traced with black designs; Clary remembered what Sebastian had said about not liking it when women disfigured their skin with Marks, and shivered inside. "Didn't you hear me saying your name?" Izzy demanded. "You really can be astonishingly single-minded."

Clary stopped and leaned against a pew. "I wasn't ignoring you on purpose."

Isabelle swung her legs down and stood up. The heels on her boots were high, making her tower over Clary. "Oh, I know. That's why I said 'single-minded,' not 'rude.'"

"Are you here to tell me to go away?" Clary was pleased by the fact that her voice didn't shake. She wanted to see Jace. She wanted to see him more than anything else. But after what she'd been through this past month, she knew that what mattered was that he was alive, and that he was himself. Everything else was secondary.

"No," Izzy said, and started moving toward the elevator. Clary fell into step beside her. "I think the whole thing is ridiculous. You saved his life."

Clary swallowed against the cold feeling in her throat. "You said there were things I didn't understand."

"There are." Isabelle punched the elevator button. "Jace can explain them to you. I came down because I thought there were a few other things you should know."

Clary listened for the familiar creak, rattle, and groan of the old cage elevator. "Like?"

"My dad's back," Isabelle said, not meeting Clary's eyes.

"Back for a visit, or back for good?"

"For a visit. He's been selected to be the next Inquisitor." Isabelle sounded calm, but Clary remembered how hurt she had been when they'd found out Robert had been trying for the Inquisitor position. "Basically, Aline and Helen saved us from getting in real trouble for what happened in Ireland. When we came to help you, we did it without telling the Clave. My mom was sure that if we told them they'd send fighters to kill Jace. She couldn't do it. I mean, this is our family."

The elevator arrived with a rattle and a crash before Clary could say anything. She followed the other girl inside, fighting the strange urge to give Isabelle a hug. She doubted Izzy would like it.

"So Aline told the Consul—who is, after all, her mother—that there hadn't been any time to notify the Clave, that she'd been left behind with strict orders to call Jia, but there'd been some malfunction with the telephones and it hadn't worked. Basically, she lied her butt off. Anyway, that's our story, and we're sticking to it. I don't think Jia believed her, but it doesn't matter; it's not like Jia wants to punish Mom. She just had to have some kind of story she could grab on to so she didn't *have* to sanction us. After all, it's not like the operation was a disaster. We went in, got Jace out, killed most of the dark Nephilim, and got Sebastian on the run."

The elevator stopped rising and came to a crashing halt.

"Got Sebastian on the run," Clary repeated. "So we have no idea where he is? I thought maybe since I destroyed his apartment—the dimensional pocket—he could be tracked."

"We've tried," said Isabelle. "Wherever he is, he's still beyond or outside tracking capabilities. And according to the Silent Brothers, the magic that Lilith worked— Well, he's strong, Clary. Really strong. We have to assume he's out there, with the Infernal Cup, planning his next move." She pulled the cage door of the elevator open and stepped out. "Do you think he'll come back for you—or Jace?"

Clary hesitated. "Not right away," she said finally. "For him we're the last parts of the puzzle. He'll want everything set up first. He'll want an army. He'll want to be ready. We're like . . . the prizes he gets for winning. And so he doesn't have to be alone."

"He must be really lonely," Isabelle said. There was no sympathy in her voice; it was only an observation.

Clary thought of him, of the face that she'd been trying to forget, that haunted her nightmares and waking dreams. *You asked me who I belonged to.* "You have no idea."

They reached the stairs that led to the infirmary. Isabelle paused, her hand at her throat. Clary could see the square outline of her ruby necklace beneath the material of her sweater. "Clary . . ."

Clary suddenly felt awkward. She straightened the hem of her sweater, not wanting to look at Isabelle.

"What's it like?" Isabelle said abruptly.

"What's *what* like?"

"Being in love," Isabelle said. "How do you know you are? And how do you know someone else is in love with you?"

"Um . . ."

"Like Simon," Isabelle said. "How could you tell he was in love with you?"

"Well," said Clary. "He said so."

"He said so."

Clary shrugged.

"And before that, you had no idea?"

"No, I really didn't," said Clary, recalling the moment. "Izzy . . . if you have feelings for Simon, or if you want to know if he has feelings for you . . . maybe you should just *tell* him."

Isabelle fiddled with some nonexistent lint on her cuff. "Tell him what?"

"How you feel about him."

Isabelle looked mutinous. "I shouldn't have to."

Clary shook her head. "God. You and Alec, you're so alike—"

Isabelle's eyes widened. "We are not! We are totally not alike. I date around; he's never dated before Magnus. He gets jealous; I don't—"

"Everyone gets jealous." Clary spoke with finality. "And you're both so *stoic*. It's love, not the Battle of Thermopylae. You don't have to treat everything like it's a last stand. You don't have to keep everything inside."

Isabelle threw her hands up. "Suddenly you're an expert?"

"I'm not an expert," Clary said. "But I do know Simon. If you don't say something to him, he's going to assume it's because you're not interested, and he'll give up. He *needs* you, Iz, and you need him. He just also needs you to be the one to say it."

Isabelle sighed and whirled to begin mounting the steps. Clary could hear her muttering as she went. "This is your fault, you know. If you hadn't broken his heart—"

"Isabelle!"

"Well, you did."

"Yeah, and I seem to remember that when he got turned into a rat, you were the one who suggested we leave him in rat form. Permanently."

"I did not."

"You did—" Clary broke off. They had reached the next floor, where a long corridor stretched in both directions. Before the double doors of the infirmary stood the parchment-robed figure of a Silent Brother, hands folded, face cast down in a meditative stance.

Isabelle indicated him with an exaggerated wave. "There you go," she said. "Good luck getting past him to see Jace." And she walked off down the corridor, her boots clicking on the wooden floor.

Clary sighed inwardly and reached for the stele in her belt. She doubted there was a glamour rune that could fool a Silent Brother, but perhaps, if she could get close enough to use a sleep rune on his skin . . .

Clary Fray. The voice in her head was amused, and also familiar. It had no sound, but she recognized the shape of the thoughts, the way you might recognize the way someone laughed or breathed.

"Brother Zachariah." Resignedly she slid the stele back in place and moved closer to him, wishing Isabelle had stayed with her.

I presume you are here to see Jonathan, he said, lifting his head from the meditative stance. His face was still in shadow beneath the hood, though she could see the shape of an angular cheekbone. *Despite the orders of the Brotherhood.*

"Please call him Jace. It's too confusing otherwise."

'Jonathan' is a fine old Shadowhunter name, the first of names. The Herondales have always kept names in the family—

"He wasn't named by a Herondale," Clary pointed out. "Though he has a dagger of his father's. It says *S.W.H.* on the blade."

Stephen William Herondale.

Clary took another step toward the doors, and toward Zachariah. "You know a lot about the Herondales," she said. "And of all the Silent Brothers, you seem the most human. Most of them never show any emotion. They're like statues. But you seem to feel things. You remember your life."

Being a Silent Brother is life, Clary Fray. But if you mean I remember my life before the Brotherhood, I do.

Clary took a deep breath. "Were you ever in love? Before the Brotherhood? Was there ever anyone you would have died for?"

There was a long silence. Then:

Two people, said Brother Zachariah. *There are memories that time does not erase, Clarissa. Ask your friend Magnus Bane, if you do not believe me. Forever does not make loss forgettable, only bearable.*

"Well, I don't have forever," said Clary in a small voice. "Please let me in to see Jace."

Brother Zachariah did not move. She still could not see his face, only a suggestion of shadows and planes beneath the hood of his robe. Only his hands, clasped in front of him.

"*Please,*" Clary said.

* * *

Alec swung himself up onto the platform at the City Hall subway station and stalked toward the stairs. He had blocked out the image of Magnus walking away from him with one thought, and one only:

He was going to kill Camille Belcourt.

He strode up the stairs, drawing a seraph blade from his belt as he went. The light here was wavering and dim—he emerged onto the mezzanine below City Hall Park, where tinted glass skylights let in the wintery light. He tucked the witchlight into his pocket and raised the seraph blade.

"*Amriel,*" he whispered, and the sword blazed up, a bolt of lightning from his hand. He lifted his chin, his gaze sweeping the lobby. The high-backed sofa was there, but Camille was not on it. He'd sent her a message saying he was coming, but after the way she'd betrayed him, he supposed he shouldn't be surprised that she hadn't remained to see him. In a fury he stalked across the room and kicked the sofa, hard; it went over with a crash of wood and a puff of dust, one of the legs snapped off.

From the corner of the room came a tinkling silver laugh.

Alec whirled, the seraph blade blazing in his hand. The shadows in the corners were thick and deep; even Amriel's light could not penetrate them. "Camille?" he said, his voice dangerously calm. "Camille Belcourt. Come out here *now*."

There was another giggle, and a figure stepped forth from the darkness. But it was not Camille.

It was a girl—probably no older than twelve or thirteen—very thin, wearing a pair of ragged jeans and a pink, short-sleeved T-shirt with a glittery unicorn on it. She wore a long pink scarf as well, its ends dabbled in blood. Blood masked the lower half of her face, and stained the hem of her shirt. She looked at Alec with wide, happy eyes.

"I know you," she breathed, and as she spoke, he saw her needle incisors flash. *Vampire.* "Alec Lightwood. You're a friend of Simon's. I've seen you at the concerts."

He stared at her. Had he seen her before? Perhaps—the flicker of a face among the shadows at a bar, one of those performances Isabelle had dragged him to. He couldn't be sure. But that didn't mean he didn't know who she was.

"Maureen," he said. "You're Simon's Maureen."

She looked pleased. "I am," she said. "I'm Simon's Maureen." She looked down at her hands, which were gloved in blood, as if she'd plunged them into a pool of the stuff. And not human blood, either, Alec thought. The dark, ruby-red blood of vampires. "You're looking for Camille," she said in a singsong voice. "But she isn't here anymore. Oh, no. She's gone."

"She's gone?" Alec demanded. "What do you mean she's gone?"

Maureen giggled. "You know how vampire law works, don't you? Whoever kills the head of a vampire clan becomes its leader. And Camille was the head of the New York clan. Oh, yes, she was."

"So—someone killed her?"

Maureen burst into a happy peal of laughter. "Not just *someone*, silly," she said. "It was me."

The arched ceiling of the infirmary was blue, painted with a rococo pattern of cherubs trailing gold ribbons, and white drifting clouds. Rows of metal beds lined the walls to the left and right, leaving a wide aisle down the middle. Two high skylights let in the clear wintery sunlight, though it did little to warm the chilly room.

Jace was seated on one of the beds, leaning back against a pile of pillows he had swiped from the other beds. He wore jeans, frayed at the hems, and a gray T-shirt. He had a book balanced on his knees. He looked up as Clary came into the room, but said nothing as she approached his bed.

Clary's heart had begun to pound. The silence felt still, almost oppressive; Jace's eyes followed her as she reached the foot of his bed and stopped there, her hands on the metal footboard. She studied his face. So many times she'd tried to draw him, she thought, tried to capture that ineffable quality that made Jace himself, but her fingers had never been able to get what she saw down on paper. It was there now, where it had not been when he was controlled by Sebastian—whatever you wanted to call it, soul or spirit, looking out of his eyes.

She tightened her hands on the footboard. "Jace . . ."

He tucked a lock of pale gold hair behind his ear. "It's—did the Silent Brothers tell you it was okay to be in here?"

"Not exactly."

The corner of his mouth twitched. "So did you knock them out with a two-by-four and break in? The Clave looks darkly on that sort of thing, you know."

"Wow. You really don't put anything past me, do you?" She moved to sit down on the bed next to him, partly so that they would be on the same level and partly to disguise the fact that her knees were shaking.

"I've learned not to," he said, and set his book aside.

She felt the words like a slap. "I didn't want to hurt you," she said, and her voice came out as almost a whisper. "I'm sorry."

He sat up straight, swinging his legs over the edge of the bed. They were not far from each other, sharing the same bed, but he was holding himself back; she could tell. She could tell that there were secrets at the back of his light eyes, could feel his hesitation. She wanted to reach her hand out, but she kept herself still, kept her voice steady. "I never meant to hurt you. And I don't just mean at the Burren. I mean from the moment you—the real *you*—told me what you wanted. I should have listened, but all I thought about was saving you, getting you away. I didn't listen to you when you said you wanted to turn yourself over to the Clave, and because of it, we both almost wound up like Sebastian. And when I did what I did with Glorious—Alec and Isabelle, they must have told you the blade was meant for Sebastian. But I couldn't get to him through the crowd. I just couldn't. And I thought of what you told me, that you'd rather die than live under Sebastian's influence." Her voice caught. "The *real* you, I mean. I couldn't ask you. I had to guess. You have to know it was awful to hurt you like that. To know that you could have died and it would have been my hand that held the sword that killed you. I would have wanted to die, but I risked your life because I thought it was what you would have asked for, and after I'd betrayed you once, I thought I owed it to you. But if I was wrong . . ." She paused, but he was silent. Her stomach turned over, a sick, wrenching flip. "Then, I'm sorry. There's nothing I can do to make it up to you. But I wanted you to know. That I'm sorry."

She halted again, and this time the silence stretched out between them, longer and longer, a thread pulled impossibly tight.

"You can talk now," she blurted finally. "In fact, it would be really great if you did."

Jace was looking at her incredulously. "Let me get this straight," he said. "You came here to apologize to *me*?"

She was taken aback. "Of course I did."

"Clary," he said. "You saved my life."

"I stabbed you. With a *massive* sword. You caught on *fire*."

His lips twitched, almost imperceptibly. "Okay," he said. "So maybe our problems aren't like other couples'." He lifted a hand as if he meant to touch her face, then put it down hastily. "I heard you, you know," he said more softly. "Telling me I wasn't dead. Asking me to open my eyes."

They looked at each other in silence for what was probably moments but felt like hours to Clary. It was so good to see him like this, completely himself, that it almost erased the fear that this was all going to go horribly wrong in the next few minutes. Finally Jace spoke.

"Why do you think I fell in love with you?"

It was the last thing she would have expected him to say. "I don't— That's not a fair thing to ask."

"Seems fair to me," he said. "Do you think I don't know you, Clary? The girl who walked into a hotel full of vampires because her best friend was there and needed saving? Who made a Portal and transported herself to Idris because she hated the idea of being left out of the action?"

"You yelled at me for that—"

"I was yelling at myself," he said. "There are ways in which we're so alike. We're reckless. We don't think before we act. We'll do anything for the people we love. And I never thought how scary that was for the people who loved *me* until I saw it in you and it terrified me. How could I protect you if you wouldn't let me?" He leaned forward. "That, by the way, is a rhetorical question."

"Good. Because I don't need protecting."

"I knew you'd say that. But the thing is, sometimes you do. And sometimes I do. We're meant to protect each other, but not from *everything*. Not from the truth. That's what it means to love someone but let them be themselves."

Clary looked down at her hands. She wanted to reach out and touch him so badly. It was like visiting someone in jail, where you could see them so clearly and so close, but there was unbreakable glass separating you.

"I fell in love with you," he said, "because you were one of the bravest people I'd ever known. So how could I ask you to stop being brave just because I loved you?" He ran his hands through his hair, making it stick up in loops and curls that Clary ached to smooth down. "You came for me," he said. "You saved me when almost everyone else had given up, and even the people who hadn't given up didn't know what to do. You think I don't know what you went through?" His eyes darkened. "How do you imagine I could possibly be angry with you?"

"Then, why haven't you wanted to see me?"

"Because . . ." Jace exhaled. "Okay, fair point, but there's something you don't know. The sword you used, the one Raziel gave to Simon . . ."

"Glorious," said Clary. "The Archangel Michael's sword. It was destroyed."

"Not destroyed. It went back where it came from once the heavenly fire consumed it." Jace smiled faintly. "Otherwise our Angel would have had some serious explaining to do once

Michael found out his buddy Raziel had lent out his favorite sword to a bunch of careless humans. But I digress. The sword . . . the way it burned . . . that was no ordinary fire."

"I guessed that." Clary wished Jace would hold out his arm and draw her against him. But he seemed to want to keep space between them, so she stayed where she was. It felt like an ache in her body, to be this close to him and not be able to touch him.

"I wish you hadn't worn that sweater," Jace muttered.

"What?" She glanced down. "I thought you liked this sweater."

"I do," he said, and shook his head. "Never mind. That fire—it was Heaven's fire. The burning bush, the fire and brimstone, the pillar of fire that went before the children of Israel—that's the fire we're talking about. 'For a fire is kindled in mine anger, and shall burn unto the lowest hell, and shall consume the earth with her increase, and set on fire the foundations of the mountains.' That's the fire that burned away what Lilith had done to me." He reached for the hem of his shirt and drew it up. Clary sucked in her breath, for above his heart, on the smooth skin of his chest, there was no more Mark—and only a healed white scar where the sword had gone in.

She reached her hand out, wanting to touch him, but he drew back, shaking his head. She felt the hurt expression flash across her face before she could hide it as he rolled his shirt back down. "Clary," he said. "That fire—it's still inside me."

She stared at him. "What do you mean?"

He took a deep breath and held his hands out, palms down. She looked at them, slim and familiar, the Voyance rune on his left hand faded with white scars layered over it. As they both watched, his hands began to shake slightly—and then, under

Clary's incredulous eyes, to turn transparent. Like the blade of Glorious when it had begun to burn, his skin seemed to turn to glass, glass that trapped within it a gold that moved and darkened and *burned*. She could see the outline of his skeleton through the transparency of his skin, golden bones connected by tendons of fire.

She heard him inhale sharply. He looked up then, and met her eyes with his. His eyes were gold. They had always been gold, but she could swear that now that gold lived and burned as well. He was breathing hard, and there was sweat shining on his cheeks and collarbones.

"You're right," Clary said. "Our problems really aren't like other people's problems."

Jace stared at her incredulously. Slowly he closed his hands into fists, and the fire vanished, leaving only his ordinary, familiar, unharmed hands behind. Half-choking on a laugh, he said, "*That's* what you have to say?"

"No. I have a lot more to say. *What's* going on? Are your hands weapons now? Are you the Human Torch? What on earth—"

"I don't know what the human torch is, but— All right, look, the Silent Brothers have told me that I carry the heavenly fire inside me now. Inside my veins. In my soul. When I first woke up, I felt like I was breathing in fire. Alec and Isabelle thought it was just a temporary effect of the sword, but when it didn't go away and the Silent Brothers were called in, Brother Zachariah said he didn't know how temporary it would be. And I burned him—he was touching my hand when he said it, and I felt a jolt of energy go through me."

"A bad burn?"

"No. Minor. But still—"

"That's why you won't touch me," Clary realized aloud. "You're afraid you'll burn me."

He nodded. "No one's ever seen anything like this, Clary. Not before. Not ever. The sword didn't kill me. But it left this—this piece of something deadly inside me. Something so powerful it would probably kill an ordinary human, maybe even an ordinary Shadowhunter." He took a deep breath. "The Silent Brothers are working on how I might control it, or get rid of it. But as you might imagine, I'm not their first priority."

"Because Sebastian is. You heard I destroyed that apartment. I know he has other ways of getting around, but . . ."

"That's my girl. But he has backups. Other hiding places. I don't know what they are. He never told me." He leaned forward, close enough that she could see the changing colors in his eyes. "Since I woke up, the Silent Brothers have been with me practically every minute. They had to perform the ceremony on me again, the one that gets performed on Shadowhunters when they're born to keep them safe. And then they went into my mind. Searching, trying to pull out any snippet of information about Sebastian, anything I might know and not remember I knew. But—" Jace shook his head in frustration. "There just isn't anything. I knew his plans through the ceremony at the Burren. Beyond that, I have no idea what he's going to do next. Where he might strike. They do know he's been working with demons, so they're shoring up the wards, especially around Idris. But I feel like there's one useful thing we might have gotten out of all this—some secret knowledge on my part—and we don't even have that."

"But if you did know anything, Jace, he would just change his plans," Clary objected. "He knows he lost you. You two were tied together. I heard him scream when I stabbed you." She shivered. "It was this horrible lost sound. He really did care about you in some strange way, I think. And even though the whole thing was awful, both of us got something out of it that might turn out to be useful."

"Which is . . . ?"

"We understand him. I mean, as much as anyone can ever understand him. And that's not something he can erase with a change of plans."

Jace nodded slowly. "You know who else I feel like I understand now? My father."

"Valen—no," Clary said, watching his expression. "You mean Stephen."

"I've been looking at his letters. The things in the box Amatis gave me. He wrote a letter to me, you know, that he meant me to read after he died. He told me to be a better man than he was."

"You are," Clary said. "In those moments in the apartment when you were *you*, you cared about doing the right thing more than you cared about your own life."

"I know," Jace said, glancing down at his scarred knuckles. "That's the strange thing. I *know*. I had so much doubt about myself, always, but now I know the difference. Between myself and Sebastian. Between myself and Valentine. Even the difference between the two of them. Valentine honestly believed he was doing the right thing. He hated demons. But to Sebastian, the creature he thinks of as his mother is one. He would happily rule a race of dark Shadowhunters who did the bidding of demons, while the ordinary humans of this world were slaughtered for the demons' pleasure. Valentine still believed it was the mandate of Shadowhunters to protect human beings; Sebastian thinks they're cockroaches. And he doesn't want to protect anyone. He only wants what he wants at the moment he wants it. And the only real thing he ever feels is annoyance when he's thwarted."

Clary wondered. She had seen Sebastian looking at Jace, even at herself, and knew there was some part of him as echoingly lonely as the blackest void of space. Loneliness drove him as much as a desire for power—loneliness and a need to be loved without any corresponding understanding that love was something you earned. But all she said was, "Well, let's get with the thwarting, then."

A smile ghosted across his face. "You know I want to beg you to stay out of this, right? It's going to be a vicious battle. More vicious than I think the Clave even begins to understand."

"But you're not going to do that," Clary said. "Because that would make you an idiot."

"You mean because we need your rune powers?"

"Well, that, and— Did you not listen to anything you just said? That whole business about protecting each other?"

"I will have you know I practiced that speech. In front of a mirror before you got here."

"So what do *you* think it meant?"

"I'm not sure," Jace admitted, "but I know I look damn good delivering it."

"God, I forgot how annoying the un-possessed you is," Clary muttered. "Need I remind you that you said that you have to accept you can't protect me from everything? The only way that we can protect each other is if we *are together.* If we face things together. If we trust each other." She looked him directly in the eye. "I shouldn't have stopped you from going to the Clave by calling for Sebastian. I should respect the decisions you make. And you should respect mine. Because we're going to be together a long time, and that's the only way it's going to work."

His hand inched toward her on the blanket. "Being under Sebastian's influence," he said, hoarsely. "It seems like a bad dream to me, now. That insane place—those closets of clothes for your mother—"

"So you remember." She almost whispered it.

His fingertips touched hers, and she almost jumped. Both of them held their breath while he touched her; she didn't move, watching as his shoulders slowly relaxed and the anxious look left his face."I remember everything," he said. "I remember the boat in Venice. The club in Prague. That night in Paris, when I was myself."

She felt the blood rush up under her skin, making her face burn.

"In some ways, we've been through something no one else can ever understand but the two of us," he said. "And it made me realize. We are always and absolutely better together." He raised his face to hers. He was pale, and fire flickered in his eyes. "I am going to kill Sebastian," he said. "I am going to kill him for what he did to me, and what he did to you, and what he did to Max. I am going to kill him because of what he has done, and what he will do. The Clave wants him dead, and they will hunt him. But I want my hand to be the one that cuts him down."

She reached out then, and put her hand on his cheek. He shuddered, and half-closed his eyes. She had expected his skin to be warm, but it was cool to the touch. "And what if I'm the one who kills him?"

"My heart is your heart," he said. "My hands are your hands."

His eyes were the color of honey and slid as slowly as honey over her body as he looked her up and down as if for the first time since she'd come into the room, from her windblown hair to her booted feet, and back again. When their gaze met again, Clary's mouth was dry.

"Do you remember," he said, "when we first met and I told you I was ninety percent sure putting a rune on you wouldn't kill you—and you slapped me in the face and told me it was for the other ten percent?"

Clary nodded.

"I always figured a demon would kill me," he said. "A rogue Downworlder. A battle. But I realized then that I just might die if I didn't get to kiss you, and soon."

Clary licked her dry lips. "Well, you did," she said. "Kiss me, I mean."

He reached up and took a curl of her hair between his fingers. He was close enough that she could feel the warmth of his body, smell his soap and skin and hair. "Not enough," he said, letting her hair slip through his fingers. "If I kiss you all day every day for the rest of my life, it won't be enough."

He bent his head. She couldn't help tilting her own face up. Her mind was full of the memory of Paris, holding on to him as if it would be the last time she ever held him, and it almost had been. The way he had tasted, felt, breathed. She could hear him breathing now. His eyelashes tickled her cheek. Their lips were millimeters apart and then not apart at all, they brushed lightly and then with firmer pressure; they leaned in to each other—

And Clary felt a spark—not painful, more like a fillip of mild static electricity—pass between them. Jace drew quickly away. He was flushed. "We may need to work on that."

Clary's mind was still whirling. "Okay."

He was staring straight ahead, still breathing hard. "I have something I want to give you."

"I gathered that."

At that he jerked his gaze back to hers and—almost reluctantly—grinned. "Not that." He reached down into the collar of his shirt and drew out the Morgenstern ring on its chain. He pulled it over his head and, leaning forward, dropped it lightly into her hand. It was warm from his skin. "Alec got it back from Magnus for me. Will you wear it again?"

Her hand closed around it. "Always."

His grin softened to a smile, and, daring, she put her head on his shoulder. She felt his breath catch, but he didn't move. At first he sat still, but slowly the tension drained from his body and they leaned together. It wasn't hot and heavy, but it was companionable and sweet.

He cleared his throat. "You know this means that what we did—what we almost did in Paris—"

"Going to the Eiffel Tower?"

He tucked a lock of hair behind her ear. "You never let me off the hook for a single minute, do you? Never mind. It's one of the things I love about you. Anyway, that *other* thing we almost did in Paris—that's probably off the table for a while. Unless you want that whole baby-I'm-on-fire-when-we kiss thing to become freakishly literal."

"No kissing?"

"Well, *kissing*, probably. But as for the rest of it . . ."

She brushed her cheek lightly against his. "It's okay with me if it's okay with you."

"Of course it's not okay with me. I'm a teenage boy. As far as I'm concerned, this is the worst thing that's happened since I found out why Magnus was banned from Peru." His eyes softened. "But it doesn't change what we are to each other. It's like there's always been a piece of my soul missing, and it's inside *you*, Clary. I know I told you once that whether God exists or not, we're on our own. But when I'm with you, I'm not."

She closed her eyes so he wouldn't see her tears—happy tears, for the first time in a long time now. Despite everything, despite the fact that Jace's hands remained carefully together in his lap, Clary felt a sense of relief so overwhelming that it drowned out everything else—the worry about where Sebastian was, the fear of an unknown future—everything receded into the background. None of it mattered. They were together, and Jace was himself again. She felt him turn his head and lightly kiss her hair.

"I *really* wish you hadn't worn that sweater," he muttered into her ear.

"It's good practice for you," she replied, her lips moving against his skin. "Tomorrow, fishnets."

Against her side, warm and familiar, she felt him laugh.

"Brother Enoch," said Maryse, rising from behind her desk. "Thank you for joining me and Brother Zachariah here on such short notice."

Is this in regards to Jace? Zachariah inquired, and if Maryse had not known better, she would have imagined a tinge of anxiety in his mental voice. *I have checked in on him several times today. His condition has not changed.*

Enoch shifted within his robes. *And I have been looking through the archives and the ancient documentation on the topic of Heaven's fire. There is some information about the manner in which it may be released, but you must be patient. There is no need to call on us. Should we have news, we will call on you.*

"This is not about Jace," said Maryse, and she moved around the desk, her heels clicking on the stone floor of the library. "This is about something else entirely." She glanced down. A rug had been carelessly tossed across the floor, where no rug usually rested. It did not lie flat but was draped over an irregular humped shape. It obscured the delicate pattern of tiles that outlined the shape of the Cup, the Sword, and the Angel. She reached down, took hold of a corner of the rug, and yanked it aside.

The Silent Brothers did not gasp, of course; they could make no sound. But a cacophony filled Maryse's mind, the psychic echo of their shock and horror. Brother Enoch took a step back, while Brother Zachariah raised one long-fingered hand to cover his face, as if he could block his ruined eyes from the sight before him.

"It was not here this morning," said Maryse. "But when I returned this afternoon, it awaited me."

At the very first glimpse she had thought that some kind of large bird had found its way into the library and died, perhaps breaking its neck against one of the tall windows. But as she had moved closer, the truth of what she was looking at had dawned on her. She said nothing of the visceral shock of despair that had gone through her like an arrow, or the way she had staggered to the window and been sick out of it the moment she'd realized what she was looking at.

A pair of white wings—not quite white, really, but an amalgamation of colors that shifted and flickered as she looked at it: pale silver, streaks of violet, dark blue, each feather outlined in gold. And then, there at the root, an ugly gash of sheared-off bone and sinew. Angel's wings—angel's wings that had been sliced from the body of a living angel. Angelic ichor, the color of liquid gold, smeared the floor.

Atop the wings was a folded piece of paper, addressed to the New York Institute. After splashing water on her face, Maryse had taken the letter and read it. It was short—one sentence—and was signed with a name in a handwriting oddly familiar to her, for in it there was the echo of Valentine's cursive, the flourishes of his letters, the strong, steady hand. But it was not Valentine's name. It was his son's.

Jonathan Christopher Morgenstern.

She held it out now to Brother Zachariah. He took it from her fingers and opened it, reading, as she had, the single word of Ancient Greek scrawled in elaborate script across the top of the page.

Erchomai, it said.

I am coming.

NOTES

Magnus's Latin invocation on page 233 that raises Azazel, beginning "*Quod tumeraris: per Jehovam, Gehennam,*" is taken from *The Tragical History of Doctor Faustus* by Christopher Marlowe.

The snippets of the ballad Magnus listens to in the car on pages 387–389 are taken with permission from "Alack, for I Can Get No Play" by Elka Cloke (elkacloke.com).

The T-shirt CLEARLY I HAVE MADE SOME BAD DECISIONS is inspired by my friend Jeph Jacques's comic at questionablecontent.net. The T-shirts can be purchased at topatoco.com. The idea of *Magical Love Gentleman* also belongs to him.

Acknowledgments

As always, I must thank my family: my husband, Josh; my mother and father, as well as Jim Hill and Kate Connor; Melanie, Jonathan, and Helen Lewis; Florence and Joyce. Many thanks to early readers and critiquers Holly Black, Sarah Rees Brennan, Delia Sherman, Gavin Grant, Kelly Link, Ellen Kushner, and Sarah Smith. Special credit due to Holly, Sarah, Maureen Johnson, Robin Wasserman, Cristi Jacques, and Paolo Bacigalupi for helping me block scenes. Maureen, Robin, Holly, Sarah, you are always there for me to complain to—you are stars. Thank you to Martange for help with French translations and to my Indonesian fans for Magnus's declaration to Alec. Wayne Miller, as always, assisted with Latin translations, and Aspasia Diafa and Rachel Kory gave extra assistance with ancient Greek. Invaluable help came from my agent, Barry Goldblatt; my editor, Karen Wojtyla; and her partner in crime Emily Fabre. My thanks to Cliff Nielsen and Russell Gordon, for making a beautiful cover, and to the teams at Simon & Schuster and Walker Books for making the rest of the magic happen.

City of Lost Souls was written with the program Scrivener, in the town of Goult, France.

Continue the adventures of
Clary, Jace, and Simon in

City of Heavenly Fire,

BOOK SIX OF THE MORTAL INSTRUMENTS.

There were dozens of unfamiliar coats and jackets hanging in the entryway of the Institute. Clary felt the tight buzzing of tension in her shoulders as she unzipped her own wool coat and hung it on one of the hooks that lined the walls.

"And Maryse didn't say what this was about?" Clary demanded. The edges of her voice had been rubbed thin by anxiety.

Jocelyn had unwound a long gray scarf from around her neck, and barely looked as Luke took it from her to drape it on a hook. Her green eyes were darting around the room, taking in the gate of the elevator, the arched ceiling overhead, the faded murals of men and angels.

Luke shook his head. "Just that there'd been an attack on the Clave, and we needed to get here as quickly as possible."

"It's the 'we' part that concerns me." Jocelyn wound her hair up into a knot at the back of her head, and secured it with her fingers. "I haven't been in an Institute in years. Why do they want me here?"

Luke squeezed her shoulder reassuringly. Clary knew what Jocelyn feared, what they all feared. The only reason the Clave would want Jocelyn here was if there was news of her son.

"Maryse said they'd be in the library," Jocelyn said. Clary led the way. She could hear Luke and her mother talking behind her, and the soft sound of their footsteps, Luke's slower than they had once been. He hadn't entirely recovered from the injury that had nearly killed him in November.

You know why you're here, don't you, breathed a soft voice in the back of her head. She knew it wasn't really there, but that didn't help. She hadn't seen her brother since the fight at the Burren, but she carried him in some small part of her mind, an intrusive, unwelcome ghost. *Because of me. You always knew I hadn't gone away forever. I told you what would happen. I spelled it out for you.*

Erchomai.

I am coming.

They had reached the library. The door was half-open, and a babble of voices spilled through. Jocelyn paused for a moment, her expression tight.

Clary put her hand on the doorknob. "Are you ready?" She hadn't noticed till then what her mother was wearing: black jeans, boots, and a black turtleneck. As if, without thinking of it, she had put on the closest thing she had to fighting gear.

Jocelyn nodded at her daughter.

Someone had pushed back all the furniture in the library, clearing a large space in the middle of the room, just atop the mosaic of the Angel. A massive table had been placed there, a huge slab of marble balanced on top of two kneeling stone angels. Around the table were seated the Conclave. Some members, like Kadir and Maryse, Clary knew by name. Others were just familiar faces. Maryse was standing, ticking off names on her fingers as she chanted aloud. "Berlin," she said. "No survivors. Bangkok. No survivors. Moscow. No survivors. Los Angeles—"

"Los Angeles?" said Jocelyn. "That was the Blackthorns. Are they—"

Maryse looked startled, as if she hadn't realized Jocelyn had come in. Her blue eyes swept over Luke and Clary. She looked drawn and exhausted, her hair scraped back severely, a stain—red wine or blood?—on the sleeve of her tailored jacket. "There were survivors," she said. "Children. They're in Idris now."

"Helen," said Alec, and Clary thought of the girl who had fought with them against Sebastian at the Burren. She remembered her in the nave of the Institute, a dark-haired boy clinging to her wrist. *My brother, Julian.*

"Aline's girlfriend," Clary blurted out, and saw the Conclave look at her with thinly veiled hostility. They always did, as if who she was and what she represented made them almost unable to see her. *Valentine's daughter. Valentine's daughter.* "Is she all right?"

"She was in Idris, with Aline," said Maryse. "Her younger brothers and sisters survived, although there seems to have been an issue with the eldest brother, Mark."

"An issue?" said Luke. "What's going on, exactly, Maryse?"

"I don't think we'll know the whole story until we get to Idris," said Maryse, smoothing back her already smooth hair.

"But there have been attacks, several in the course of two nights, on six Institutes. We're not sure yet how the Institutes were breached, but we know—"

"Sebastian," said Clary's mother. She had her hands jammed into the pockets of her black trousers, but Clary suspected that if she hadn't, Clary would have been able to see that her mother's hands were tightened into fists. "Cut to the point, Maryse. My son. You wouldn't have called me here if he wasn't responsible. Would you?" Jocelyn's eyes met Maryse's, and Clary wondered if this was how it had been when they'd both been in the Circle, the sharp edges of their personalities rubbing up against each other, causing sparks.

Before Maryse could speak, the door opened and Jace came in. He was flushed with the cold, bareheaded, fair hair tousled by the wind. His hands were gloveless, red at the tips from the weather, scarred with Marks new and old. He saw Clary and gave her a quick smile before settling into a chair propped against the wall.

Luke, as usual, moved to make peace. "Maryse? Is Sebastian responsible?"

Maryse took a deep breath. "Yes, yes he was. And he had the Endarkened with him."

"Of course it's Sebastian," said Isabelle. She had been staring down at the table; now she raised her head. Her face was a mask of hatred and rage. "He said he was coming; well, now he's come."

Maryse sighed. "We assumed he'd attack Idris. That was what all the intelligence indicated. Not Institutes."

"So he did the thing you didn't expect," said Jace. "He always does the thing you don't expect. Maybe the Clave should plan for *that*." Jace's voice dropped. "I told you. I told you he'd want more soldiers."

"Jace," said Maryse. "You're not helping."

"I wasn't trying to."

"I would have thought he'd attack here first," said Alec. "Given what Jace was saying before, and it's true—everyone he loves or hates is here."

"He doesn't *love* anyone," Jocelyn snapped.

"Mom, stop," Clary said. Her heart was pounding, sick in her chest; yet at the same time there was a strange sense of relief. All this time waiting for Sebastian to come, and now he had. Now the waiting was over. Now the war would start. "So what are we supposed to do? Fortify the Institute? *Hide?*"

"Let me guess," said Jace, his voice dripping sarcasm. "The Clave's called for a Council. Another meeting."

"The Clave has called for immediate evacuation," said Maryse, and at that, everyone went silent, even Jace. "All Institutes are to empty out. All Conclaves must return to Alicante. The wards around Idris will be doubled after tomorrow. No one will be able to come in or get out."

Isabelle swallowed. "When do we leave New York?"

Maryse straightened up. Some of her usual imperious air was back, her mouth a thin line, her jaw set with determination. "Go and pack," she said. "We leave tonight."

Before Clary and Jace there were Tessa,
Will, and Jem. Discover their story in

Clockwork Angel,

BOOK ONE OF THE INFERNAL DEVICES.

Southampton, May.

Tessa could not remember a time when she had not loved the clockwork angel. It had belonged to her mother once, and her mother had been wearing it when she died. After that it had sat in her mother's jewelry box, until her brother, Nathaniel, took it out one day to see if it was still in working order.

The angel was no bigger than Tessa's pinky finger, a tiny statuette made of brass, with folded bronze wings no larger than a cricket's. It had a delicate metal face with shut crescent eyelids, and hands crossed over a sword in front. A thin chain that looped beneath the wings allowed the angel to be worn around the neck like a locket.

Tessa knew the angel was made out of clockwork because if she lifted it to her ear she could hear the sound of its machinery, like the sound of a watch. Nate had exclaimed in surprise that it was still working after so many years, and he had looked in vain for a knob or a screw, or some other method by which the angel might be wound. But there had been nothing to find. With a shrug he'd given the angel to Tessa. From that moment she had never taken it off; even at night the angel lay against her chest as she slept, its constant *ticktock, ticktock* like the beating of a second heart.

She held it now, clutched between her fingers, as the *Main* nosed its way between other massive steamships to find a spot at the Southampton dock. Nate had insisted that she come to Southampton instead of Liverpool, where most transatlantic steamers arrived. He had claimed it was because Southampton was a much pleasanter place to arrive at, so Tessa couldn't help being a little disappointed by this, her first sight of England. It was drearily gray. Rain drummed down onto the spires of a distant church, while black smoke rose from the chimneys of ships and stained the already dull-colored sky. A crowd of people in dark clothes, holding umbrellas, stood on the docks. Tessa strained to see if her brother was among them, but the mist and spray from the ship were too thick for her to make out any individual in great detail.

Tessa shivered. The wind off the sea was chilly. All of Nate's letters had claimed that London was beautiful, the sun shining every day. Well, Tessa thought, hopefully the weather there was better than it was here, because she had no warm clothes with her, nothing more substantial than a woolen shawl that had belonged to Aunt Harriet, and a pair of thin gloves. She had sold most of her clothes to pay for her aunt's funeral, secure in the knowledge that her brother would buy her more when she arrived in London to live with him.

A shout went up. The *Main*, its shining black-painted hull gleaming wet with rain, had anchored, and tugs were plowing their way through the heaving gray water, ready to carry baggage and passengers to the shore. Passengers streamed off the ship, clearly desperate to feel land under their feet. So different from their departure from New York. The sky had been blue then, and a brass band had been playing. Though, with no one there to wish her good-bye, it had not been a merry occasion.

Hunching her shoulders, Tessa joined the disembarking crowd. Drops of rain stung her unprotected head and neck like pinpricks from icy little needles, and her hands, inside their insubstantial gloves, were clammy and wet with rain. Reaching the quay, she looked around eagerly, searching for a sight of Nate. It had been nearly two weeks since she'd spoken to a soul, having kept almost entirely to herself on board the *Main*. It would be wonderful to have her brother to talk to again.

He wasn't there. The wharves were heaped with stacks of luggage and all sorts of boxes and cargo, even mounds of fruit and vegetables wilting and dissolving in the rain. A steamer was departing for Le Havre nearby, and damp-looking sailors swarmed close by Tessa, shouting in French. She tried to move aside, only to be almost trampled by a throng of disembarking passengers hurrying for the shelter of the railway station.

But Nate was nowhere to be seen.

"You are Miss Gray?" The voice was guttural, heavily accented. A man had moved to stand in front of Tessa. He was tall, and was wearing a sweeping black coat and a tall hat, its brim collecting rainwater like a cistern. His eyes were peculiarly bulging, almost protuberant, like a frog's, his skin as rough-looking as scar tissue. Tessa had to fight the urge to cringe away from him. But he knew her name. Who here would know her name except someone who knew Nate, too?

"Yes?"

"Your brother sent me. Come with me."

"Where is he?" Tessa demanded, but the man was already walking away. His stride was uneven, as if he had a limp from an old injury. After a moment Tessa gathered up her skirts and hurried after him.

He wound through the crowd, moving ahead with purposeful speed. People jumped aside, muttering about his rudeness as he shouldered past, with Tessa nearly running to keep up. He turned abruptly around a pile of boxes, and came to a halt in front of a large, gleaming black coach. Gold letters had been painted across its side, but the rain and mist were too thick for Tessa to read them clearly.

The door of the carriage opened and a woman leaned out. She wore an enormous plumed hat that hid her face. "Miss Theresa Gray?"

Tessa nodded. The bulging-eyed man hurried to help the woman out of the carriage—and then another woman, following after her. Each of them immediately opened an umbrella and raised it, sheltering themselves from the rain. Then they fixed their eyes on Tessa.

They were an odd pair, the women. One was very tall and thin, with a bony, pinched face. Colorless hair was scraped back into a chignon at the back of her head. She wore a dress of brilliant violet silk, already spattered here and there with splotches of rain, and matching violet gloves. The other woman was short and plump, with small eyes sunk deep into her head; the bright pink gloves stretched over her large hands made them look like colorful paws.

"Theresa Gray," said the shorter of the two. "What a delight to make your acquaintance at last. I am Mrs. Black, and this is my sister, Mrs. Dark. Your brother sent us to accompany you to London."

Tessa—damp, cold, and baffled—clutched her wet shawl tighter around herself. "I don't understand. Where's Nate? Why didn't he come himself?"

"He was unavoidably detained by business in London. Mortmain's couldn't spare him. He sent ahead a note for you, however." Mrs. Black held out a rolled-up bit of paper, already dampened with rain.

Tessa took it and turned away to read it. It was a short note from her brother apologizing for not being at the docks to meet her, and letting her know that he trusted Mrs. Black and Mrs. Dark—*I call them the Dark Sisters, Tessie, for obvious reasons, and they seem to find the name agreeable!*—to bring her safely to his house in London. They were, his note said, his landladies as well as trusted friends, and they had his highest recommendation.

That decided her. The letter was certainly from Nate. It was in his handwriting, and no one else ever called her Tessie. She swallowed hard and slipped the note into her sleeve, turning back to face the sisters. "Very well," she said, fighting down her lingering sense of disappointment—she had been so looking forward to seeing her brother. "Shall we call a porter to fetch my trunk?"

"No need, no need." Mrs. Dark's cheerful tone was at odds with her pinched gray features. "We've already arranged to have it sent on ahead." She snapped her fingers at the bulging-eyed man, who swung himself up into the driver's seat at the front of the carriage. She placed her hand on Tessa's shoulder. "Come along, child; let's get you out of the rain."

As Tessa moved toward the carriage, propelled by Mrs.

Dark's bony grip, the mist cleared, revealing the gleaming golden image painted on the side of the door. The words "The Pandemonium Club" curled intricately around two snakes biting each other's tails, forming a circle. Tessa frowned. "What does that mean?"

"Nothing you need worry about," said Mrs. Black, who had already climbed inside and had her skirts spread out across one of the comfortable-looking seats. The inside of the carriage was richly decorated with plush purple velvet bench seats facing each other, and gold tasseled curtains hanging in the windows.

Mrs. Dark helped Tessa up into the carriage, then clambered in behind her. As Tessa settled herself on the bench seat, Mrs. Black reached to shut the carriage door behind her sister, closing out the gray sky. When she smiled, her teeth gleamed in the dimness as if they were made out of metal. "Do settle in, Theresa. We've a long ride ahead of us."

Tessa put a hand to the clockwork angel at her throat, taking comfort in its steady ticking, as the carriage lurched forward into the rain.

Discover Emma and Julian's story in

Lady Midnight,

THE FIRST BOOK IN CASSANDRA CLARE'S

NEW SERIES, THE DARK ARTIFICES.

Emma took her witchlight out of her pocket and lit it—and almost screamed out loud. Jules's shirt was soaked with blood and worse, the healing runes she'd drawn had vanished from his skin. They weren't working.

"Jules," she said. "I have to call the Silent Brothers. They can help you. I *have* to."

His eyes screwed shut with pain. "You can't," he said. "You know we can't call the Silent Brothers. They report directly to the Clave."

"So we'll lie to them. Say it was a routine demon patrol. I'm calling," she said, and reached for her phone.

"No!" Julian said, forcefully enough to stop her. "Silent Brothers know when you're lying! They can see inside your head, Emma. They'll find out about the investigation. About Mark—"

"You're not going to bleed to death in the backseat of a car for Mark!"

"No," he said, looking at her. His eyes were eerily blue-green, the only bright color in the dark interior of the car. "You're going to fix me."

Emma could feel it when Jules was hurt, like a splinter lodged under her skin. The physical pain didn't bother her; it was the terror, the only terror worse than her fear of the ocean. The fear of Jules being hurt, of him dying. She would give up anything, sustain any wound, to prevent those things from happening.

"Okay," she said. Her voice sounded dry and thin to her own ears. "Okay." She took a deep breath. "Hang on."

She unzipped her jacket, threw it aside. Shoved the console between the seats aside, put her witchlight on the floorboard. Then she reached for Jules. The next few seconds were a blur of Jules's blood on her hands and his harsh breathing as she pulled him partly upright, wedging him against the back door. He didn't make a sound as she moved him, but she could see him biting his lip, the blood on his mouth and chin, and she felt as if her bones were popping inside her skin.

"Your gear," she said through gritted teeth. "I have to cut it off."

He nodded, letting his head fall back. She drew a dagger from her belt, but the gear was too tough for the blade. She said a silent prayer and reached back for Cortana.

Cortana went through the gear like a knife through melted butter. It fell away in pieces and Emma drew them free, then sliced down the front of his T-shirt and pulled it apart as if she were opening a jacket.

Emma had seen blood before, often, but this felt different. It was Julian's, and there seemed to be a lot of it. It was smeared up and down his chest and rib cage; she could see where the arrow had gone in and where the skin had torn where he'd yanked it out.

"Why did you pull the arrow out?" she demanded, pulling her sweater over her head. She had a tank top on under it. She patted his chest and side with the sweater, absorbing as much of the blood as she could.

Jules's breath was coming in hard pants. "Because when someone—shoots you with an arrow—" he gasped, "your immediate response is not—'Thanks for the arrow, I think I'll keep it for a while.'"

"Good to know your sense of humor is intact."

"Is it still bleeding?" Julian demanded. His eyes were shut.

She dabbed at the cut with her sweater. The blood had slowed, but the cut looked puffy and swollen. The rest of him, though—it had been a while since she'd seen him with his shirt off. There was more muscle than she remembered. Lean muscle pulled tight over his ribs, his stomach flat and lightly ridged. Cameron was much more muscular, but Julian's spare lines were as elegant as a greyhound's. "You're too skinny," she said. "Too much coffee, not enough pancakes."

"I hope they put that on my tombstone." He gasped as she shifted forward, and she realized abruptly that she was squarely in Julian's lap, her knees around his hips. It was a bizarrely intimate position.

"I—am I hurting you?" she asked.

He swallowed visibly. "It's fine. Try with the *iratze* again."

"Fine," she said. "Grab the panic bar."

"The what?" He opened his eyes and peered at her.

"The plastic handle! Up there, above the window!" She pointed. "It's for holding on to when the car is going around curves."

"Are you sure? I always thought it was for hanging things on. Like dry cleaning."

"Julian, *now is not the time to be pedantic*. Grab the bar or I swear—"

"All right!" He reached up, grabbed hold of it, and winced. "I'm ready."

She nodded and set Cortana aside, reaching for her stele. Maybe her previous *iratzes* had been too fast, too sloppy. She'd always focused on the physical aspects of Shadowhunting, not the more mental and artistic ones: seeing through glamours, drawing runes.

She set the tip of it to the skin of his shoulder and drew, carefully and slowly. She had to brace herself with her left hand against his shoulder. She tried to press as lightly as she could, but she could feel him tense under her fingers. The skin on his shoulder was smooth and hot under her touch, and she wanted to get closer to him, to put her hand over the wound on his side and heal it with the sheer force of her will. To touch her lips to the lines of pain beside his eyes and—

Stop. She had finished the *iratze*. She sat back, her hand clamped around the stele. Julian sat up a little straighter, the ragged remnants of his shirt hanging off his shoulders. He took a deep breath, glancing down at himself—and the *iratze* faded back into his skin, like black ice melting, spreading, being absorbed by the sea.

He looked up at Emma. She could see her own reflection in his eyes: she looked wrecked, panicked, with blood on her neck and her white tank top. "It hurts less," he said in a low voice.

The wound on his side pulsed again; blood slid down the side of his rib cage, staining his leather belt and the waistband of his jeans. She put her hands on his bare skin, panic rising up inside her. His skin felt hot, too hot. Fever hot.

"I have to call," she whispered. "I don't care if the whole world comes down around us, Jules, the most important thing is that you *live*."

"Please," he said, desperation clear in his voice. "Whatever is happening, we'll fix it, because we're *parabatai*. We're forever. I said that to you once, do you remember?"

She nodded warily, hand on the phone.

"And the strength of a rune your *parabatai* gives you is special. Emma, you can do it. You can heal me. We're *parabatai* and that means the things we can do together are . . . extraordinary."

There was blood on her jeans now, blood on her hands and her tank top, and he was still bleeding, the wound still open, an incongruous tear in the smooth skin all around it.

"Try," Jules said in a dry whisper. "For me, try?"

His voice went up on the question and in it she heard the voice of the boy he had been once, and she remembered him smaller, skinnier, younger, back pressed against one of the marble columns in the Hall of Accords in Alicante as his father advanced on him with his blade unsheathed.

And she remembered what Julian had done, then. Done to protect her, to protect all of them, because he always would do everything to protect them.

She took her hand off the phone and gripped the stele, so tightly she felt it dig into her damp palm. "Look at me, Jules," she said in a low voice, and he met her eyes with his. She placed the stele against his skin, and for a moment she held still, just breathing, breathing and remembering.

Julian. A presence in her life for as long as she could remember, splashing water at each other in the ocean, digging in the sand together, him putting his hand over hers and them marveling at the difference in the shape and length of their fingers. Julian singing, terribly and off-key, while he drove, his fingers in her hair carefully freeing a trapped leaf, his hands catching her in the training room when she fell, and fell, and fell. The first time after their *parabatai* ceremony when she'd smashed her hand into a wall in rage at not being able to get a sword maneuver right, and he'd come up to her, taken her still-shaking body in his arms and said, "Emma, Emma, don't hurt yourself. When you do, I feel it, too."

Something in her chest seemed to split and crack; she marveled that it wasn't audible. Energy raced along her veins, and the stele jerked in her hand before it seemed to move on its own, tracing the graceful outline of a healing rune across Julian's chest. She heard him gasp, his eyes flying open. His hand slid down her back and he pressed her against him, his teeth gritted.

"Don't *stop*," he said.

Emma couldn't have stopped if she'd wanted to. The stele seemed to be moving of its own accord; she was blinded with memories, a kaleidoscope of them, all of them Julian. Sun in her eyes and Julian asleep on the beach in an old T-shirt and her not wanting to wake him, but he'd woken anyway when the sun went down and looked for her immediately, not smiling till his eyes found her and he knew she was there. Falling asleep talking and waking up with their hands interlocked; they'd been children in the dark together once but now they were something else, something intimate and powerful, something Emma felt she was touching only the very edge of as she finished the rune and the stele fell from her nerveless fingers.

"Oh," she said softly. The rune seemed lit from within by a soft glow.

Turn the page to read

Becoming Sebastian Verlac,

A NEW SCENE SHOWING JONATHAN MORGENSTERN'S FIRST MEETING WITH SEBASTIAN VERLAC.

It was a very small bar, on a narrow sloping street in a walled town full of shadows. Jonathan Morgenstern had been sitting at the bar for at least a quarter of an hour, finishing a leisurely drink, before he got to his feet and slipped down the long, rickety flight of wooden stairs to the club. The sound of the music seemed to be trying to push its way up through the steps as he made his way downward: He could feel the wood vibrating under his feet.

The place was filled with writhing bodies and obscuring smoke. It was the kind of place demons prowled. That made it the kind of place demon hunters frequented.

And an ideal location for someone who was hunting a demon hunter.

Colored smoke drifted through the air, smelling vaguely acidic. There were long mirrors all along the walls of the club. He could see himself as he moved across the room: a slender figure in black, with his father's hair, white as snow. It was humid down here in the club, airless and hot, and his T-shirt was stuck to his back with sweat. A silver ring glittered on his right hand as he scanned the room for his prey.

There he was, at the bar, as if he was trying to blend in with the mundanes even though he was invisible to them.

A boy. Maybe seventeen.

A Shadowhunter.

Sebastian Verlac.

Jonathan ordinarily had little interest in anyone his own age—if there was anything duller than other people, it was other adolescents—but Sebastian Verlac was different. Jonathan had chosen him, carefully and specifically. Chosen him the way one might choose an expensive and custom-tailored suit.

Jonathan strolled over to him, taking his time and taking the boy's measure. He had seen photographs, of course, but people always looked different in person. Sebastian was tall—the same height as Jonathan himself, and with the same slender build. His clothes looked like they would fit Jonathan perfectly. His hair was dark—Jonathan would have to dye his own, which was annoying, but not impossible. His eyes were black, too, and his features, though irregular, came together pleasingly: he had a friendly charisma that was attractive. He looked like it was easy for him to trust, easy to smile.

He looked like a fool.

Jonathan came up to the bar and leaned against it. He turned his head, allowing the other boy to recognize that he could see him. "*Bonjour.*"

"Hello," Sebastian replied, in English, the language of Idris, though his was tinged faintly with a French accent. His eyes were narrowed. He looked very startled to be seen at all, and as if he was wondering what Sebastian might be: fellow Shadowhunter, or a warlock with a sign that didn't show?

Something wicked this way comes, Jonathan thought. *And you don't even know it.*

"I'll show you mine if you show me yours," he suggested, and smiled. He could see himself smiling in the grimy mirror over the bar. He knew the way the smile lit up his face, made him almost irresistible. His father had trained him for years to smile like that, like a human being.

Sebastian's hand tightened on the edge of the bar. "I don't . . ."

Jonathan smiled wider and turned his right hand over to show the *Voyance* rune on the back of it. The breath went out of Sebastian in relief, and he beamed with delighted recognition—as if any Shadowhunter was a comrade and a potential friend.

"Are you on your way to Idris, too?" Jonathan asked, very professional, as if he were in regular touch with the Clave. *Protecting the innocent*, he projected to the world and Sebastian in particular. *Can't get enough of that!*

"I am," Sebastian replied. "Representing the Paris Institute. I'm Sebastian Verlac, by the way."

"Ah, a Verlac. A fine old family." Jonathan accepted his hand, and shook it firmly. "Mark Blackthorn," he said easily. "The Los Angeles Institute, originally, but I've been studying in Rome. I thought I'd come overland to Alicante. See the sights."

He'd researched the Blackthorns, a large family, and knew they and the Verlacs had not been in the same city for ten years. He was certain he would have no problem answering to an assumed name: He never did. His real name was Jonathan, but he had never felt particularly attached to it, perhaps because he had always known that it was not his name alone.

The other Jonathan, being raised not so far away, in a house just like his, visited by *his* father. Daddy's little angel.

"Haven't seen another Shadowhunter in ages," Sebastian continued—he had been talking, but Jonathan had forgotten to pay attention to him. "Funny to run into you here. My lucky day."

"Must be," Jonathan murmured. "Though not entirely chance, of course. The reports of an Eluthied demon lurking about this place, I assume you've heard them as well?"

Sebastian smiled and took a last swallow from his glass, setting it down on the bar. "After we kill the thing, we should have a celebratory drink."

Jonathan nodded, and tried to look as if he were very focused on searching the room for demons. They stood shoulder to shoulder, like brother warriors. It was so easy it was almost boring: All he'd had to do was show up, and here was Sebastian Verlac like a lamb pushing its throat on a blade. Who *trusted* other people like that? Wanted to be their friend so easily?

He had never played nicely with others. Of course, he had not ever been given the opportunity: His father had kept him and the other Jonathan apart. A child with demon blood and a child with angel blood—raise both boys as yours and see who makes Daddy proud.

The other boy had failed a test when he was younger, and been sent away. Jonathan knew that much. He had passed every test their father had ever set for him. Maybe he had passed them all a little too well, too flawlessly, unfazed by the isolation chamber and the animals, the whip or the hunt. Jonathan had discerned a shadow in Father's eyes now and then, one that was either grief or doubt.

Though what did he have to be aggrieved over? Why should he doubt? Was Jonathan not the perfect warrior? Was he not everything his father had created him to be?

Human beings were so puzzling.

Jonathan had never liked the idea of the other Jonathan, of Father having another boy, one who made Father smile sometimes, without a shadow in his eyes at the thought of him.

Jonathan had cut one of his practice dummies off at the knees once, and spent a pleasant day strangling it and disemboweling it, slitting it from neck to navel. When his father had asked why he'd cut off parts of the legs, he had told him that he wanted to see what it was like to kill a boy who was just his own size.

"I forget, you'll have to excuse me," said Sebastian, who was turning out to be annoyingly chatty. "How many are there in your family?"

"Oh, we're a big one," Jonathan replied. "Seven in total. I have three brothers and three sisters."

The Blackthorns really were seven: Jonathan's research had been thorough. He couldn't imagine what that would be like, so many people, such untidiness. Jonathan had a blood sister, too, although they had never met.

Father had told him about his mother running off when Jonathan was a baby and she was pregnant again, inexplicably weepy and miserable because she had some sort of objection to her first child being improved.

But there had been a second child. A girl. Only a few weeks ago, Father had met Clarissa for the first time, and on their second encounter Clarissa had proven she knew how to use her power as well. She had sent Father's ship to the bottom of the ocean.

Once he and Father had taken down and transformed the Shadowhunters, laid waste to their pride and their city, Father said that Mother, the other Jonathan, and Clarissa would be coming to live with them.

Jonathan despised his mother, who had apparently been such a pathetic weakling that she'd run away from him when he was a baby. And his only interest in the other Jonathan was to prove how superior he was: Father's real son, by blood, and with the strength of demons and chaos in that blood as well.

But he was interested in Clarissa.

Clarissa had never chosen to leave him. She had been taken away and been forced to grow up in the midst of mundanes, of all disgusting things. She must have always known she was made of different stuff from everyone around her, meant for utterly different things, power and strangeness crackling beneath her skin.

She must have felt like the only creature like her in all the world.

She had angel in her, like the other Jonathan, not the infernal blood that ran through his veins. But Jonathan was very much his father's son as well as anything else: He was like Father made stronger, tempered by the fires of hell. Clarissa was Father's real daughter too, and who knew what strange brew the combination of Father's blood and Heaven's power had formed to run through Clarissa's veins? She might not be very different from Jonathan himself.

The thought excited him in a way he had never been excited

before. Clarissa was *his* sister; she belonged to no one else. She was his. He knew it, because although he did not dream often—that was a human thing—after Father had told him about his sister sinking the ship, he had dreamed of her.

Jonathan dreamed of a girl standing in the sea with hair like scarlet smoke coiling over her shoulders, winding and unwinding in the untamable wind. Everything was stormy darkness, and in the raging sea were pieces of wreckage that had once been a boat and bodies floating facedown. She looked down on them with cool green eyes and was not afraid.

Clarissa had done that, wreaked destruction like that, like he would have. In the dream, he was proud of her. His little sister.

In the dream, they were laughing together at all the beautiful ruin around them. They were standing suspended in the sea. It couldn't hurt them; destruction was their element. Clarissa was looking down as she laughed, trailing her moonlight-white hands in the water. When she lifted up her hands they were dark, dripping: He realized that the seas were all blood.

Jonathan had woken from his dream still laughing.

When the time was right, Father had said, they would be together, all of them. Jonathan had to wait.

But he was not very good at waiting.

"You have the oddest look on your face," Sebastian Verlac said, shouting above the beat of the music, bright and jagged in Jonathan's ears.

Jonathan leaned over, spoke softly and precisely into Sebastian's ear. "Behind you," he said. "Demon. Four o'clock."

Sebastian Verlac turned, and the demon, in the shape of a girl with a cloud of dark hair, stepped hastily away from the boy it was talking to and began sliding away through the crowd. Jonathan and Sebastian followed it, out a side door with SORTIE DE SECOURS written across it in cracked letters of red and white.

The door led to an alley, which the demon was swiftly running down, nearly disappearing.

Jonathan jumped, launching himself at the brick wall opposite, and used the force of his rebound to arrow over the demon's head. He twisted in midair, runed blade in hand, hearing it whistle through the air. The demon froze, staring at him. Already the mask of a girl's face was beginning to slip, and Jonathan could see the features behind it: clustered eyes like a spider's, a tusked mouth, open in surprise. None of it disgusted him. The ichor that ran in their veins ran in his.

Not that that inspired mercy, either. Grinning at Sebastian over the demon's shoulder, he slashed out with his blade. It cut the demon open as he'd once cut open the dummy, neck to navel. A bubbling scream rent the alley as the demon folded in on itself and disappeared, leaving only a few drops of black blood splattered on the stones.

"By the Angel," Sebastian Verlac whispered.

He was staring at Jonathan over the blood and the emptiness between them, and his face was white. For a moment Jonathan was almost pleased that Sebastian had the sense to be afraid.

But no such luck. Sebastian Verlac remained a fool to the end.

"You were amazing!" Sebastian exclaimed, his voice shaken but impressed. "I've never seen anyone move that fast! *Alors*, you have got to teach me that move. By the Angel," he went on. "I've never seen anything like what you just did."

"I'd love to help you," Jonathan said. "But unfortunately

I've got to get going soon. My father needs me, you see. He has plans. And he simply can't do without me."

Sebastian looked absurdly disappointed. "Oh come, you can't go now," he coaxed. "Hunting with you was so much fun, *mon pote*. We have to do this again sometime."

"I'm afraid," Jonathan told him, fingering the hilt of his weapon, "that won't be possible."

Sebastian looked so surprised when he was killed. It made Jonathan laugh, blade in hand and Sebastian's throat opening beneath it, hot blood spilling onto his fingers.

It wouldn't do to have Sebastian's body found at an inconvenient time and the whole game ruined, so Jonathan dragged the body through the streets as if he were carrying a drunken friend home.

It was not very far at all to a little bridge, delicate as green filigree or a dead child's moldy, fragile bones, over the river. Jonathan heaved the corpse over the side and watched it hit the rushing black waters with a splash.

The body sank without a trace, and Jonathan forgot it before it had even sunk all the way. He saw the curled fingers, bobbing in the currents as if restored to life and begging for help or at least answers, and thought of his dream. His sister, and a sea of blood. Water had splashed up where the body went down, some of it splattering his sleeve. Baptizing him with a new name. He was Sebastian now.

He strolled along the bridge to the old part of the city, where there were electric bulbs masquerading as gas lanterns, more toys for tourists. He was headed toward the hotel where Sebastian Verlac had been staying; he had scoped it out before coming to the bar, and knew he could scramble up through the window and retrieve the other boy's belongings. And after that, a bottle of cheap hair dye and . . .

A group of girls in cocktail dresses passed him, angling their gazes, and one, silvery skirt skimming her thighs, gave him a direct look and a smile.

He fell in with the party.

"Comment tu t'appelles, beau gosse?" another girl asked him, her voice lightly slurred. *What's your name, pretty boy?*

"Sebastian," he answered smoothly, with not a second's hesitation. That was who he was from now on, who his father's plans required him to be, who he needed to be to walk the path that led to victory and Clarissa. "Sebastian Verlac."

He looked to the horizon, and thought of the glass towers of Idris, thought of them enveloped in shadow, flame, and ruin. He thought of his sister waiting for him, out there in the wide world.

He smiled.

He thought he was going to enjoy being Sebastian.

You
Tube

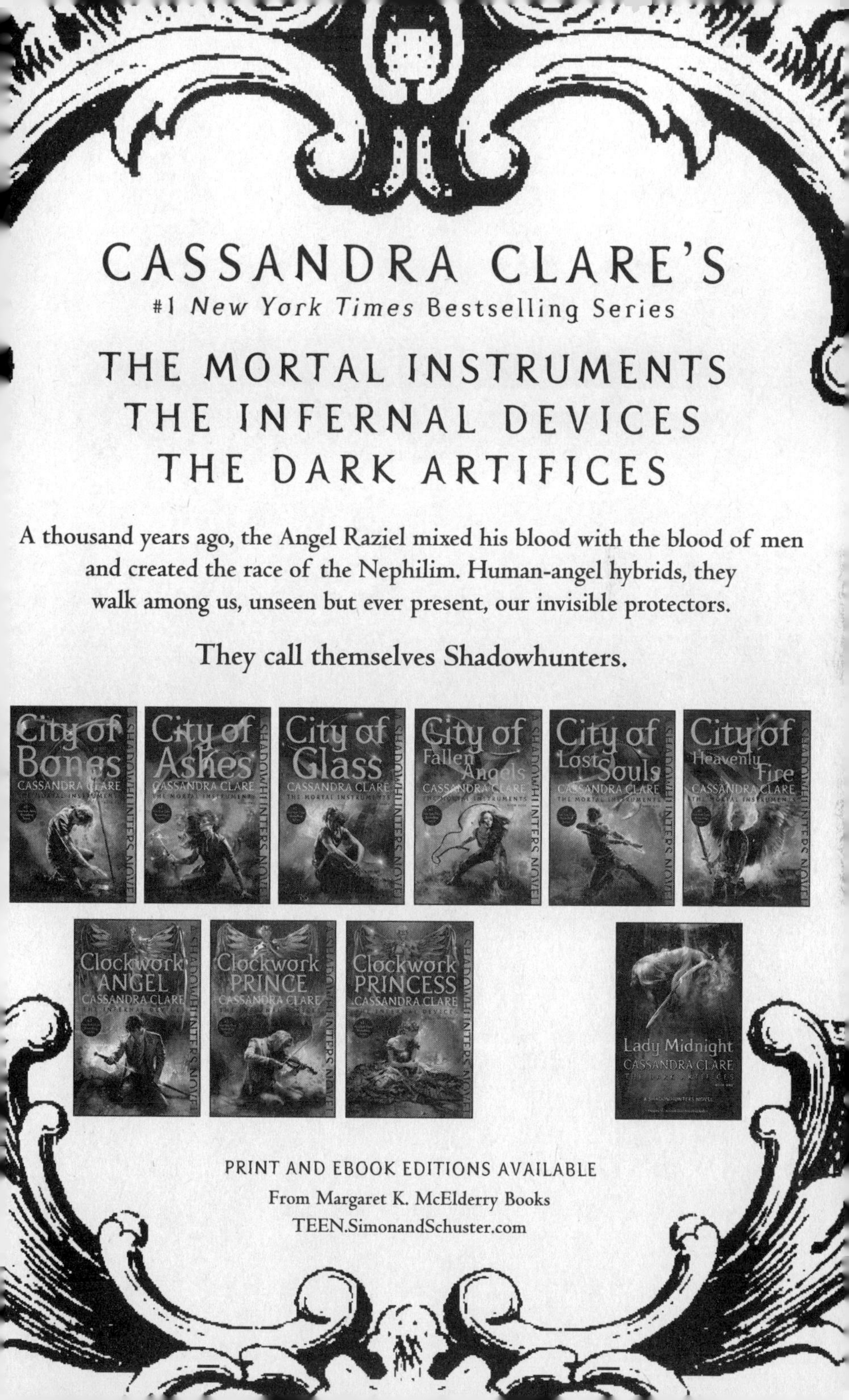
CASSANDRA CLARE'S
#1 New York Times Bestselling Series
THE MORTAL INSTRUMENTS
THE INFERNAL DEVICES
THE DARK ARTIFICES
A thousand years ago, the Angel Raziel mixed his blood with the blood of men and created the race of the Nephilim. Human-angel hybrids, they walk among us, unseen but ever present, our invisible protectors.
They call themselves Shadowhunters.
City of Bones
CASSANDRA CLARE
City of Ashes
CASSANDRA CLARE
City of Glass
CASSANDRA CLARE
City of Fallen Angels
CASSANDRA CLARE
City of Lost Souls
CASSANDRA CLARE
City of Heavenly Fire
CASSANDRA CLARE
Clockwork ANGEL
CASSANDRA CLARE
Clockwork PRINCE
CASSANDRA CLARE
Clockwork PRINCESS
CASSANDRA CLARE
Lady Midnight
CASSANDRA CLARE
THE DARK ARTIFICES
PRINT AND EBOOK EDITIONS AVAILABLE
From Margaret K. McElderry Books
TEEN.SimonandSchuster.com

Go deeper into the world of the Shadowhunters with

THE SHADOWHUNTER'S CODEX,

the essential guide to becoming one of the Nephilim.

PRINT AND EBOOK EDITIONS AVAILABLE

Explore the legends and legacy of Magnus Bane in

THE BANE CHRONICLES

What happens when Magnus meets Marie Antoinette?
And what *really* happened in Peru?
Find out the answers in this illustrated short-story
collection featuring everyone's favorite warlock.

PRINT AND EBOOK EDITIONS AVAILABLE

From Margaret K. McElderry Books | TEEN.SimonandSchuster.com

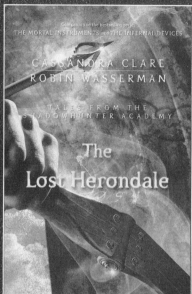

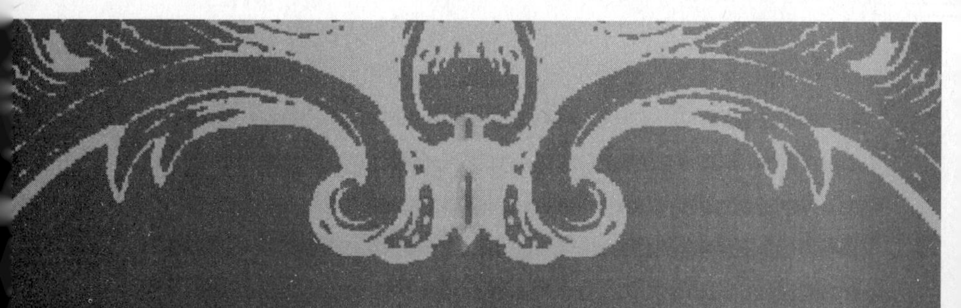